He's the Duke of Death and she's his last chance…

Michael, Duke of Blixford, was all Lady Jane Lennox ever wanted in a husband. Growing up with her gregarious widower papa and six raucous older brothers, Jane was drawn to the handsome, taciturn duke and purposefully set her cap for him. Unfortunately, despite his attraction to her, the duke was less than impressed with her unladylike skills, and after he ruined her, then proposed at the same time he called her his *very last* choice as his duchess, she fled to Scotland.

To keep the ducal title and holdings from reverting to the crown, Michael needs a wife to give him an heir – but he doesn't need to love her. Called the Duke of Death, a pariah said to have demon seed, Michael has lost three wives in childbed. His worst nightmare is following his father into grief driven madness after the woman he loved died. His iron discipline failed him four years ago when he succumbed to his fascination with Jane, and his fury was great when she jilted him. Now, she's returned to London and, just as he is her only choice, she is his last chance.

She's determined to have a real marriage; he's determined to hold her at arm's length. But when the past catches up and old ghosts demand their due, Jane is devastated, and Michael risks everything to save his last duchess from permanent ruin. All he has to do is not fall in love.

The Last Duchess

THE LENNOX SERIES
BOOK ONE

STEPHANIE
RITA© AWARD WINNING AUTHOR
FEAGAN

DEDICATION

For Michael – They're all for you.

ACKNOWLEDGEMENTS

Many thanks to Tanya Saari for her marvelous editing, and to lovely beta readers Sarah Evans, Brooke Kenjura, Kathy Gee, and Anita Learned. Thanks to Kim Killion for the beautiful cover design. And thanks to the Beau Monde chapter of RWA for being such a great resource of historical information and the minutiae of the Regency period I love so much. Any mistakes in this story are all mine.

CHAPTER 1

"Jane, he simply won't do. The man's a stick. Surely becoming a duchess can't be that important. You've never shown the slightest interest in marrying for consequence."

Casting a look at her brother, Lady Jane Lennox pulled a face. "My interest in Blixford has nothing to do with rank. I happen to be madly in love with him."

Robert barked a loud laugh, startling her horse and sending the mare into a skittish dance across the road. Handling the beast with ease, Jane brought her back into line and frowned at Robert. "Laugh if you like, but there it is."

"When did you develop a *tendre* for the stick?"

"Do stop calling him a stick. It's the height of disrespect."

"There was a time you'd have agreed with me that he's dry as toast and has all the humor of a graveyard. Please, Jane, rethink this and you'll see how ill-suited you are to be his duchess."

Staring ahead, vaguely angry, she scarcely noticed the beauty of the narrow country lane, dappled with early-morning sunlight. Ordinarily, she'd have been invigorated by the clear air, the cloudless sky, the moist, heady scent of dew-laden, freshly cut hayfields stretching out to the north. But this morning, her mind was in turmoil, solely focused on one goal, allowing little room for appreciation of the glorious morning. "Is this lecture the only reason you asked me to ride early with you?"

"Largely, but I also believe you could do with a bit of a respite from Lady Bonderant's house party. I've watched you act the perfect lady for upwards of a week now, and it's painful to witness." His eyes were laughing at her. "You're dying to run, aren't you?"

Of course she was, but admitting it didn't seem wise. Robert was certain to pounce upon it as a method of illustrating how dour the consequence of her marrying the Duke of Blixford. "I shouldn't say *dying*, but yes, it would be lovely to let this mare have her head."

"Very well, we will run, as soon as you explain how you came to fall wildly in love with the Duke of Dullford."

Ignoring Robert's further insult of Blixford, she said, "Do you recall two summers past, before my coming out, when I went to visit Annabel during her confinement?"

"I have recollection of a letter from Sherbourne mentioning your visit, as well as Annabel's untimely death. I was still at Cambridge, so never learned particulars. Was it dreadful, Jane, being there when poor Annabel died?"

"It was. She was a sweet soul, the heart of kindness."

"She was forever scolding us when we were children, do you remember?"

Jane smiled, despite the sad memory of Annabel's death. "Yes, and all the while, she was neck-deep in the prank herself." Jane glanced at her handsome brother. "I always believed she had a sweet spot for you."

"And I for her, but it was doomed from the outset. I'm the youngest son of an earl with six sons, my title prospects dismal. Despite being well lined in the pocket, I was unsuitable for Annabel, whose mama set her sights quite high. She got her wish and Annabel became a duchess, but I wonder what cold comfort that must be to Lady Margaret now?"

Remembering, Jane said, "She was overset in the extreme when she arrived at Eastchase Hall and realized her daughter was dead. For all our years of resentment toward Lady Margaret's high-handedness and presumptuous manner, I've never felt such depth of sympathy for anyone. The entire affair was horrid and sad. Annabel was frightened when her labor began too early, and I, of course, knowing nothing of these matters, was at a loss. I sent for the midwife, as well as Blixford, who was in London, and Lady Margaret, who was to come a week later, to finish out Annbabel's confinement, but she died before her mother arrived. All alone but for me, the midwife, and the vicar's daughter, Bella. Blixford didn't arrive until the following day, just in time to witness his wife and infant son entombed in the family crypt."

They rode in silence for a while before Jane finished her story. "He's an outwardly cold man, not one to be demonstrative. I was put off by his manner during the service, astonished a man could bury his wife with such dispassion." His face, she remembered, looked as though carved from granite. Even his dark eyes had held no warmth, no emotion. "At the conclusion of the service, he thanked me for my assistance, for my kindness in attending Annabel, and turned to leave, but before he walked out of the chapel, his gaze caught a spray of roses at the front. Roses were Annabel's favorite, you know." Turning, she looked earnestly at her brother. "Robert, I have never forgotten his expression. He was . . . bereft."

He was clearly unimpressed. "Bereft, indeed. I'd gather from his look he was severely aggravated that the heir he covets didn't live. What you witnessed was not a husband mourning his wife, but a duke's annoyance at losing his heir. It's paramount he beget an heir, Jane. As the last male of his line, his titles, holdings, and wealth will revert to the crown upon his death. Centuries of Blixford dukes will fairly spin in their graves should he allow such a catastrophe. It is, I believe, why he's here, at his sister's house party. Everyone knows Blixford detests social events, yet here he is, attending a veritable stable of young ladies, yourself included, from which he will choose his next brood mare." Robert nudged his gelding close and reached out to touch her arm. "I would wish much better for you, Jane. He can never love you, and I have my doubts that you love him. It is only your sympathy and frankly, imagination, that have captivated you. Please trust me about this, and set your cap elsewhere besides Blixford."

Jane listened to Robert, as she always did, and accepted his counsel for what it was; the concern of her closest brother, borne of love and respect for her. But she wouldn't heed it. He didn't understand, and she could never adequately express her reaction to that minuscule moment when the ducal mask fell away and she witnessed the man beneath. She'd never forgotten. Every suitor she acquired during her first Season was soundly rejected, solely due to her desire to marry Blixford as soon as he was ready to try again.

That time was now, and she would *not* be dissuaded from pursuing him. Her chances were excellent, she thought. He seemed to pay particular attention to her, although he did appear to be impressed with Lady Letitia's ability at the pianoforte. Jane was dismal at the pianoforte. She was also not adept at stitching, or painting, or idle conversation. Lady Letitia was a model of decorum. Jane was not.

But she was of impeccable birth and great fortune, the only daughter of an earl. Her mother's death and father's refusal to take another wife meant she assumed the duties of a large household at a very early age. She was well qualified to step into the role of duchess, despite her failings in the drawing room. Blixford was bound to see this, and assuredly would offer for her within the fortnight, before the end of Lady Bonderant's house party.

"I'm truly confounded by this infatuation of yours. He's six years your senior, a great lummox of a man, not considered handsome in the least. If you marry him, your brats shall all sport rather large noses."

Jane's back went up. "I'm ashamed of you, Robert. How can you be so unkind? Yes, Blixford has a strong Roman nose, but it's his best feature. Unique. Frankly, I find him quite attractive." Much more than quite, but she could not say so to her brother. He'd keel over in a dead faint if she told him what her imagination had conjured during the previous week. Most definitely not ladylike. Low, common and terribly earthy. As for Blixford's size, being on the tall side herself, she found his height and breadth intriguing.

"I suppose he does cut a fine figure, but he positively glowers. I suspect he's foul tempered, and you would dislike living with anyone not jolly." He gave her a solemn look. "You should know our father feels as I do. He won't stop you marrying Blixford, if indeed the man asks, but he won't like it."

"Perhaps he won't offer, and yours and Papa's concern will be for naught."

"One can only hope." He caught her expression and hastened to add, "I'm not being cruel, Janie. I would see you happy in marriage, and I'm convinced Blixford is incapable of making you anything but miserable. He would hide you beneath a basket with his foot firmly atop, and you would smother." He nodded ahead. "He wouldn't allow you to run."

"Ah, but he need never know. I'm here, now, about to beat you soundly to the end of the lane. Blixford is undoubtedly fast asleep and none the wiser."

She watched her brother closely. As usual, he heard only the challenge. Robert slowed his gelding and met her gaze, a wide smile lighting his face, his sober expression vanishing. "Ready?"

"At your will."

He laughed, as did she, and they took off, thundering down the lane, neck and neck, shouting insults at one another.

"Bloody sloppy, sir!"

"Damned incompetent!"

"Disgrace to horseflesh!"

"You ride like a *girl*!"

It was a splendid run, a welcome reprieve from the sedate riding she'd been forced to do all week. She would return to the house and dress for breakfast in a new morning gown. She would partake of her eggs and coffee, then change back into her habit and go for a ride with the others, prim and perfect. It would not feel so confining, because she had already had a run.

She shouted at Robert, "Any slower and you'll be a blasted statue!"

"Poor loser!" He nudged ahead and she concentrated more fully on the race, laughing with exhilaration.

From a bluff edging the southern end of the extensive formal gardens at Margrave Park, Michael Benedict Deveraux, twelfth Duke of Blixford, sat his horse and watched Lady Jane and her brother race down the lane edging a hayfield. She was a beauty; vibrant, filled with laughter and *joie de vive*. Hers was a nature of passion, everything in her life taken on with determination and single-minded purpose.

For reasons Michael couldn't fathom, she'd taken him on. He was amused by her attempt to cloak herself in a mantle of decorous behavior, to vie for his attention amongst the other young ladies his sister, Lucy, had invited to her late summer house party.

Lady Jane was earnest in her pursuit of him and he admired her dedication, even if he had no intention of acting upon it. She was unsuitable for his needs, and the sooner she realized it and moved on to other possibilities, the better off she would be.

"She's in love with you."

Without glancing at his sister, who sat her horse beside him, Michael nodded. "Yes, I'm aware."

"She doesn't care about the title."

"I know."

"Nevertheless, you won't marry her."

"Not on a bet, Lucy." He glanced at her and admired her seat. She'd always been an excellent rider. Nothing in the league of Lady Jane, but quite competent. "I recall you mentioned her while you visited me in London this past Season. I believe I told you we wouldn't suit."

"How could you know, having barely met her? You refused to attend any functions, so you didn't see her as I did."

"I don't live in a cave. I'm well aware she was the toast of the Season, but I'm also aware she's Sherbourne's only daughter, raised with six older brothers. She rides neck-or-nothing and discusses unladylike subjects. She shoots pistols."

"Yes, I know," Lucy said, a gleam in her dark eyes. "As I said, she's perfect for you."

"You invited her, no doubt certain I would be unable to resist her after two weeks of constant company."

"How astute you are, and yet, how obtuse. Lady Jane would make a fine duchess, and make you extremely happy. I so wish to see you happy, Blix, to have something meaningful in your life that has nothing to do with sums and crops and shipping investments."

He turned his attention back to the race. "I intend to offer for Lady Letitia at the end of the week."

Lucy was quiet for a moment, watching Lady Jane

and her brother as they raced to the finish. "Lady Letitia will make a fine duchess, but she'll never make you happy."

"It is not my aim to be happy. I need an heir, and an acceptable wife willing to provide one. My choice is adequate."

"Your choice is a woman whom you'll never love. You can't bamboozle me, Blix. You chose Annabel for much the same reason. For an educated, intelligent man, you can be annoyingly short-sighted."

"You married Bonderant because you loved him. Now you have lost him. Only last evening, you cried again. He's been gone over a year, yet you continue to mourn him. Would you wish me the same misery?"

Lady Jane won the race. He could hear her voice, carried on the breeze, just as her earlier very unladylike shouts had reached him. "By God, Robert, I may ride like a girl, but I have bested you, yet again. I demand you bow before my superior horsemanship, at once."

Robert was a good-natured sort, as were all of Sherbourne's brood. He laughed and bowed in the saddle.

She returned his laugh as they turned back toward the house.

Lucy watched and murmured, "I don't regret one moment I had with Matthew, and even had I known he would be taken from me far too soon, I'd marry him all over again. We had one glorious year of deep happiness and contentment. I have his son. I live in his house. His memory will never die. You see this as misery. I see it as honor and hope and something intrinsic I can't name. Yes, I mourn my husband, but I'm far from miserable, Blix. Were you to marry Lady Jane, and if she were to die in childbed, as our mother did, as Annabel did, you would go on, and you wouldn't be miserable. You'd be glad for the time you had."

Michael refocused on the riders along the lane.

"She's very beautiful, and spoiled by Sherbourne. She would most likely demand attention and distract me from my work."

"You should be distracted. You work too hard, Blix. Life is not meant to be lived riding the farms and toting up accounts."

"It's been my life since our father died, Lucy." He glanced toward her and lifted a brow. "There was a time when you didn't mind my working so hard. Your coming out was not inexpensive, and I spared nothing to see you had an excellent Season."

She returned the favor and lifted her own brow. "You can't guilt me into silence, brother. Yes, you've worked hard to regain all that Papa lost, but you've done so a hundred times over. How rich must you be? There's only so much money one can spend in a lifetime, and what is it for if you've no one to share it with?"

"I will share with Lady Letitia. I intend to marry her, and there's an end to it."

His gaze returned to Lady Jane. She was more than simply lovely. There was a charisma about her, an undeniable draw. Even her competition couldn't dislike her, though perhaps they didn't see her as worthy competition. A frisky puppy would be more adept at the pianoforte than Lady Jane. When it came to painting, no doubt an infant could claim a more advanced artistic ability. The lady's attempts were terrible enough to draw laughter from her friends. She took it in stride and laughed along with them, telling a story of her watercolors instructor, a woman so worn down by her hopeless student, she retired to the country to grow turnips and was never heard from again.

The art of polite conversation was also lost on Lady Jane. At times, she crinkled her forehead and became almost fierce in her discourse on matters not generally considered genteel, polite, or appropriate for the drawing room. Only last night, she debated the merits of crossbreeding sheep with young Lassiter and trumped him soundly. To his discredit, he didn't appear offended in the slightest. On the contrary, he was besotted with her. They all were.

Except Michael.

She was to be disappointed, but would soon realize all was for the best. They wouldn't suit. Not at all. Lady Jane required a younger man, one open to her lifestyle of riding neck-or-nothing, her mannish interest in farming, her tendency to shout unladylike curses in a hayfield.

He still couldn't figure out how, when, or why she'd developed such an infatuation with him. He'd scarcely met her before the beginning of the house party. If memory served, he was introduced at his wedding to Annabel. She was there with Annabel when she died, and he spoke to her for a few moments after the burial service. How did a woman develop an infatuation in such a short matter of time? It was a puzzle. Not to mention, most young ladies just out of the schoolroom were afraid of him. He didn't doubt Letitia was afraid of him. At the very least, she was intimidated.

Lady Jane was not afraid, or intimidated.

She gazed at him far too long and too many times, her wide blue eyes filled with yearning. It was damned near impossible not to respond, but he was careful not to give her any encouragement. In less than a week, Lady Jane would return to her father's home and come spring, another Season, when she would find a man able to fully appreciate her passionate nature.

When she and her brother disappeared from sight, he turned to Lucy and realized she was staring at him. "Have I a smudge?"

"Yes, quite. It's just there, in front of your eyes, clouding your vision."

Unwilling to follow her lead, determined to kill any further conversation about Lady Jane, he nodded toward the north. "Shall we go?"

Lucy shook her head. "I've lost the ambition, Blix. You go on and I'll ride along the lane there before I retire to the house and check on breakfast."

He eyed her curiously. "Would you run, Luce?"

She cocked her head and said thoughtfully, "It has been rather a long time. I believe I will." Nudging her mare, she turned and headed toward the slope of the hill that led down to the lane. She called over her shoulder, "Care to join me?"

For one mad moment, he thought he would. But he was to visit several of the Margrave Park tenants this morning and he didn't think it advisable to procrastinate. He waved to her and turned the opposite direction. As he made his way down the edge of the back lawn toward the road, he heard the sound of hooves pounding the ground.

Before he could talk himself out of it, he bent forward and murmured a command, gratified by the feel of the magnificent stallion's muscles bunching beneath him, springing forward with breathtaking speed. There was only one thing more pleasurable than running a horse, and as his prospects for that activity were exactly none, at least for the foreseeable future, he'd take a run and enjoy it.

Hell and damn. Five days left of this interminable house party. Five remaining days to avoid Lady Jane's lovely blue eyes. Her *yearning*, lovely blue eyes. God save him from infatuated misses. Never mind that Lady Jane was the only miss ever infatuated with him. All the others saw only the title, and the money. Incredibly, Lady Jane appeared to have developed something of a *tendre* for him.

All the more reason to stay well clear of her.

Only five more days.

From a dark corner of the vast front hall at

Margrave Park, a stately clock chimed the hour of two. The house was asleep, including the servants. Confident she wouldn't be discovered, Jane made her way down the stairs and crossed to the library, a candle lighting her way. She carefully opened one side of the double doors and slipped inside, closing the door behind her. The fire had long since died, leaving only the faint glow of embers to dimly illuminate the room. Holding her candle aloft, Jane glided across the floor on bare feet, straight to the third shelf of the east wall. She scanned the titles, searching for one book in particular. *Mr. Paisley's Discourse, In Three Parts, of Australian Aboriginal Tribes, With Accompanying Etchings.* Ah, there it was. Turning, she set the candlestick on the small table to her left and just behind before reaching for the book.

It was shockingly naughty of her to look, but her curiosity managed to get the best of her. Not to mention, she was positively dying for some diversion – something, anything that could be considered exciting.

Lady Bonderant's house party had become exceedingly tiresome. The past three days, Blixford had cooled considerably toward her, and she rather thought her chances of betrothal to him were narrowing to somewhere near nothing. She was at a loss how to go on. She tried harder, and the result was such a strain she thought she'd go mad. Just this morning, she'd gotten up before dawn, dressed in her habit, and went for a run, all by herself, hopeful that some new method of attracting Blixford's attention would come to her.

It did not.

He was clearly set on Lady Letitia, and Jane was left out in the cold.

Her heart would surely break when an announcement was made. She would return home with Robert and Sherbourne and nurse her disappointment until the start of the Season. Then she supposed she would return to London and see if she could make a go of it with another suitor.

What else could she do? Living her life on the shelf was unthinkable. She would not be a doddering, maiden aunt to her brothers' children, if and when any of them finally married and had any.

For now, she was certain she was bested, and had decided to have what bit of fun she could while suffering through the remainder of what had become a detestable house party. If she could pull it off without severe rudeness and ill-mannered consequence, she'd pack and leave, straightaway.

The book was terribly disappointing. Letitia had lied. Or perhaps Letitia's expectations were less than Jane's. She expected 'horrid masculinity of the sort no lady should ever look upon.' Jane was determined to look. Squinting in the dim light of the single candle, she peered at the etchings. How very curious. Her sole experience with a male member was limited to horses. She was intelligent enough to realize a man would not be so large as a horse, but the men in the etchings seemed hardly adequate. Proportionately, it was confounding. She continued turning the pages, but each etching was less impressive than the last. Nothing resembling horrid. Not even particularly masculine. The etchings might be of breastless women with appendages smaller than her fist between their legs.

She yawned. How tiresome. She'd stayed up late for this.

Then she noticed a slip of paper peeking out from the back spine of the book. With a tug, she withdrew it and her eyes widened considerably. This was well worth losing sleep over. She stared down at a charcoal sketch of a nude man, his member extraordinarily large. Oh my. It was a bit awkward, wasn't it? How peculiar to have something like that between one's legs.

What was between her legs made itself known and she shifted her weight from one bare foot to the other. Surely she would be torn apart by a man whose maleness was that spectacular. Was the duke thusly endowed? She blushed furiously, but didn't replace the charcoal in the book. She laid it there, on the table, while she replaced Mr. Paisley's dry discourse upon the bookshelf.

When she turned back toward the table, she let out a squeak of alarm.

The Duke of Blixford stood just to the other side. He was still in his evening clothes, looking devastatingly handsome. In his hand, he held the charcoal of the nude man with the imposing member.

Jane rather thought she'd like to die.

"Well," he said. "*Well.*"

He managed to give a sermon in two words. One word, actually. Spoken twice, undoubtedly for effect.

Choosing to ignore the obvious atrociousness of the situation, Jane reached for the candlestick with one hand and clutched the neck of her dressing gown with the other, straightening her spine until she grew another inch, composing her features into one of haughty formality. "My sympathies, Your Grace. You are similarly afflicted with insomnia. I shall bid you good night, then, and pray you sleep well." Moving around the table, she struck out for the door, certain she would faint of embarrassment. Why had her curiosity got the best of her? Oh, how she wished she'd gone straight to bed after the evening's entertainment was done, instead of reading until the hour grew late enough to slip down to the library.

"Will you not wait for my reply, Lady Jane? It's customary to delay departing until you've heard an answering good night."

With her hand upon the door-knob, she waited, counting each beat of her heart. She got to twenty before she realized he wasn't going to say good night.

He wouldn't allow her to escape this humiliation. Seeing her hopes of marriage to her duke disappear altogether, she turned, slowly. "Was there something you wished to discuss, Your Grace?"

He moved toward her, the offending charcoal in his long fingered hand. His black breeches fit him like a second skin, highlighting the strength of his muscled thighs. Broad shoulders filled his elegant, superbly fitted evening coat. She was made further aware of her state of undress by the contrast of his clothing to hers. Her feet were bare. Curling her toes beneath the hem of her dressing gown, she truly wished the floor would open up and swallow her.

The picture was there, between them. She would not look at it again. She could not. Her gaze remained on his face, noting that his lips were perfection, not too full, not too thin. His eyes were dark, as was his hair. Winged brows rose above those eyes. The duke had an unnatural ability to move them about, making his wishes clear without making a sound. It was said that entire armies of servants and underlings jumped to the command of one single set of eyebrows.

The only feature he possessed that was not handsome was his nose. Slightly on the long side, it was a true Roman nose that otherwise marred the perfection of his face. Jane loved that part of him best of all.

At the moment, he stared down that length with a firm look that neither approved, nor disapproved. "You will, of course, explain to me how you knew this charcoal was hiding in Mr. Paisley's boring discourse."

"I should be only too happy to explain, if I had prior knowledge of it."

"You did not?"

"I did not."

"Then you will tell me when your interest was sparked by the societal study of Australian aboriginal tribes."

She'd really rather not. If she lied and claimed a true interest, he might see her as a bluestocking. But to tell the truth, that she was desirous of seeing for herself what a male member looked like, would surely cause him to look upon her as a naughty woman. Or worse, an inquisitive child. Her mind cast about for possible explanations, but she realized, as he stood there staring at her, he already knew. Lying could only make the situation worse —if that were possible. Blushing so fiercely, she feared her face must surely catch fire, she murmured, "Mere curiosity brought me to the library, Your Grace. I can only plead your pardon and indulgence in not judging me too harshly."

He stepped closer and held the charcoal so that the candlelight shone on the man. And his member. "It's not a very good sketch, is it?"

Jane cleared her throat, never taking her eyes from his face. "Having no point of reference, Your Grace, I wouldn't know."

His gaze met hers. "You're mortified, are you not?"

"Quite so."

"It occurs to me that your embarrassment extends only to this badly rendered drawing of a naked man. That you are wandering about Lady Bonderant's home, half dressed, in the middle of the night, appears not to bother you at all."

"On the contrary. It's only that the picture in your hand is of such breathtaking humiliation, my state of dishabille and the late hour pale in comparison."

He stared at her again. After a time, he said in a low, modulated voice, "You wish to marry me." It was baldly stated.

"Yes, Your Grace. Above all things."

"And you believe this episode has ruined your chances."

She dropped her gaze to the floor. "I am quickly coming to that conclusion, yes. You're known for your insistence upon decorum, and this can hardly be considered decorous behavior on my part."

"No, it cannot. It's shocking, actually."

Her heart sank. She was doomed. Letitia Rawlings would marry her duke and Jane would die of a broken heart.

"Though not at all surprising."

Eyes wide, she jerked her gaze to his. "I beg your pardon?"

"I daresay curiosity concerning the opposite sex is a natural thing, perhaps more pointed in yourself because of your nature and your advancing years."

"I am eighteen!"

Something glittered in his dark eyes. Not humor. The duke was not a man for humor. What then? She swallowed.

"You might have waited merely a few months, Lady Jane, and put your curiosity to rest in the same manner as all gently bred young ladies who become brides. As it is, you've put yourself into a compromising position."

"I am not compromised. Beyond we two, no one need ever know I was here, in the library, in my dressing gown."

"Looking at a naked man."

His disapproval began to nudge aside her crushing disappointment of certainty that he would not, after all, ask for her hand. "He's but a one-dimensional rendering, Your Grace. A few strokes of charcoal."

Did he move closer still, or was it only her imagination?

"Ah, but the charcoal man is not the only one in the library, is he? There is me, Lady Jane, and I am far more than a few strokes of charcoal."

He was definitely closer. She caught the vague scent of brandy on his breath and the lovely odor of his cologne. And him. Musky, and male. Her back was against the library door. "You are a gentleman. I'm not afraid."

"Suppose I were not a gentleman? I might ravish you there on the sofa and you would be ruined."

She'd never know what possessed her to say it, but before she gave it an instant of thought, she whispered, "Then I would delight in my ruination."

He kissed her then, touching her with only his lips. She still held the candle. He still held the charcoal. A shot of desire pierced her center, far stronger than the faint quiver she'd felt when she first saw the sketch. *Oh, my*. His lips were soft, yet firm. He turned his head slightly and deepened the kiss, touching his tongue to her lips, gently forcing them open that he could slide it into her mouth. *Oh, heaven*. She tentatively touched her own tongue to his, some part of her brain wondering why such an odd thing could have such a powerful effect. The shot of desire became a demand. She lifted her free hand to rest it against his shoulder. He was warm beneath the coat. Solid. Hard.

His large hand slipped beneath her hair to close around the nape of her neck, holding her there as his mouth moved across hers and made her dizzy with longing.

Abruptly, he stopped. Stepping back, he raised one dark brow. "Just as I thought, Lady Jane. You're a woman ruled by your passions. Most unfitting for a duchess."

He'd sought to prove a point, and so he had. What he didn't know was that she loved him. Otherwise, she'd never have allowed him to kiss her. Certainly she would not have responded with passion. She debated telling him, right out, but knew it wouldn't help her in the slightest. A declaration of love would only further damage her already tattered chances, for it was surely not at all decorous to tell a man he was loved before the gentleman expressed the sentiment first.

The game was up. She had lost.

Anger replaced disappointment. Raising one brow,

she stared him down. "Inexperience explains my response to your forced attentions. I daresay most women find their first kiss . . . stimulating."

"You are wrong."

"Am I to assume then, that other young ladies do not respond in kind, but rather, turn and run screaming into the night?"

"Not quite so dramatic an exit, but something like that." He stepped close again. "They don't allow a gentleman to open his mouth, nor do they answer by opening their own. Lady Jane, you have the disadvantage of being raised in a houseful of males. I would counsel you, for your own sake, to have a care where gentlemen are concerned. When you receive your second kiss, do not part your lips. The results could be dangerous."

"You're hardly in a position to give me counsel, Your Grace, considering it is you who just forced me to do what you advise against. I'd not thought you a hypocrite."

"Ah, but I did not force you, Lady Jane. That is the point."

"And you always make your point, Blixford, do you not? You're a tiresome man." Talking about the kiss was almost as stimulating as the kiss itself had been. He would not marry her, but she sincerely wished he'd kiss her again. Just once more. She moistened her lips with a swift swipe of her tongue.

His dark eyes became darker. Turning his face without his gaze leaving hers, he pursed his lips and blew out the candle in her hand. "Drop it," he commanded.

Her fingers loosened and the moment the candlestick clattered to the floor, he enveloped her in his arms, crushing her against the hard length of him, from her knees to her thighs, her belly and breasts, all the way to her lips, which he kissed with barely leashed passion. He speared her with his tongue and she didn't follow his advice. She opened her lips and drew him in, twisting her tongue with his, shaking with desire, her body yearning.

Hands twice as large as her own moved along her back, one falling to cup her buttocks and draw her closer, making her very aware that Blixford was at least as well adorned as the charcoal man. Perhaps he was merely making another point, driving home another lesson.

Jane didn't care. If he would teach, she would learn. Never could she allow another man to do this to her, but he was not another man. He was Blixford, whom she loved madly.

One hand moved from her back to her front, deliberately untying the neck of her nightgown and drawing it down, sliding beneath her dressing gown to close over her naked breast. The core of her swelled and demanded she assuage the need.

"So full, so beautiful," he whispered, dragging his lips away from hers, running them down her throat before closing them around her puckered nipple.

Diving her fingers into his silky hair, she clutched his head and moaned, deep in her throat. Good God, but this was delicious. He raised up and kissed her again, both arms about her, holding her so close, she could feel the beat of his heart against her breast.

Then he did a very odd thing. He dropped one hand and began to gather up the skirt of her dressing gown, bringing the gown along with it, exposing her legs. This he did while still kissing her, and she was barely aware, drowning in sensation. The feel of his breeches against her thighs brought home her nakedness, but she made no move to remove his hand and cover herself.

His fingers tangled in the curls between her thighs and she willed him to continue, to touch her there, where she was hot and needful.

He did.

Oh blessed heaven, how much better than anything her untried mind might have imagined.

"You're ready for me," he murmured, sounding surprised.

"I've been ready for quite some time," she replied, inhaling his scent, aware that her own mingled in the air.

"Sweet innocent, you've no idea how precarious your situation."

"You've no notion how very much I want you."

"Is it so important to be a duchess?"

"It is only important I be *your* duchess. Oh!" She started in his arms. "Your Grace, what are you doing?"

"Ravishing you." He kissed her again, his hand between her legs, his finger slipping within her, making her quiver and shake. "Now I shall have to marry you."

"Because you've ravished me?"

"Precisely." His kiss became harder, more insistent. His fingers worked magic, building her desire, even as he whispered fiercely, "Damn you, Jane. Damn your infernal curiosity, your misplaced affection, those *yearning* eyes."

Deliriously happy, caught up in him, it took a moment for his words to sink in. Drawing back from his mouth, she looked into the dark shadow of his face, scarcely visible in the dim glow of the smoldering coals in the grate. "You would damn me, sir, in the midst of ravishing me?"

"You're the very last woman I'd choose. Do you hear me? The very last." His finger plunged deeper. His thumb ran circles against the most tender of spots. "Give over, Jane. Close your eyes and let yourself go."

She did as he said, closing her eyes, concentrating on his hand, on her center, on the dizzying kiss he gave her. Her body took on a will of its own, shaking uncontrollably, warmth and powerful contractions radiating from the middle of her. Never in her life had she felt thus, and nothing in life had ever been so enjoyable. Nothing. Ever. When she stopped shaking, when she could breathe normally, she opened her eyes and stared at him. "Your Grace, that was . . . spectacular. Is it always like that?"

"No. It's not." He removed his hand and the hem of her dressing gown fell to the floor, once again. Grasping her hand, he laid it across the front of his breeches. He was rock hard, his member impressively large, straining against the black cloth. "It's something typically only enjoyed by men. Hardly surprising you'd find fulfillment your first time out. You do, I believe, enjoy many pastimes ordinarily dominated by men."

Frowning, she pulled her hand away and stepped back, until she was once again against the library door. "That was an insult, I'm certain."

He was angry, but she could not fathom for what reason.

"Of course it's an insult. You're halfway to a hoyden, riding faster and harder than most men, taking up pistols for God's sake, and harboring a very unfeminine interest in farming. You're too loud, too bold. You even *sound* like a man on occasion." He crowded her against the door, his hands in her hair, holding her head while he rained incongruous kisses across her cheeks, her chin, her nose. "Is it any wonder you would climax with scarcely a few minutes of stimulation? You are far too passionate, everything I *do not* want, but now must have because I couldn't resist those eyes."

The full import of his words finally settled into her mind, quickly clearing the haze of desire. Jerking away from him, she moved toward the fireplace, suddenly chilled to the bone.

"If I'm repulsive to you, I wonder why you'd insist on marrying me?"He stalked toward the fireplace and faced her, his scowling face reflecting his anger. "Because I've just assaulted you. Can you know so little of propriety, you don't realize you've been completely compromised? Ruined? I will speak to Sherbourne first thing in the morning."

Jane considered reaching for one of the glowing embers and dropping it into his breeches. If she wouldn't burn her fingers, she would. And enjoy his pain. Drawing herself up, she forgot she was in a dressing gown, that it was past two in the morning, that his hand had only just been in her most private place, that he'd offered what she wanted above all things. All she could think of were his cutting, hurtful words. He would marry her because he had to. Not because he wanted to. "Rest assured, I won't hold you to any such terrible fate, nor will I thrust my passionate personage upon you in the future. Don't touch me again, or you'll become a man with one hand. Don't speak to my father, or you'll become ridiculous. You've taken me to the height of passion, then disparaged me cruelly. My love for you is indeed misplaced, a mistake I'll not make again."

"You're but a child, Jane. What would you know of love?"

It appeared he was not done insulting her. "Evidently, nothing at all. I always thought myself of above average intelligence, but I'll have to reconsider after tonight. I'm clearly no cleverer than a bleating ewe, following the herd, regardless of peril. I misjudged you entirely and I'm perplexed by my lack of insight." She allowed her gaze to travel the length of him, uncaring of her insolence. "What a pity such masculine beauty is wasted on one so cold, cruel, and self-righteous. Perhaps I'm a child –a *mannish* child – but I'm quite capable of giving and receiving affection. You sir, are not, and for that, I'm sorry for you." She stopped her perusal at his eyes, noting he looked angry, and maybe a little astonished she would speak so rudely to him, a duke. "You've all the warmth of a block of granite and I pity any woman who must call you husband. Good night, Your Grace."

She turned and walked out, closing the door behind her. In the dark, she found her way upstairs and reached the quiet solitude of her room.

She didn't cry, she packed. And grew up, having left the last vestige of childhood and fairy tales in the Bonderant library.

The devil with Blixford. She would return to London in spring and make the most of her second Season. There was a gentleman out there who would not disapprove of her, who would appreciate her unconventional talents, who would not disparage her passion. There must be, and she would find him, marry him and give him children.

Blixford could rot in Hell for all she cared. He was, indeed, a dreadful stick. Robert was correct. The look she'd seen on Blixford's face after Annabel's burial was simple aggravation that she'd had the audacity to die and take the heir he coveted with her.

But even as she thought it, she didn't really believe it. At that moment, he had truly looked bereft, lost, completely vulnerable.

It did not, could not matter. He would never allow whatever softness lay within his soul to rise to the surface, but instead remain a hard, cold, imperious man, incapable of expressing affection and quite capable of cruelty.

Mannish, indeed. How she despised what he'd said, and it naturally followed, she despised him for saying it.

After tomorrow, they would all be gone, thank God. Lucy lay in her bed and listened to the clock in the hall downstairs as it chimed the hour, yet again. Three o'clock, and still she couldn't sleep.

Deciding to give up, she threw back the covers and reached for her dressing gown. She went to the fireplace, retrieved the coal spade, and tossed a few lumps upon the embers, stirring them about until a small fire blazed. She lit two candles and sat at the secretary positioned before one of the windows in her chamber. Pulling her latest drawing from a narrow, hidden compartment, she gazed at it critically. It wasn't right. It was disproportionate, the man's legs too large for his torso. Her last attempt had the man's legs too thin, not nearly muscled enough. The etchings in Mr. Paisley's discourse had not been much help to her, his aborigines rather on the diminutive side. She desired her drawing to reflect a man of tremendous masculinity, his physique impressive. It was necessary for proportion, in order for his cock to be large enough for her purposes.

Lucy sighed and withdrew another drawing, taking heart as she gazed at this one. She'd managed to master capturing a feminine figure, and she thought her charcoal woman was lovely; full figured, with long, shapely legs, a definite dip to her waist, and round, plump breasts topped with perfectly sized nipples.

Her gaze returned to the man and she frowned. "You are not worthy of her, sir. I vow, your legs would crush the poor thing." She chuckled at the thought then sobered as something occurred to her. Perhaps she was going about this all wrong, trying to perfect each of them individually. If she drew them together, would not the proportion work itself out naturally?

Anxious to see if the theory was correct, she retrieved a fresh sheet of drawing paper and her charcoal and began to sketch, concentrating carefully, memory her only guide —and even that couldn't be very dependable. She'd never actually seen a man and a woman coupling. It wasn't as though she'd ever had the ability to see herself while engaged in the act. It was entirely up to her imagination to determine how she and Matthew had fit together.

As the drawing took shape, her memories

threatened to overwhelm her. Despite more than a year gone since last he'd held her in his arms and made his body a part of hers, she remembered with aching detail how it had been, and how much she had loved him.

Her core flooded with desire, hot and needful. She continued to draw, first their heads, lips meeting in a passionate kiss, downward to their necks and torsos. Here, she stopped. Face to face, body to body, what was there to see? Hmm.

She started again, this time drawing the woman's head and body turned forward and the man's face just behind, peering over her shoulder, eyes cast downward. Yes, that was good, for he would surely be fascinated with her round, perfect breasts. His hands would be caressing them . . . no, only one hand, caressing one breast. The other would be just there, at the apex of her thighs, touching her as his very impressive cock slid between her legs, up and into her.

Legs. They had no legs. She eyed the drawing carefully, determined to get it right. Where would her legs be, if she were in front? Perhaps he was sitting, and she in his lap? Inspired, she hurriedly sketched their legs, and the legs of a chair, beneath them.

She spent another hour filling in details, concentrating carefully on her task, getting up to poke the fire when it burned down and her light dimmed.

She heard the clock strike five just as she finished. Holding the drawing up, she gazed at it with a critical eye. She still needed to work on his legs, but they were much better proportioned than her earlier attempts. Perhaps she could get the hang of this, eventually. She had no notion what she might do with her erotic drawings, would likely keep them locked away, only to be brought out and viewed for her own enjoyment. She was never quite sure where her imagination might lead her and had no notion how or why her mind insisted on such startling mental images, but she felt a need to draw what she imagined, to give her carnal thoughts shape and form, a reality of charcoal on paper, because reality in truth would never come to pass.

Sighing, she locked away her night's work and returned to her bed, slipping out of her dressing gown, pulling her night rail over her head, sliding naked beneath the covers. In the darkest hour of night, just before dawn, she closed her eyes, caressed her breasts with one hand and reached between her thighs with the other. Swollen and slick, begging for a deep, filling thrust, her core, the center of her, sometimes her only source of pleasure, was once again resigned to naught but her fingers.

Afterward, she rolled to her side and wept. God, how she missed him.

Jane had not attempted sleep, certain she was far too agitated. Instead, she spent the remaining hours of the night packing and making out a list of manly attributes she would search for in a prospective spouse. When she was done, she looked it over and determined Blixford had none of them, with the sole exception of his looks. He was a fine figure of a man. Pity his body housed such a despicable person.

The sky was pearl gray with the beginning of dawn when she let herself out the garden door and strode toward the stable. She would ride and vent some of her anger, then change into a morning gown and await Sherbourne in the dining room. As soon as he appeared, she would plead some female malady and ask him to accompany her home, back to Hornsby Grange in Oxfordshire. He would do so, without question.

A sleepy groom was already up and about and made little comment when she requested he saddle the mare she'd ridden since arriving at Lady Bonderant's house party. Clattering out of the stable yard, she turned toward the lane that crossed the hayfields, speaking to her mount in quiet tones.

The lane stretched enticingly before her and after a short canter to warm up the mare she urged her into a full out run. Her thoughts were a tangle, far from the lane, the hayfields, or the run itself. Lack of concentration, coupled with the pounding of the mare's hooves was the only explanation of how she failed to notice another rider approaching from behind.

Not until he surpassed her and moved ahead did she see that Blixford was also enjoying an early dawn run. In truth, he did not appear to be enjoying it. He looked his usual expressionless self. Did he never smile?

He didn't so much as glance at her as he passed, but overtook her and forged ahead.

The instinct to increase speed and beat him to the end of the lane tugged at her, but she resisted. To do so would naturally result in the necessity of speaking to him, and she'd really rather eat a clod of dirt.

She slowed the mare to a walk, turned her about, and set her to canter back toward the house, severely aggravated he had ruined her run. Scarcely a minute later, the duke pulled up next to her and called out for her to slow down, that he wished to speak with her.

Manners overrode anger and she did so, biting out a greeting. "Good morning, Your Grace."

"Lady Jane, I wish to impress upon you the significance of what transpired in the library. I ask that you accept my hand and allow me to make reparations for my thoughtless actions." His face reflected such strong distaste, he looked as though he'd sucked a lemon. Was this the same man who so passionately ravished her against the library door?

"The only significance to me is the realization that I have been a fool for two long years, and entirely wasted my first Season and an impressive number of suitors, waiting for you to come out of mourning." She glared at him. "In point of fact, I should probably thank you for a harsh dose of reality." She looked ahead, away from his cold stare. "You are forgiven, and there's an end to it. I do not wish to marry you, can think of no greater travesty, and I suggest we put the matter behind us and forget about it."

"It's not a matter of forgiveness, nor avoidance. You are ruined, and I *will* make reparations."

"Oh, for pity's sake, Blixford, I'm not ruined. My precious maidenhead is still intact, and will be until I take a husband, who will never know I was previously ravished by a blackguard of a duke." She wouldn't look at him again. She was half afraid she would be tempted to plant him a facer.

"Nevertheless, I intend to speak to your father this morning, as soon as possible."

"Will you tell him what transpired in the library?" She almost hoped he would. Sherbourne would definitely plant him a facer.

"I see no reason to upset the man needlessly. It's no secret I'm currently searching for a wife, and I have chosen you. I will ask your father for your hand."

"Ask if you like, but you'll look a fool when I refuse you. You may not have my hand," she said coldly, "nor any other appendage. I beg you ask Lady Letitia for hers, as I'm certain she would cut it off and feed it to the hounds if you directed her to do so and made her a duchess at the same time. She's a perfect lady, Blixford, and perfect for you. Not mannish at all. I daresay she would not have allowed you to ravish her in the library, and it's debatable whether she will allow it after you're married, but you clearly have a preference for passionless ladies who paint divinely and play the pianoforte with elegant mastery. I'm sure you'll be very happy together."

Shocking her, he rode close, reached out and grasped her arm. "Don't be a fool. You're allowing emotion to override good sense. Only think for a moment, and consider if anyone saw you go into the library. Your reputation will be in tatters."

Jerking free of him, she urged the mare away. "You grow tiresome, Blixford, and I grow hungry. I wish you a good day and every happiness." She pressed her heel against the mare's flank and set her into a canter, gratified when Blixford made no move to follow.

Michael watched her ride away and clenched the reins in frustration, as angry with himself as he was with her. What had come over him in the library? He was not a debaucher of young ladies. He was not a particularly amorous sort, content to keep a sedate mistress to mollify the physical side to his nature. A wife was for procreation. His wife would be a duchess, responsible for overseeing five different houses, managing whatever minuscule social engagements he was required to hold or attend, and raising their offspring competently. He didn't want a wife he lusted after.

Regardless of what he wanted, that was precisely what he was about to have. She was all he never sought in a wife; courageous, beautiful, desirable, intriguing and passionate. He didn't want her for his wife, but he couldn't deny he wanted *her*. After last night, he wanted her with something that bordered on obsession. He'd not slept. Instead, he sat in the chair beside the fire in his bedchamber and considered how he might convince her to accept his hand. Close to dawn, he hit upon the notion of going for a ride on the off chance she would be out early again.

She had. He proposed. She refused.

Now what? He continued toward the house, deciding just as he reached the stable yard, he would tell Sherbourne she was compromised. Her father wouldn't allow her to refuse him. They would be married by tomorrow morning. He'd bed her by tomorrow night. By the time she was with child, hopefully sooner than later, he would be done with this insanity-inducing desire. He would keep his distance, except when they shared a bed, and he would not know her beyond that. He couldn't allow it, for he was absolutely certain, just as Lucy believed, he would grow attached. Already, he liked Lady Jane. Rather a lot. His horrible words in the library had shocked her, but she couldn't know he'd been equally shocked. It was unlike him to be cruel, but he'd been desperate to gain some distance, to kill her desire, for he'd been dangerously close to hauling her over to the sofa and taking her, right there, damn the consequences or the possibility of someone walking in on them. She'd have allowed it, not because she hoped to force his hand, but because she wanted it.

Incredible. She was simply incredible. And she would be his wife.

It would be difficult in the extreme not to become attached, even to fall in love with her. And then where would he be? If she died in childbed, as his own mother had, he might perhaps lose his mind, become a madman, like his poor, demented papa. He would lose all he'd gained, would further disgrace the family name, the ducal title. Hundreds of people would suffer, as they had when his father went mad, all because he lost the wife he loved so much, and subsequently, his handle on reality.

No matter what, he could not love Lady Jane. He would allow himself to enjoy their marriage bed, but out of it, in the light of day, he would stay far away from her. When she became pregnant, he would leave her at Eastchase Hall until she was delivered. He would return, see the babe, perhaps get her pregnant again, to ensure an heir in case the first succumbed to death in childhood, then leave again. If she died in childbed, he would feel terrible, of course, and he would mourn the passing of one so young and full of life. But he would not go mad.

He thought of Annabel and flinched. He had not loved her, but he'd felt a certain amount of affection for her, and her death had been a blight on his soul. In point of fact, he was not yet fully recovered. Thinking of Annabel brought on dull pain and a gloomy outlook.

He tried not to think of her and, as a general rule, was successful. Of late, he was able not to think of Annabel at all, unless he was in his cups. Regrettably, he'd been close last night. He'd made his way to the library and overindulged his brandy, feeling morose after a decidedly tedious evening of entertainment. He'd suffered through Lady Letitia's recital, Miss Harriet Sutcliffe's monologue of a scene from *Hamlet*, and a game of charades, the best performance, of course, by Lady Jane. He'd not joined in because it was beneath his dignity, electing to remain in the corner, conversing with Sherbourne about crop rotation and an interesting investment opportunity. Otherwise, he found the evening irksome, the culmination of almost two weeks of constant companionship with a group of people he'd ordinarily avoid at all costs.

Tomorrow would be an end to it. He'd thought to offer for Lady Letitia, but no more. He would have Lady Jane. Perhaps she was a hoyden, but she would make an adequate duchess. She was well acquainted with running Sherbourne's household, and with the guidance of her aunt she'd not be hard pressed to provide entertainments in his home. She had a great amount of health and vitality. She would, no doubt, produce an heir without too much trouble.

Set upon his course, he'd only just stepped into the house through the garden door when Lucy rushed toward him and dragged him into the conservatory. "Blix, did you meet Lady Jane in the library last night?"

Gazing at his sister's bright eyes, her flushed

cheeks, he could see she was rather excited at the prospect. "It was accidental, but yes, I did see her in the library when all the house was asleep."

"Oh, Blix, how marvelous!"

"Not precisely how I'd phrase it, Luce. How did you know?"

Her brows rose. "Mrs. Sutcliffe, of course. She's a horrid woman, but I do adore her daughter, Harriet, so I had to suffer inviting her in order to have Harriet."

Michael blessed the horrid Mrs. Sutcliffe. She'd inadvertently made all of this much easier for him. "Did she happen to mention why she was up and about at two in the morning?"

"Claims she suffered dyspepsia and couldn't get an answer to her ring. She went to the kitchen for a bromide and on her return, saw Jane leaving the library. Directly afterward, you opened the door and looked after her, and Mrs. Sutcliffe reached her own conclusion." Lucy's eyes, if possible, became brighter. "Was she correct?"

"Really, sister, do you expect me to kiss and tell?"

"Oh, Blix, how lovely. You will offer for her, of course?"

"Immediately." He stepped back, sketched a slight bow and left her, headed for the front of the house to enquire whether Sherbourne had descended as yet.

Lucy's butler met him and spoke before he could ask. "Your Grace, the earl has requested you meet him in the library."

Ah, so Sherbourne was already aware. Michael stepped to the door and opened it without pausing.

Tomorrow night. He'd have to keep that in mind while he faced her irate papa. And Jane herself, who would undoubtedly make him more than uncomfortable before it was said and done. He wouldn't mind. His discomfort now would be made up for tomorrow night.

CHAPTER 2

She'd be gone from Margrave Park within two hours, and if Blixford kept to his usual antisocial behavior and avoided society engagements, she might never see him again.

That would be a relief. Even now, as angry and hurt as she was, she could not forget how he had made her feel for only those few moments. It would be embarrassing to see him in the company of others, knowing he'd had his hands and lips on her in such a shockingly intimate fashion. She ruefully admitted her embarrassment would be as much for his obvious dislike of her as for his physical attraction to her. It was humbling and degrading to realize he thought her a dreadful person, even while he lusted after her.

She left the stable and walked to the house, deciding to take breakfast before she went up to change into a morning gown. This time, she went through the front door, into the open, airy hall. The clock was chiming eight as she stepped inside.

Sherbourne was there, lying in wait, it appeared, his normally smiling face a thundercloud of fury. "Daughter, I will see you in the library this instant."

Doom impended. Her parent was rarely angry with her, and she could only conclude that someone had witnessed her library visit.

He closed the door behind her and instantly verified her fear. "Mrs. Sutcliffe has just informed me that you came to the library in the wee hours of this morning in your dressing gown, and Blixford was here. You will tell me what transpired."

She didn't like to lie, particularly to her father, but she could see no reason to tell the truth. The consequences were too horrible, and what was one small lie, after all? "I was unable to sleep, so I came down in search of a book. I was on my way out when I realized the duke was here, in that chair close to the fire. He'd evidently nodded off and I woke him when I opened the door to leave." She kept her expression bland. "It was nothing, sir. I bade him good night and left." How had Mrs. Sutcliffe been aware? Was the wretched woman lurking in the shadows out in the hall?

Her papa looked distressed. "Jane, I've done my best by you, but perhaps I erred in failing to take another wife, to provide you a feminine hand in your upbringing."

"There is Aunt Northern, sir. She sponsored my coming out and has always been helpful to me. You mustn't chastise yourself. I've not turned out so badly, have I? There are some who would say I'm a bit mannish in my interests, but I'm certain I can find a gentleman who won't mind." She reached out and touched his arm. "Please don't allow my library visit to concern you. It was entirely innocent, and you should recall who made it her business to tell you. Mrs. Sutcliffe is a terrible gossip and frequently driven by whatever bee she has in her bonnet. To be frank, she's a mean-spirited woman."

He actually looked more grieved. "Don't you see? It's her nature to gossip, and by the time the rest of the party has risen and come downstairs, everyone will know what happened. Innocent, or not, your reputation is damaged and the only course of action is to demand Blixford offer for you."

Seeing her world turn upside down, she hastened to

save herself. "Please don't do that. I have no wish to marry him."

His eyes narrowed. "What's this? You've clearly set your cap for him, insisted we accept Lady Bonderant's invitation to this house party for the sole purpose of pursuing him. Events have made it so you may have what you wished. When and why have you changed your mind?"

She turned and paced to the fireplace, tapping the skirts of her habit with the head of her crop. "Last night, actually. I came to the conclusion that he is, indeed, a stick, and I would be miserable married to him."

"Ah, Jane, surely you can see it doesn't matter now? I've no choice but to insist you marry him."

Wheeling around, she met his gaze. "I don't like to cross you, sir, but I *will not* marry Blixford."

The hateful man made an appearance then, stepping inside the door and closing it behind him with a soft click.

"Your Grace, we are in the midst of a private conversation," she said with righteous indignation. "I'd ask that you leave us to continue."

He ignored her and focused on her father. "Sherbourne, will you do me the honor of granting me Lady Jane's hand in marriage?"

Her papa shot her a harsh glance before facing Blixford again. "Is she compromised?"

Without so much as a blink, the duke said, "She is. I will travel to London this afternoon and obtain a special license. We will be married tomorrow morning."

Blixford looked like a man en route to the gallows. Her pride stung. Her feelings were bruised and bleeding. She was accustomed to acceptance, even admiration from her friends and suitors. That this arrogant man could make her feel like so much dirt beneath his boots made her want to hit something.

And cry. She never cried, and his ability to make her want to infuriated her.

Alarmed, she moved forward and stood between them, turning her back on Blixford to face her father. "Sir, I implore you not to force me into what will surely be a life of misery."

"I can't allow you to ruin yourself and become a pariah. Only think of your brothers. They've yet to find brides, and what lady will have any one of them if their sister is ruined?"

"How grossly unfair of you to use guilt."

His anger returned and she saw her future grow exceedingly dim. "You should have considered the consequences of visiting the library in the middle of the blasted night, half dressed. God's blood, daughter, *what* were you thinking?" Suddenly, his eyes widened and he jerked his gaze to Blixford. "Was there an assignation?" He grew another inch, his back straight, his hands balling into fists. "Did you ask her to meet you here, Blixford?"

"Papa, you're overset. There was no assignation. It happened just as I said. I came down to get a book, Blixford was here, and that's all there is to it."

"I had not yet retired when Lady Jane arrived, and she did, indeed search for a book. She hastened to leave and I detained her. I took liberties, Sherbourne. Afterward, I was less than kind and Lady Jane was deeply offended. Rightly so. I have apologized and assured her in future I will treat her with the utmost respect and deference."

His honesty spurred her into action. "He dislikes me dreadfully, Papa. He said I am *mannish*. Would you have me married to a man who thinks so little of me? I will be miserable."

"Nonsense, Jane." He cut her a look. "A man does not take liberties with a woman he dislikes, dreadfully or no. You have no choice, child. If you refuse to marry him, I will have to kill him."

He said it calmly, rationally, much the same as he might say he'd have to invite Blixford for dinner. "Sir, do not jest."

Sherbourne moved to the fireplace and stood with his back to them, his hands folded behind him. "I do not jest, Jane."

She did not like her father to be unhappy with her. Devil take the rest of the world, but Sherbourne frowning at her, disappointed in her to this extent, made her feel ill.

Turning toward Blixford, her rage surged forth. "Arrogant, meddlesome *clod*. I told you not to speak to him, or suffer the consequences. Why are you doing this? You don't wish to marry me, and for all that, I'd rather marry my father's poorest tenant farmer than shackle myself to the likes of you. Withdraw your offer, this instant."

"Jane, be quiet," her father said. "You will marry him, and say no more on the matter."

Wheeling about, she looked to the only parent she'd ever known. "I warn you, sir, this will end very badly. For his sake, don't make me do it."

"This has nothing to do with him." Papa turned and scowled at Blixford. "Were it not my own child's reputation on the line and his life necessary to make reparations, I'd kill him with my bare hands."

"Understandable," Blixford said dryly. "Were I not the only thing standing between my title and the crown, I believe I might welcome it."

"Death is preferable to marrying my daughter?" Sherbourne's blue eyes, exactly like her own, were cold and hard. "It will be a joyless day when I'm forced to call you kin." He cast a look at Jane. "You've broken my heart, daughter. I can only thank merciful God your mother isn't here to witness your disgrace." He stalked to the door, but paused with his hand on the knob. "We're leaving. Immediately. Have your bags brought to the front hall. Blixford, I will expect you at

Hornsby Grange tomorrow morning. We will discuss the marriage settlement at that time." Then he was gone.

Turning to face the duke, Jane noted he looked very tired. Had he slept at all? "The travesty of this only becomes worse. My father loves me and I have broken his heart."

"He'll get past it in time, Lady Jane. We shall make the best of things."

She moved toward the door. "You may do as you wish, Your Grace. I certainly intend to."

"Have a care, Lady Jane. I am not a man to be trifled with."

She glanced over her shoulder. "You really think I'm filled with false objections and missish aggravation, don't you?"

"Yes. You've made it clear you wish to marry me. You now have your wish. I apologize for speaking harshly to you last night and assure you, it will not happen again. I believe my sensibilities were dulled a bit by too much brandy."

"Is this also how you excuse ravishing me?"

"I'm not ordinarily a slave to passionate emotions, Lady Jane. It would seem your fair charms were my undoing."

How had she ever considered that she loved him?

"No doubt you despise coming undone, because it necessitates a show of emotion, and God forbid you reveal an ounce of humanity, for it is surely beneath your dignity. Good day, Your Grace." She walked out, certain she would never see him again. And never, most assuredly, would be too soon.

As promised, Michael presented himself at Hornsby Grange in Oxfordshire the following morning, well before ten o'clock. As his carriage rolled up the drive to the house, he noted the grounds were immaculate, the fountain out front in good working order, and the house itself was an attractive Palladian style. An attentive groom rushed forward to assist his driver with the horses and as soon as Michael alighted, the front doors opened. Sherbourne stepped out, flanked by his eldest son and heir, James, and the next in line, Jack. The resemblance between all three men was striking. Michael recalled all the Lennoxes were similar, dark haired and blue eyed.

"Good morning," he said, refusing to feel the slightest bit awkward.

"Welcome, Blixford," James said, extending his hand.

Sherbourne didn't smile. "I trust your journey was comfortable?"

"Yes, thank you. I traveled to Glendon last night, to the Blue Hound."

"Excellent steak and kidney pie at the Blue Hound," Jack said as he shook Michael's hand.

Sherbourne turned and waved toward the door. "Please come inside. I've something to say to you."

The front hall of Hornsby Grange was narrow, but beautiful, the paneled walls edged in gilt, the soaring ceiling adorned with a fresco of frolicking wood nymphs. His host led him up the stairs and into the drawing room and as soon as they all were seated and the butler closed the doors, Sherbourne focused on Michael. "She's run off, Blixford. Her maid delayed telling me until only a few moments ago. Julian has gone in search of her."

He was shocked. "How long has she been gone?"

"Since last evening," James said gravely. "She's at least twelve hours ahead of Julian. Cursed full moon, or she'd not have been able to travel in the night."

"Is she in a traveling coach?" She could be caught up with if in a coach.

"She took her mare and told her maid she would write soon with instructions for her belongings to be sent to her." Sherbourne sighed heavily and stared down at his hands. "It appears she will ruin herself, hell or high water. I would offer an apology, Blixford, but you'll forgive me if I'm unable to voice it." He looked up and met Michael's eyes. "I blame you for this disaster."

Her brothers also stared at him, and he felt an undercurrent of rage so strong, it was a living, breathing thing within the room. He didn't blame them. Had a man compromised Lucy, he'd have killed him without blinking. On the other hand, Lucy would not be so cowardly as to run away. She would own up to the situation and do the right thing.

Lady Jane was not Lucy. She was spoiled by her doting papa, too used to getting her way. "Is there any suspicion of foul play?"

"None. Her maid said she waved her goodbye, after her mistress told her she would be gone for quite some time."

Jack said conversationally, "She's taken quite a dislike to you, Blixford."

"Rather along the lines of hate, I'd say," James added with a nod.

How could they be so unconcerned? "Do you have any idea where she may have gone, evidently without benefit of even a maid? She's in danger, and I have to wonder how the three of you can remain so calm in the face of it."

James shrugged. "Jane is resourceful. She will be fine, I assure you."

He knew then, they were well aware of her whereabouts. "I assume one of you will have the good grace to tell me where she has gone."

They exchanged a glance before James said evenly, "Scotland. Our mother's family is in Scotland and Jane indicates she will live there until we are all married, or she dies."

"You say Julian has gone in search of her. Will he

bring her home?"

Sherbourne got to his feet and went to the window to stare out at the gardens stretching beyond the back of the house. "She won't come, Blixford. Julian follows only to see that she is settled in Scotland and funds are available to her that she won't be dependent upon anyone. You are, it would appear, off the hook, and I ask you to leave my home with all due haste. It's becoming increasingly difficult not to kill you."

"Where in Scotland might I find her?"

James crossed one leg over the other and regarded him levelly. "Would you go and fetch her home, then?"

"I can't in all good conscience not do so."

"Yes," Jack said, "you can, and will. Leave her be, and there's an end to it. If she would go to this extreme to avoid marriage to you, we won't insist, or allow you to demand it of her."

Michael was well and truly astounded. He stood and looked from one to the other of them, including Sherbourne's back. "She will be ruined! Her life will be nothing but a shuffle from house to house, with nowhere to call her home. She won't be received. She will have no friend, no family of her own. *Nothing.* You would allow this?"

James slowly rose to his feet, his usually smiling face dark with anger. "Jane is well aware of how it will be, and assured me she'd prefer to live the rest of her life in reclusion than be your wife. For God's sake, Blixford, she despises you, and I'm given to understand you do not hold her in high regard. We will not force her to marry you. I wish you good day, sir."

And so, dismissed and despised, Michael turned on his heel and left Hornsby Grange.

In the days and weeks that followed, he fell into a deep depression, not unlike his frame of mind after Annabel's death. But there was still his duty to produce an heir, and if he accomplished nothing else in his life, he would do that, at least.

Five weeks to the day that he was supposed to marry Jane, he took Lady Letitia Rawlings to wife. He recalled what Jane had said, that Letitia would cut off her hand and feed it to the hounds if it meant becoming a duchess. He'd been married less than three days when he discovered the truth to it. His bride demanded many things and refused him her bed if he was not forthcoming. He advised her of the error of her assumption that he would jump to her will, and told her she would give him an heir, or return to her father's home. She complied, but hated him ever after. Whatever meager friendship they had when they began was quickly gone, replaced by cold silence.

Late in the night, mercifully alone in his bed after performing his conjugal rights and praying to God she would quickly conceive, he thought of Jane, remembered her determined face, just before she walked out of the library.

And cursed himself for a fool.

CHAPTER 3

Four Years Later

Michael arrived at the Manderly ball at precisely eleven in the evening. In keeping with his wealth and position, he was dressed in the finest clothing and accoutrements. In keeping with his mission of visiting death upon innocent females, every garment upon his person was black, save the froth of lace at his throat.

Not that his undertaking dictated his choice of apparel. Far from it. Of late, he always dressed in black.

He was announced. Lady Manderly sailed toward him, a vision of true horror in a puce satin gown, her graying hair styled in odd corkscrew curls that bounced about her forehead. "Your Grace, how lovely to receive you!"

He accepted her chubby gloved hand and sketched a slight bow before releasing it. "Good evening, ma'am."

She tapped his shoulder with her fan, a useless, flimsy gewgaw possessed of numerous dangling lines of ribbon, each adorned with a glass bead. The damned thing's noise was annoying in the extreme. "I'll warrant you're here to take a gander at the Season's marriageable misses." Her pale-blue eyes were lit with satisfaction. "I'm honored you've chosen my humble ball to begin your search."

Humble, indeed. It was a crush. As for him taking a

gander at the Season's offerings, it was ludicrous, perhaps a cruel joke on Lady Manderly's part, for she knew quite well, he might gander all he wished, but none save the most desperate and unsuitable would have him. Fixing her with a cold stare, he neither agreed nor disagreed. Instead, he got right to the point. "I would beg to know if Lady Jane Lennox is in attendance."

Lady Manderly's cheeks instantly colored and her thick lips pursed with disapproval. "Your Grace, with all due respect, I cannot countenance your reason for asking, unless it's simply your wish to avoid her, which would be understandable, of course. The forward, impertinent baggage was not invited. She isn't received by anyone. If you actually have some wish to see her, especially after—"

"I've made an enquiry. You decline to answer. We won't belabor the reasons." He'd expected her to beat him about the head with indignation, but was compelled to ask, nonetheless. He wanted everyone in the expansive ballroom to be buzzing. He needed Lady Jane to be the sole person of interest, if she were not already. As soon as he turned away, Lady Manderly would do her duty and spread his enquiry far and wide. Within five minutes, every man and woman in attendance, even the older generation who played cards in the salon, would know he was there, asking after Lady Jane. Particularly, so would Lady Jane.

She was ruined.

She was a beautiful termagant, bursting with passion and vibrant life, ruled by her emotions, the worst possible woman to become his duchess.

She was his only hope.

Turning, he walked away from his hostess and moved to the topmost step leading into the ballroom, his gaze sweeping the throng until he found her father. At fifty, the Earl of Sherbourne was still a fine figure of a man, on the tall side, his dark hair silvering at the temples, his face given additional character by the appearance of laugh lines edging his mouth and crow's-feet near his eyes. Sherbourne and his brood were a lively, jolly lot, prone to raucous laughter, mischievous pranks and riding neck-or-nothing. They were all dark haired, blue eyed, big boned. They were all males. Excepting Lady Jane. She'd never known her mother, that woman having expired scarcely six months after giving birth to her seventh child and only daughter. It was said Jane emerged from the womb alternately laughing and shouting and had not stopped in two and twenty years. Unlike her good-natured brothers, Lady Jane was sometimes possessed of a nasty tendency to rage.

Michael was well acquainted with that rage.

He supposed there must necessarily be some duality to her passionate nature. She laughed with good humor, and stormed in her anger. She would undoubtedly be equally ardent in bed. That much was clear from her reaction in Lucy's library, four years ago. He ground his teeth. What despicable fate had landed upon him this turn of events? What bitter irony that the only suitable woman in all England who would have him —and she *would* have him —who wouldn't be afraid of him, was the one woman he would never wish to marry. The woman who jilted him and ran off to Scotland to avoid him.

Mentally, he shook himself. How many events in his life had he managed to overcome through sheer force of will? He would likewise deal with marriage to Lady Jane and the possible consequences. If she died in childbed, there would be the cruel guilt of his demon seed killing yet another flower of England, but he wouldn't grieve. He would bury her and move on. He cursed his duty. Damned his father for losing his mind and thus failing to remarry and beget more heirs. Railed at the travesty that was his life.

There was the possibility she wouldn't die. He'd

heard it said, only the good die young. If that were true, Lady Jane was destined to hit the century mark. And then there were her hips. Coming from a long line of big boned, healthy stock, Lady Jane was a picture of robust vigor and stamina. The midwife attending Letitia had said in ominous tones on the day of delivery, "Her Grace will have a hard labor. Her hips are too narrow." Letitia's hips hadn't given an inch and the baby he'd planted in her belly killed her. If any woman could bear a son of his and live to see him grow to manhood, surely it must be Lady Jane Lennox. She would not die. But if she did . . .

Moving toward Sherbourne, Michael's gaze traveled from the earl and focused on his daughter, standing just to his left. Head held high, blue eyes twinkling, she was eye to eye with Sir Samuel Mowbry, an expressionless chap evidently possessed of great wit. Lady Jane appeared ready to laugh right out loud.

She was magnificent.

Her dark hair was piled atop her head in an artful arrangement of curls, from which several tendrils fell across her neck, resting intriguingly close to her bosom, barely contained within the bodice of a stunning gown of midnight blue, shot through with streaks of glittering silver. Unsurprising to him, he experienced a frisson of sensual awareness as he moved closer to the small group occupying the center of the east wall of the ballroom. He realized she'd matured in four years. What had once been fresh, innocent beauty was now the flawless face and figure of a woman full grown. In spite of two wives and a string of mistresses in four years, he had not forgotten Jane, occasionally wondering where she was, how she fared, whether she regretted her impulsive flight. Did she feel even the slightest amount of guilt over humiliating him?

He'd been murderously angry. When Sherbourne told him she'd gone to Scotland, he seriously considered riding after her and demanding she stand up and do her duty, by God.

But he hadn't. Pride, or stubbornness, or perhaps a deep realization that she still would not come to heel made him stay home.

Scarcely more than a month later, he married Lady Letitia. A year after that, she was dead. But he wasn't done. A year after Letitia died in childbed, he married Miss Grace Dowling. Poor Grace hadn't made it to labor. She miscarried at five months, hemorrhaged, and died. Each of his wives had died horribly, in great pain, their only comfort as they left this world the gentle kindness of Bella, the vicar's daughter, who had befriended Annabel in the very beginning and was a steadfast friend to Letitia and Grace.

He was cursed with demon seed, it was said. Behind his back, polite society called him the Duke of Death. He'd once been the best catch in all England. Now, he couldn't find a bride amongst suitable young ladies. Matchmaking mamas gave him a wide berth, less enthusiastic to see their daughters become a duchess. After all, how could one enjoy one's status as such if one were dead?

Then Jane returned from Scotland. He didn't know, not until he stopped into his club and was soundly roasted. "Your bride's back in town, Blix. Word has it she's been rusticating in Scotland, lo these four years. Never married. And here you are, widowed again. Shall we call upon the bishop and put in for another special license?"

Michael took it in stride. Had the shoe been on the other foot, he'd undoubtedly have given in to at least one pointed jab. He looked a fool, and hated it, but he would not, could not show a crack in his demeanor. He'd raised his quizzing glass and said evenly, "Deuced bad tempered, the Scots. I daresay a laird wouldn't be interested in marrying one of equal disposition, and thus it's not surprising the lady didn't find a highland husband."

They laughed, as he'd intended. He took a seat and had a brandy before taking his leave. He went home and started to plan. She'd returned to England despite not one of her brothers yet married, and long before she was dead. He surmised her reason was to find a husband —namely, him, for who else would have her? It had taken four years, but she had finally seen reason. He was so certain of it, he made careful enquiries to determine how best to meet her for the first time. He hit upon Lady Manderly's ball when he heard rumors that Jane would be there, despite not being received, or, in fact, invited. Something told him she would attend for the sole reason of seeing him. It was neutral ground.

She would marry him. He would not believe otherwise.

But she wouldn't do it on his terms. Only hers.

Michael would allow her the illusion.

Her father spotted him as he approached, and frowned. "Blixford."

"Sherbourne."

Michael returned the earl's grudging handshake.

The earl nodded toward the cluster of men around him. "I don't reckon introductions are necessary?"

Michael shook more hands and greeted each of them. He noted there were no ladies within the group. No lady would come within twenty feet of Lady Jane, lest her ruination cast any of its dismal shadow across their pristine womanhood.

At long last, he'd performed the necessary courtesies and could now ask Lady Jane to dance. She'd left off listening to Mowbry's droll observations when Michael came up, and turned her attention to him, her gaze considering him curiously.

Sherbourne was called away to the card room by Lady Manderly, who exclaimed Lord Twykham had fallen asleep and another hand was needed to finish his game.

Michael saw it as the ruse it was. Everyone wanted her father out of the way, to see if perhaps Lady Jane would do something untoward in his absence.

She swept into a curtsy, one befitting a duke, and when she rose, extended her gloved hand. He grasped her fingers and bent low before releasing her and meeting her eyes. They were quite an extraordinary shade of blue. On the dark side. "It's a pleasure to see you again, Lady Jane."

She was above average height, requiring her to bend her neck but a small amount to look him in the eye. "One must wonder, Your Grace, why you are come to a ball. It's well known you despise balls. And one must further wonder why you've particularly singled me out. Word of your enquiry reached me even before you appeared." Her voice was low, with a smoky edge. Seductive. "Your repute as a serious man precludes the notion of your seeking me out merely as a curiosity. I daresay your inquisitiveness is confined to matters of import, primarily those which directly concern you, and the remainder of life's odd curiosities pass you by without notice. There are those who find cause to see me in much the same vein as they might scurry to Mr. Medford's Curiosity Fair to ogle the two-headed lady, or the albino crocodile. You, sir, would not be interested."

Michael raised one brow. "How very astute you are, Lady Jane." And impertinent. But then, he'd expected that. A waltz was beginning. Michael bent his arm. "Would you care to dance?"

Without hesitation, she accepted his arm. "I'd be delighted."

The roar of the ballroom became deafening. A ruined woman, dancing with the Duke of Death, the same duke who had ruined her, and from whom she'd run away. Did gossip get any better? At the edge of the dance floor, she withdrew her hand from his arm and faced him. She curtsied. He bowed. Then reached for her. Her height matched with his in just the right fashion. He placed his hand upon the curve of her spine and she rested her hand upon his shoulder without much of a reach. Her gloved fingers lay within his palm and they began to move among the other dancers. It didn't take long to realize, she was very accomplished. It also didn't take long for most of the other couples to move away from them, a great number of them leaving the dance floor altogether. It took less time to remember how she'd felt in his arms, crushed against him, her heart beating wildly.

"You are a pariah, ma'am." He swung her into a twirl and she never missed a step.

"Do you take a particular fancy to pariahs, Your Grace?"

"Not particularly, no."

"There is little left to life that surprises me, but I find myself intrigued by your singling me out. I'm quite appreciative, surely, because I do love to dance, and despite their willingness to speak to me, my family's friends can't be quite so brave as to squire me about the floor."

She smelled of lemons. How appropriate. "There is a distinction between bravery and a wish for self destruction, Lady Jane."

Her eyes were lit with amusement. "And you are bent on self destruction?"

"Of course not. Our dancing together isn't condoned, but I'm above reproach. Your lessons in peerage must surely have made that clear."

Her lips curved into a smile. "Dukes behaving badly must be countenanced?"

"Precisely." She was a divine dancer, quite light on her feet. He pulled her a bit closer. She did not withdraw.

"Shall I puzzle it out then?"

"Please do."

"I've already discounted the notion that your interest is based upon idle, rude curiosity. You've no need for female companionship, owing to the fact you have a mistress, and even if your intentions were so dishonorable as to include making me your mistress, my father would kill you, duke or no."

In spite of himself, he was shocked. But he remained mute.

She laughed. Right in the midst of a waltz, with all of London society looking on, she laughed at him. "I have a tendency to plain speaking, Your Grace."

"So I've been told." Was she not going to speak plainly of their marriage that did not happen? Could she simply ignore their history?

"I assume, from your stunned expression, that my second guess is inaccurate. You don't wish to make me your mistress, despite my ruination. Can it be that your intentions are honorable? Are you searching for a duchess to produce the heir you covet?"

"There was a time when the idea of marriage to me pleased you."

Her smile never failed. "Yes, I remember it well. What was it you said? I am ruled by passion and would make a most unsuitable duchess. I would be your *very last* choice of a duchess. Yet here we are, four years later, and I've suddenly become quite the thing to you. What fascinates me is how I can now be so attractive to you. Not only am I ruled by passion, I'm totally and completely ruined. My reputation is destroyed." Her gaze never wavered. "For a large man, you are really quite an excellent dancer."

Michael deeply suspected she was not one to idly offer flattery. "Thank you."

"Of all women, why me?"

Her waist dipped in above her hips with an enticing curve. Lady Jane was born in the wrong era of fashion; the high waistline of the current mode did not allow a man to adequately appreciate her hourglass shape.

"Why not?"Her eyes widened in disbelief. "Sir, you insult me. Shall I request pen and paper and list out the reasons? I believe it will require two sheets of Lady Manderly's stationery."

He couldn't very well say right out loud that she was his only choice. For all that he was a man of few words, he wasn't an addlepated clod. In his fashion, he was bent on wooing her to accept his hand. There must necessarily be some semblance of a courtship. "I find you very attractive." It was not a lie. She was a beautiful woman. Bedding her would definitely be a step above unpleasant. Many steps, actually. He was still obsessed, it appeared. Despite harsh, silent commands to the contrary, his cock was beginning to make itself known. He did not recall ever having such a thing occur merely by dancing with a woman. He inhaled her scent, once again. How intriguing that she smelled of lemons.

"There are several dozen unmarried ladies in this very room who are also attractive. They are not ruined and would make quite the nice duchess. I repeat, why me?"

"Perhaps I am merely altruistic, desirous of saving you from your fallen status. Had you thought of that?"

"Yes, quite. And maybe I'm the long lost daughter of an Indian nabob, kidnapped at birth and brought here to wreak havoc on the poor sensibilities of the *ton*."

Hell and damn. "If plain speaking is your desire, by all means, let us speak plainly. We will suit. That is all."

She was quiet for a long moment before she said, without the ghost of a smile, "Your Grace is as much a pariah as I, and I do believe you're correct."

"I generally am, you'll discover."

"Have you no anxiety that I might leave you at the altar again?"

"None at all." He swung her about a bit faster, enjoying the heightened color in her cheeks. Lady Jane benefited from exertion. "You've had your revenge and I my humble pie. You need your respectability restored. I need a wife."

"Why do you presume I would marry you when no one else will?"

"Because you want a husband, family and respectability, and much as I am faced with one clear choice, so are you. You surmise, rightly so, I have acquired humility due to the unfortunate circumstances of my previous marriages. I am brought to heel, Lady Jane, and am now and ever will be, your servant. If you will allow it." It was a calculated gamble to say so. He actually had no idea. She might tell him to go to the devil.

Her look was filled with knowing. "Has it come to that, then? I really am your only choice, your last chance, am I not?"

"Yes, Jane, it has come to that." He stared down at her and drew her closer still, his thighs brushing hers as they moved in ever faster circles. "We are beyond polite banter."

"I should hope so, Your Grace. Polite banter with a man who ravished me seems hypocritical in the extreme."

"For reasons I'd prefer not to enumerate, I feel it best to marry a woman whom I respect, but do not love. In fact, I prefer not to harbor the slightest affection for a wife. I most certainly do not want a wife ruled by a passionate nature. To be brief, Lady Jane, I am drawn to you. I find I still want you, even after what you did to me, after four years and the death of two wives. It bothers me to marry you, and I will say right out, I will never allow myself to tender an affection for you. But we will rub along well, I believe." His hand dropped an inch, until his wrist touched her hip. "And I am convinced you will not die."

"Because I have adequate hips?"

"Precisely."

"How very romantic, Blixford. I may faint, I am so overcome with passion."

Her eyes glittered with anything but passion.

"You're angry, but it's misplaced, Lady Jane. I mean no offense, and am sincere. You asked for the truth and I have given it to you." He glanced over her shoulder, noting they were now completely alone on the dance floor and the room was lined with all of polite society, surreptitiously gawking behind fans and glasses of punch. Perfect. "Look about you, Jane. These are our people, those whom we must befriend for the sake of our families and our children, if not for our own need of human companionship. They are judging us, finding us lacking. Marriage will bring both of us back into the fold, but no one else will have you, and no one will have me. You were never meant to be a spinster, Jane. Marry me."

Her gaze moved to one side of him and she watched as he swept her past the faces of those who would not accept her unless and until she obeyed the rules.

"I will consider it, Your Grace, under one condition."

"What is that?"

She met his gaze. "You must give up your mistress."

"How do you know I have one?"

"Because I followed you there, just last night. Her house is in a neighborhood known as a haven for mistresses. She is quite lovely, and I'm sure an able companion for you, but I simply won't share. Give her up, or find another bride."

He missed a step.

"Oh, do stop glowering at me, Blixford. Try to remember, it's been four years since you saw me last. A great many things can happen in four years. I am no longer a child, and you no longer hold all the best cards in your large hand."

"My hands are large?"

"Huge. I always loved your hands." She peered up at him and smiled, perhaps the first genuine smile of the evening. "And your nose."

"My nose is generally considered my worst feature."

"It is striking and ruins your beauty. This is not a bad thing, for certainly a beautiful man is less a novelty than an anomaly."

He was surprised into silence.

"You do realize, if you marry me, you'll be laughed at unmercifully?"

Once more, he twirled her about the floor, completely unhindered by others. "You do realize I don't give a damn?"

"Well, then," she said as the music came to an end, "shall I expect you to call on the morrow?"

He offered his arm. "Will you receive me?"

"Of course. You are a duke and it would be the height of rudeness not to. I am plain spoken, Your Grace. Never rude."

"That was not my question, Lady Jane. If I call, will you be receptive to a brief courtship?" She looked up at him as they walked from the dance floor. "Yes, Your Grace. My aversion to matrimony only extends to toads."

"And I am not a toad?"

"Not tonight."

Well. That was something, wasn't it?

"Incidentally, why are you here, uninvited?" He wondered if she would tell him the truth of it and was pleased when she attempted no artful dodge.

She stopped when she reached the periphery and faced him. "To see you, of course. Sherbourne nearly went into apoplexy, but he sees it is the only way."

"Do you mean to say you knew I'd come, knew I'd offer again?"

Her eyes were frosty. "As I said, Your Grace, a lot can happen in four years. You are not the only one for whom time did not stand still."

"You sound positively mysterious, Lady Jane."

"Nothing of the sort. I am only grown up, you see."

Grown up, indeed. Her height was the same, but she had bloomed into a ravishing beauty, her bosom full, her arms graceful and slender. "Why did you follow me last night? Come to think of it, *how* did you follow me?"

"I am furlongs ahead of you, Blixford. When I decided to come home, I knew it would not be permanent unless I could redeem myself, and my only avenue to redemption is marriage. It took me all of one day to determine that no one but you will suit. Without the benefit of my previous friendships and associations, I was unable to gain any satisfactory information about you, thus my discreet investigation. I've actually been following you two days past." She frowned slightly. "You really should attend to your driver a bit more closely. While you stopped off at your club, he entertained a woman within your coach. I was quite shocked." Her frown disappeared. "As to how I followed, I'd rather not say."

"I'd rather you did."

"I will demonstrate at a later date."

"I'll look forward to it. In the meantime, I ask that you leave off shadowing me, Lady Jane. I find the thought unnerving."

"Never fear, Your Grace. With the exception of your visit to your mistress, your activities are exceedingly dull. I daresay two days of boring reconnaissance were quite paid off by that." The frown returned. "You *will* give her up, will you not?"

She was perfectly safe from death by his demon seed. This marriage would kill him long before he could get her pregnant. "I will give her up. By this time next week, she'll be another man's responsibility."

"Do be sure to give her a large settlement."

"That is hardly something with which you should concern yourself."

"I am to take her place as your lover. It would soothe my conscience to know she's been handsomely taken care of."

"You will be my wife, Lady Jane. There is a difference."

Her gaze was direct and halfway to icy. "I'm merely a brood mare, then? You will get a child on me with due haste and perform the duty without passion?" She nodded. "Of course you will. It is what I'd expect of you, a man of controlled emotion."

She was insulting him. "I am not an automaton, ma'am."

"And I will not be merely a brood mare. I fully expect to find pleasure in our marriage bed. Whether or not you enjoy the experience is entirely up to you."

"Well." He took a deep breath and let it out on a huff. "*Well*."

"My brothers are correct. You *are* a stick. Perhaps this is a mistake. Perhaps I should return to Scotland and marry MacDougal, after all. He was most insistent and, I think, heartbroken when I left."

She was a sly one. Michael caught himself enjoying their conversation, in spite of the true wretchedness of his situation. "Idle threats can sometimes have a way of haunting one, Lady Jane. In future, once we are married, I'd prefer never to hear the name MacDougal again. I'd also prefer you give off attempting to goad me by pointing out what you and your brothers perceive to be character flaws. If I am a stick, you are a hoyden."

"I'm very much a hoyden, as you well know. We are ill matched on all accounts and I foresee a turbulent marriage." She stepped a bit closer and lowered her voice. "However, despite four years and additional experiences, I have not forgotten my ravishment, and I will not be coy and say I am not anticipating further exploration of such."

"Additional experiences, ma'am?"

"Yes, Your Grace, all quite illuminating."

Hell and damn. "I see. In what way, may I ask?"

"No, you may not. Suffice it to say, I would not

conceive of marrying you if I did not anticipate some measure of fulfillment. I will accept no one in my bed but you, so it will be up to you to provide what I need. Are you comfortable with this? If not, speak now and I shall return to Scotland."

"I believe the subject bears further analysis. We will discuss it tomorrow."

"I look forward to it."

Sherbourne returned just then. He scowled at Michael before he turned his attention to Jane. "Well?"

"The duke will call on the morrow."

"Very well. Come along, daughter. I've had enough of the fishbowl tonight."

Michael watched them leave, his mind turning over all that she'd said. Obviously, Lady Jane believed she held the upper hand, that he was desperate enough for a wife, for an heir, he would dance to her tune, whether the melody pleased him or not.

Michael took his leave of Lady Manderly and made his way to his carriage. Once inside, he glanced about and noted a stocking wedged between the squabs. Hmm. He'd definitely have a word with his driver.

He alighted on Marchmont street and rapped at the door of a sedate, attractive row house. Miriam opened almost immediately, her pretty face beaming a welcome. "Blix! I hadn't expected you this evening."

Hard and frustrated, feeling damned to eternal Hell, Michael stepped inside and reached for her as the door closed behind him.

CHAPTER 4

"Jane, are you absolutely sure? I admit, the thought of you married to him bothers me no small amount. He's an autocrat. He has a tendency to cold arrogance."

At the breakfast table, glancing at Robert over her coffee, Jane smiled. He was closest to her in age, just two years her elder. At four and twenty, he was a strapping man– actually the tallest of the brothers, taller even than Sherbourne. She noted her papa was also staring at her, awaiting a reply. Her gaze moved to his right, to her brother, Bram. At five and twenty, Bram was the most serious of them all, although, even in his seriousness, he couldn't match Blixford.

"I'm quite sure. So long as I'm ruined and shunned, it will be difficult for any of you to find suitable brides. It's my duty to marry Blixford."

"Nonsense!" Jack said with a scowl. "If you've no wish to marry the scoundrel, do not do so on our account. Respectability can be yours again regardless of whom you choose to marry."

Jack was second oldest, married at one and twenty and widowed three years later, while he was in the Peninsula with Wellington. His had been a love match and he'd yet to try again. Jane well understood his insistence upon marrying for love. Owing to their family's great wealth, each of them had the luxury. Oddly, Jack was the only one who'd thus far walked down the aisle.

They were all there, even the eldest, Sherbourne's heir, James. Upon her return from Scotland, her brothers rallied about, determined to put to rights what had gone so wrong four years earlier. When she declared herself ready for London, they'd each traveled along, four of them taking up residence with her and Papa in the house on Grosvenor Square. Only James and Julian were not staying with them; James having his own house in Cavendish Square and Julian electing to stay with him, due to late hours he said were certain to disrupt the household.

This morning, in anticipation of the duke's call, of the beginning of his courtship, they were all there, a wall of masculine support. Jane would find it humorous if they didn't each one look as though they'd love nothing more than to murder Blixford. His title meant nothing to the Lennox brothers. He was a man before he was a duke, and he'd taken liberties with their sister. He deserved to die, and she didn't doubt Julian could accomplish such without mishap, without detection. The duke would simply disappear and none would ever find evidence of a Lennox hand in the matter.

"He's a dreadful stick, Janie. Chances are he won't permit you much freedom." James stirred a spot of cream into his coffee. "Once you've married, he'll have rights upon your movements."

"He may have rights, but I don't have to obey."

They all exchanged glances. Julian cleared his throat and said in his silky voice, "If I felt a farthing of sympathy for the man, I might pull him aside and warn him."

"I daresay the chap's well aware," his twin, Henry, said around a bite of his toast. "She did leave him holding a useless special license, did she not?"Laughter erupted and the memory was gone over, once again. Even Jane couldn't help a smile.

Her father, however, was not amused. "There are elements of life subject to ridicule. Your sister's marriage doesn't qualify. I expect each of you to treat Blixford with all due respect. No shenanigans. Do I make myself clear?"The table quieted, each of her brothers acquiescing through his silence.

The earl got to his feet and made his way round the dining room, reaching out to pet her hair. "You're a willful brat, Jane, but I will hate to see you leave my house, so soon after returning."

She looked up at his dear face. "I won't be far away, Papa."

His expression was odd. Almost sad. "Perhaps not in distance, but you will be out of my reach." His hand fell to her shoulder. "I'll be in the library until he arrives and will speak to him before he attends you in the drawing room."

When he was gone, her brothers became far more animated and open, tossing out bits of advice.

"Let him know, right up front, what you'll tolerate and what you will not."

"You'll not be a guest in his home. You'll be a duchess, and mistress of all. Take charge, sister, and don't be cowed by anyone."

"The first available opportunity, host a grand ball, but only invite a select few. Make the rest wait."

"Yes, Jane, and be very discerning about whom you receive. By God, put a bit of it back in their eye."

"If he hurts you, I expect to be informed."

Silence reigned. They turned to look at Julian.

He shrugged. "The man's lost three wives, all due to complications involving childbirth. Has it occurred to no one that the circumstances are a bit over the top? I cannot forget how the duke's own mother met her end."

Jane's heartbeat steadily increased. "I am unable to forget as I never knew to begin with."

Julian looked at her from his place at the far end of

the table. "She was in confinement with her third child when she died and it was generally thought complications killed her. But word has always been the old duke thought he'd been cuckolded and murdered her before she could foist another man's child upon him. He loved her, you see, and her betrayal sent him into temporary madness. After her death, he became a hermit and no one ever saw him again."

With a loud huff of disgust, James dropped his spoon into his cup. "Charming, really. Nothing says I love you like murder."

"It's all hearsay, of course. She was alone at Eastchase Hall, with only her young son and daughter for company. The duke was insanely jealous and possessive of her and chances are her betrayal was simply a figment of his imagination."

James looked thoughtful. "I've heard it said she had a particular friendship with Viscount Radcliffe's father, whose lands adjoin Blixford's."

Julian never took his eyes from Jane's. "The elder Radcliffe was shot by a highwayman not long after the duchess died. One has to wonder why a highwayman would choose a barren, scarcely traveled country road upon which to search for prey. One must also take into account the fact that most highwaymen are merely thieves —not murderers."

"Are we allowing our Jane to marry the son of a killer?"

Julian finally looked away, to Jack, whose face was thunderstruck. "In all fairness, a son can't be held accountable for his father's sins, nor can his character be judged by that of his parent." He returned his gaze to Jane's. "And we must remember, this is all rumor and speculation. It may well be the duchess did indeed die of complications in childbirth and Radcliffe was in fact shot by a highwayman. My concern is for Jane, and this I do insist —if your husband mistreats you in any way, you will come to one of us, immediately."

I most certainly do not want a wife ruled by a passionate nature.

I feel it best to marry a woman whom I respect, but do not love.

I will never allow myself to tender an affection for you.

She'd thought his speech was predicated upon his fear that she would die, that he would grieve if he loved her and lost her. He was protecting himself from pain.

Had she been wrong? Was his insistence of marriage to a woman he respected but did not love, a woman of no passion, based upon his father's insane jealousy regarding his mother? One could hardly experience insane jealousy when one's heart wasn't involved. A woman of no passion would never dream of straying, would she? Jane considered Annabel. A sweet, soft-spoken miss, content to tend to her gardens and homes, far more interested in needlework than bedroom activities. Letitia had been cut from the same cloth. Jane had never met his third duchess, Grace, but from all she'd gathered, that miss was equally reticent, decorous and purely devoid of a passionate nature.

She, on the other hand, had allowed him to ravish her in the library. Had he not said such cruel things to her, she had no doubt he would have completed the task and she would have allowed him to do so. She'd been quite captivated by it all.

"You have my word, Julian, but I don't anticipate mistreatment from Blixford. I rather think my greatest obstacle will be indifference."

Every one of her brothers stared at her, astonishment on their faces.

"Jane, you are sometimes unaccountably silly. No man would be indifferent to you. None. Not even a stick like Blixford."

If they only knew. "We shall see." She rose and they followed suit. "Bear in mind, will you all, I am a better shot than most men. If Blixford gives me too much trouble, I'll shoot him and point out the error of his ways."

That earned a laugh, as she'd intended. They made their way to the drawing room to wait upon the duke.

Michael supposed some men might feel uncomfortable and awkward, but he did not. For any injustice he'd visited upon her, Lady Jane adequately earned her recompense by jilting him. Her ruination would be set aside after they were married, with little to no lingering effects. He wouldn't place himself in a position of perpetual apology to Sherbourne, or his daughter.

After a stiff, formal meeting with his future father-in-law, wherein a marriage settlement was agreed upon to their mutual satisfaction, he walked with Sherbourne up the stairs and across the hallway, into the drawing room. Dressed in a fetching gown of soft yellow, topped by a spencer of dark blue, Lady Jane sat close to the fire, a book upon her lap. In the seat facing her, James Lennox, Viscount Hildebrand and heir to Sherbourne's earldom, was likewise employed with reading. Julian Lennox, whom Michael had once considered a friend, having known him since they were boys together at Eton, sat at the pianoforte and played a lovely tune far more adeptly than his sister was able. Her remaining brothers, Jack, Henry, Bram and Robert, were playing cards, jesting with one another, bluffing their hands and generally being loud and raucous, as was their nature.

As soon as he and Sherbourne cleared the doorway, they all rose and greeted him in turn, shaking his hand, welcoming him with the courteous formality one offers to another in polite society, despite the nature of true feelings.

Behind their affable smiles, Michael was well aware they would each take great enjoyment from shoving a rapier between his ribs.

In the midst of a platoon of champions, Jane smiled beatifically and accepted his bow over her hand. "Good morning, Your Grace. How lovely of you to call."

"My pleasure, Lady Jane."

"May I offer tea?"

"Thank you, no. Perhaps you'll do me the honor of accompanying me for a drive in the park."

She'd already been riding, he guessed, her person wafting the scent of the outdoors, her cheeks still flushed with wind and exertion. As always, she looked good enough to eat. And to return to for extra servings.

"I'd be delighted."

Accepting his arm, she walked with him to the doorway. No one spoke a word until Michael paused and glanced over his shoulder. "Good morning, gentlemen."

They each nodded curtly, smiles gone, replaced with fierce looks Jane would not see unless she turned.

She did not.

When they were at the foot of the stairs, the butler handed her a bonnet then stepped away to open the door. As she tied the ribbons beneath her chin at a rakish angle, Michael said dryly, "I shall have to remember to handle you with kid gloves, lest your army of brothers descend upon my house to defend you."

"Your Grace would be advised to be wary of your wife before you give a thought to my brothers."

"I stand duly warned, Lady Jane."

She jerked a look at him as he handed her up into his curricle. "Are you laughing at me, Blixford?"

"Hmm, perhaps a little. I doubt many men receive warnings of bodily harm from their betrothed."

She settled in and adjusted her skirts around her,

leaving room for him as he took his seat and gathered up the reins from the footman. "We are not yet betrothed. We have, I believe, an item of some importance to discuss before I'm satisfied."

"Ah, yes. The important item." He took them off down the street, heading for the park. "As I recall, you were most insistent I afford you the pleasure you expect in the marriage bed. I assure you I will do my best, but there must necessarily be some effort on your part."

"Yes, of course, but you may have misinterpreted my meaning. I've no doubt we will find mutual satisfaction with one another, but only if we're together. I won't be packed off to Eastchase Hall for the duration of our marriage, made to wait upon your whim."

He turned a corner a bit too sharply and she leaned into him, her breast resting against his arm rather nicely. "It's customary for an increasing wife to stay out of the public eye."

"I'm aware, Blixford, but I won't take kindly to being left alone for the duration of my confinement, nor will I be happy if I'm abandoned after the birth of your heir. In short, I don't wish to be merely a brood mare, set out to pasture once I've delivered. I expect to continue to enjoy conjugal relations, and if this is unacceptable to you, I suggest you turn round and take me home."

This was unexpected, and he didn't want to lie to her, but he could not, would not agree to stay with her. He pondered his response while she looked ahead, to the park, evidently enjoying herself immensely.

Her dark-blue eyes sparkled. "We'll be able to converse without interruption, as I'm shunned and no one will speak to me."

"Ah, the silver lining. That will change, of course, once we are married."

"Yes," she said simply. When they were within the

park gates and on the long portion of the drive, they passed the first carriage, an open barouche housing Lady Mowbry and her daughter, a pasty-faced young woman with wide, staring eyes, terrified at the sight of the Duke of Death. Michael lifted a brow and resisted the odd urge to growl. Insolent chit.

They'd only just passed the Mowbry carriage when he said, "Ah, here we have the Marchioness of Bloomsbury. Shall we call out a greeting and flummox the old battle-axe?"

Jane chuckled in her low, throaty voice. "Behave, Blixford."

Nevertheless, as the marchioness's carriage drew near, Michael tipped his hat to her and called out, "Good morning, Lady Bloomsbury! Lovely weather, is it not?"

The woman's chins actually shook with indignation. But she couldn't ignore him, regardless of his passenger. He was a duke. "Quite," she said with a snap of her head before she turned to look the other way.

He glanced at Jane, expecting a wide grin and merriment dancing in her eyes. Instead, she stared straight ahead, a deep flush along her pretty cheeks. "I beg your pardon, ma'am. I've embarrassed you."

"Indirectly, yes. It matters not to me that I'm shunned. I asked for it. But it grieves me for others to feel embarrassment on account of my presence."

"What a fascinating revelation. I'd never have guessed. Please tell me how grieved you were after you ran away from marrying me, four years ago."

Turning her face toward him, she said soberly, "It was a very wrong thing to do to you, and I'm ashamed of myself for treating you with such disregard and disrespect. My only hope is that I may make it up to you in the future and pray you will find it within you to forgive my childish, selfish behavior. You spoke cruelly to me and forced my hand, but you didn't deserve such a public humiliation."

He saw deep sincerity in her eyes.

Michael returned his focus to the horses and they clipped along in silence for some time. He didn't do more than nod to anyone else they passed. His mind continued to assess Jane's demand, but he couldn't find an adequate response. The truth of it wasn't something he would speak of. He wouldn't tell her of his fear of following his father into madness, that he couldn't allow himself to become attached to her, and the only way he could be certain of it was to keep her at a distance. He would have to come up with an alternate reason, or he'd have to lie.

He wondered how she'd spent her time in Scotland, if that had some bearing on her insistence of enjoying conjugal relations. "What manner of man is MacDougal, and what was the nature of your relationship?" He noticed she stiffened, ever so slightly, but her words were easy and open.

"My mother, as you surely know, was half Scots, her father a third son who traveled to London to find a bride. He and my grandmother alternated their years between England and Scotland, but my mother always considered herself more Scot than English. She had many cousins, but favorite amongst them was Elizabeth, who married a man named MacDougal. They have five children, the oldest being Brian MacDougal. He and his family once visited at Hornsby Grange, and we all got along famously. When I decided to travel to Scotland, I went to his parents' home at Castle MacDougal. They invited me to stay indefinitely, and over time, I became well acquainted with my extended family. A year ago, Brian proposed."

Why did it take three years for him to ask? "You declined?"

Her nod was brief. "I didn't love him in the way a wife should love her husband."

"You've agreed to marry me, yet do not love me in

the way a wife should love her husband. I fail to distinguish the difference." He was fishing, compelled to cast the line because she so conveniently provided the lake.

"I yearned to return home, to be nearer my father and brothers. Had I married MacDougal, I'd live the rest of my life in Scotland and, despite my love for the highlands and my mother's family, I'm a child of England and wish to live here."

"Am I a means to an end, then?"

"In a manner of speaking. As you said, we may accommodate one another."

He was dissatisfied and didn't know why. He didn't want her to feel anything for him beyond friendship, didn't want the guilt of being unable to return her affections. Why, then, did her bald statement cause him this discomfort? He continued to watch the ears of his matched bays as they twitched in response to the sounds around them.

"You're not jealous, surely, because to entertain jealousy would necessarily mean your affections are engaged, and you've made it abundantly clear such is not the case."

He glanced at her and saw that she was earnest. What a pompous man he had become. She accepted him to reinstate herself within society and if any lingering feelings remained, he'd undoubtedly squashed them completely with his Thou Shalt Not Love Thy Spouse speech the night before. Her request for continued sexual relations with him was not, it appeared, anything to do with him, but with the act itself. He ruthlessly squelched the distant howling within him. He should be glad. Never mind that he was not. "I'm not prone to jealousy. It's a wasted emotion, of which no good can come. While I expect you to remain faithful until such time as I have an heir, perhaps two, your life after that will be your own, to do with as you please. I daresay a woman of your passionate nature would, indeed, require continued . . . stimulation."

"Are you saying you wouldn't be averse to me taking a lover?"

His gaze returned to the drive while the howling increased volume in his head. "That is what I'm saying."

"Do you disremember what I told you last night? I will accept no man in my bed but you, and if this is unacceptable, I suggest we disassociate ourselves from one another and make alternate plans."

"Would you marry MacDougal then? A man you don't love? Would you expect *him* to remain your bed partner for life?" He was astonished to realize he was angry.

"I would indeed." She drew herself up in that way she had. Very much like a straitlaced, aristocratic, entitled duchess, about to give someone a frigid setdown. "It's becoming clear that you still find me repugnant, that as much as you will welcome a son because you'll have done your duty by your ancestors, your true joy will be found in your freedom from my attentions."

Her voice became deeper as she spoke and he was aware she attempted to avoid weeping. He'd rather made a mess of things, though he was at a loss just how so. Was this a portent of their marriage? He suspected it was, and his anger increased. "I don't find you repugnant in the slightest, Lady Jane. I've told you I desire you. Must I prostrate myself at your feet and blather on about your beauty, your lovely eyes, luxuriant hair and soft, inviting body? Would you have me circle you like a stallion, pawing the ground and baring my teeth at the other rutting animals who would dare look at you? Perhaps I should bite you, as a stallion does a mare, to place my mark upon you that all will know you are mine, that they must keep their distance. Would this give you comfort and assurance that I find you desirable?"

She stared ahead, a veritable statue. When she spoke, it was a whisper. "I think I hate you, sir, for you have this ability to hurt me by your cruelty. I don't love you, and thank God for that, because were I foolish enough to love you, I've no doubt you would destroy me."

Michael was dumbfounded. Had he been cruel? *Of course he had not.* She was being overly sensitive, imagining a slight where none was intended. "All this because I gave you my permission to take a lover of your choosing once you've discharged your duty to me? And here I believed I was being rather grand in my gesture. How have I become the villain in this piece?"

Turning her face to his, her gaze was cold. "Has it not occurred to you that I don't consider giving you children to be a duty, that I desire children because it's within my nature to want them? Or do you blithely assume my interest in children is in the same vein as yours, merely a commodity, necessary to retain a title? I assure you, it is not. I don't give a damn about your title."

He was more confused than ever. "If you don't love me, why does it matter that it's me in your bed? A woman of your beauty and charm will have no lack of choice in lovers."

Rage took hold of her. Fascinated, he watched her eyes grow darker and her cheeks bloom with color. "I will *not* be unfaithful. I will *not* cuckold my husband, whom I've sworn to honor until I die. And I *will not* spend the rest of my life with only a bloody warming brick as a bedmate. I believed you understood, but it's apparent that you do not. Take me home. Immediately."

Michael turned the curricle from the main drive onto a meandering path through the trees.

"This is not the direction of home, Blixford. I insist you turn about, this instant."

"We aren't done, Lady Jane."

"I am done. What you do or say is no longer of any consequence to me." Her gloved hands twisted together, an outward sign of her inner turmoil, which belied the blank expression of her lovely face.

He turned the curricle once more and after a time, drew to a stop within a small, narrow clearing, the sunlit grass dotted with wee, white flowers nodding in the breeze. He set the brake and loosened his hold on the reins, allowing the horses to graze while he turned his attention to Jane. Reaching for the ribbons of her bonnet, he tugged until they were undone and removed it from her head, laying it aside before he grasped her shoulders and pulled her about to face him. She was so soft, so beautiful, her dark hair gleaming in the sunlight. Once again, she smelled of lemons. How had he never fully appreciated the scent of lemons?

"If you kiss me, I shall scream. Then I will slap you."

"If you scream, I'll kiss you again. If you slap me, I won't care. For now, however, I have but one question and beg you do me the honor of answering honestly."

She might have doused a blazing fire with her freezing stare. "One question."

"Last night, you mentioned additional experiences. I believe you said they were *illuminating* additional experiences."

"If you expect me to tell you anything at all, you're not nearly so intelligent as I thought."

"What I expect you to tell me is whether you responded in the same manner as you did with me, all those years ago in Lucy's library."

"No."

He frowned slightly. "No, you won't tell me, or no, you didn't respond the same way?"

"Blixford, you're a tiresome man! No, I didn't respond in the same way. In point of fact, it was my total lack of interest which I found so illuminating. Frankly, I didn't like it. While I'm certain this can only serve to fan the flames of your male importance and give you ammunition with which to wound me at a later date, I tell you only because you asked for honesty. Now will you take me home?"

His elation could only be disguised pride, surely. "As soon as I've kissed you."

"You, sir, have been warned."

His fingers tightened against her shoulders and he drew her closer to him. "You're entirely wrong, you know. If I'm cruel, it's never intentional."

"Untrue, Blixford. You were deliberately hateful to me that night. That you could say such things, after ravishing me, is unconscionable."

"I have apologized. You have accepted. I prefer never to speak of it again, but I'll leave the subject by pointing out how very close I was to taking you on the sofa." He drew her nearer still. "I'm not ordinarily a man given to losing my head, but I was half drunk, feeling rather sorry for myself, and there you were, in your dressing gown, more beautiful, more desirable than any woman I've ever known, and you were sneaking a peek at etchings of naked men. You're an innocent, and have no comprehension of what this signals to a man. Had you not left when you did, we would be married four years now. I'd have bedded you right there in the library, and no amount of running away would keep you from marrying me."

Her eyes were wide, her breath quicker. "You said those things because you knew it would make me angry enough to leave?"

"In retrospect, yes, I believe I did. It's not my nature to be cruel, and truth be told, I find your choice of pastimes unique and intriguing, no matter the impropriety. So you see, all this talk of me finding you repugnant would be laughable, if you were not so convinced of it, and so certain I'll be anxious to set you out of my bed." He would be anxious to do so, but certainly not because he found her undesirable. Ironically, the exact opposite. He found her too desirable, too intriguing, and entirely too tempting in her manner and character. If he stayed too long with Jane, he had no doubt he would become attached, would fall in love with her, and it was simply not something he could allow.

"You do realize this casts you in something of a bad light?"

"Of course it does. I appear to be a weak man where you're concerned, unable to control myself, forced to resort to desperate measures, including abandonment of my manners and regard for you by hurling childish insults. Take now, for instance. You've threatened to scream and mete out an injury to my person if I kiss you, but I'm compelled to do it anyway because you're close enough to smell, so close I can feel the warmth of your body, so close, it would be really very foolish of me not to kiss you."

And so he did. She didn't slap him, nor did she scream.

His lips met hers and within seconds, he recalled quite clearly why he'd been compelled to ravish her, against his better judgment, almost against his will. She was the essence of vitality, of throbbing, pulsing life, her body an endless, unexplored frontier of soft curves and intriguing scents. She quivered beneath his hands, ever so slightly, as though her very soul shook with passion and desire. He parted his lips and touched hers with his tongue.

She drew back slightly and whispered, "Promise you won't lecture me."

"Let me in, Jane," he commanded, slanting his mouth across hers, plunging into her moist heat, sucking her bottom lip between his teeth, kissing her as no gentleman ever kisses a lady. If passion was what she expected, he would give it to her, consequences be damned. He carefully ignored the voice in his head that told him he was powerless to respond to her in any way less than unbridled passion. As he lifted his head and looked down into her dark-blue eyes, her lids heavy with desire, he couldn't help but compare her to his first three wives. Bedding them had been almost as painful for him as it had been for them. They stoically waited for him to finish and he felt a brute, had even apologized to Grace, for she cried into her pillow, every single time.

He suspected Lady Jane wouldn't cry unless she failed to climax, and even then, he'd be the one most likely to cry. She'd surely unman him.

As his hands fell away from her shoulders and his arms went round her to draw her against him, her arms circled his neck and she gave as good as she got, opening her mouth to him, returning his kiss with a fervor that made a lie of her insistence that she was done with him.

She was far from done with him, and he was only just beginning with her.

"I won't wait a month, Jane," he murmured against her mouth. "This afternoon, I'll acquire a special license and we'll be married tomorrow morning. Is this acceptable to you?"

"Hmm, yes, good . . . fine . . . " She tangled her fingers in his hair, knocking his hat off as she kissed him. After a time, she drew back and looked into his eyes. "You will agree, then, to keep me with you, to stay in my bed, to engage in a true marriage?"

She had to marry him. There was no other choice. He ignored the voice in his head telling him he could, indeed, find another bride. She might be of common stock, perhaps not quite fit to be a duchess, but she'd do. The singular drawback to any other woman was simply that she would not be Jane. With her there, in his arms, her lips plump and pink and wet from his kiss, he knew it had to be Jane. He would figure a way out of the agreement, could, perhaps, convince her it was in her best interest to live apart from him. Later. He'd wait until she conceived and worry about it then. Staring into her lovely eyes, he murmured, "Yes, Jane, I'll agree."

Her response was a blinding smile and another kiss that completely silenced the distant howling in his soul. After a time, she pulled back a bit and grinned cheekily. "Blixford, how very odd it will be to see you without your clothes."

Michael raised a brow. "I daresay I'll enjoy seeing your naked body far more than you'll enjoy mine. You are grace and beauty and mystery, while I . . ." He shook his head. "Men, I'm afraid, are rather awkward. I shall try not to frighten you, Jane."

"Don't be absurd. The only oddity to seeing you naked will simply be that you are naked. You are something of a stick, you know, and oh-so-proper in your manner and dress. I wouldn't want you to be offended if I wonder at the peculiarity of it all."

Humor disappeared and he snatched her close again. "Appearances can be deceiving, Jane. Never make assumptions based upon the face one shows the world. Tomorrow night, you'll tell me if you still believe me to be a stick."

"And you will tell me if you still believe me a hoyden."

"A fair trade. Consider it done." He kissed her once more before he replaced her bonnet and his hat, gathered the reins and released the brake. As he turned about and drove from the clearing, he said, "I believe we may enjoy certain elements of married life, Lady Jane, don't you?"

"I concur, Your Grace. We may never love one another, but we will enjoy procreation."

We may never love one another. Perhaps she had loved him once, but that was long ago, when she was still not much more than a child.

It did not matter.

It could not matter.

If anything, it was a blessing. They would come together as lovers, but they would not love.

Yes, that was as it should be.

They were within sight of the park gates when she asked, "Have you discharged your mistress?"His mind flashed to a picture of Miriam's tear streaked face. "Yes."

"Was she overset?"

"Is it any concern of yours?"

"Not in the slightest. Was she?"

"Quite, although I couldn't be certain how much was true sorrow at my dismissal, or a very pretty act to encourage my guilty conscience to increase the settlement."

"I asked you to be generous."

"I was beyond generous and downright ridiculous. We will not speak of her again, Jane. Is that clear?"

"Oh, yes, quite."

He noted she was smiling happily. "You are pleased with the turn of events?"

"Very pleased, Blixford. Thank you. I find I'm anxious for tomorrow to arrive."

Turning his attention to the street beyond the gates, Michael realized that while he might be loath to admit it, so was he.

CHAPTER 5

Just after dawn the following morning, Jane soothed her mare, explaining she would have to wait a bit before having her head. "As soon as Blixford arrives, you shall run. Until then, we must be patient."

Grendel tossed her head, clearly unhappy with the notion of patience.

At long last, Blixford appeared, riding toward her at a leisurely pace. Why had he not heeded her request to hurry? Had he assumed her note was sent as a lark, merely meant to entice him for an early morning ride? The man had quite a lot to learn of her.

"Good morning, Lady Jane," he said amiably as he rode up. His buckskin riding breeches were tucked into polished, black boots. He wore a black coat and black waistcoat, the darkness broken only by the froth of his white linen shirt and loosely knotted neckcloth. He looked very handsome, as he always did, but clearly, he had dressed in a hurry. In fact, he had forgotten his hat and riding gloves.

Mollified, but not all together, she said, "You are tardy, Your Grace. This is most annoying. Did you not read my note carefully?"

"But of course I did. You indicated you had something of great import to tell me and I should meet you at Rotten Row at first light." He nodded to the east. "I see the sun just peeking out. It is first light, and you, my lady, are your usual termagant self. All is as it should be. Now, what is this news that cannot wait until our wedding?"

Worrying her bottom lip with her teeth, she allowed Grendel to prance about while she collected her thoughts. How best to tell him? She decided straight out was the only way. Easing the mare to a standstill, she looked across at Blixford, sucked in a deep, calming breath and released it slowly. "I would not go forward with our plans until I have made you aware of certain truths. I believed I could do so, that it would not be of importance, but after a restless, trying night, I find I must tell you. To begin our marriage without truth and honesty would seem the height of stupidity, as well as a dishonor to you and your consequence, both as a duke and a gentleman. I'll not have you accusing me of any betrayal."

His expression grew dark as she spoke. "Suppose you tell me, right out? What is this secret that kept you tossing and turning last night?"

"You will not be my first."

His eyebrows shot up, but he remained silent.

"I was not forthcoming about MacDougal. It is my hope that what I'm about to say will remain between us, Your Grace. For all that MacDougal grievously wronged me, I do not wish him dead, and were my father and brothers to discover the truth of things, he would most certainly be killed with all due haste."

Incredibly, his expression grew darker. Thunderous, even. He nudged his stallion closer to Grendel. "Have you no fear that I pose a similar threat?"Oh dear. She had inflamed his masculinity, and his honor. This was not something she anticipated. Treading carefully, she kept her gaze upon his. "My honor was adequately avenged, Blixford. His death will not reinstate my maidenhead. It would, in fact, cause me a great deal of anxiety if he were killed."

He set the stallion to walking and jerked his head that she should catch up. Glad to be moving, she did so and their horses walked along Rotten Row. "Perhaps you should tell me all of it, Jane."

"Yes, well, you see, MacDougal was quite fond of me. I was fond of him, but failed to realize until after some time that his fondness was of a romantic nature. When this became apparent, I told him I couldn't return his affections. He was persistent for a time, but eventually, we settled into a companionable friendship."

She drew in a deep breath before she continued. "Then MacDougal traveled to Edinburgh on a matter of business, and while there, he met with someone recently from London. He returned home and informed me he knew of my ruination. After that, he began his pursuit of me in earnest. He said I was ruined to London, that I would never secure a husband here, and surely I did not wish to be on the shelf. He wanted to marry me, he insisted. Over time, he wore down my protests. One afternoon, after I received a letter from home, I accepted him. He was quite amorous and assured me he would leave straightaway the next morning to visit my father at Hornsby Grange, that we would be married in two weeks' time." She stopped talking and swallowed, the memory paining her. "Instead, that very night his father announced his betrothal to a local lass, who was dining at Castle MacDougal, along with her parents."

Blixford was silent for several long minutes. At last, he asked evenly, "What manner of revenge did you plot?"

Looking ahead, she wondered if he would call off the wedding? "I shot him."

"And he did not die?"

"I did not wish him to die. I wished him to be incapacitated."

"How so?"

Meeting his gaze, she lifted one brow.

"Good God, Jane! You did not!"

"He recovered, but I am unclear whether he will ever father children. He took what was not his to take and I took it back. In a manner of speaking." She faced ahead once more. "There you have it. I am used, Blixford, and I would not marry you without your full knowledge. I'm aware this is something of a prideful thing to a gentleman, and if you care to withdraw your offer, I understand completely. I will cry off, of course, because this is how it's done. Although I do not believe anyone would be the wiser. The banns not having been read, I daresay no one is aware of our betrothal at this point."

They rode in silence for quite some time before he asked in a dead calm voice, "Do you wish to marry me, Jane?"

"I find the notion more appealing every moment I am with you. There was a time when I fancied myself in love with you. In truth, my decision to finally accept MacDougal came on the heels of news from home that you had taken a third bride." She met his gaze directly. "For all that I despised you at the moment I ran from home, it did not last."

"Are you saying that you—"

"Nothing of the kind, Blixford. I see now that what I felt for you was in the nature of infatuation, a very clear attraction to your person, and your demeanor. Nevertheless, after four years of considerable thought, I am come to the conclusion that I overreacted most grievously and proceeded without reasonable consideration. And I have never forgotten the episode in the library. Nor have I experienced anything remotely like it since."

"MacDougal was not—"

"Sir, he was not. I was overset by the whole matter, wondering what I'd got myself into, imagining myself tied to him for the rest of my life. Afterward, I experienced bitter regret. Then the announcement of his betrothal came and I thought surely I would kill him for his duplicity. Even now, I can elicit enough rage against him to start a fire without a tinder box." She shrugged one shoulder. "I've come to learn, however, that raging against events has little effect on the outcome of things. One must accept and move on, mustn't one? To do otherwise is surely madness."

"Did you return to England because of what transpired?"

"I returned to England for the reasons I have already told you. I wanted to be closer to my family, I wish to remain in England as I grow older, and I desire a husband and family of my own. As to what transpired, I moved far away from Castle MacDougal and took up residence in Sherbourne's fishing lodge, actually quite a lovely and spacious cottage. My maiden Cousin Sarah and her plethora of cats moved in with me to act as companion and chaperone. I lived there almost a year, until I received news from home that you were widowed, once again."

"And had you not received this news . . . ?"

"I would be anticipating summer in the highlands."

"So, may I surmise your return to England was specifically with the intent to marry me?"

"Of course you may, for that is the truth. And lest you think you are truly my only choice, I hasten to say, you are not. I have a considerable fortune, as you know, and there are several impoverished titles who would be happy to overlook my ruination and subsequent ill treatment of you four years ago if it gave them access to my funds. Marriage to any one of them would reinstate me in polite society."

"But you do not wish to marry any of them?"

"I wish to marry you, Blixford. However, as I said, if you withdraw, I will not cry foul."

"Suppose I did withdraw. What would you do?"

She swallowed again. "I believe I would hire a companion, travel the Continent for a few years, and return to England when I am too old for anyone to care about my ruination. I would live out my days as a maiden aunt to my brothers' children. Perhaps I would raise horses. Or teach pistols to intrepid young ladies."

"You would not marry another?"

"Doubtful, Your Grace. Frankly, after my experience with MacDougal, I find the thought of marriage to anyone but you repugnant. At one time, I didn't think it mattered so much, that one could grow to love one's husband and experience satisfactory intimacy. I was very foolish."

They were nearing the end of the lane. "Tell me, Jane, how and when you became infatuated. I admit to curiosity. I'd barely met you before Lucy's house party."

"The day of Annabel's funeral, you were your usual stalwart self, rather emotionless, I thought. As you were leaving, you looked toward the front of the chapel and saw the pink roses I had placed there. Your expression was genuine and heartfelt and I believed I glimpsed the man behind the duke, so to speak. Perhaps it was fanciful, and it's possible I read much more into it than was actually there. But I was intrigued and certain I was meant to fall in love with you." She glanced at him, noting he was staring ahead, looking lost in thought. Had he heard her? "I was sixteen at the time, yet to come out. Still a child, really."

"And yet, you pursued me when the time was right, did you not? I didn't imagine it, did I?"

"No, Your Grace. I pursued you tenaciously, convinced you would see what an excellent match we'd make. You wounded me grievously in the library and I didn't think I could ever forgive you for it." She gave him a sad smile. "Would that you had finished things. We'd be married these four years past, you'd have your heir, I would not have been used so vilely by my cousin, and all would be well."

"Would that you hadn't scurried off to Scotland."

"I suppose all things are more clearly seen at a distance, are they not?"

"Hmm, yes. I suspect, were I to withdraw, I would regret the decision in the not so distant future."

Her spirits rallied. "Oh? Why is that?"

"Perhaps I feel responsible in some way for what happened to you. And there is my need for an heir. As I've said before, Jane, I desire you. What you've told me, while upsetting, doesn't alter my decision. We'll be married in a few hours and won't speak of MacDougal again."

"Yes, Your Grace. Thank you."

"Now," he said with an uncharacteristic smile, "I believe we shouldn't waste this opportunity. No one is yet about, not even grooms exercising mounts, and we have this fine horseflesh beneath us. What do you say we run to the other end of Rotten Row?"

"Shall we race?"

"You're at a disadvantage, Jane. Pendragon is a Thoroughbred, built for speed."

"Ah, but Grendel doesn't like to lose. I believe we're up to the challenge. Unless you're afraid you might lose?"

"I'm afraid of nothing, my lady. Are you ready?"

"Lead on, sir."

She urged Grendel ahead and the mare leapt into a run, delighted at last to have her head. They thundered down Rotten Row, neck and neck. She bent lower and urged Grendel to make haste. The mare was all heart, bunching her muscles to give everything she had to the race.

Unfortunately, the stallion was more powerful, and as they neared the end, he pulled ahead and won by a neck.

Blixford appeared well pleased with his win, even had the audacity to crow about it. "Blood will tell, always. I daresay horsemanship has something to do with victory, as well."

"Grendel, we've been maligned. Will you suffer the indignity without a word?"

The mare danced toward his stallion and nipped at his flanks, causing him to jump forward. He turned about and bared his teeth at her.

Wisely, Grendel backed up.

"I believe the spoils are mine, my lady. I would have my forfeit now."

Bowing low, Jane said, "Your servant, sir."

"Nothing of the kind. Come here."

She nudged Grendel closer, despite the mare's resistance. Leaning over, she pecked his cheek in a decidedly matronly manner. "There. Satisfied?"His eyes glittered. "No." He snatched her from Grendel's back and settled her in front of him before he bent his head and kissed her deeply and soundly. "Now, I'm satisfied."

Jane found her smile dying as she stared into his dark eyes. "You're a remarkable man. I promise you won't regret marrying me."

"If I thought there was the slightest likelihood I'd regret it, I wouldn't marry you."

"I thought I was your last chance."

He dropped several kisses across her face. "Like you and your fortune hunters, there are those who would risk death to become a duchess. Few and far between, but they are there, available."

"It's comforting to know I'm not the *only* means to an end. That you chose me, despite the fact that your other choices are somewhat unsavory, does marvelous things for my feminine pride."

He kissed her again, rather ardently, especially considering they were atop a horse, and didn't stop until the sound of applause caught their attention. Turning her head, Jane saw a group of riders congregated nearby. In the lead was her brother, Robert. He winked at her.

Blushing furiously while Blixford set her back upon

Grendel, Jane murmured, "Are you terribly grieved, Your Grace?"

"Bloody hell, Jane, we are to be married. It's the crack of dawn. If they're offended, it serves them right for intruding."

She decided against pointing out their location in a public park. "On the contrary, Blixford, I believe they were applauding."

"Yes, so they were." When she was seated properly, he turned his mount toward the street and she followed, daring one last glance at Robert and his friends. Her brother saluted her. The remaining gentlemen followed suit.

Despite words to the contrary, Michael experienced momentary anxiety when the kindly Reverend Hastings reached the portion of the ceremony involving questions. To her credit and his relief, Jane said in a firm voice, "I do."

Shortly, it was done. He had a new wife. Another duchess. He offered a silent, fervent prayer to God that she would not die.

Lucy was in attendance, having come up to London last evening, as soon as she received his note. She appeared to be the sole personage, save perhaps the reverend, who was pleased with the proceedings. Sherbourne and his sons didn't smile and gave grudging congratulations. They did demonstrate significant affection toward Jane, each embracing her fiercely before they made their way to the dining room for a wedding breakfast.

Michael knew it was irrational, but he was unaccountably angry with all of them over what happened to Jane. It appeared they took her strong, resilient nature at face value and assumed she could hold her own in any situation. Why had they not sent a female relative, a paid companion, someone, *anyone*, to

Scotland to keep an eye on her? From his conversation with Sherbourne, he'd ascertained none of them had paid her a visit during her sojourn. She'd not returned home, hadn't seen any of her family in four years. It was as though they were glad to have her out of sight, and took it a step further by placing her out of mind as well.

He didn't doubt they held her in high regard and great affection. Their thoughtless, if unknowing, abandonment of her was simply a product of their arrogant assumption that no one would dare take advantage of a Lennox. He was a duke, for God's sake, and even he was not so presumptuous, particularly when it came to his sister.

He'd dissuaded several suitors in the years since Bonderant's death, pointing out very clearly that their advances were not appreciated. Lucy assured him she was capable of spurning eager suitors, but Michael knew some men didn't hear the word *no* nor could they comprehend why a lovely woman like Lucy would remain alone in her widowhood. They also couldn't resist Bonderant's wealth, left to his son and within Michael's care until he reached his majority. Lucy was tempting to any man, but particularly to those in need of funds. Michael saw it as his duty by her, and Bonderant's memory, to apprise the more wily of them that further pursuit of his sister would result in dire consequences.

As her brother, he took particular care to see to her well-being, and saw it as a fiduciary responsibility to assist her in managing the estate at Margrave Park. He was considerate of her feelings, and her loneliness, traveling to visit at least three days of every month, issuing an open invitation for her to come to Eastchase Hall at any time, for as long as she liked. For damn sure, at no time would he allow her to traipse off across the country, unprotected.

Sherbourne raised his glass and offered a toast to

their prosperity and happiness. Michael thought he had some difficulty forming the words. The man despised him. His sons were less than enthusiastic in their acknowledgement of the toast.

Lucy, however, was vocally appreciative. "Well said, my lord! I look forward to furthering my acquaintance with my new sister."

"Thank you, Lady Bonderant," Jane said with a smile.

She looked very fetching in a gown of pale blue silk, adorned about the neckline with intricately woven ribbons of varying shades of blue. Additional ribbons wound through her dark curls, affixed to her head in an artful arrangement. Michael wondered how many pins he'd need to discard before it came tumbling down. Was her hair still to her waist, as it had been four years ago? He hoped so. Was there anything more pleasing than a woman's hair swaying against her naked back?

Turning his attention to his breakfast, he conversed with Robert, seated to his left. "Are early rides something of a standing tradition amongst your family?"

"Yes. Riding neck-or-nothing later in the day is frowned upon, and while we're known to thumb our noses at some of the strictures of society, we do try not to step too far outside the lines." He swallowed the remainder of his champagne and waited for the footman to refill his glass before he turned his blue eyes, so like Jane's, back toward Michael. "For instance, I daresay none of us have ever exhibited a public display of affection, regardless of provocation. It's not really the thing, is it?"

Before he could get his back up, Michael noted the distinct gleam of humor in Robert's eyes. He was funning him, perhaps offering approval in his own way. Lifting his flute, he took a drink, then said gravely, "Not the thing at all. I'd assume a gentleman caught in such shocking behavior had surely lost his head in the moment, perhaps too exultant in victory to remember he was in plain sight of passersby. In fact, besting a woman known for her superior skills on horseback might lead a gentleman to demand a forfeit and devil take the consequences."

"By damn, Blixford, I believe I may have to like you, after all." He clinked his flute to Michael's and grinned. "Dashed fine of you to beat Jane. She's far too superior and needs a comeuppance on occasion. Be warned, however, she'll exact revenge by beating you soundly next time."

"In truth, it was a matter of superior horseflesh that allowed the win."

"Undoubtedly, but you see, Jane will appear for the next race on a horse certain to outdistance yours. She does hate to lose, and will go to great lengths to assure it doesn't happen again. In fact, I've no doubt her first purchase as your bride will be of a four-legged variety. Prepare to spend a fair portion at Tattersall's, very soon."

"Most ladies would ask for jewels or bonnets."

"You've not married most women, Blixford. You've married Jane. I advise you to set all preconceived notions of femininity aside. She'll never fail to surprise you."

"Yes, I've already found this to be true." He met Robert's gaze. "Nevertheless, she is a woman and as such, in need of protection, don't you agree?"

"Of course. Do you doubt it?"

"Not at all, although I confess I'm curious how she managed to travel to Scotland all on her own. It's not something gently bred young ladies do."

"I suggest you ask Jane. I believe the answer may surprise you. In fact, you should know all there is to know about your bride, and were I in your shoes, I'd demand she come clean and sally forth." He took another drink of champagne before he set back to work on his smoked trout, eggs and sausages. "You no doubt believe us to be lackadaisical to have allowed Jane such freedoms, but she would have it no other way, I assure you."

Michael doubted that very much. His anger at the Lennoxes grew. He glanced to his right and saw that Jane was deep in conversation with the reverend. He refocused on Robert. "I find it odd in the extreme that no arrangements were made for a female relative, or other woman of gentle breeding, one with Jane's best interests at heart, to attend her and provide chaperonage during her stay in Scotland."

"Odd? How so? She was with family, Blixford. Our own mother's favorite cousin, in fact. Can't get much better chaperonage than that, can one?"

He had a point, but Michael still couldn't understand their carelessness when it came to Jane. She could ride and shoot as well as many men, but dammit, she was not a man. She was vulnerable to men without honor. "She did mention the MacDougals," he led, hoping Robert would follow.

"Sound Scottish family," Robert said with a nod. "Landed and titled, though I forget just now of what rank is Elizabeth's husband." He rested his fork and knife upon his plate and looked at Michael. "I daresay we won't see any of them again, however, or further acknowledge our kinship. Evidently, Jane took umbrage to something said by their eldest son, Brian, and lost her temper. Most women would leave it at a rude shout and be done. Jane shot the man. I'm certain she aimed for his leg, but due to her heightened state of anger, she was agitated and missed. Practically unmanned him, if you see what I mean."

Michael stared at him, unable to comprehend how he could be so dimwitted. "I've been led to believe your sister is a crack shot. Have you considered the possibility that she didn't miss?" He lifted one brow suggestively.

Robert's eyes widened. "Of course not! Jane would never do such a thing. That she shot him is shocking enough, but to insinuate she aimed to unman him is out of the question."

Resisting the urge to shake Robert by the shoulders until his teeth rattled, Michael drank his champagne and let the subject turn. He was struck with wondering if he, himself, was sometimes this obtuse? A novel thought and one he would have to ponder.

In future, her family's neglect wouldn't matter. She was his responsibility now, and he would make certain she was protected from any and all threats to her person, her well-being, and her happiness. He looked to his right and caught her gaze. "After breakfast, you and I will be on our way to Beckinsale House in Kent. It is the smallest of my estates, actually somewhat cozy. I believe you'll enjoy a brief stay there before we return to London for the closing sessions of Parliament."

"I'm certain it will be delightful, thank you."

Something in her manner seemed off kilter. Her eyes, ordinarily boldly meeting his, were firmly fixed upon his shoulder. "Is anything amiss?"

Astonished, he watched her cheeks flush pink. "I find myself feeling out of sorts and a trifle awkward."

"Because your family dislikes me?"

"They don't dislike you, Blixford. They would react in this manner to any man I chose to marry. Give them time and they'll warm up, I assure you."

"Well, then, if your agitation is not due to your family, why are you feeling awkward?"

The blush deepened. "Perhaps this is a subject best left for later, when we're alone." She smiled across the table at Julian, then very prettily said to Michael, "I believe I'm done with breakfast and anxious to be on our way." She glanced at his plate. "You've not finished your trout."

He lowered his voice and said conspiratorially, "I actually dropped my previous serving into the joyous jaws of the mouser lurking about beneath the table. Deuced butler replenished me immediately and the damned cat has abandoned his post beside my chair."

"Do you mean to say you don't enjoy smoked trout?"

"I confess, 'tis true. Poached, perhaps, or even thrown about with butter and lemon, but something about smoked trout is unpalatable."

She met his gaze and grinned, as he'd known she would. "I've married a finicky man. Blixford, you're a wealth of surprises."

"As are you, my dear. Shall we rise and call an end to this, then?"

"I should like that above all things. Not only am I ready to go, I find these new slippers pinch and I'm most anxious to cast them into the fire at the first opportunity."

In her bedchamber, Jane changed from her morning gown into a traveling dress of plum velvet, trimmed with pink ribbon and tiny rosettes. When she was buttoned up, she dismissed her maid and finished her toilette by herself, in order to converse more openly with Lady Bonderant, whom she'd asked to accompany her.

She lounged in a chair before the fire, her pretty silk slippers resting upon a dainty footstool. "What a lovely bride you are," she said warmly. "I vow, it's as it should be, you married to Blix. I said as much four years ago, but my brother is the obstinate sort and he wouldn't consider it. That is, until his own nature overrode his will." She caught Jane's startled look and smiled. "We shall have no secrets. We're sisters now. I'm fully aware of what happened, and truth be told, I didn't blame you for jilting him. Blix is at heart a kind soul, but he's an autocrat. I demanded he tell me why you left, for I was most certain you felt an affection for him and your actions belied any affection."

"Did he tell you?"

"He did. Oh, no details, mind, but I got the gist of things. I informed him it was all badly done, that no lady would find honor in marrying a man who spoke so cruelly. He was perplexed, of course, quite angry, in fact, but he eventually conceded he handled the whole affair very badly."

Sitting before her glass, Jane set her hat upon her head and affixed it with pins before she dabbed a bit of scent to her wrists and turned to pull on her half boots. "I was a fool, Lady Bonderant. It's kind of you to voice an understanding of my motives, and exceedingly wonderful of you not to hold a grudge against me for wronging your brother as I did. But the truth to the matter is that I behaved like a spoiled, peevish child. I've told Blixford I will make it up to him."

"Perhaps you will feel comfortable to address me by my Christian name of Lucy? I'd like that very much."

"Yes, of course. As you must call me Jane."

"Thank you, Jane. Now, as to making it up to Blix, I would offer a bit of sisterly advice to you, if I may speak plainly?"

Her boots firmly upon her feet, nothing left to do but gather her reticule, Jane sat up on her dressing bench and faced Lucy squarely. "I'm a great advocate of plain speaking. Do tell."

Lucy removed her feet from the stool and moved to perch at the edge of the chair, her expression earnest. "You've married a complicated man, Jane. As time passes, I'm certain you'll discover why, but until you have a complete understanding, I counsel you to stay the course. He can be very cold, as you've witnessed, but it's only his manner of avoiding things which cause him discomfort. Do you understand what I am saying?"

"I believe I do."

Her new sister-in-law looked conflicted. "I beg you

not to lose heart, or back down. He's determined to feel nothing for you but friendship, and it simply won't do, Jane. I love him very much. He's my brother, but he's also the only parent I've ever known. My father was never the same after my mother's death, when I was but four and Michael eight. We were sent to live with his sister, a hard, bitter woman who forever resented us in her home. Blix never forgave our father for farming us out like that, and I believe his bitterness has hardened him, made him determined not to extend affection to anyone, lest he be hurt."

Jane got to her feet and paced along the edge of her bed. Julian had failed to mention that Blixford and his sister were sent away after their mother's death. Was it any wonder he was so distant from society, that he avoided social engagements and went about his business in all but total solitude? It broke her heart to think of him and Lucy, at the mercy of an ill-willed aunt. She'd met Lady Reid several times, and couldn't think of a colder, more arrogant woman. The Marchioness of Bloomsbury was a jolly warm soul in comparison. She slowed and looked at his sister. "You don't appear to have followed the same course, Lucy. I've long admired your grace and kindness, and while you do seem a bit reclusive at Margrave Park, it's understandable, having lost your husband whom you loved so much."

Lucy smiled sadly. "Who can say why we are different, Jane? Perhaps each of us is born predisposed to go through life in some manner, and circumstance tends to exacerbate the disposition. I left it behind and retain an optimistic outlook. Blix did not. Maybe because he's male, or because he's older and better understood what was taken from us."

Jane resumed pacing. "I've no idea how to go on. I cannot demand he tender an affection for me, and if he's determined to keep me at arm's length, I don't see a way around it. I did insist, before I agreed to marry him, that he not leave me rusticating at Eastchase Hall, that I expect to be with him, as a wife should be."

"Did he agree?"

"Yes, but it was clear he didn't like the notion. I thought it was because he thinks me mannish, even unlikable. I see now, he didn't lie when he assured me he doesn't dislike me, or find my pastimes repugnant. It's perhaps because he fears he may like me too much. What a coil! And how unexpected. I suppose I must retain my distance, else I'll put him off all together."

"Ah, this is my point, Jane. That is exactly what you *must not do*. The key to Blix is the element of surprise, to keep him on his toes and never let him become complacent. You should go about your life as you would if he were not hindered by his fear of rejection. I don't imagine you love him, but it's obvious you hold him in high regard. You must be your normal, vivacious self, act as though you *are* wildly in love with him and proceed accordingly. If he exhibits the slightest tendency to shut you out, you should remember his reasons and defeat his efforts. I've said all of this only so you will stay the course and help him realize his full potential. He's truly a kind soul, with a great capacity to love. I sometimes believe he's like two persons —the man he shows the world, and the one deep within, wishing to get out. I also believe you are the one to set him free, but you'll have to be quite cagey about it."

Jane stopped pacing and looked carefully at her sister-in-law. She was a woman of quiet, dignified beauty, with the dark hair and eyes of the Devereauxs, a model of propriety. Just now, however, she was uncharacteristically animated. "Lucy, your eyes are positively sparkling. You've a devious mind."

She laughed, well pleased, it appeared. "It's a necessity when dealing with Blix, you'll soon find." Rising from the chair, she crossed the room and embraced Jane. "I foresee you and he will be supremely happy." She leaned back and grasped Jane's shoulders, her expression now quite serious. "But it will take much courage on your part. I beg you not to lose faith, and please, if you ever feel the need for a friendly face who well understands your dilemma, you've only to send for me. I expect you to visit me as well, Jane." She dropped her arms and looped one through Jane's, to walk with her to the door. "I'll leave you now and go and say goodbye to Blix and your family." She looked askance at her. "It must have been . . . interesting, growing up in a houseful of males, all of them, shall we say, rather overtly masculine?"

"Indeed," she agreed before she impulsively pressed a kiss to Lucy's cheek. "All the more reason for my appreciation of you. How dear you are to counsel me."

Smiling warmly, Lucy grasped her hand and squeezed. "Goodbye, Jane. Do have a lovely honeymoon and write when you can."

"Yes, I will. Goodbye, Lucy." She watched her slip from the room then turned to gather up her reticule, her mind turning as she faced a different dilemma than what she'd originally thought. He was not so much afraid of losing her in childbed as he was simply afraid to let her too close. She'd thought that once she became pregnant, was delivered of a child, and recovered nicely, Blixford would come around. Now, she saw that she was wrong.

Still, she couldn't regret marrying him, even if the necessity of doing so was a bit of a mystery to her. She'd determined she didn't love him, but there was something about Blixford she couldn't ignore, as if he had that which she needed desperately. Just what it was, she had no idea. She'd returned home to marry him, and so it was done. Whatever the future held in store, she would face it and make the most of it.

Beginning right now.

With a light step, she took one last look around her

bedchamber to ensure she hadn't left anything of import, then went out into the hallway. She heard voices raised and wondered what was afoot.

At the top of the stairs, she looked down into the front hall and was immediately dizzy.

Blixford stood there, just inside the front door, embracing his mistress, who sobbed uncontrollably. Sherbourne was shouting, as were James and Jack. Lucy stood by, her face pale, her lips trembling.

It appeared, from what she could glean from the shouts and the mistress's wailing voice, that she was expecting Blixford's child, that she expected him to marry her, and she was most displeased that he had married another.

CHAPTER 6

Jane started down the stairs, wondering if hers was always to be a life of contention. Sometimes, she sincerely wished she'd been left on the steps of a French convent, to be raised by quiet nuns. Surely without the presence of men, life would be infinitely more peaceful.

No one had yet noticed her. Stepping into the fray, she said calmly, "Perhaps this is a matter best left inside the door, Your Grace? I daresay the neighbors are all quite thrilled to know you're to be a papa, but I don't believe this is precisely the way you should announce it." She noticed then that he wasn't embracing the woman. Rather, she clung to his neck, sobbing and keening her unhappiness all over his coat.

He stepped back, effectively dragging her along so that the butler could close the door. "Miriam, you must control yourself," he said sternly, attempting to disengage her.

Sherbourne looked angry enough for the top of his head to come right off. "The marriage will be annulled, immediately. Reverend Hastings, you are witness to this and will plead the annulment to the bishop, will you not?"

Poor Reverend Hastings was beside himself with agitation, holding his hands folded in front of him as if in perpetual prayer, murmuring pointless things such as, "Good heavens!" and "Mercy me!" and "Gracious

God!" The instant Sherbourne said his name, he looked just as he might if Moses were to appear on the stairs and command him to part the Thames. Wide eyed, he looked up at her father and stammered, "My . . . my lord, sure . . . surely we must think this through? I've no idea how this might be . . . be met by the bishop. I shall have to . . . to—"

"That won't be necessary, sir." Jane patted his shoulder and gently nudged him toward the door. "You've done your duty this morning, for which I'm most grateful. I shall see you at services three weeks hence." Rothschild, bless his soul, had opened the door, once again, and waved to John Coachman to pull forward. Jane continued nudging the reverend toward the doorway. "Please have a lovely day, there's a good man, and I'm certain we can count on your discretion in this matter?" She saw his nervous nod. "I thought so. Well, goodbye then, sir, and do be careful of the steps—" She flinched. "Ah, you've not sustained an injury after all. Excellent."

Turning away from the door as it closed she looked at her dear papa and brothers and said in a loud voice that brooked no argument, "I believe this is a matter between my husband, myself and his previous mistress. We will discuss it in the study, the three of us, and return shortly."

Sherbourne was not to be dissuaded. He moved closer and shouted, "You *will not* remain married to the scoundrel."

Looking him straight in the eye, she said evenly, "If Blixford is a scoundrel because he had a mistress, then I'd warrant at least three other men standing in this hall are also scoundrels."

For perhaps the first time, at least the first time she'd ever noticed, her father looked shocked. He fairly shook with indignation. "Daughter, *you go too far*. I will not stand by and allow you to ruin your life with that man. Go upstairs and let me handle this."

Blixford stepped between them, almost as tall as her father, practically nose to nose with him. "We will speak privately, Sherbourne."

"Yes, I believe we will. Shall we adjourn to the garden?" He turned and stalked away, Blixford on his heels.

Her husband of less than two hours called over his shoulder, "Miriam, you will await my return in the study." Then he was gone.

"Good heavens. Will there be fisticuffs?" Lucy asked, looking horrified.

"Certainly not," James said, turning to offer his arm. "My apologies, ma'am. You are distressed, of course. Please accompany me to the drawing room and I'll have tea brought up."

Lucy thanked him before she looked toward Jane. "Will you come along?"

"I think not, thank you. I'll stay and have a visit with . . . " She looked to the woman beside her, who was still sobbing a trifle hysterically. "Madam, you are overset. Stop it, at once."

She did. Staring at Jane, she stiffened her spine and dabbed her eyes with the edge of her handkerchief. "I beg your pardon, m'lady. I've created a scene, haven't I?"

"Yes, quite." She touched the woman's arm and nudged her toward the study, across the hallway from the dining room. "I must beg *your* pardon, madam, I don't believe we've been introduced."

"Miriam," she whispered. "Miriam Wendover."

Jane kept urging her forward. "Rothschild, if you would be so good as to bring tea to the study as well, I'd be most appreciative."

Lucy went up the stairs with James and Jack and the rest of her brothers while Jane stepped into the room and closed the pocket doors. Miriam moved toward the window and stared out at the street, affording Jane the opportunity to study her. Her walking gown was the first stare of fashion, a pale pink affair with two flounces, a high neck, and lace around her wrists. Her little hat was a dear thing, a confection of pink and white, with a short, jaunty feather. With her golden hair and fair skin, pink was just right. Jane experienced a stab of something she decided must be jealousy. Or resentment. Here was a woman who'd seen Blixford without his clothes on numerous occasions, had, in fact been extremely intimate with him. Enough to conceive his child. Jane suppressed the instinctive urge to rush forward and snatch the woman's hair from her head.

"I'm terribly sorry, m'lady," his mistress said. "Please understand, it wasn't my intent to upset your wedding day, except that you have married the father of my child. I sent a note round to him this morning, but he didn't respond. I assumed he was ignoring me, and I was hurt and angry. I went to his house, and was told he was not home. After I demanded to know where he'd gone, his valet arrived and said he was here, marrying you." She wheeled around, head held high. "Blix always said if I became with child, he would marry me. That day is now, and he has promised."

Jane didn't believe it for an instant. "Please, won't you sit down?" She waved her toward a chair and followed suit as soon as the woman took a seat. "Now, suppose you tell me the whole of it, so I may decide for myself what course I should take."

Miriam's pretty green eyes widened. "Do you mean to say, you really would seek an annulment?"

"Oh, but of course! If the duke promised to marry you in the event you conceived his child, most certainly he must honor his word."

She clutched her handkerchief as though it would save her from drowning. "I didn't believe you could do so. Get an annulment, I mean."

"I most certainly can, and will. Please tell me

exactly when the duke made his promise."

"Well, it was more in the manner of a jest, you see, but all the same, he did say he would do right by me."

Jane saw directly through the woman, but she wouldn't humiliate her by saying so. She was with child, and no doubt concerned about her future, now that motherhood loomed. "You and the duke are friends, are you not?"

"Oh, yes, m'lady. I may be his mistress, and you of course understand the nature of this sort of relationship, but we have always got along rather famously. He is a kind man, very considerate. And terribly smart. He's taken some time to educate me, buying me books, insisting I learn to speak and write properly."

Jane glanced toward the door when she heard a knock. "Come."

Rothschild stepped inside and rolled the tea cart close to her chair. "Will there be anything further, Your Grace?"

"Thank you, no."

When he was gone, Jane poured, then settled back to continue her interrogation. "When faced with a dilemma, I like to apply the anything can happen and all things are possible theory. I suggest we do so now, Miss Wendover. If anything can happen, if all things are possible, with no negative consequences, only what is best for you, how would you see this scenario wind up? Would you be his duchess, responsible for entertaining the beau monde, the members of Parliament, perhaps even the royals? Do you see yourself managing five different households? Will it intimidate you to be presented at court? I daresay you will require extensive coaching on matters of society, but then, you are clearly very bright and I'm certain an apt pupil."

Miriam sipped her tea and didn't respond. She appeared somewhat befuddled. "Perhaps this is not actually what you desire. Do you see yourself settled in a comfortable home, somewhere in the country, with a few servants to see to your needs, and a handsome yearly allowance? Can you imagine raising your child there, allowing Blixford to provide for the child's requirements, including his or her education? The child will be the bastard of a duke, and certainly entitled to an upbringing above that of commoner children, don't you agree?"

"Yes, m'lady, that sounds perfect. I'm just not certain Blix will agree to it. He was most emphatic when he left last, that we would not see one another again, that his settlement would be the last money I would receive from him."

"You didn't know about the babe at that time?"

"I suspected, but wasn't certain until yesterday, when I went to the midwife for an examination. She says I'll deliver sometime in October." Miriam set her tea upon the small table to the left of her chair and bent forward to meet Jane's gaze. "I've no wish to marry him, not really. I beg of you not to get an annulment. If you could perhaps stand beside me and help me convince him to take responsibility for the child, that is all I want."

"What of you, Miss Wendover? Have you no thoughts of marriage?"

She waved the handkerchief as if in surrender. "I knew I would never marry after young Benjamin, a stable hand at my father's farm, ruined me in a pile of hay, just after my sixteenth birthday. I knew then what men are about, and I've no need of one, except to make my living. My papa set me out and told me never to come back, so I made my way to London and have earned my keep by making gentlemen happy." She eyed Jane carefully. "If you don't mind a bit of advice, m'lady, a man has needs and if he can't get them at home, he'll go elsewhere. You don't strike me as a broomstick, so perhaps you'll forgive my bluntness."

What a bizarre turn of events. "Yes, of course. Thank you, Miss Wendover." She sipped her tea and waited a moment before she said, "Well, then, we are decided? You won't hold Blixford to his promise of marriage, but will be content to retire to the country and raise your child?"

"I do believe I would be most content, Your Grace."

Ah, so she was finally going to acknowledge Jane's recent elevation in rank. "Very well, then, you may consider it done. If Blixford takes any notion not to provide you with what you need, I'll do so myself."

"You, ma'am?"

"I'm an heiress, with funds at my disposal. I'd consider it a privilege to see to your welfare, and that of your child."

"Well, that's something. Not a broomstick at all. I'm most thankful, Yer . . . Your Grace, and I do apologize again for disturbing your wedding day with such outrageous behavior."

"I daresay, were I in your position, I might do the same." She rose and waited for Miriam to follow suit. "We are to leave for Kent in a short while, and will return to London in a fortnight. I'll speak to Blixford, and his agent will contact you to work out details about the settlement. As I said, if he refuses, which frankly, I can't imagine, I'll provide for you. Please don't concern yourself. Take the next two weeks to enjoy your retirement, perhaps make some purchases necessary for your new life."

"God bless you, Your Grace."

Jane smiled at the woman and nodded. "Thank you, Miss Wendover. I'm sure we'll meet again, many times, as the duke will want to have some interaction with the child. We will be friendly, will we not?"

"I'm humbly grateful for your warmth, but it wouldn't be proper, would it?"

"Probably not, but we will be friendly nevertheless." She walked with Miriam toward the door. "I would make one request of you, and trust you will honor it."

"Anything, Yer . . . Your Grace."

Just at the door, Jane turned to face the woman and rested her hand upon her arm. "Do not ever become intimate with my husband again. If you do, if I discover he's in your bed, I'll take severe action against you and you will not like it. Are we very clear, Miss Wendover?"

Shocking her completely, the young woman threw her arms around Jane's neck and laughed out loud. "Oh, you are a love! I vow I'm happy for Blix." She stepped back and grinned at Jane. "You're just the thing for him, yes you are. I offer my congratulations, Your Grace, and wish you every happiness. You need not worry about me, truly. I was his mistress. I performed a service, just as that stiff butler performs a service to you and your family. Now that he has you, Blix won't be in need of those particular services any longer, will he?"

Jane couldn't resist returning the woman's smile. "No, he will not."

Michael leaned against a Grecian column, one of five placed along the garden path, and watched his father-in-law pace the bricks before him. He was terribly upset. Michael believed, if the man would ever allow it, he might cry. He stopped and faced Michael. "If you won't betray her confidence, if you insist on speaking in riddles, have the good grace to tell me if my conclusions are correct."

"You must ask Jane. If you don't ask, if you don't take action, it will be as though she's been mistreated all over again. Surely you can see this? I intend to take care of the problem myself, but I won't stand aside and allow you to browbeat her over marrying me, when something of such consequence is a dead weight around her happiness and peace of mind, ignored in favor of pointing out my myriad faults."

"You say she met you in the park this morning to tell you?"

"She did."

"And you agreed to go ahead with the wedding?"

"I did. Sir, your daughter didn't ask to be hoodwinked, nor did she place herself in a dangerous situation. She was within the bosom of her mother's family, seemingly safe. That this happened to her is alarming, and distressing, and I in no small way place some of the blame upon you. When she ran off to Scotland, did it not occur to you to visit on occasion? Had you been a presence there, she would have established that someone was looking out for her, that someone would demand answers from anyone who dared mistreat her."

Sherbourne had the good grace to look ashamed. He didn't argue. He resumed pacing, running his hand through his hair again and again. "Jane's always been a strong girl, backbone of steel and all that. Rides and shoots better than most men, never was afraid of anything."

"She is not a man, of course, but a woman, in need of protection from unsavory sorts, which doesn't include me, regardless of your opinion. You hold a grudge about what happened at my sister's house party, despite my clear intention to do the right thing. As for my recently dismissed mistress arriving on your doorstep, I'm quite certain she is either not actually breeding, or she's in want of additional funds with which to care for the child. As you well know, children do occasionally result when one takes a mistress. I believe at last count, you have three bastards, scattered about England."

"Yes, but I don't have a wife."

"Neither did I, until two hours ago. As I said, she's my previous, recently dismissed mistress. I'll take responsibility for the child, of course, and that will be an end to it. I've gone out on a limb to discuss it at all, but I don't wish to continue this thrust and parry with you. Either accept me for what I am, as your daughter's husband, or say you will not, so that I may in future not return to your home and cause my wife undue anxiety and unhappiness."

Sherbourne stopped pacing again and faced him. "Hell and damn, Blixford, I've muddled things all out of sorts, and *goddamn*, I am perplexed and enraged that anyone would violate her and not make it right. I've a mind to take off for Scotland within the hour."

"I'd ask you to speak to Jane, without delay. Your consideration will be of greater help to her at this point than rushing off to defend her honor." He raised one brow. "I understand she went a long way toward defending her honor already."

"Blast! I'd forgotten. We thought she was overset and missed her aim, but by God, she didn't, did she?"

"I'd say she was right on target." He pushed away from the column. "As for finishing the task, I believe, as her husband, it's my right to do so. I'd ask your forfeit of any right, Sherbourne, and allow me to gain satisfaction."

"You'll have a fight on your hands from my sons. Dashed fond of Jane, they are."

"Yes, quite. However, I'd not recommend they ever be the wiser, Sherbourne. This is a matter of pride to Jane, and I'll not have her ashamed before her brothers. You are her father, and it's important she have your respect and regard, that she understands she is not at fault, and you take responsibility for failing to protect her. As for her brothers, other than Julian's initial visit at the very beginning, they didn't take it upon themselves to travel to Scotland either, did they?"

"No," he said, shoulders slumping as he walked toward the house with Michael. "Her mother would be heartbroken and mad enough at me, she'd no doubt pull out her father's broadsword and make mincemeat of my liver. Damned if I wouldn't deserve it." He slowed and looked at Michael. "I've failed her, Blixford, and I don't mind telling you it's a pain from which I'll never recover."

"Sir, if you'll allow me to be blunt, your pain is not at issue here. Your daughter needs to know you approve of her marriage, that she remains in your affections, regardless of what has happened. She was most emphatic that I not say a word, because she was afraid you would kill the man, but I suspect she frets you will find fault with her, that this will lower her in your esteem."

"Ridiculous!"

"Yes, but what else might she think if you say nothing? You've made it clear you disapprove of me, yet no one questioned her reasons for shooting a man in his bollocks."

"I will speak to her, Blixford." He stopped and extended his hand. "It would appear I've misjudged you, sir, and I offer my apologies. I wonder what manner of man you are, after all? Not many would have gone through with the wedding."

Michael returned his handshake and lifted one brow. "Not many would have offered in the first place, Sherbourne, but I am not a man of many." They turned to walk again. "Perhaps you should wait until our return from Kent to speak with her. I don't doubt today's events have taken a toll on her, and it might not be the best time to broach a sensitive subject."

"Worried she'll realize you've broken her confidence?"

"Not at all, for I have not. I mentioned that I thought it odd she didn't marry anyone in Scotland, and that she met me in the park at first light on a matter of great importance, something that occurred in Scotland, and you drew your own conclusions. I sincerely hope you will stress to her that I did not, in fact betray her confidence?"

"Absolutely." Sherbourne slapped him on the back. "Have a restful sojourn in Kent, Blixford, and I'll look forward to having you and Jane for dinner, as soon as you've returned."

"Thank you."

"Now, suppose I at least tell her I've decided not to kill you, after all?"

"Excellent notion, Sherbourne. Not killing her husband will go a long way to strengthening the familial bond."

As they passed through the garden door and stepped into the small conservatory, Sherbourne glanced at him with a gleam of anticipation. "Much for pheasant hunting, Blix?"

"On occasion, yes. Perhaps you'll visit Eastchase Hall in autumn and we might go out a bit. My steward tells me we should have an adequate population by fall."

"Yes, I'll plan on it, thank you."

They made their way to the front hall, only to find it empty. Rothschild moved close and nodded to Michael. "Her Grace awaits you in the study."

"Miss Wendover?"

"Has only just left," the butler said without expression.

"She left? Are you certain?"

"Very certain. I might add she appeared well pleased after a brief visit with Her Grace."

"The devil you say."

"Yes, Your Grace. Quite."

Striding toward the pocket doors, he slid them open and stepped inside, noting his bride stood close to the window, gazing out at the street. Without turning, she said, "Have you and Sherbourne come to blows?"

"Nothing of the sort," her father replied before Michael could, smiling as she turned a startled look toward him. He went to her and swept her into a protracted embrace. "As usual, your good sense has led you to a wise decision. I believe I shall approve of Blixford, after all."

She stepped back and looked up at him. "Sir, you amaze me. What brought about this startling change of heart?"

Patting her shoulder, he said heartily, "Turns out the man has an adequate population of pheasants within his park."

Jane laughed. "You won't tell me, then. All right. So long as I know every family meet won't include the risk of fisticuffs and cursing, I'm pleased."

Sherbourne dropped a kiss atop her head and turned back toward the door. "I'll leave you to discuss what needs be discussed, and ask you to join me in the drawing room before you take your leave."

Michael nodded and waited for the doors to close before he approached Jane.

"You've charmed him, or cast a spell upon him, surely."

"Nothing of the sort. We merely cleared the air of some misconceptions." He stood beside her at the window. "I'm grieved by the morning's events, Jane, and would know what you discussed with Miriam."

She calmly told him of their conversation and he couldn't decide whether to laugh, or lecture her on the propriety of having tea with his previous paramour. He opted for neither, and instead slipped an arm about her shoulders to draw her to his side. "You are a compassionate woman, I see, willing to offer assistance to a woman it must surely be your instinct to dislike."

"I did have the very low desire to snatch a handful of her hair and stomp upon her lovely hat. I realize, however, that she's not competing for your affection, that she's merely concerned for her future, as any woman in her position would be." She looked up at him and said soberly, "I did warn her that if she were ever to be intimate with you again, she would regret it bitterly."

"Did you, Jane? I'm flattered, I must say. But it does take two, so I wonder what vengeance you might mete out to me?"

Her face fell and she looked away. "I find I cannot jest about this, Blixford."

"Of course not." He turned her so that he might draw her closer, within his arms. "Never fear. I will be faithful."

"As will I." She lifted her face to his. "May we go now? I'm terribly anxious."

"Is this why you were awkward at breakfast?"

"It's telling, I know, but I'm nervous about it all, afraid you will find me lacking in some way. I've somehow got it in my head that we should hurry up about it, get past the initial discomfiture, and all will be well. Until then, I will be on tenterhooks."

Her anxiety was oddly endearing. "You are all bluster, wife. I see now, you are not the brave woman I thought, but a frightened girl, hiding behind her pistols."

Her eyes darkened. "I am *not* frightened. Merely fretful. There *is* a difference."

He bent his head to hers. "Kiss me, Jane." Far from the pliant, soft woman of yesterday, she was stiff as a board, her lips cold. He ignored the instinct telling him to step away. Moving his mouth across her cheek, he nibbled the lobe of her ear, inhaling her scent at the same time. "Lemons can be tart, sometimes even sour, but add a bit of sugar and they're divine."

"Do you consider yourself sugar?"

He growled softly and gathered her nearer. "Not hardly." He wanted her. As soon as possible. What a novel thought, to desire one's wife to such an extent. He'd found it difficult to muster the enthusiasm necessary to bed his first three wives. Truth be told, he'd lost a great deal of his enthusiasm for Miriam the past few months. She was a gentle woman with a sad life, and he hoped she'd find some measure of happiness. He considered her a friend, in spite of her choice of work, and would certainly support her child, as was his duty. But he wouldn't miss her bed.

In a manner of speaking, he felt as though it had been a very long time, despite having bedded Miriam only two nights ago. Running his hands along Jane's back, he absolutely considered drawing the draperies and taking her upon yon sofa. She'd suggested they hurry up about it. Her reason was anxiety; his was pure, unadulterated lust. This was something he'd held in the back of his mind all of the four years since he ravished her in Lucy's library.

But he couldn't consummate their marriage on her father's sofa. It was too ghastly common, by half, and she deserved better. He kissed her again and met the same response. "You are reacting to Miriam, and I ask you to put her out of your mind. I certainly have."

"You lie."

"No, Jane," he whispered into her hair, "there is only you."

"Prove it."

"Would you have me love you in your father's study?" He shocked himself by hoping she'd say yes.

"I think not." She stepped away from him and he dropped his arms. "Let's leave now."

"The coach awaits your pleasure."

She moved toward the doors. "I've changed my mind about the coach. If you've no objection, I'd prefer to ride. We can make good time and lunch at the Red Lion on the Dover road." Glancing at him over her shoulder, she was sober as a church. "I've heard they have lovely private rooms there."

Forcing himself not to look the way he felt, Michael nodded as solemnly as she'd spoken. "Luncheon at the Red Lion would be an excellent beginning to our honeymoon. Will you be donning a habit, Jane?"

"Yes. I'll meet you in the drawing room shortly."

He watched her leave and ruthlessly squelched the ridiculous shout of gladness forming in his throat. He must remember his goal where she was concerned. Get her pregnant as quickly as possible and leave directly afterward. Spending additional time with his beautiful wife was unwise at best, potentially disastrous at worst.

Clearing his throat, he remained in the study and considered the spines of Sherbourne's books until he was once again in control of his person, able to present himself to the occupants of the drawing room without embarrassment.

CHAPTER 7

Lucy was relieved when Sherbourne appeared in the drawing room and announced he and Blix had come to an understanding, that by Jove, he would undoubtedly make Jane a fine husband. The Lennox brothers appeared to relax, and anxious to ask questions, but clearly didn't want to embarrass her.

The next quarter hour was spent discussing mundane topics over tea, which she had been requested to pour, being that no hostess was present. As she gazed about at Jane's family, she wondered why none of them were married, for surely there were not more handsome men to be had in all England. She'd heard they each held a considerable fortune in their own right, a legacy of their mother's father, a Scottish tradesman who made his money in woolens. It seemed curious that none of them had taken a wife, although she did recall the second eldest, Jack, was a widower.

Sherbourne himself was something of a puzzle. He was a devilishly handsome man and cut a fine figure, even in middle age. With his black hair beginning to silver at the temples and laugh lines about his mouth, he looked very much like a man who enjoyed life, but retained a certain aristocratic dignity. Perhaps he had loved his wife too much to contemplate marrying again. She could well understand that, if it was true. After Bonderant, she'd not been inclined to consider a second marriage. One was fortunate indeed to experience true love and happiness in marriage, and it was unlikely one could find such a fortunate union twice in one lifetime.

James, Viscount Hildebrand, asked politely, "How is your son faring, ma'am?"

"Very well, thank you. William has reached the grand age of five, and considers himself quite grown and capable. It proves difficult to convince him otherwise."

Sherbourne laughed right out loud. "Deuced tricky to raise sons, Lady Bonderant. I should know, having done so with these six lummoxes you see before you." He beamed at his lummoxes, clearly mad for each of them. "Connie, m'wife, that is, up and left me when James was but eleven, and Jane a mere infant. I suppose a feminine hand was what was needed, but strangely enough, every female I brought on the place took one look at these rapscallions and immediately decided to leave."

Robert, the youngest of the brothers, chuckled. "Don't let him bamboozle you, ma'am. Sherbourne simply didn't want any interference in his favorite pastimes of hunting and horse breeding, which surely a wife would pose."

Lucy watched Sherbourne smile, intrigued by the faraway look in his blue eyes, and his wistful expression. "Not ashamed to admit, m'lady, I never found a wife who could replace Constance, and so I did the best I could with all these brats, and in the process, have grown into the crusty bachelor you see before you."

She couldn't resist a grin. "Sherbourne, I'd not describe you as crusty, just yet."

He took a sip of his tea while holding the delicate china saucer in one long fingered hand. "Perhaps I've a few years left in me." He set the saucer and cup aside and rested his elbows against the arms of his chair, steepling his fingers before him as he gazed at her. "Reckon we're family now, in some manner, so I hope you won't think me forward in offering my assistance to you in the event you're ever in need. I know something of raising sons, and if there is a question of how to go on, I'd be honored to provide advice or help." He nodded toward his own sons. "For all that they appear unlikable, in light of the fact they cannot find a woman who will have them, they didn't turn out so badly."

Lucy's smile faded and she said seriously, "I believe you've done outstandingly well, my lord. Thank you very much for your kind offer. Don't be surprised if I have the temerity to take you up on it."

Their eyes met and it seemed to Lucy an understanding passed betwixt them. Ah, yes, he did indeed know what it was like to raise the child of one loved dearly, but no longer there to provide support and encouragement. The many lonely nights, the worry of going about things all wrong, the uncertainty of childrearing made doubly difficult due to no help at all.

"I don't offer merely as a courtesy, and you shouldn't hesitate if the need arises."

"I won't hesitate, Sherbourne."

Julian stood and said, "What we need is a bit of entertainment." He went to the pianoforte and began to play a lively tune –a Scottish highland song, it appeared. His brothers stood and went to stand close and join in. It didn't take long for her to surmise it was a rollicking song of love and marriage, something undoubtedly sung after highland weddings.

It was delightful, for they harmonized and Bram beat a staccato rhythm with his palms against the gleaming wood of the pianoforte. Lucy was delighted, and laughed when they sang a line about the boy finally winning the bonnie lass by gifting her with a pair of sheep, a ewe and a ram, who stood up with them as they exchanged their vows, and provided many sheep in the years that followed.

She caught Sherbourne's eye again and noted he didn't appear to enjoy the song quite so much. He looked a trifle sad, actually.

The last of the song came about and she understood why. The bonnie lass went out to see about the ewe and the ram and her lovely herd of sheep, but never returned, taken by the ice and wind of a sudden, highland storm. Julian slowed the tempo and the song took a decidedly somber turn, ending with a warning to all bonnie lasses to love their husbands regardless of gift or fortune, for love was all important and eternal, and the other merely fleeting.

When the last note faded away, Lucy looked down at her hands and wished it hadn't been so very sad. Her eyes had welled with tears and she was embarrassed. She blinked quickly and thought of Blix and Jane, determined not to be a damper.

Thankfully, Julian began another tune, this one about a lady in a loch, who tempted young men to their deaths with her siren song. Much like the wedding song, this one proposed a lesson, though Lucy was a bit at a loss why any young man would dive into a frigidly cold loch after a watery woman.

Sherbourne said evenly, "I see your confusion, and agree. If a young man is fool enough to go after a woman who lives in a lake, he damn well deserves to die. Never did comprehend this song, though it was one of Connie's favorites."

"Perhaps it's a warning to avoid dangerous women?"

He shrugged. "Can't see how falling for a dangerous woman would lead to death. I'd far rather consort with a lady of mystery than one of strict propriety." He smiled at her most charmingly. "But that's no doubt my age speaking. One does reach a level of maturity that finds all the pomp and circumstance a bit tiring." He was not merely looking at her, but actually staring at her curiously. "How old are you?"

It was a rude question, for which he did not apologize. Lucy decided not to mind, for she suspected she was going to become friends with Sherbourne. There was something of a similarity between them and she found she rather liked him. "I'm four and twenty." She blinked. "And you, sir? How old are you?"

"Fifty, just a month ago. Close to doddering, I expect."

It was so ludicrous, she laughed. "Doddering, indeed! You're a jokester, I see." She nodded toward the brotherly choir in the far corner. "What a grand time you must have had, raising them. They provide tremendous entertainment. Julian is very accomplished."

"True enough, it's been a jolly ride, all these years, and you're correct about Julian. I daresay poor Jane didn't inherit her mother's musical talent, but instead, took after me. I'm unable to carry a tune, was, in fact, asked to lower my voice at services. Seemed there was some concern the good Lord would leave the building if he heard my abuse of sacred hymns."

Once again, she laughed. "Not quite that bad, surely."

His blue eyes twinkled with good humor. "I'd demonstrate, but you'd no doubt run away, and that would be a shame." He continued to stare at her. "Why do I not remember you being so animated four years past, when you hosted that house party?"

"It was but a few months past a year since I lost Bonderant. I was out of mourning, but still mourned. The notion of a house party was not my favorite, but Blix needed a wife, and I thought to do him a kindness." Her eyes widened. "Oh, dear, I've wandered into a most awkward subject, which I regret." She glanced at the tea cart. "May I pour you some more tea?"

"No, thank you, and you shouldn't feel awkward, for

all's well that ends well, and I suspect Jane and Blixford may wind up with a dashed fine marriage, after all. Sometimes adversity isn't a bad thing, wouldn't you agree?"

Lucy gazed at him thoughtfully. "I believe it requires a great deal of distance to see what strength adversity may bring. In the midst of it, there seems no end in sight, no other manner of living than misery."

The brothers began yet another song, and she realized she and Sherbourne were quite intimate, in a manner of speaking, with all the others disengaged from conversation. He kept his gaze on hers and asked quietly, "What of your life now? Do you still go about in misery?"

"No, I am actually quite content. I like living somewhat reclusively at Margrave Park, raising my son. There are neighbors, of course, so I'm not a true hermit. And Blix is very good about visiting. He's been a great help to me with the estate, although by now I believe I'm perfectly capable." She smiled fondly. "Far be it from me to say so, however. He does appear to take pleasure in looking after me."

"But you feel you don't require looking after?"

"Not from a business standpoint, no. On the other hand, he is my only family, and we're quite close, so I do look forward to his visits."

Sherbourne appeared confused. "What of your aunt? Lady Reid?"

Lucy's smile stayed in place, but it was not nearly so sincere as before. "Yes, Aunt Reid, my father's sister."

"You don't consider her family?"

Lucy floundered about in her mind, seeking an answer. At long last, she said bluntly, "Not unless absolutely necessary, I regret to say. You may think me vulgar and unkind, but there it is."

He was thoughtful before he said, "Never did mind one speaking the truth, and she is a difficult woman to like. She's a few years older than me, but I remember her from my salad days as a young man about town. Remember she gave the cut direct to Constance and I wished she were a man so I could call her out." He reached for his teacup, realized it was empty and handed it to her as he continued. "She'd married a marquess, a step down from her position as the daughter of a duke, but she carried herself as a princess, demanding respect, even from her peers. Constance was the daughter of a Scottish sheep farmer turned merchant, and far beneath Lady Reid, so when she was introduced to her, Lady Reid refused the introduction and gave her the cut. Connie didn't care, but I was incensed and insulted on her behalf, as you can imagine." He accepted the filled teacup with thanks, then settled back and asked, "Didn't you and Blixford live with her for a time?"

Lucy decided to be honest, to avoid further discussion. "Yes, Sherbourne, we did. If you don't mind, I'd prefer not to talk about Lady Reid. It's certain to ruin my happiness of the day, and it is, for me, a very happy day."

"Beg pardon, ma'am, of course it is a depressing subject, and you're correct." He sipped his tea and smiled again. "You're pleased, then, that your brother has married Jane?"

"Oh, very happy, indeed. I thought she was the perfect bride for him the instant I met her and discovered her interests, as well as her personality. I believe they will suit marvelously."

As though her words had conjured him, Blix came into the drawing room just then. Lucy was glad to see him smiling, and more glad when Sherbourne stood and welcomed him, as did Jane's brothers. Miriam was not mentioned, and all appeared to be comfortable, the earlier tension having dissipated.

She was a bit surprised, however, to realize she was disappointed her conversation with Sherbourne was at an end. It had been a very long time since she felt the kinship of a new friend. It had been a much longer time that she'd felt any manner of attraction to a man, and that she did so with the Earl of Sherbourne seemed almost funny. Why, then, did she feel no urge to laugh? He truly was an impressive looking man, and quite a happy soul. She was undeniably drawn to him, and thus she explained her disappointment that their *tête a tête* was at an end.

It was just as well. As soon as she returned to Blix's townhouse in Cavendish Square and packed, she would be en route to Margrave Park in nearby Sussex. She'd not brought William to London, since she was only to stay one night and did not wish to disrupt his routine. He'd been sad, but she assured him she would return the very next day. Because she was to go directly home, it would be impossible to pursue a new friendship, so she put it out of her mind and concentrated on speaking to Blix.

"You must write and let us know how things progress at Beckinsale House," she said.

"Yes, do that," Sherbourne agreed with a nod. "I'm curious to know the advancement of your breeding program."

Blix agreed to write and winked at her, signaling he would not write much, because he would, after all, be on his honeymoon.

Lucy blushed, and Blix looked toward Sherbourne. "Jane's taken it into her head she'd prefer to ride, so she's changing into her habit, and I've asked your head groom to saddle Grendel. I hope this is acceptable?"

"Of course! You'll make better time on horseback, and with this exceptional weather, it'd be a shame to be cooped up in a traveling coach, would it not?"

"Yes, I had much the same thought." He glanced down at his formal attire before he looked to Lucy. "If you're ready to go, we'll take you up in my carriage. I'll have to stop by the house to change and saddle my own mount for the trip."

From a distance, she recalled her wedding day. Matthew had bedded her just after their wedding breakfast, in the first inn they passed on their way to Margrave Park. He'd said he could not, would not wait, and she had felt the same. How lovely it had been, how patient and kind he was.

How awkward it would have been if anyone had been with them. Perhaps Blix had another agenda during his stopover at home. She would be in the way, and feel decidedly uncomfortable. Blushing furiously, she managed to say, "Actually, if you don't mind, I believe I'll stay here a while longer. Sherbourne's offered to show me his conservatory and a new, exotic plant he's obtained. I'm certain he or one of Jane's brothers won't mind escorting me home." She turned a smile toward Sherbourne, who took the cue without missing a beat.

"I'd be delighted, Lady Bonderant, and I'm honored you'll stay and allow me to boast of my acquisition."

She couldn't be certain, but she thought Blix looked relieved. He came close and kissed her cheek before stepping back to shake Sherbourne's hand.

Jane came in then, dressed in a beautiful habit of gold velvet, with braided cording around the waist. Her bountiful bosom wasn't overly exposed, but one could see the soft swell of pale skin above the neckline, and Lucy felt a moment's envy. She'd not been gifted with lovely, round breasts. Hers were less than round, and her nipples, rather than a soft, pretty pink, were the color of earth, a dusky brown. Matthew hadn't seemed to mind, but she always felt a bit self-conscious about them.

She kissed Jane goodbye, as did all of her family, and within moments, the newlyweds were gone.

Jane's brothers were not far behind, each of them making their excuses to leave, undoubtedly in pursuit of some entertainment for the remainder of the day. They were all very jovial as they bade her farewell, and James offered to wait and escort her home, but Sherbourne told him to go on along, that he would see to her safe transportation.

"Well," he said when the room was empty, "it appears all that remain are the settled folk." He offered his arm. "Shall we take a stroll through the conservatory, Lady Bonderant? I happen to have something of interest to show you."

She chuckled and laid her hand upon his arm. "You're a dashing good sport, Sherbourne. Quick on your feet as well."

"That I am." He smiled down at her. "It would appear I'm not into my senility as yet."

They made their way down the stairs and circled back toward the garden door, but turned to the left before reaching it and stepped inside the conservatory. It was not so large as hers, but then, this was a townhouse, and Margrave Park was an extensive estate house.

Nevertheless, what it lacked in size was made up for by an exotic array of unusual flora. They strolled along the path that wound in and around the foliage and he pointed out some of the more unique specimens. He stopped when they came upon an extraordinary lily, a lovely delicate bloom, the color of sunset. "A friend of mine brought this to me from India. It's said to have magical powers that confer eternal youth and beauty to all who inhale its fragrance."

"Do you believe it?"

"Complete claptrap." He smiled another of his twinkling smiles at her. "Nevertheless, I make it a habit of a morning to come in and take a good sniff, just in case there's any truth to it."

Lucy laughed, truly enjoying herself. "Perhaps there is. You've the vitality of a man half your age."

He sobered a bit and continued to escort her through the indoor garden. "One tends to consider his mortality as he ages, and I have to confess I'm much more comfortable with life now than I was at twenty-five. I was happily married, with several children already, but still in the throes of proving myself." He glanced at her. "Young men feel the need to do so, you know."

"Yes, I know."

"It bears remembering as your William grows up. There will come a time when he'll want to do something you either don't approve of, or that frightens you because his life and limb may be at risk. The difficulty in raising children, ma'am, is letting them go." He waved his arm, indicating the house. "I'm fortunate that my children visit often, but it's very different now that none of them actually live with me."

"You're lonely?"

"Occasionally." He patted her hand on his arm. "I like you very much, Lady Bonderant. 'Tis a shame you must go home directly, for I'd enjoy furthering our friendship. And I believe we are becoming friends, are we not?"

"Oh, yes, quite. I've taken a liking to you, as well." She looked up at him. "Perhaps our budding friendship will forgive my rudeness, but I'm terribly curious to know why you never remarried. Is it truly because you did not want a wife who might interfere with your pastimes?"He slowed and stopped at a low bench, handing her down to it while he stood by and propped one boot upon the seat, bending to rest his forearms across his knee. "I didn't find another wife for what I suspect are your reasons for not finding a new husband." His gaze was solemn on hers. "Time has a way of fading memories, and I won't pretend I live each day in the past, or that I still mourn. But in the beginning, I certainly did, and had no interest in another marriage, for I knew no other could compare. It wouldn't be fair to any woman to hold her to such a standard. I'm uncertain dear Connie could have held up to my memory of her, if you see what I mean."

"Oh, yes. Bonderant has become quite saintly in death."

"By the time I was past miserable and beginning to feel more the thing, my children required a great deal of my attention, and I became somewhat obsessed with my horse breeding program. Years slipped past and it became less and less a matter of necessity to remarry. I did fine on my own, I thought. Looking back, however, I realize I missed the opportunity to build a satisfying relationship with someone. I now face the prospect of growing old alone, and it's not appealing in the slightest."

He touched her shoulder briefly, as if he wished to make his point very clear. "I'd not wish to see one as lovely and interesting as yourself wind up like me. Don't wait too long to come back to life. It's been five years, and while I'm sure you believe there is no one who will suit, who can possibly make you happy, I would disagree."

"You're right, I'm certain, but for several reasons this is all much easier to speak of than to put into practice. For one thing, I'm reclusive at Margrave Park. Unless I were to marry my neighbor, Sir Edmund, who's close to eighty, or take up with my gardener, or perhaps convince the good vicar to abandon his wife, I have no prospects. There's my steward, Mr. Timms, but he's a dreadful dull sort, and I'd no doubt spend the rest of my life dozing off at inopportune moments. The notion of coming up to London in search of a spouse is distasteful."

"And the other reason?"

She met his gaze directly. "I've yet to feel the desire." It was not a good choice of vocabulary, but she realized, after she said it, how accurate it truly was. At least, it was accurate until approximately an hour ago. What was it about him? She was shocked at her reaction to him, and wondered what he would think of her if he knew she was interested in him *that* way?

"Perhaps you should come up to London with William, stay a while and take him about, and perhaps enjoy some social engagements. I daresay you lack female companionship, rusticating in the country. Not a woman of my acquaintance who doesn't enjoy her friends. You and Jane seem to have struck it well, and she'll be back within a fortnight. In fact, if you decide to spend some time in London, I'd consider it a privilege to escort you wherever you wish to go."

"You'd attend a ball with me?" She almost laughed. Most men didn't like attending balls.

He surprised her when he nodded. "If you wish to go, I'll take you." He touched her shoulder again. "I'd like to help you find someone suitable, and while I'm no matchmaker, I do have some idea about who's who and what's what. It wouldn't do for you to fall into the clutches of a fortune hunter."

"Not at all. It's my duty to retain all of William's holdings and wealth until he reaches his majority. Indeed, Blix worries much over me being taken advantage of." She grinned up at Sherbourne. "It becomes apparent, I presume, that my brother still regards me as a mere child, incapable of understanding the less than noble motives of some men."

"It's aggravating to you, no doubt, but there may come a time when you're glad to have him at your back. I confess I misjudged your brother and have a newfound appreciation for his honor and character."

"I'm so glad. He's a good man." She looked away, toward the lily. "Would that I could find a man of like nature and integrity, one whom I might feel the slightest attraction to, I might consider remarrying."

"It will be impossible if you don't make yourself available. But that's stating the obvious, isn't it?"

She looked at him again and nodded. "Perhaps I'll come up to London with William. Spring is here, and the Season in full swing. I can take him into the park, and to Gunther's for an ice, and in the evenings, I can attend a few parties. Are you sincere about escorting me?"

"Most sincere." He blinked then and smiled wryly. "How very peculiar this conversation is. Does it seem so to you?"

"On the contrary. I have the oddest feeling that I've known you for years."

Their gazes met and something very different and far beyond friendship passed between them. He dropped his foot and stood straight. "Good God, Lady Bonderant, this won't do at all. I believe I should take you home now."

She rose to her feet and faced him. "Yes, undoubtedly wise, Sherbourne, but I'd really rather you made good on that look. I vow my curiosity is killing me."

"I'm old enough to be your father."

"But you are not my father, and your gaze is not in the least fatherly."

He looked somewhat pained. "This is absurd! You are still young, while I am—"

"Not old. Mature, but not old. I daresay old men don't contemplate what just went through your mind. Do not deny it."

He stared at her with those deep-blue eyes, fringed with dark lashes, lined with years of laughter. Lucy stood outside herself for a moment and tried to tell herself she was being ridiculous, that she didn't *really* want the Earl of Sherbourne to kiss her.

She told herself to be quiet, that yes, she really did. More than she'd wanted anything in a very long time. "Either kiss me, or say you absolutely do not wish to. I may go mad, standing here, waiting."

"It should be James, or Jack, or any of the others escorting you about this bit of paradise, wondering if you'll allow them to kiss you. I am ludicrous, ma'am."

"You are incredibly attractive, and I haven't wished

to kiss anyone in five years. If you're a gentleman, you'll grant me my wish and stop blathering on about it."

"Blathering, am I?"

"Oh, good heavens." Lucy moved very close and slid her arms up the front of his coat, round his neck and tilted her head back. He was a fair amount taller than her, so she really couldn't kiss him without his cooperation. "Now I shall die of humiliation if you don't kiss me, and surely a friend wouldn't allow the other death by mortification?"

"Devil take it, Lady Bonderant, this is just not right." His hands grasped her waist and he bent his head to hers for a chaste kiss, before he stepped back, forcing her to drop her arms.

Lucy didn't know what had come over her. She'd not been aware of a man in this way since Matthew, but she appeared to be making up for lost time. Her body fairly hummed and her center flooded with heat and longing. "Please kiss me as you want to, and my curiosity will be assuaged, and you may take me home and pretend it never happened."

"Do I have your word?"

"My solemn word."

He reached for her then, and drew her to him slowly, his eyes on hers, his expression a disparate blend of doubt and desire. One arm slid over her shoulder and his hand splayed across her back, drawing her nearer, while the other arm moved about her waist to pull her body snugly against his. "You are so very beautiful, it's unnatural, perhaps even a crime for you to lock yourself away as you do."

"I'm trying to rectify things, if only you would cooperate."

He bent his head until his nose was close to hers. "I'm far too old and jaded for you."

"If you're too old, why do I feel the evidence of your desire against my belly?"

"I'm old, not dead."

That was putting it mildly. "You don't actually know me at all, so as to being jaded, perhaps I've my own manner of experience. Had you thought of that?"

"No. You were an innocent when you married, and your husband was taken from you a year later. You've as much as said you've been with no other, so I fail to see where you might have become experienced. Bonderant was not much older than you, so I doubt he might have taught you anything out of the ordinary."

He was correct, of course, but he couldn't know what was in her head, how vast was her imagination. What would he think if he knew how she spent a great many of her nights while sequestered at Margrave Park? She'd never know what he thought of it, because she would never tell him. Or any other living soul.

Thinking of her creative work, of her drawings and writings, her vivid thoughts, she wondered how it would be to actually engage in those activities. Sherbourne may not have remarried, but he had no doubt gone through a string of mistresses. He would know a great many things, could show her, lead her, and teach her. All that she imagined might be reality, if he was so inclined.

If he could be convinced into willingness.

She swept her eyes closed as his lips touched hers and slid one arm about his middle, the other round his neck, enjoying his height, his heat, his scent. He truly smelled wonderful, and tasted of tea and something indefinable, perhaps simply him —his unique flavor. He held her more tightly, kissed her more deeply, languidly stroking the interior of her mouth with his tongue, inviting her to reciprocate.

What began as desire and longing stretched out into full scale need, and her mind exploded with images and possibilities.

One kiss was not going to be enough.

He drew his lips away from hers and looked into her

eyes. He seemed almost surprised. "You've not grown rusty, it would appear."

"No, but I do grow restless. I really do not think one kiss is going to suffice."

"You gave me your word."

"Yes, but I beg you not hold me to it. I didn't know how very good this would be. I only suspected."

He kissed her again, more passionately, his arms beginning to move against her back, one hand dropping to cup her buttocks and press her ever closer to his very strong erection. Lucy trembled and wished to feel him inside of her, though she strongly suspected she could climax with only the movement of his fully clothed member against her core. It had been such a great, long, lonely time, and she had ever loved the physical side to her marriage. How wonderful it would be to lay with him, to feel his hard nakedness against her, within her.

But he was hesitant even to kiss her. How on earth might she convince him to lay with her?

When next he drew his lips away from hers, she whispered, "Do you suppose, just once, we could—"

"No, we could not. We absolutely . . . positively . . . could . . ." He was kissing her again, and their hands didn't stay where they ought if this was to be only a kiss, even only a passionate kiss. His hand gently massaged and stroked her buttocks through the silk of her gown, and his other hand moved to her neckline, tugging until her breasts were released. Still plunging his tongue against hers, still holding her lower body tightly to him with one hand, he caressed her swollen bosom and paid particular attention to her nipples, rubbing them softly before gently rolling their peaks between his warm fingers.

Her hands were equally employed, one set of fingers exploring the definition of his buttocks, enormously intrigued by the rounded, tight perfection of him, while the other set of fingers stroked and investigated the feel of his stiff cock, straining against the fabric of the fall fronting his breeches.

Years of loneliness welled up within her, demanding relief. She'd thought pleasuring herself would always be enough, that she could hold the memory of Matthew's hands upon her, his body within her, long enough to sustain her throughout the rest of her life.

She was mistaken. Until now, she'd not fully realized how very lonely she was, how much she missed a man's touch, or how desperately she craved intimacy. That her desires were focused on a man twice her age bothered her not at all. He certainly didn't seem twice her age. On the contrary, he was imminently desirable.

His mouth was hot, firm, seductive. His body against hers was hard and lithe, not in the least dissipated. She moved her arms beneath his coat, traveling further, beneath his waistcoat, tugging his shirt from his breeches that she could touch the warm skin of his back.

"Lady Bonderant, you really should not—"

"Lucy. You will call me Lucy, and I will not hear the words *should not* from you again. I'm a widow, a mother, a woman particularly mature for my age. If I shock you, Sherbourne, I don't care. It's very clear you desire me as much as I want you, so do stop protesting and let us enjoy one another."

His gaze was less surprised than smoldering. "I can only think we'll regret it. I'll feel ridiculous."

"Not before me, surely, and who else will know?"

He was silent and still for a moment, then murmured, "Who else, indeed? Are you quite certain this is what you want, Lucy?"

"Yes, quite." She glanced about her and added, "We've not the luxury of darkness in the conservatory, Sherbourne, and I would rather be shot than caught groping the master of the house by a gardener who happens by."

He closed his eyes and sucked in a deep breath, which he released slowly as he opened his eyes again. "You would accompany me, then, to my bedchamber? It's shocking, truly, for it's not yet time for luncheon."

"I fail to see what luncheon has to do with it. I'm not at all hungry." She nipped at his lower lip with her teeth and scratched his back with her nails. "At least, not for food."

She could see from his demeanor the instant he stepped across the line between hesitation and determination. He moved back a bit and adjusted her bodice, then grasped her hand and walked her rather quickly toward the front of the house. Rothschild was not about, thankfully. Neither was there a footman or any other servant in the hall. They climbed the stairs silently, though several meaningful looks passed between them. At the landing, he turned to the right and she followed him to the last door of the hallway. Just before he opened it, he turned to her once more, his expression serious.

"Are you certain, Lucy? Speak up now, for once we are set upon the course, it will be difficult to turn back."

"Oh, do open the door, Sherbourne. I'm fair shaking, and eager, and crazy for you."

In bare seconds, they were locked within his chamber and he was quickly divesting her of her small hat, her hair pins, her morning gown, her stays and chemise, her slippers and stockings. When she was naked, she reached for his cravat, his coat, waistcoat, shirt, boots, breeches and drawers. They stood apart for a moment and looked their fill.

"Honestly, my lord, you are beautifully put together." His chest was broad and well formed, sprinkled with dark hair that grew into a line that led to his groin. His hips were narrow, and his thighs boasted impressive muscles, no doubt the result of years in the saddle. Sherbourne's first love was said to be horses. Was he larger than Matthew had been? It was difficult to remember. One thing was certain, however –Sherbourne was very well endowed. She audaciously moved toward him and grasped his heavy, thick cock within her hand, filling the other with the weight of his bollocks. "Old, indeed. You're spectacular."

His hands were not idle, swiftly moving across her skin, touching her arms, her throat, her back, her belly, and her breasts before he drew her close to the bed and tossed back the tester. He turned to her and smiled with a twinkle. "Let us see how well the old man holds up in the face of your beauty and grace and extremely luscious body, shall we?"

"Luscious, Sherbourne? I'm anything but luscious."

His smile faded, replaced by a look of burning intensity. "You've been alone too long, I fear, without benefit of a man's appreciation. I'd thought yours a quiet beauty, dignified and refined, but now, seeing you naked, with your lovely hair about your shoulders, your dark nipples peaked with desire, I can only describe you as luscious, tempting and not the least refined. It's infinitely appealing, for I've never had a taste for refined ladies. Perhaps you're the daughter of a duke, the widow of a viscount, but damned if you aren't the very earth itself." He reached for her and kissed her hungrily, holding her close whilst his hand moved between her legs. "You're like a ripe peach, lush, sweet and deliciously . . . juicy."

She shoved him backward and fell upon him as he hit the bed.

"You're also decidedly impetuous and lusty, my lady."

On her knees, her center was close to his cock when she stopped and gazed down at him. "Do I go too far? Am I too bold? If so, you must forgive me, but it's been a very long time, and I cannot wait another moment."

"Not too far, at all, and I find your boldness

intoxicating." He bent his knees and raised his feet to the bed to propel himself farther along the mattress, taking her with him until they were in the center, though still sideways. His hands reached for her waist and held her loosely as she settled herself along the length of him, all the way down, until the head of his cock touched her womb.

She melted with pleasure and fulfillment. Ah, how lovely it was, how right it felt. Slowly, she moved against him, gyrating her hips to create the friction and heat she craved. It wouldn't take long, she realized as she gazed down at him between the curtain of her hair. "The very earth, Sherbourne? How poetic you are."

His hands tightened about her waist and suddenly, without warning, he flipped her to her back. He crouched above her, his laugh lined face no longer filled with good humor, but rather a certain dark expression of deeply carnal intent. "I sense a certain wildness and erotic knowledge within you, and I have to wonder from whence it comes." He withdrew and plunged deep before pulling back, almost leaving before thrusting once more.

"I read . . . oh! . . . a great deal."

"Not anything available at an ordinary bookshop." He thrust again, then lingered on the back pull, appearing to find great pleasure in the process.

She stared up at him, willing herself to hold on, to not let go just yet. She wanted to last and last, to enjoy him as long as possible. "No, my lord, they don't come from a bookshop." How would he react if she told him they were her very own books, handwritten, with original art, bound by her own hand and read by no one but herself?

"I've seen such books, Lucy. They typically include drawings, as well. Very realistic renderings of what we're doing at this very moment, and a number of things we're not doing."

He filled her again, withdrew again, maddeningly slow, but she wouldn't hurry him. She was determined to make it last. "I confess, it's my nature to be keenly curious to know what some of those other things might feel like, if they'd be as enjoyable in reality as it seems in my imagination. I find the imagination can be quite . . . stimulating."

He surprised her when his expression became almost sad. "Poor Lucy, alone in your grand house, but for erotic picture books. I trust you're enjoying yourself now, rather more than being alone?"

She understood his meaning and smiled up at him. "Sherbourne, I can't recall when I last felt this much pleasure. You fill me completely, and it's taking a great amount of effort not to go off too quickly."

His thrusts became more rhythmic, deeper and harder. "By all means, allow yourself to release."

"I don't wish for this to be over so soon."

"Neither do I, but all this talk of your wicked books and the thought of you pleasuring yourself, alone in your bed, is far too stimulating. I'd thought to outlast you, but now it appears doubtful."

Her hands clasped his thickly muscled upper arms as she rose to meet each stroke of his body in hers. He bent low and licked her lips before turning his head to kiss her deeply. Their bodies slid together with a fine sheen of perspiration, slick, hot, perfectly matched in rhythm.

She didn't follow her usual pattern of slow build into a soft, pleasing climax. Instead, she was taken by breathless surprise when her entire body began to shake uncontrollably. Her back came up from the bed into an arch. Finally, at long last, saints be praised, she cried out her immense euphoria. Had it been thus with Matthew? It had been marvelous, she was certain, but had it been like this?

She didn't know. She didn't think it mattered at all. There was here, and now, and Sherbourne, and that

was all that mattered at the moment.

He stared at her with wonder before he dropped his weight to hers, pressing her into the mattress while his thrusts became ever more powerful. She wrapped her legs around his hips, her arms around his middle, and held on to the last shred of her sanity.

It didn't help.

As he completed and pumped himself into her, she went off yet again, her needful, too-long-untouched body responding enthusiastically to his.

When the last of their fulfillment settled into a gentle peace, he remained there, above her, within her, his breathing labored, his head resting beside hers, half of his face buried in her hair. She turned her head and met his blue gaze. "Do you feel ridiculous?"

"No, not ridiculous, but somewhat of a villain. Although I'm deeply honored you've chosen me with which to break your fast, I feel I've taken advantage of your loneliness. I'm older, wiser, more experienced, and should have discouraged you. Instead, I've bedded you."

"Did you enjoy it?"

He smiled and raised a hand to brush her hair from her face. "More than I should, I'm afraid."

"Why so?"

His fingers traced her profile, down to her throat, where he caressed her tenderly. "Because it can only be this time and no other, Lucy, and having known you, it'll be difficult to resist knowing you again."

"Yes, I see your point, although I fail to see why we might not enjoy one another so long as we wish. I'm a widow, not a virginal miss."

He sighed and rolled off of her, though he took her along and held her close to his side. "I won't dishonor you by making you my mistress. I suppose I could marry you, but it would, indeed, announce to the world that I'm ridiculous, would it not? I, myself, have chuckled with the rest of them when an old man marries a young woman. I have only to remember the laughing jibes we poked at Twykham when he married Miss Moring last year."

"Honestly, Sherbourne, how you do go on. Twykham was a year from eighty and Miss Moring barely seventeen when they married. The comparison of Twykham to yourself is absurd. Consider Hollister, if you will. He married Miss Emily Smitherman when he was five and forty and she but twenty. She went on to bear him five children and they are to this day quite happily living in Shropshire. I don't recall that he was held up in jest, or that anyone so much as blinked in surprise."

He was quiet for a while, considering, she supposed.

"This conversation has taken a decidedly interesting turn. Do you mean to say you would consider marrying me? We've not known one another long at all."

She raised up on her elbow and gazed down at him. "I suppose it is a bit presumptuous of us to talk of marriage. But you won't take me as a mistress, and I don't wish to return to my matronly life of loneliness, so what's the alternative?"

His expression was sober. "Perhaps you should send for William and stay in London a few weeks, as we discussed earlier. I'll honor my promise to escort you out and about, and we'll arrange to meet privately on occasion. After a fortnight, perhaps this attraction will become less . . . intense, and we'll be able to judge the situation with cooler heads. I'd also like for you to take a look around, perhaps single out a gentleman you'd find desirable as a husband. A *younger* gentleman."

Admittedly, she didn't pay close attention to all he suggested, rather focusing on his willingness to arrange for additional private meetings. She was delighted and said so. "Do you suppose we might try some different things, Sherbourne?"

His eyes widened. "You're serious?"

Slightly embarrassed, though not enough to back up

and deny her seriousness, she dropped her head to his shoulder and nodded. "I've no doubt you have a great lot of experience in these matters. Would it bother you to teach me what I beg to learn?"

He chuckled then and held her closer. "It wouldn't be a bother, I assure you, but I'll be curious to see how far you're willing to go in your education."

"I look forward to laying your curiosity to rest."

His chuckle became a laugh. "You'll be the death of me, won't you? I'll die in the midst of a lesson and be sent straight to Hell for debauching an innocent woman."

"Innocent, indeed!" If he only knew. Yes, she was physically still quite innocent of anything beyond coupling, always beneath, usually in the dark, but mentally, she was not at all naïve. She wondered, yet again, what he would think if he knew of her books?

She further wondered if her interest in erotic writing and drawing would wane after today, after a fortnight of intimacies with Sherbourne? She suspected it might. They had served to sustain her since Matthew's death, but with a living, breathing, very virile male in her bed, she thought words and drawings upon paper would definitely pale in comparison.

"I'll send for William as soon as I return to Blix's house in Cavendish Square."

"Please make use of my footman, and send your request from here. While we await his arrival, we'll have luncheon, and then perhaps enjoy a drive in the park. Or a ride, if you prefer." He shot her a concerned look. "You do ride, Lucy?"

She laughed. Had she ever laughed this much? "Being that you're a very accomplished horseman, it would sound the death knell to your interest in me if I didn't, so I'm fortunate to say that yes, indeed, I do ride. I've been told I've an excellent seat, so I shall ride with you this afternoon and bravely bear your scrutiny."

"Death knell? I think not." His hand dropped to her thigh and slowly made its way to the apex, where he drove a finger within and waggled it about, grinning as she squirmed beneath him. "If you didn't ride, I would teach you. If you do not ride well, I will teach you to do so. I believe I'm going to enjoy teaching you a great many things." He kissed her again, still grinning.

"I'll enjoy learning." Her eyes widened. "But, Sherbourne, I've only just realized, I don't have a suitable mount."

He leaned over her, his fingers continuing to fondle her while he smiled into her eyes. "I've just the mount for you, m'lady."

Lucy stared up at him and sighed happily. "I've no doubt, my lord, no doubt at all."

CHAPTER 8

Jane couldn't fathom what had come over her. As they traveled along the Dover road, she tried to enjoy the splendid spring day, the plentiful sunshine and new growth all around. She conversed with Blixford, who was being a dear, really, talking far more than was his wont, undoubtedly attempting to put her at ease, but she was only half listening to him, her mind unable to let go of worry.

She hadn't told him, would never tell him, the truth to what happened in Scotland. Yes, she'd been willing, up until a point. Regrettably, she learned there is a moment in a man's time when he might still leave off, and once that point is past, he's compelled to finish things. MacDougal hurt her far more than his betrayal. She'd felt torn to bits, and thinking of the act occurring once again was frightening in the extreme.

Blixford was so *large*, it followed his member would be proportionate, didn't it? She shifted in her saddle, praying she would be able to accommodate him, that it wouldn't be too painful.

When the Red Lion was within sight, he abruptly changed the subject, though she was unclear which subject he'd been on. Something about sheep?

"Jane, you're a world away."

"Never say it. I've followed along most studiously."

"Now it's you who lies. I just suggested we attempt to crossbreed a Merino ewe with a Hereford bull, that the resulting animal would be significantly large. Complete balderdash, and you merely nod and say, *Yes, excellent notion, Blixford.*" He urged Pendragon closer. "Tell me what's on your mind."

"I'd rather not."

He reached over and squeezed her shoulder before dropping his hand. "I'm not a brute, you know. We'll take our time and nothing will happen that you don't wish to happen."

"I'm sure I don't know what you're implying," she said with what she hoped was convincing astonishment.

"Ah, I see, and mere hours ago, you gave such a pretty speech about how our marriage would begin with truth and honesty."

"Bloody hell," she mumbled.

He looked off down the road. "I'm quite hungry and looking forward to luncheon. Wonder if they'll have steak and kidney pie? It's a favorite of mine."

Jane scowled at Grendel's ears. Dash it all, she had the insane feeling she might cry. What was wrong with her? It vexed her to be this intimidated. She tried to think of other things, but she invariably came back to the matter at hand, that as much as she wanted Blixford, she was scared to death of him. Oh, what a tangle! He'd never stay in her bed if she was a cold fish, a frightened little rabbit.

"Ah, here we are."

Jerking her head up, she realized they were, indeed, approaching the yard of the inn. A groom ran out to greet them, tipping his hat as he came. "Would ye be stayin' the night, m'lord, or would ye be here to partake of the mistress's tasty victuals?"

"Luncheon, my good man," Blixford boomed with a wide grin. "We've only just married and I desire to impress my bride with a feast." He dismounted and reached for Jane, his large hands circling her waist to swing her clear of the saddle. When her feet were upon the ground, Blixford tossed a coin to the groom and offered his arm to her.

Inside, the public room was crowded; mingled voices forming a dull roar. The proprietor, a portly man with a florid face and bulbous nose, smiled as he approached. "Welcome to Red Lion, sir, ma'am! I'm Bertram Osgood, proprietor." He sketched a brief bow and summed them up, all at the same time. "How might I be of service to you?"

Blixford handed Mr. Osgood his card. "The duchess is quite exhausted from our journey, and I believe it would suit her to rest a while. Perhaps a spacious room in which we might enjoy luncheon and a rest?"

"I'm honored, Your Grace! Please, step this way." Posthaste, they were escorted to the stairs and shown to a room at the farthest end of the first floor hallway. It was spacious, bright and airy, with windows along two walls, it being a corner situation. The bed was an old fashioned canopy with light, muslin hangings and what appeared to be three mattresses beneath the tester. A floral patterned rug stretched across the polished floor, just to the edge of the hearth. "I'll have a maid bring up hot water, Your Grace, and be back shortly with some of the wife's victuals. I'm a cobbler without shoes if you don't agree she's a fine cook." He bowed himself out, and they were alone.

"Are you tired, Jane?"

She stared out the window at the countryside behind the inn and shook her head.

"Hungry?"

"Vaguely, but I'm not sure."

He went to the window and threw open the sash. "How fortunate we are to enjoy such lovely weather. Are you up for riding the remainder of the way to Beckinsale House?"

"Yes, Blixford."

He glanced over his shoulder. "You've no idea how far it is."

Moving to stand beside him, she sighed. "It can't be too terribly far, for we've already traveled a good distance into Kent, have we not?"

"Yes. We're but five or six miles from our destination."

"Why, then, did you agree to stop here?"

"Because you wanted it, and I'm beginning to believe your theory is correct."

She jerked a startled look to his face. He stared down at her with a strange intensity. "You do?"

"Yes, Jane. It's very clear that you're afraid, which is understandable, but I don't think there's anything I can say to alleviate your fear. I'll have to demonstrate why your fright is groundless."

She felt herself blush, but didn't look away from him. "I loathe and detest this, you know."

He turned and gathered her next to him. "I'll not ask why you're afraid, but I will say fear isn't a bad thing. It's our instinctual manner of avoiding pain, perhaps even death. No soldier goes into battle without a healthy dose of fear. We run from predatory animals because we fear them, but there's no shame in self-preservation." He held her closer. "You'll have to trust me. Try and remember that I'm your husband, and hold you in high regard." He paused, then added, "Perhaps it would help if you remember the library and put any other memories from your mind."

"I'll try. Thank you."

He moved his hands to her head, carefully removed her hat and set it upon the low dressing table. Returning to her hair, he slowly removed the pins, lying each one aside before resuming the task. Eventually, her hair fell about her and he murmured, "Ah, beautiful. I'd hoped you hadn't cut it." His fingers combed through the curls, all the way to the ends, somewhere close to her waist.

A knock sounded at the door and he went to open it, allowing a maid to enter with a pail of steaming water.

She poured it into the pitcher before she curtsied and left. Directly, Mr. Osgood arrived, along with another maid, who laid out a lovely repast on the small table to the opposite corner of the room. A bottle of wine was produced, opened and poured before the man and his helper inquired as to further instructions.

"I believe that will be all," Blixford said. "You'll see that my wife is not disturbed?"

"Of course," he said with another wide smile. "My groom tells me you're newly wed, Your Grace. May I offer felicitations?"

"Yes, thank you."

At last, the man was gone and they were alone, once again.

Blixford turned from locking the door and walked a few steps into the room. "Come here, Jane."

She did.

"Turn round."

She did so without question and stood stock still while he moved her hair over her shoulder and began to unbutton her habit. When he was done, he slowly tugged the garment until it fell to her waist, then nudged it along until it went into a heap upon the floor around her feet. He bent and grasped the fabric. "Step out." He took it to one of the chairs before the fireplace and laid it out carefully before he returned and bent to remove her boots. "These are unusual for a woman."

Balancing herself with one hand upon his shoulder, she replied, "I have them made especially for riding. Most women's riding boots are terribly inadequate."

He rose, returned to her back, and loosened her stays, tossing them to land atop her habit. She was down to her shift, a fine lawn garment with dainty lace trim. Moving around her, he bent to one knee and lifted the shift to concentrate on her garters. He untied them slowly, his movements almost reverent, anticipatory. Her stockings followed, each rolled down in turn, and she lifted her foot that he could remove them entirely.

When he was done, he stepped back and devoured her with his gaze. "Just as I thought."

"Beg pardon?"

"You're lovely, Jane." He reached for his cravat and removed it without fanfare before he shrugged out of his coat. "Does it occur to you that I may be nervous, as well?"

She watched him remove his waistcoat. "Not at all. You're quite accomplished at this, I'm sure."

"Perhaps," he admitted as he unbuttoned his shirt and pulled it over his head, "but not with you." He met her gaze as he tossed the shirt toward the other chair by the fireplace. "You've already informed me you will find it humorous to see me without clothes, so I'm ready to take the humiliating plunge."

A smile tugged the corners of her mouth, even while she stared openly at the expanse of his chest. He was very well formed, muscular and masculine, with a thatch of dark hair that followed a line down to the edge of his riding breeches. "I didn't say I'd be amused, Blixford. I said it would be odd, that I would wonder at the peculiarity of seeing you naked."

"Yes, I remember. Why was that, Jane? Because I'm a stick?"

"It was thoughtless of me to say so, and I'm quickly concluding that you're not at all a stick. It's merely an affectation."

"Similar in nature to your bluster without blush, announcing to all within your sphere that you're fearless." He stood there, gazing at her. "I find I'm unable to complete the task of undressing. You're going to laugh and I will be crushed with the indignity of it all."

"Oh, pish! You're funning me, sir, and I don't appreciate it."

"Not at all," he said quietly, moving closer. "I'm a man of great pride, Jane, and I'd not want to disappoint."

He was serious! It hadn't once entered her mind that such could be the case, but he was actually anxious about bedding her. Was it merely a reaction to her fear? The thought brought another urge to weep. Her hateful jitters were going to ruin it for him. He would not enjoy their coupling. He would leave her bed and find another. One who wasn't a ninny.

Oh, God, how had she come to such a pass?

"Your face is a map to your soul, you know." He reached out and fiddled with her hair, watching it curl about his fingers. His very long fingers, attached to his very great hand. "Mine, I believe, is not, so I'll tell you exactly what I'm thinking." Without meeting her gaze, his eyes fixed to the hair within his fingers, he continued softly, "I've taken three wives, and each was a lady of strict decorum and staunchly conservative morals. Carnal thoughts didn't enter their minds, most likely because they were raised to believe such is not ladylike. Otherwise, my experiences have been with women like Miriam, for whom fulfillment is generally an unexpected benefit. Do you understand what I'm saying?"

"Yes."

He raised the other hand and combed his long fingers through her hair, brushing against her breasts as he did so. "You, Jane, are unlike any other woman I've lain with. You are my wife, a gently bred lady, but one of a passionate nature. On the other hand, you're inexperienced." Finally, he met her gaze. "What happened in Scotland doesn't qualify as experience. I find myself perhaps as nervous as you, because I want to erase the memory from your mind, and the only way to do that is to make lying with me infinitely better."

"Be assured, it would not take much to be better."

His smile was gentle. "Was it so bad then, Jane?"

The damned tears came, in spite of a valiant effort on her part. Multiple swallows couldn't hold back the knot in her throat. Rapid blinking did nothing but encourage the escape of the dreadful things. They coursed down her cheeks, mocking her by dripping onto her breasts. "I'm so sorry, Blixford. This is a disaster of epic proportions, is it not?"

She expected him to embrace her and assure her that it was not, to lie and make her feel better, despite what was surely great disappointment. He'd married a woman who was not so far from his first three wives after all.

Instead, he turned toward the bed, flung back the tester and underlying sheet, then returned to her. He lifted her shift over her head, threw it aside, and swung her up into his arms before he carried her to the bed and laid her in the center, where she was enveloped by the mattresses. Wide eyed, her tears aborted by surprise, she watched him remove his boots and stockings, then stand and release the fall of his breeches before he hastily unbuttoned them. He shoved them off, along with his drawers and bent a knee to the bed, sliding next to her, pulling the covers over them before she got a very close look at his member. But she'd seen enough. He was, indeed, proportionate. Dear God. He would kill her, surely.

Then he was pulling her next to him, one arm beneath her, and the other against her waist, kissing her forcefully, plunging his tongue into her mouth, demanding a response. All the while, his free hand wandered. Across her belly to her breasts, kneading each in turn and then running along her ribcage to her waist, and down to the curls between her legs before returning to her breasts. He tasted of the wine he had sampled before Mr. Osgood poured. He smelled very male, of soap, sweat, horse, and musk, mingled with his cologne. He felt hot and hard and powerful, muscles moving beneath his skin as his hand traveled up and down her body.

Jane couldn't be certain when she'd begun to kiss

him back, but at some point, she did. Of their own volition, her arms reached for him, one curling about his neck, the other circling his middle. He was solid and thick, much larger even than she'd thought. He moved his lips away from hers and kissed her brows, her cheeks and chin before he made his way to her throat, then lower, to her breast. He ran his tongue around her nipple, his big hand kneading the breast beneath, sending sharp pangs of desire though her center.

He raised up and moved closer still, resting his weight along his forearm, his chest lying against hers as he kissed her again. He found her curls, his fingers dipping lower, parting her, deftly stroking. She willed herself not to clamp her legs together, concentrated fiercely upon it.

He slowed and returned his hand to her waist. Lifting his head, his face mere inches from hers, he said in his deep voice, "I thought it best never to speak of it again, but perhaps I was wrong. Will you tell me the truth of how it was?"

"I would prefer not to."

"Undoubtedly, but do so anyway. There's another man in this bed and the only way I may rid us of him is to know him as you do."

She wanted to look away. A part of her wanted to get out of the bed, don her habit, fetch Grendel and ride back to London, to her father.

He wouldn't have it. "Stay just there, Jane. Look at me and speak."

Clearing her throat, she rested her hand against his upper arm and began tentatively. "Castle MacDougal is a lovely place, with many outbuildings, most of them fallen into disuse in modern times. Cousin Elizabeth altered an old fish hatchery, set beside the loch, into a summer pavilion of sorts, a place to rest and view the lake in comfort. I'd gone there to read my letter from home. I was distressed and thought to have a moment alone."

"Was your distress due to news within the letter?"

"I have told you so. You'd taken a third bride."

"Did you expect I wouldn't?"

"I don't know what I expected. I only know the news was terribly depressing. MacDougal came up at a bad moment and offered comfort."

"A bad moment?"

She frowned at him. "You have the singular distinction as the only man with the ability to make me weep, even hundreds of miles away and our friendship some three years lost."

"My apologies, ma'am. Unintentional, most certainly." He lifted his hand and brushed her hair away from her temple. "Go on. You were weeping in the pavilion beside the loch and MacDougal offered comfort."

"I allowed it, and he kissed me. He proposed, yet again, even went on bended knee, so sincere, so convincing that I would waste my life pining after something that was never meant to be. A gust of wind tossed the letter into the loch and I confess I saw it as a sign. I impulsively said yes and he became quite amorous. I allowed liberties, I suppose because we had just become betrothed. He was my dear cousin, my friend, a man I trusted." She stopped, remembering, feeling a fool.

"Go on, Jane. Tell me all of it. Don't be embarrassed."

Sucking in a deep breath, she let it out slowly. "I didn't see or comprehend what was happening, not until it was entirely too late. My gown was suddenly above my hips, his breeches were undone and I said . . . no." She squeezed her eyes shut and swallowed violently. *Please, God, do not allow me to cry. Grant me a shred of dignity.*

God, it appeared, was busy elsewhere. As the memory descended, she felt one hot tear creep from beneath her lid. "Perhaps he didn't hear, or perhaps he ignored me. I was frightened, and said so. He assured me it was natural to be afraid, that the first time is generally painful, but I should be still and accept it, that the next time would be pleasurable." More tears followed the first. "I do so hate to weep, Blixford. This is dreadful! And our wedding day! You think me horrid, do you not?"

"Shh, no, I do not. I want to hear all of it, Jane. Please continue."

She opened her eyes again and saw that he was concentrating fiercely, his gaze steady on hers. "It was much worse than merely painful. I thought I might die of it, and I do not exaggerate. He finished with me and stood to adjust his breeches. My most vivid memory is the expression on his face as he stood there, looking down at me. He was displeased and insisted I get up quickly, that I was bleeding on his mama's divan. Naturally, I did, quite horrified. We walked back to the castle, and he went off for a ride without even a goodbye. I thought surely I'd reached the depths of despair. How could I live my entire life with such a cruel and thoughtless man, but how could I not, having given him what belongs to a husband?"

Her eyes moved from his and focused on the canopy above. "That night, when his father announced his betrothal to Mary Anna MacGruder, he smiled at me, as if to say he'd had me and I was a fool. He made a comment about fine Scottish lasses making better brides, for they have strength of character lacking in the English. I realized then he resented me and my family, my father's position and wealth. Inasmuch as he violated me, he did so to my entire family. We had all been disparaged by an arrogant Scot. I didn't consider my actions, nor did I think of the consequences. I excused myself from table, fetched my pistol, returned to the dining room and shot him, with all of his family and the MacGruders looking on.

Cousin Elizabeth's husband wanted to call the constable and have me arrested. I informed him, if he did so, my father and brothers would learn of his son's perfidy and he would be dead, instead of merely wounded. I was gone from Castle MacDougal at first light."

He said nothing for a very long while. Instead, his hand continued to pet her hair and he dropped soft kisses against her face. At last, he raised up again and said, "You've more courage than any man I know, Jane. You're a woman of great pride, which I find relatable. I applaud what you did. He deserved much worse, in fact, and in my estimation, you were far kinder than most would be."

"Thank you, Blixford, but surely you understand, I have no shame for what I did to him? Had I all of it to do over, I would still shoot to unman him. I gained satisfaction for myself and my family. Unfortunately, no amount of satisfaction can take away the memory of how horribly painful it was. No amount of courage will allow me not to fear you."

She expected him to get up, get dressed and take her back to London, to demand an annulment.

He didn't do anything of the sort.

He gathered her up and rolled to his back, nestling her against his side, arms enveloping her. "You're sensible and bright. Only consider how many men and women have engaged in sexual congress throughout the ages. Do you suppose, if it were always horribly painful for the female, they would continue to allow it? Think of those with multiple children. What woman would continue to submit to something dreadful? Think back to our interlude in Lucy's library. You enjoyed it, did you not?"

"Rather a lot. The memory has sustained me for a very long time, and is, in fact, one of the reasons I returned to my pursuit of you. I thought surely you must know something others do not."

"I know a woman needs time to become ready, for her body to accept a man's." He reached for her hand and moved it to the apex of her thighs. "Touch yourself, Jane. You're slick and swollen."

She blushed. "Indeed."

"I suspect MacDougal didn't allow you any time to become ready. Other than a kiss, which was undoubtedly not overly passionate, he afforded you nothing in the way of building your desire. This would make it painful for any woman, but for one untried, still virginal, I don't wonder it was terribly painful for you."

"Forgive me for prying and feel free to deny an answer, but how did you manage with your previous brides?"

He didn't answer right away. Eventually, he said evenly, "There are creams available. I daresay half or more of polite society utilize them for purposes of procreation."

"And the other half?"

"Are fortunate enough to be married to women who have no need of creams." He tightened his hold. "Before you ask, the answer is no, I don't have any and don't anticipate a need to purchase any. We'll work through this, Jane, and you'll find pleasure with me, I swear it."

She sighed and nestled her head in the nook of his neck, her arm circling his middle. They lay quietly for some time, the distant sound of voices from the yard drifting around the building and through the open window. Birds twittered happily in the trees beyond the inn. "You're a remarkable man, Blixford. What have you gotten into with me?"

"I believe it is a bed, ma'am."

Chuckling, she traced circles across his chest, playing in the soft, springy hair. "Have you lost the moment?"

"Not entirely."

"Why don't we eat a bite and try again in a little while?"

"Hmm, the idea has merit. I'm fair starved after feeding most of my breakfast to the cat." He raised his head and looked into her face. "Perhaps some wine would serve to relax you a bit more. Already, you seem less anxious."

"You're wise. I didn't believe speaking of it would serve any purpose, but I do feel somewhat better."

"Always best to face demons straight on, Jane. Deal with them and put them in their proper place." He drew away and reached for his breeches, standing to pull them on, giving her a fair view of his backside.

Such a lovely, masculine man.

Her stomach growled and he jerked his head around, eyes wide. "Ye gods, woman, would you devour me before I can get you to table?"

Jane laughed and caught her shift when he tossed it toward her. "You didn't notice, Blixford, but the cat abandoned your chair for mine."

"Do you mean to say you disposed of your trout in the same manner?"

"I did. Like you, I detest smoked trout. I was also beset with anxiety, so didn't eat much else." Her gaze moved to the table. "I vow, Mrs. Osgood's victuals do look tempting."

Lucy's son was beautiful, with great dark, soulful eyes, just like his mother's. Sherbourne fell in love with him on sight. Damned if the child didn't remind him of Henry at the same age. He'd been such a serious little one, the boy who hung back, who carefully weighed every situation, who sometimes didn't join his brothers in whatever mischief they'd got up, claiming it was a bad idea, or that the consequences of getting caught —and they generally always got caught —were too dire. On his own, Henry got into much more serious scrapes than his brothers ever did, simply due to his quiet, pensive determination to conquer the world.

Even at five, William, Viscount Bonderant had all the makings of a man who would always take the high road, the difficult journey, the path to greatness, if not glory.

Lucy had explained to him that Blixford spent as much time as possible with the boy, but as he didn't live with them, his interaction was necessarily limited. She worried the lack of any steady male influence was detrimental to William. Sherbourne tended to agree and actually felt sorry for the wee mite, living all alone as he did at Margrave Park, with his mother as his only companion. He would go to school in a few more years and be far behind the other boys, who were bound to be cruel to him for his lack of experience and knowledge.

He should be catching toads and leaving them in his nurse's bed, sneaking sugar into the salt cellars, fencing with long, dangerous sticks, climbing the tallest tree in the estate park, despite his terror, all on a dare. "Does he ride?" he asked Lucy as they strolled in Hyde Park and watched William run along the banks of the river, collecting stones.

"Oh, yes, he has his own pony and is as accomplished as might be expected for a boy of five. He's also learning the pianoforte, and I've employed a watercolor instructor for him. She comes on Tuesdays, and William usually goes missing on Tuesdays. I once found him a half mile away, in the upper reaches of the folly, hiding."

He thought for a moment, then asked, "Although it's not my place to offer comment, advice, or criticism, would you permit me to do so anyway?"

She looked up at him earnestly. "Please do."

"Lucy, the boy needs to be active, to get rid of all that energy. Forcing him to sit or stand still and paint with watercolors is cruel and undignified for him. Watercolors are a feminine endeavor, suited to young misses."

"But William doesn't know this. He can't have an aversion to it because he thinks it's only for girls."

"You should understand, every boy has an innate sense of masculinity, of what he's capable of, and he will constantly stretch the limits, to test himself and see if he's strong enough, if he's worthy. I'm not at all surprised he runs off on Tuesdays. If it were me, I'd run three miles away and hide in the village bell tower to avoid anything so distasteful as watercolors. How does he take to music lessons?"

"Better, but he does complain a lot." She was thoughtful before she asked, "What manner of lessons should I be providing?"

"Archery would be good. I will purchase a bow and quiver of arrows for him and teach him the fundamentals, straightaway. It's a good precursor to pistols. Teaches aim."

Her eyes were wide and worried. "Arrows, Sherbourne? He might poke out his eye."

"Yes, and he will adore you for allowing him the risk. Truthfully, it's not dangerous at all, if you consider he'll always be lobbing the arrow away from his person." He grinned at her. "It's the poor chap in the line of fire who must be careful. You'll need to stand well behind him when he practices."

She appeared to accept the notion. "What else do you recommend?"

"Are there no other children living nearby?"

"None other than the tenants'. I've not allowed him to interact with them, simply because they run wild, and get into scrapes."

"William should run wild and get into scrapes. He'll learn much more from his mistakes than he'll ever learn from your patient lectures. If he's allowed some freedom to roam about and play with other children, he'll learn independence. He'll feel proud of himself that he can wander off, tempt death in the form of tall trees to climb and dangerous fish to catch and great, awful beetles to toss at girls, but still make it back home to his nursery and his cot."

She sighed and squeezed his arm as they strolled. "Thank you, Sherbourne. I see the wisdom to what you say. I confess, Blix and I are not adept at this, no doubt because our own upbringing was so dismal. I went to live with Aunt Reid when I was but four, and didn't get away until my father died, ten years later, when Blix came from Cambridge to collect me and take me back to Eastchase Hall." Her gaze as she looked at her son was wistful. "I often rail against fate for taking Matthew so soon after I had William. There was no possibility of other children, natural born playmates. How fortunate your children were, and still are, to have one another."

He patted her hand. "He'll be just fine, Lucy. The key is to relax, to not hover, to allow him to grow up. He's young yet, probably still likes to climb up in your lap, if no one's looking, and have you read to him of a night before he goes to sleep. But every day older, he'll pull away a bit more, and you can't hold him back."

Her gaze was curious. "Did your children climb in your lap? Did you read to them at bedtime?"

"Every last one of them did. Bram was the most affectionate, and to this day, he's the most demonstrative. At five and twenty, he still kisses my cheek to say goodbye. Tells me he has no mum to kiss, so he has to settle for his papa."

William had discovered the joy of sailing twigs downstream. No sooner had he realized he could set them afloat and watch them meander away, he had the brilliant notion of spearing a large leaf with the twig, fashioning a sailboat. They slowed to a stop and stepped off the path to watch him.

"Perhaps a toy boat would be in order?" she asked.

"Hmm, maybe, but it would not be nearly so much fun as crafting his own, now would it? I recommend a good, sharp knife. He can whittle canoes from twigs."

"A knife, Sherbourne? A *sharp* knife?"

"Absolutely. Let's finish our stroll and go for an ice at Gunther's, and just afterward, we'll take him to pick out his very own knife."

"Good heavens, I may never survive seeing William wielding a knife."

"Fear not, for it will be a small one, just the size for his small hand. He'll immediately cut himself, of course, and try not to cry, and you'll bandage him up and scold him and he'll be infinitely more careful in future. Buck up now, Lucy." He grinned down at her, enjoying himself immensely.

She gave him a hesitant smile and nodded. "I shall do my best."

What a beautiful woman she was, and how dedicated she was to her son, as well as the memory of her long dead husband. If her carnal need was not so strong, he suspected she might remain celibate the rest of her life, to remain faithful to his memory.

But the thought was ludicrous. Lucy was a woman of serious, deep passion and strong, dark desires that would never remain repressed, regardless of how hard she tried to contain them. He'd encountered very few women in his life who came close to Lucy's needful nature. Come to think of it, not since Connie had he lain with a woman who could climax with absolutely no stimulation other than the thrust of his cock. He'd suspected Lucy would go off just after she climbed atop him and impaled herself.

He was enchanted. He was sexually charged and eager to take her again, soon. He was ridiculous.

But he'd promised her a fortnight, and silently, he'd promised himself, as well. They would spend the next two weeks exploring one another, perhaps engaging in some risky lovemaking and interesting positions, and then it would be over. She would tire of him, naturally, and eventually see him for what he was –an aging peer who'd someday be unable to keep up with her lusty appetites. She'd return to Margrave Park, perhaps more enthusiastic to seek out another husband, one who would fulfill her desire. As for himself, he'd remain in London until the end of the Season, then return to Hornsby Grange for summer. If she conceived, he'd marry her immediately, ridiculous, or no. If not, well, she would be a fond memory he would never forget.

It struck him as particularly odd that their age difference didn't seem to matter, wasn't noticeable to him. She was, indeed mature for her age, her soulful, dark eyes filled with a certain knowing, an understanding of the world many never achieved, regardless of how many years they lived. He supposed he didn't actually think of himself as old. He enjoyed life, could see no reason for a gloomy outlook. He'd had his share of misfortune and heartbreak, but what was the point dwelling on it? Best to move on and see what life held in store.

For instance, how could he have imagined the day would turn out this way when he awoke this morning? He'd been anxious and grievously concerned about allowing Jane to marry Blixford, wondering if, yet again, he was doing the wrong thing by letting her have her way. It had always been so damned easy to spoil her. How he adored her, and how he had missed her while she sojourned in Scotland.

He thought of what had transpired, and although he knew no details, he knew she had come to harm, and it fair broke his heart. It also made him deadly angry. If Blixford didn't exact proper satisfaction, by God, he would. He'd kill the blackguard.

But that was something to fret about another day. For now, he was enraptured by the lovely surprise that was Lucy, and additionally, her captivating son. He anticipated the next fortnight with great enthusiasm. Not only would he have the pleasure of a child's company, something he missed now that his own brood were grown and gone, he would undoubtedly find enormous gratification in Lucy's sweet, beautiful body. She was, indeed, luscious. The very earth.

"Come along, Wills," he called to the boy, "and I shall buy you an ice."

Well behaved, not prone to ill temper, the child turned obediently and walked to Sherbourne's side, gazing up at him with round eyes. "Sir, what is an ice?"

"It is a treat all boys love a great deal, including this one."

"Do girls like it, as well?"

"Oh, indeed. I daresay your mother will enjoy one along with us, will you not, Lady Bonderant?"

"I may enjoy two of them, my lord."

They continued along the path beside the river and he was aware of the curiosity of friends and acquaintances who drove or rode past on the park drive nearby. Tomorrow, he would accompany Lucy as she made calls to announce that she was in town, and open to invitations. She'd no doubt receive one for Twykham's ball, to be held tomorrow night in honor of his first anniversary of marriage to Miss Moring. Sherbourne wondered if the fellow would stay awake long enough to entertain his guests.

He would escort Lucy and dance with her and assist her as she took a look about at the eligible gentlemen in attendance. Perhaps Wrotham? No, he was a bit stiff. And not in a good way. He considered Holtzbrink and dismissed him out of turn. The man had a predilection for lightskirts. Lucy's husband couldn't expire himself anywhere but in her bed. It would be grossly unfair to her. Dillingham? Hmm, now there was a possibility. But he sometimes had an annoying demeanor, and his speech was atrocious, for he was wont to spray those he conversed with. Too wet by half.

Sherbourne considered his own sons and set the thought aside almost immediately. He couldn't sit at table with Lucy in future, knowing one of his sons was intimate with her. It would drive him mad, and perhaps drive a wedge between him and one of his sons. No, he'd ruined the chance for a match between Lucy and any of his boys the instant he led her up the stairs and down the hall to his chamber.

He couldn't be sorry. He'd found her desirable from the moment he laid eyes on her this morning. Had she not insisted he kiss her, and then boldly propositioned him, he'd have taken her home and continued to admire her and lust after her in his own mind and nothing more. But it still would have bothered him if one of his sons courted her.

His thoughts turned to Blixford. It would be noted that Sherbourne was squiring Lady Bonderant about town, and someone was sure to alert her brother. He hoped there wouldn't be any altercation over it, but he suspected there well might be. It was odd, almost humorous, how they each seemed predisposed to needle the other, via their female relatives.

He thought of Jane and smiled. He so hoped she'd be happy, that she'd find what she was looking for in Blixford. He'd concluded the man ran with very deep, still waters indeed. Jane would enjoy discovering the depth of him, he was certain. She'd always loved a challenge, and Blixford would ever be that.

They were close to his carriage, which awaited them close to the park gates, when William asked, "Sir, do you ride?"

"All the time. And you, Wills? Do you ride?"

"Oh, yes, sir. I've a pony named Biscuit and he's a grand champion."

"Is he? Then I hope you ride him well, for surely a grand champion would be dishonored by a lackadaisical rider."

The boy was quiet for a while, then asked, "Sir, what does lackadaisical mean?"

Lucy chuckled and tapped his ribs with her elbow, her gaze merry, daring him to explain.

If she only knew how many things he'd explained over the years. This was child's play. "Well, it's not a good thing, that's what. If you're lackadaisical, you're sloppy, your seat improper and your legs misplaced. Biscuit can only do as you tell him, and if you're lackadaisical, you may unwittingly tell him to do something you never intended. Why, he might run about in circles, making you dizzy, or take off at a gallop and toss you into the lake. He might bolt into the house and eat your mama's flowers."

Ah, at last, the boy smiled. Grinned, actually. "That's silly! He couldn't open the door!"

Was ever there a sweeter sound than the voice of a child? Sherbourne was a bit overcome, remembering. He ruffled William's hair and nodded ahead to the carriage before he pulled a lump of sugar from his pocket. "Go and give Portia a treat, and perhaps she'll get us to Gunther's that much quicker."

The boy took the sugar and dashed off, waving it about as he ran, calling out to the horse. Sherbourne watched as John Coachman smiled indulgently at the lad. The man had been in Sherbourne's employ for years upon years, had watched out for his brood on thousands of occasions. Sherbourne thought the older man looked pleased to have a lad about again, feeding a treat to his carriage horse.

"Lucy, he's a delight, he really is. You've done marvelously with him."

"Besides turning him into a girl?" she asked with a laugh.

"Nonsense. You might dress a boy in a silk gown and teach him to stitch, but the boy will always out. Same for girls, you know. Only look at my Jane.

Taught her to ride and shoot, took her about the sheep farms, but no part of her could be considered masculine. 'Cept maybe her voice. She's got her mother's odd, low voice. That aside, however, she's all girl, so her masculine accomplishments are not to her detriment."

Lucy nodded, still smiling. "To my mind, they are what make her most charming, and what will drive my poor, wound up brother to distraction." She looked up and met his gaze. "Is it wrong that I secretly laugh at what I'm sure she'll put him through?"

"Undoubtedly, but do go ahead. In fact, we'll discuss it at length a bit later."

"Later?"

He winked at her. "Don't be alarmed if there's a scratch at your chamber door when you least expect it. And don't assume it's your maid and tell her to go away."

"Oh, Sherbourne, how lovely! Will you really sneak about like a spy, to gain entrance to my bed?"

His grin faded and he became quite serious. "I'd climb the deuced ivy to your window, or slide down the chimney, and if all else failed, I'd walk through the front door, come upstairs in plain sight, and threaten to kill anyone who spread tales. But I don't believe such drastic action will be necessary. I'm merely alerting you to keep your eyes open and be ready to take a cue."

"Yes, my lord, I will, I'm sure, be very ready."

Jane ate a great deal and had two glasses of wine, appearing to find comfort and ease in his presence, despite her lack of any clothing beyond her shift and him in his shirtsleeves.

For his part, Michael was bedeviled with desire, smoldering hotly as he watched her, his gaze unable to draw away from her long, curling hair, the manner in which it moved with her body, teasing him with glimpses of her breasts, her rosy nipples outlined clearly beneath the thin lawn of her shift.

He felt sorry for her, well aware she would despise his pity. But he couldn't help it. She'd been at the mercy of a cad, a bounder, an evil scoundrel who deserved death. Remembering her at eighteen, filled with inquisitive, uninhibited passion, he wanted to shout his anger. He wanted to find MacDougal and crush him beneath the heel of his boot, pummel him into oblivion, visit a terrible fate upon him for destroying her innocence, her natural curiosity, the essence of her.

Eventually, he would do so. He'd demand his own satisfaction and he would have it. Until that time, he was determined to bring back the woman he'd ravished in his sister's library. She was still there, he was certain. He had but to coax her out of hiding.

They talked of Beckinsale House and some of the things he had planned for their stay. She revealed she enjoyed swimming and he promised, if the weather was warm, he would take her to the lake within the park and they would bathe there. Sated and drowsy, she leaned back in her chair and watched him from eyes the color of the sky at dusk. "Had you enough to eat?"

"Yes, quite."

"Are you disappointed there was no steak and kidney pie?"

"A bit, but I expect I can convince Cook to prepare one during our stay."

She cast a look toward the screen in the corner behind him. "I'd like to freshen up a bit."

Feeling the need of a privy himself, he nodded and rose to his feet. Dressing quickly, no doubt sloppily, he went to the door. "I'll be back directly, Jane."

"I look forward to it." She was already headed for the screen.

Downstairs, he found what he needed, then spent a while visiting with Mr. Osgood, asking about local personages and the state of the year's crops. He was a kindly man, with a twinkle in his eye and a ready laugh. He was pleased with Michael's praise of his wife's cooking, clearly proud of her efforts. "'Twas Mrs. Osgood's idear to buy the inn, Your Grace. Took a bit of work to polish 'er up, but we've been pleased."

Glancing about the common room, beginning to thin of its crowd, the hour for luncheon having just passed, Michael nodded. "Very polished, indeed, sir. You're to be commended for your hard work."

"Oh, but, Your Grace, credit is due to Mrs. Osgood as much as myself. The Lord was good to me, sending her into my wee shop in London, twelve years ago. Struck it well, right off, and after we married, she happened upon the notion of an inn and here we are. Not many will admit owing their good fortune to their wife, but I'm not too proud to say so. Reckon I'd still be squinting at watchworks, scraping by, but for the missus."

That sterling woman made her entrance just then. Michael might have stared if he were not a gentleman. She was so similar in appearance to Mr. Osgood, it was uncanny. Her face was flushed, undoubtedly from the heat of the kitchen, her nose ended with a slight bulb, and her gray eyes sparkled with good cheer. The Osgoods were like bookends. She curtsied before him. "Your Grace, 'tis an honor to have you visit with us, and your beautiful bride. Is there aught we might do to make Her Grace more comfortable?"

"I think not, thank you, Mrs. Osgood. She's quite replete after sampling your fine cooking."

The woman looked happy enough to begin clapping her hands. "Your Grace is too kind. I'm so pleased your duchess enjoyed my simple fare."

"Oft times, simple is what's wanted and needed, ma'am, and we much enjoyed it."

"Oh, thank you! And please, express to Her Grace my felicitations on her marriage to such a fine gentleman."

"I will do that, Mrs. Osgood." He glanced toward the stairs. "Perhaps I'd best return and see to her."

They exchanged a glance and beamed at him. "You've only to ring should you need anything at all, Your Grace."

He decided they knew exactly what was to transpire in the room in the corner. He returned their smile and nodded his head before he turned for the stairs. Shouldn't he feel some measure of discomfiture? Oddly, he did not. Even Mrs. Osgood's giggle, quickly shushed by her husband, didn't irk him in the slightest. On the contrary, he was grinning as he made his way down the hallway. He rapped once and opened the door when he heard her call out.

She was in bed. Naked. Looking at him boldly.

His grin remained.

"Your Grace is happy?"

"His Grace is supremely happy." He strode to the bed, discarding his clothing as he went. "And I suspect His Grace is about to be even happier."

"You mustn't overset yourself."

"Never fear, madam wife." He bent his knee to the bed and stretched out beside her, reaching for her in the same movement, pulling her on top of him, plunging his hands into her hair to hold her head whilst he kissed her deeply. "You will not be afraid. You will touch me as I touch you. You will enjoy this."

"Ducal edicts?"

"Leave the duke out of it. This is your husband speaking."

She ducked her head and rolled away to the opposite side of the bed.

"Where are you going?"

"Just over here to see if you will follow."

He turned until he was flush against her, snaking

his arms around her to haul her close. "I will always follow, Jane." Ah, she was light and life in his arms, and looking that much more at ease. His hope grew and he held her to his breast most tenderly. Her hair was soft and clean, her face freshly washed, her scent in the air. Lemons and female, with a dash of horse. A heady combination, and one he wouldn't forget. He kissed her then, gently, carefully. Her lips were supple and soft beneath his. He stifled a groan when she slipped her tongue against his mouth, seeking entrance.

In what remained of rational thought, it occurred to him he'd never spent a terribly long time merely kissing a woman. He did so now, finding a great deal of satisfaction in the process of wooing her with naught but his lips and a gentle hand upon her back. Her full, soft breasts pressed against his chest, but he made no move to touch them, all of his concentration remaining on her mouth, intrigued by the sheer eroticism of her feel and taste.

She sighed and he felt her relax more completely, her body molding to his with intimate trust. Michael was a bit overwhelmed, his determination to please her somehow melding with his desire for her, neither overriding the other, despite their seemingly disparate objectives. His was a nature of all-consuming passion, taking a woman with his ultimate satisfaction uppermost in his mind. Her fulfillment was important, but he suspected it was merely for his own gratification, to enhance the experience of lovemaking.

In the corner bedchamber of the Red Lion Inn, he wanted to be selfless, to lead Jane back to where she began, unschooled, but eager. In the process, he discovered certain truths about his own need and was a trifle astounded. As he progressed in his effort to coax her passion to the fore, he found his own desire increased ten-fold. Had he ever wanted a woman this much? He didn't think so. And yet, he was in no hurry to seek release, finding that he enjoyed what he ordinarily considered something of a chore.

Far from work, moving his hands across her soft, silky skin, touching her everywhere, returning to her lips again and again for deep, passionate kisses, served to inflame him with a slow burn that was as intriguing as it was gratifying. He shook with it, and when she looked into his eyes, her lids heavy with desire, and whispered, "Now, Michael. I'm ready," he wondered that he'd ever considered himself learned of women. He was as unschooled as she, it seemed.

Raising up, he got to his knees and moved on the bed, placing her feet flat upon the mattress, alongside his thighs. Reaching beneath her, he lifted her hips and positioned himself there, just at her curls. Jane was beautiful, everywhere. He drew his gaze up and met her eyes. She was still afraid, but willing to brave it out. "You will tell me to stop if you're in discomfort."

Her eyes widened. "You can do that?"

His smile was wry. "I can do whatever you wish." With his eyes remaining on hers, he pushed inside of her with a languid stroke, without hesitation, but also without hurry.

Her eyes widened further and her pretty lips formed a round 'O' of surprise. "I'd not thought it possible."

He moved his hand to where they were joined and pressed firm, rhythmic strokes against her soft, wet heat as he slowly withdrew and returned as gently as he began. He shook with need, with the insistent, instinctive urge to plunder her with abandon, but he determinedly shoved it aside and continued to make slow love to her, in and out, easily, unhurriedly, watching her face, fascinated by her constantly changing expressions; surprised, anxious, relieved, surprised again, concentrating, puzzled, and then she looked . . . pleased. Her lips curved into a slow, seductive smile.

"Oh, my," she murmured, watching him.

"Yes." He was strangely unwilling to finish, to interrupt the moment. He felt as though he knew her thoughts, was inside of her in more ways than one. His fingers remained within her softness, constantly stroking, and he knew she was close to release, could feel her muscles working around his shaft with every slow thrust.

"I wonder . . . " She began, blushing before she finished the thought.

"What do you wonder, Jane?"

"Am I to . . . wait? It's becoming difficult to do so, but I'm not sure what you want."

The need inside of him increased exponentially and threatened to take him over. Exultant, as pleased for Jane as he was for himself, he moved his hand away and shifted position, stretching above her without withdrawing, resting his weight along his forearms until his body was flush with hers. "Do not wait," he whispered as he kissed her. "Give over, Jane. Let yourself go."

Her legs wrapped around his hips and he allowed the beast to consume him, increasing the speed of his thrusts until she panted short, gasping breaths, her body shook beneath him, and her muscles contracted around him. Scarce moments later, he shuddered and poured into her, ending with a glad sigh.

He'd barely caught his breath before she was raining sweet kisses across his face. "Thank you . . . oh, thank you! What a remarkable man you are, and how fortunate I am."

"Ah, Jane, you're not nearly so fortunate as I." He returned her kisses, well aware his weight must be pressing the air from her lungs but not ready to move away. Not yet.

"Is this something we'll do again soon?"

He listened for a strain of fear, for any sign of hesitation or dread. He didn't hear it. All he heard was curiosity, perhaps tinged with a certain eagerness. He wanted to laugh and shout his satisfaction. Instead, he kissed her again before he rolled off of her, dragging her with him to tuck next to his side, throwing a possessive leg across hers. "I daresay we'll most definitely do this again, very soon."

She yawned and settled against him, mumbling something about waking her when he was ready before she drifted off to sleep. He recalled she'd said she had a fairly sleepless night, fretting about whether to tell him her secret. How much it must have taken for her to meet him this morning and reveal something that clearly caused her great grief and consternation.

Not for a moment had he considered withdrawing. He was set on marrying her, and by God, it was done. She was his wife now, as she should have been four years ago.

Lying there, holding her soft body close to his, listening to her deep, rhythmic breaths, he was well aware the danger of falling in love with her was as great, if not perhaps greater, than it had been four years ago. All the reasons he'd had then for resisting her were alive and well.

He would resist. He would not contemplate otherwise. He didn't doubt he would grieve if she died, but he would soldier on. Without love, he could bury her and retain his peace of mind.

Without love, he could calmly, rationally bear witness to the attentions of other men, which was inevitable because where there was a woman of Jane's beauty and vitality, there were men who paid homage. He would not allow himself to feel threatened. She pledged to be faithful and he had no reason to disbelieve her.

He gathered her closer. She stirred and tightened her arm about his middle. "So drowsy . . . so sorry. Perhaps you might catch a wink yourself?"

He recalled he hadn't had a particularly restful night either. His valet had awoken him while it was still dark to deliver Jane's urgent note to meet her in Rotten Row at first light. Odd to think it was only that morning. It seemed days past.

The scent of lemons and sex curled about his nostrils. Lovely. He sighed, relaxed and closed his eyes, unaware when he faded into slumber.

CHAPTER 9

Not far from the Red Lion Inn, they had turned off of the Dover road and onto a country lane that wound its way through fields of newly sprouted barley and wheat just beginning to thrive in the warmth of spring. Occasional copses of trees along the way provided welcome shade as they passed beneath. Jane took notice of everything, finding delight in the journey, in the day, in all that had transpired.

She also found herself prone to shyness, a discovery she faced with astonishment. Each time she recalled the afternoon, she blushed anew and paid particular notice to what lay to her right, keeping her face averted from him, trying to hide her immature bashfulness. He would surely admonish her, and why not? Good heavens, it was preposterous, this funny feeling of shyness after all they had done.

But fully clothed, in the bright light of outdoors, it was easy to forget the intimacy they shared and not focus on her shocking behavior. She had awakened to find him asleep, his face in repose very peaceful and handsome. Such a feeling of affection and attraction had bubbled up within, she shamelessly moved atop his slumbering body to caress and kiss him boldly, until he awoke and made love to her all over again. It had been the same, yet very different. He'd been more aggressive, more powerful, moving her body with authoritative control, bringing her to the peak of passion until she was limp with exertion.

It was incredible.

He was incredible, her path to redemption in the eyes of society, but also, unexpectedly, the way to healing the hurt she'd carried with her since that afternoon in Cousin Elizabeth's pavilion. What a grand gesture it was of him to insist she tell him all, to listen and comprehend the abject misery she endured. He did, she was certain, and sought to alleviate her fear through gentle wooing and a patient hand.

Her instincts had been right. The Duke of Blixford was a man of vast complication, deep emotion, and strong character. He was not at all a stick.

How easy it would be to fall wildly in love with him. She suspected she would, despite the rationale behind not allowing it and her best intentions. It would take a very long time, if ever, to bring him round to love her. He would resist vehemently, according to Lucy, who knew him as no other. The years and his experiences appeared to have mellowed him considerably and lessened his strict demand for proper, ladylike behavior. He had raced her in Rotten Row, something he'd never have done four years ago. But he remained guarded in his affection and she didn't doubt that loving him would bring her much pain.

Much better to hold him in high regard, enjoy his company, and his bed, and live her life earnestly and helpfully. What did it matter if he loved her to distraction? Or if she lived and died by his love? Love was a fickle emotion, even at best. Theirs would be a marriage of mutual respect and friendship, bound by law and what transpired in their bed.

"You're very thoughtful, Jane."

"Yes, I was wondering what crops you grow at Beckinsale House, and if you might take me about to see the fields. I do so love to look at them. It's terribly elemental, growing things that will clothe and sustain people." She cast him a sidelong glance. "It's also quite nice to earn money from them, but I shouldn't say so and point out my more mercenary character. You'll think me avaricious."

"I don't find the prospect of earning money to be avaricious. In fact, I'm rather keen on the pursuit of income, from all sources."

"Tell me about your investments."

He did so, though not in great detail. There were several captains whose shipping ventures he supported, along with a conglomerate of other gentlemen. He was also invested in a woolen mill in York, a steel smelt in Manchester, and a coal mine in Wales. Perhaps most interesting, he dabbled a bit in the literary world, funding a small publisher in London. "Mr. Pipkin is slowly gaining some notoriety, though earnings are still not close to balanced with expenses. It's more of a hobby or an interest than a real investment. I suspect it will never earn anything, but continue to be a black pit of lost funds."

"How noble of you to support the literati, Blixford. Are you something of a bibliophile, then?"

He looked at her and raised one brow. "Something of the sort. You'd be interested to know that you perused one of the first books we published."

"Oh?" She should have known by the gleam in his eye, but she did not.

"Mr. Paisley's discourse about Australian aboriginal tribes is a Chase East publication. In fact, I've met Mr. Paisley and discussed his travels at length. I was asked my opinion as to which etchings should be included in the volume. Tell me, do you concur with my selections?"

She stared at him a moment, attempting to determine if he was in jest. He was not. Jerking her head round, she looked straight ahead and bit her lip.

"What? No opinion, Jane? And I'd thought you held such a fascination with the subject."

"Incorrigible! You should be ashamed, leading me on

like that."

"I'm not at all ashamed, ma'am. I'm still awaiting an answer, by the way."

Determined not to laugh, for surely he would be wounded by it, she managed to say in an even voice, "Excellent choices, Blixford, though perhaps redundant. I believe several of the etchings were much like the others. Perhaps a bit of variety might have been called for?"

"Interesting observation, one I'd not considered."

"Oh? Why is that?"

"Because each etching represents varying elements of daily life amongst the aborigines. Hunting, building shelters, preparing food, cultivating crops." He appeared to be pondering her comment with serious consideration. "The particular tribe Mr. Paisley lived among for almost a year is somewhat unique in that they rarely don garments of any kind. He considered adding some manner of loincloth, but I assured him he should remain true to the reality of their world, for surely no reader would solely focus on the nudity, but would, instead, study the etchings for their visual description of daily life amongst the tribe."

Jane cast him a chilling look. "Oh, do cut line, Blixford. Come right out and accuse me of being a naughty brat for ogling etchings of naked men, failing to distinguish the actual portrayal and merely seeing what I wished to see. I'll simply plead curiosity and you'll have a good chuckle at my expense. Let us skip through all of that and move on to the chuckle, shall we?"

He didn't chuckle. He laughed right out loud.

"Are you quite finished?"

"Not . . . quite." He laughed again.

"Horrible man." His laugh was deep, rolling and marvelous.

He nudged Pendragon close and leaned over to plant a kiss on her cheek. "If I live to be very old, I'll never forget just how you looked when you turned away from that bookshelf and saw me there. If you were the type who swoons, you'd have crumpled into a heap upon the floor."

"I tried to make an escape, which you didn't allow."

"True. I was compelled to keep you there, to see how you might bluster your way out of such a mortifying situation."

"It was most unsporting of you to approach me with the sketch of the nude man. By the by, who do you suppose drew him?"

He remained close until Grendel turned her head and nipped at Pendragon, who danced away from her teeth. Blixford allowed it, casting a look at the mare. "She's not fond of him, is she?"

"She's still humiliated by this morning's loss and won't forgive him until she's able to best him." It was a silly notion, of course, but she didn't like to admit Grendel had less than a sweet nature. The mare sometimes had a nasty disposition.

"Tomorrow, perhaps."

"Tomorrow, for certain." She looked ahead again. "You were going to tell me the name of Mr. Charcoal's creator."

"Ah, yes. I'm certain it was Lucy. She's an artist, though she doesn't display her work."

"Because her subjects are nude men?"

"Her oils are usually pastoral scenes, devoid of humans, nude or otherwise. I briefly considered why she might have drawn the charcoal man, though truthfully, owing to her situation as my sister, the consideration was very brief." He looked askance at her. "It's a distinction of male relatives to harbor the fantasy of their female relatives' enduring innocence."

"This despite your sister's marriage and subsequent son?"

"As I say, it's a fantasy, not subject to the strictures of reality. To imagine the end of one's sister's innocence is unsettling."

Jane found it amusing, but didn't say so. He appeared to be in earnest. "Then I suppose, even were I to present you with an entire brood, my brothers would continue to believe me virginal."

"I didn't pretend the notion held a whit of logic, Jane. It's not so much the concept of a sister or daughter retaining her virginity as the avoidance of imagining her in the throes of passion with a man."

"How very curious. Why would one imagine such a thing?"

He didn't answer for a moment, his expression thoughtful. "It's surely not done with forethought. I daresay all men have a tendency to vivid imaginations where women are concerned. It's only when the image is their female relative, a woman obviously to be cherished and loved in the purest sense, that the imagination shies away."

She gazed ahead, her curiosity awakened. "Do you have a vivid imagination, Blixford?"

"I would answer truthfully, except I know the logical question to follow, and I've no desire to answer it."

"Why-ever not? Are you embarrassed?"

"No." He moved Pendragon close, once again. "I suspect, were you to learn the truth, you'd find great sport in attempting to read my mind. Not to mention, I'd prefer you retain an impression of me as a serious man of responsibility, respectability, and consequence."

Turning to meet his gaze full on, she saw that he was not in jest, but very solemn. "No one is all of one thing or the other, though we are each of us prone to certain characteristics which dominate. I assure you, I'll never find you anything but what you are, which is a man of honor and integrity who sometimes ferociously guards himself from those who would come too close." She watched his face, noting his expression didn't change. "So you see, answering my question is not likely to result in my attempting to read your thoughts, or to reconsider my impression of you."

His voice lowered to a deep timbre, almost husky and gruff. "Very well then, wife, I will tell you, I do indeed have a tremendous imagination, my mental pictures generated in great detail."

"As you predicted, I really must ask the nature of your imaginings."

His gaze remained on hers. "You may be disappointed to know they aren't what you would consider romantic. I imagine neither conversation nor convention. It is, after all, the nature of our imaginations to run free and unhindered from censure. All things which are improbable in reality are entirely possible in one's imagination."

"Am I to assume your imaginings are of a sexual nature?"

"Not entirely, of course, but I'd guess 'tis true with far greater frequency than yours might be."

She looked ahead. "How very arrogant of you to assume you know what my imagination might hold."

"Perhaps. Tell me, Jane, what did you imagine at Lucy's house party?"

Turning, she gave him a steady look, then focused on his mouth. "I imagined what it would feel like were you to kiss me." Her gaze moved to his hand, loosely grasping Pendragon's reins. "I was intrigued with your hands, because they are so large and well formed, and I imagined how they might hold me about the waist while you kissed me." She looked to his eyes again, noticing they were darker, and he appeared intensely alert. "I confess, after the incident in the library, my imagination was much enhanced by experience, and I embellished the memory with alternate conclusions as the years passed." She turned to face forward once again. "After MacDougal, despite his brutality and hostility, I suppose I had a better understanding of things and I weaved all manner of imaginings around how it might have been with you."

"Better, I hope?"

"Infinitely." She blushed and wondered if there would ever come a time she wouldn't do that when she thought of the intimacy they shared.

"You're remembering this afternoon, are you not?" His voice was low and husky again.

"Well . . . yes. It bothers me that I blush, because it seems missish and coy, neither of which are in my character."

He reached across the space between them and stroked her cheek with the backs of his fingers. "Uncharacteristic, maybe, but you've no idea how charming you are, looking away and blushing." He dropped his hand and moved Pendragon, widening the distance. "As for your imagination, I stand corrected, ma'am. In future, I suspect it may be me who attempts to read your mind, instead of the other way round."

"You're welcome to try," she said with a wide smile. Glancing at him, she noticed his seat was much relaxed, so much so that he was almost leaning back. "What of you, Blixford? I doubt you remember much at all of me from our first two meetings, but it would interest me to know what, if anything, you imagined when we met again at Lucy's house party."

"I assure you, Jane, I imagined quite a lot, none of which is seemly, and all of it ungentlemanly."

Her entire body was awash in a warm languor. "Do tell, Blixford. My curiosity is keen."

He was quiet for a long while before he moved close again and looked at her skirts, settled across Grendel's girth. While she watched, his gaze slowly moved upward, lingering at her breasts. "I imagined how you might look without your traveling gown. It was purple, and exposed a fair amount of your bosom." His gaze moved to her hair. "You wore a pretty bonnet and when you removed it in the front hall, part of your hair escaped its pins, so I knew it was long. I imagined what it would look like, all of it down, across your naked back. I wondered how soft it would feel against my own skin."

Her languor slowly began a metamorphosis. He recalled the color of her gown?

Now he looked at her mouth. "Your lips were plump and pink and I knew kissing you once would never be enough." His eyes met hers. "You have beautiful eyes, Jane, an unusual shade of blue. I'm certain anyone would agree, and had you simply looked at me with cool composure, I'd not remember with such clarity the effect they had on me." He leaned toward her, staring into her eyes. "No woman ever looked at me as you did, before or since."

The warmth of the day increased and she became flushed with heat. "I thought myself wildly in love with you. Is it any wonder I looked as though I'd like you for breakfast?"

"Ah, but I didn't know, couldn't fathom why a young miss would boldly stare back at me with as much hunger as I felt."

"Hunger, Blixford? You mock me."

"No, Jane." His hand reached out and caressed her jaw, stroking downward to her throat. "I stood in my sister's front hall and allowed my imagination to race off with you to my bedchamber, where I stripped you of your clothes, laid you across the bed and had my wicked way with you." His lips curved into a sinful smile. "The finer points I'm unwilling to share, primarily because you wouldn't understand, can't conceive such things are possible."

Jane licked her suddenly dry lips. "Do you suppose you might demonstrate the finer points in the near future?"

"It will be my pleasure," he said, leaning closer. His hand moved to the nape of her neck and he tugged her toward him that he could capture her mouth with his – moist, hot, and promising. Desire stabbed through her center, all the way down her inner thighs.

He released her and drew back. "You'll think me insatiable."

She eyed him carefully, noting the bulge at his crotch that pressed against the saddle. Now she understood why he appeared to lean back a bit. Realizing her own state of arousal was equal, though not nearly so obvious, she sat up in her saddle as she looked ahead. "How far did you say we are from the house?"

"Less than a mile, I believe."

"Hmm. Pity the horses are tired, or we might run the remainder of the way."

Although she didn't turn her head, she knew he jerked a startled glance toward her.

She calmly added, "It's been a tiring day and I believe I'd prefer to have supper in my room and retire early, if you've no objection."

His voice was deep when he drawled, "You may have whatever you wish, Jane. We are, after all, in the country, and it's expected we keep country hours."

This he said, despite the fact that sunset was still at least an hour away. Even country hours didn't dictate bedtime before sunset.

Beckinsale House was a lovely old manor, in the style popular a hundred years ago, its rose bricks mellowed with age and its corners lovingly embraced by creeping ivy, neatly trimmed lest it encroach completely. The relative warmth of southern England and its milder winters meant the windows were large, oversized even, and this lent an air of brightness to the interior, highlighting the warm honey paneling and shining oak floors. A small hall in the entry was flanked by a study to one side and a parlor at the other, the dining room farther back, its wide windows facing south, overlooking a free-form garden, just beginning to burst into spring bloom. Farther along, past the garden, was a wilderness, carefully cultivated, Blixford said, to remain a wilderness. "We'll walk there tomorrow," he said, "and I'll show you a secret place no one knows about but me."

"Really, Blixford, I'm not such a green girl to fall for anything so melodramatic."

He was mysterious when he said, "Ah, a skeptic. You shall see."

The housekeeper was a rotund, cheerful woman by the name of Hester, and her counterpart —her husband, in fact —was an equally rotund man named Clive. He was a proper butler, but it was difficult to take him too seriously because he chuckled often, setting his belly to quivering in a comical way.

Hester listened to their plan of retiring early and had such a look of knowing in her merry, blue eyes that Jane blushed furiously. Naturally, Blixford noticed, and as they followed the chattering housekeeper up the stairs, he whispered, "I may become adept at mind reading, Duchess."

"Behave!"

She quickly became aware that they didn't have adjoining rooms, that there were none among the six bedchambers. They would share the largest room, as well as the dressing room. The traveling coach had arrived over two hours prior to their arrival and his valet and her maid had already unpacked their trunks. Jane found it oddly, warmly intimate, their brushes and bottles and such resting side by side upon the dressing table.

She believed, from the look of surprise on Blixford's face, he'd expected her to be situated in another room, but he said nothing. She wondered if he would have her things moved? Surely staying with her in the same room would bring a sense of warmth and intimacy to their marriage, even if only for a fortnight, that would severely threaten his determination to keep her at a distance. Thinking of Lucy's counsel, Jane decided if he asked her maid to remove her to another room, she would protest.

Hester said in her happy voice, "A Mr. Hopping built this house from money he earned as a purveyor of small boats. It's said he was a fine craftsman and his boats were beautiful and sturdy. You'll notice a nautical theme in some of the furnishings, the ones that remained with the house through the years, and the balustrade is a series of carvings representing sailor's knots. Out beyond the wilderness is a small lake, which Mr. Hopping liked to use to test his boats. Those that failed are still resting at the bottom of the lake." She smiled and nodded, her hands folded across her ample midsection. "There are two there that didn't fail, that have been kept well over the years. Perhaps His Grace will take you about in one tomorrow."

"That would be lovely," Jane agreed, already thinking she'd love to learn to row. She glanced at Blixford and her heart skipped a beat. He stared at her. He looked . . . *hungry*. Doubtful he'd heard a word of Hester's house history, but then, he would already know all of it. She quickly returned her gaze to the housekeeper and smiled politely.

"Well, then," Hester said with a wide grin as she walked toward the door, "you've only to ring when you're ready for supper. In the meantime, I'll just have Polly and young John bring up your bath and light the fire. It's been a nice, warm day, but sunset will bring a chill." She chuckled and looked at each of them. "You'll have to argue amongst yourselves as to who may go first. When you're done, ring and fresh hot water will arrive." She left in the midst of Jane's thank you and closed the door behind her.

As soon as the latch clicked, Blixford swept her into his arms and bent her backward, kissing her with as much desire as though they'd been parted for weeks, as though they hadn't made love to one another a scarce few hours ago. Insatiable, indeed.

Jane decided she was equally so, her arms about his neck, her fingers tangling in his silky hair. All their talk of imagination had set her to yearning for him again and she made no protest when he reached for the skirt of her habit and jerked it up to thrust his hand between her legs.

"Jane, you astonish me." His fingers moved greedily within her as he raised her upright and urged her backward, until her thighs bumped the bed.

Dropping her arms, still kissing him, she felt her way across the fastenings of his fall, quickly releasing it, then deftly unbuttoning his riding breeches. As he had done with her, she daringly reached for his privacy within his drawers, shoving them out of the way that she could grasp his shaft, impressed all over again, and fearing him not at all.

"'Tis a bold one, you are, wife."

Before she could say a word, his hands wrapped about her waist and he lifted her up to set her upon the mattress, then none too gently pushed her backward before he reached for her booted ankles and lifted her legs to either side of his waist. He quickly hitched her skirts up and moved close to the bed, his gaze upon hers when he thrust inside of her, filling her quickly before withdrawing and plunging again. The lack of pain still amazed her, made her look upon him with something close to worship. In place of pain was a feeling like nothing else in all the world, a warmth and intimacy she found infinitely appealing and addictive to her feminine soul. Her desire increased with every drive of his thick, heavy shaft and the look in his drowsy, smoldering eyes was intoxicating.

"I've no hope of lasting, Jane. You're closing around me too sweetly to resist." His smile was slow and sinful. "And I confess, doing this to you while fully clothed is very stimulating."

He was still in his coat. She was still in her boots.

He was correct. It made it all somehow enormously erotic and as she watched him begin to lose his control, she felt her body take on a mind of its own, her back arching from the bed, bringing her center ever closer to his, delicious waves of pleasure thrumming through her. As her climax slowed, he found his own and his head went back, his eyes closed and he groaned. She felt the pulsing of him within and smiled her pleasure.

What a wondrous thing to make love with him.

He was still buried within her body, both of them breathing rapidly and heavily, when a knock came at the door.

Jane's eyes widened in horror.

Blixford chuckled as he withdrew, stepped back and reached for her hand. In one smooth movement, she was upright, her skirts covering her, once again. He quickly did up his breeches then called out, "Come."

She hastened to the window, hoping to appear as though she were merely enjoying the view of the wilderness through the large panes of glass, instead of catching her breath and forcing her legs not to shake. Listening to the sounds of the servants laying out the bath, the rush of water, the clang of metal against metal, the duke's softly spoken instructions, she felt the trickle of him as it made its way down her inner thigh and stopped at her garter. Good heavens. How could something like that make her smile like a cat in the canary cage? She was surely low and common to find such pleasure in him, such delight with him *in her*.

At last, the servants were gone and they were alone again. He came up behind and circled her with his arms, tugging until she rested her back against his chest and belly. His mouth moved close to her ear. "You're embarrassed, Duchess?"

"No, merely thoughtful."

"I'd attempt to read your thoughts, but you don't play fair, keeping your face averted toward the window. Mayhap you'll simply tell me what you're thinking?"

She did, feeling as though she might say anything to him at the moment. "I recall you seemed put off by my response to you in the library, all those years ago. I hope you won't find cause to disapprove of my enjoyment in you now. It would make the entire process lose a bit of its luster."

His response was slow in coming. Finally, he murmured, "Has it luster, then, Jane?"

"I'm fascinated with you, and anticipate what is yet to come."

He turned her to face him and his look was sober. "I assure you, at no time in our lives will I ever disapprove of anything we do in privacy. It's my hope that you will always be comfortable, relaxed, not shy, and well satisfied. A man may find his pleasure with fair ease. It's not always so for women, and you have to tell me what it is you want or need." He pressed a soft kiss to her forehead. "It gives me the greatest pleasure to give you pleasure, and in no way do I disapprove of your enjoyment."

She felt another drop of liquid as it slid down her leg and she smiled, ducking her head to rest it against his shoulder.

"You're grinning. Why?"

Looking up to meet his eyes, she blushed furiously. "You'll think me low and common."

"Doubtful."

Raising up, she moved her mouth close to his ear and whispered the cause of her amusement. "Isn't it shocking to find such a thing so tantalizing?"

His answer was not in words, but action; his arms crushed her against him, his big hands splayed across her back. He held her so close she lost a bit of her breath.

"You're not shocked?"

He made an odd sound, deep in his throat, and it

was a while before he murmured, "No, not shocked. Not at all."

Jane began to wonder if he would hold her like this until the room was completely dark of daylight and illuminated only with the cheery fire in the grate. The sun was set, but the room was still lit with dusk.

How strange was his reaction. He made that odd sound again and she could only wonder at his thoughts. It would appear she'd moved him in some way, though she was at a loss why what she'd said could be considered touching in the slightest.

Men were very strange, she decided. Fascinating, sometimes wonderful, sometimes not, but decidedly strange.

At long last, he released her and turned away toward the bath, a copper tub, just the size for one. "Would you care to be first, Jane? I'll be gallant and soap your back." He glanced at her and waggled his eyebrows.

Laughing, she nodded. "Very well. I suppose, this being our wedding night, we'll dispense with my maid and your valet's services?"

"I think it best. You're mine for the evening and I will gladly play lady's maid to you." He shot a glance at his breeches. "I daresay you'll do adequately well as valet, considering how quickly you divested me of my fastenings."

She nodded and said gamely, "I've had some experience with men's breeches, growing up with a father and six brothers."

He stared at her, dumbfounded. "Why would you have anything to do with their breeches?"

"Laundry, sir. It's a massive undertaking, of which you wouldn't be aware, being a man and such things beneath you."

"You're the daughter of an earl! Why on earth would you have your hand in laundry?"

She shrugged and presented her back for him to

undo her buttons. "Mostly for demonstration purposes. We rotated housekeepers on a regular basis because my brothers were so slovenly and difficult. I was always very particular about the laundry. Ruining garments is a horrid waste. So I demonstrated to each new housekeeper how I preferred it to be done. In all that, I learned to handle fastenings and buttons with great dexterity." She glanced over her shoulder.

He stepped close and his warm fingers soon had her naked of all. He summarily picked her up and set her into the tub, then stood back and gazed at her. "Is the water to your liking, my little laundress?"

"It's perfect, thank you." She gazed up at him, flushing as much from his heated look as from the warm bathwater. "If I didn't know better, I'd think there's something about me having a hand in laundry that's appealing to your masculine nature."

"Damned if it isn't appealing, and I haven't any idea why. Can't say I've ever found the concept of a woman performing menial labor alluring." He shrugged and turned to divest himself of his coat and waistcoat. He returned and rolled up his shirtsleeves before kneeling beside the tub and reaching for the soap. While he lathered her back, he spoke softly. "I've been thinking about when we return to London. Would you be averse to hosting a small affair of some type, a soiree or musicale, perhaps, to test the waters?"

"I'd be delighted." She wished he'd continue soaping her back for another year or so. His big hands upon her were positively wonderful, such an ease to her tired muscles. "If we choose to hold a musicale, however, I'll politely decline to perform. It would dampen any hope of easing back into the fold. In fact, I've no doubt we'd be run out of town by an angry mob."

"You'll forgive me if I agree?"

"Of course. It's a stretch to call my ability at the pianoforte ability at all. We should call it an attempt and leave it at that." She leaned forward and moaned. "You've a talent with your fingers, sir. I daresay I'll be unable to repay the kindness in like manner."

"Ah, Jane, having your hands on me in any capacity is pleasurable. Is this good?"

His fingers rubbed firm circles against her shoulder blades and she nearly fainted with pleasure. "Oh, it's far better than good. Wherever did you learn to do this?" She realized what she'd asked the moment she said it, and hastened to say, "Never mind, Blixford. I'd rather not know."

"Actually, it was Lucy. I've long had muscle spasms in my back, and she eased the discomfort just like this. I believe she learned the technique from her husband, who spent some time in India and came home with a wealth of foreign notions."

"I shall have to ask her to teach me then, so I can ease your discomfort."

"You would do that?"

Turning her head, she met his eyes. "Why would I not? You're my husband and I'm committed to providing you a comfortable life, a happy home and hearth, a restful sojourn at the end of every day."

He startled her when he threw his head back and laughed.

"Really, Blixford, I fail to find any amusement in my vow to be kind to you."

Instantly, he sobered, though laughter still lurked in his eyes. "Forgive me, it's just that this picture of domesticity, of you chafing your lovely hands in laundry, fetching my slippers and brandy come time for bed, and massaging away my aches gives me pause. I'd not thought it of you, Jane."

She sniffed and turned her back to him again. "You know so little of me, really. Blinded, I suppose, by my pistols and horses and talk of sheep. Did I not say, only recently, we are all perhaps dominated by certain characteristics, but none of us are all of one thing and none of the other? I find the lure of domesticity rather enticing, if you'd know the truth. I look forward to children, and supervising servants and seeing to your welfare. Mayhap I'll ride neck-or-nothing at dawn, visit tenants of a morning to check on their crops and sheep, and shoot pistols in the afternoon, but I'll be a grand duchess and take my responsibilities and duties to heart. You're unkind to laugh at me, sir."

"Devil take it, Jane, I was merely funning you. Of course you'll be a marvelous duchess, and a good wife of whom I shall be proud."

"Except when I play the pianoforte?"

His hands slid about her and began to lather her breasts. "Even then, I will applaud the effort, for I know how much you dislike it."

The combination of slick soap bubbles and his giant hands massaging her breasts brought on yet another bout of yearning.

"I confess, this is about as close to true domesticity as I have ever been. It's a bit of a novelty to give a woman a bath."

"Hard work is its own reward."

"Yes, I begin to comprehend." He slowed his hands and gently tweaked her very erect nipples. "Jane?"

She looked toward the window. It was now completely dark outside. Night had fallen. "You surely know a woman's bosom is something of an erotic place, and mine has just been attended to with loving care. Did you expect I wouldn't react at all?"

Bending close, he kissed her cheek and made his way to her lips. "Hold the thought, and I'll show you something of interest after supper."

"I look forward to it."

Raising up, he cupped his hands to fill them with water, which he cascaded across her back and front before he stood and reached for a towel. "The water grows cold and I'll not have you taking a chill. Besides, I'm ready for my turn."

Dutifully, she rose from the bath and allowed him to wrap her in the towel before he lifted her free of the tub and set her on the rug to finish the task of drying her body. She wasn't a child, and perfectly capable, but she didn't stop his ministrations. In his shirtsleeves, splashed with water spots, the Duke of Blixford knelt at her feet and rubbed her legs dry with concentrated care. She thought domesticity suited him. How original. And endearing. "Thank you, Blixford."

He stood and tossed the towel aside. "Would Your Grace care to choose a night rail?"

"No, she would not. I'd prefer my maid to make the choice."

Striding to the dressing room, he disappeared around the doorway and she heard the sound of a wardrobe door opening, the rustle of fabric, and the door closing. He reappeared with a nightgown of pale yellow silk and a matching dressing gown that was nothing but lace. It was the one she'd acquired specifically for her wedding night, something made more for the benefit of masculine eyes than functionality, and she was pleased he'd chosen it. Not surprised, because it was far different from her ordinary sleeping attire, but pleased, nonetheless.

He didn't dress her in the gown just yet. Instead, he moved her to the dressing table, sat her upon the stool and methodically removed her pins. When her hair was loose, he took up her hairbrush and gently brushed out the curls, his concentration focused on his task. She watched his face in the glass and warmed at the sight. "You've something of a predilection for a woman's hair, haven't you?"

"Not any woman's, Jane. Yours. Your hair is so soft, and shining, and beautiful, especially against your bare back."

She couldn't be certain of course, but she deeply suspected his imagination at the moment involved her hair and his naked skin.

He glanced at her in the glass and smiled slowly. "You're wondering what I'm thinking."

"Yes, and I've a fair idea, I believe."

He laid the brush aside and ran his hands through her hair, nodding. "I believe you are correct. You won't plait it before bed?"

"No." She stood and turned to remove his shirt. "But we'll never get to bed if we don't move along. Let's get you in the bath so we can have our supper and turn in."

"Are you hungry, Jane?"

Her hands flew over his buttons. "Starving."

He was solemn when he said, "Life takes many strange turns."

"It's what makes it all worthwhile, to my mind. I never know what's just ahead, around the corner, and I'm always eager to find out. Granted, sometimes what lies in wait is unpleasant, but then there are those moments that make up for all of it, that are such genuinely lovely surprises, we continue on in hopes of finding another." She watched his eyes as he sat on the chair by the fire, his breeches undone but still riding his hips, and she knelt to remove his boots. "Do you consider our marriage to be a strange turn?"

He nodded.

She raised up and on her knees, between his thighs, bent forward to wrap her arms around his middle and rest her cheek against the soft hair of his chest. "You're a remarkable man, and I'm grateful for your patience, and your kindness."

He stroked her hair and they stayed like that for a very long while, until she heard the clock in the hall downstairs chime the hour. Then she went to the pull and rang for fresh water.

CHAPTER 10

Jane was a quick study and appeared to trust him absolutely. He'd not sprung anything overly shocking on her after they turned in, but she never batted an eye when he rolled her over, hoisted her hips from the bed and mounted her from behind. Actually, she batted both eyes quite a lot before she cried out and her soft, curvaceous body quivered beneath his hands.

Afterward, she said it was most enlightening, and she'd like to try it again tomorrow, to make certain she liked it, if he didn't mind.

He assured her he did not mind before he tucked her close to him and began to drift off to sleep. Tomorrow, he supposed he would have her maid remove her to the bedroom next door. Having her in the same room, sleeping all the night through with her, was unwise at best, dangerous at worst. Hester had taken it upon herself to put them both in the same room, despite his instructions to the contrary. Though to be fair, he didn't exactly recall that he'd been very specific in his letter to her.

It was no matter. Tonight, she would stay here, beside him, curled up like a purring cat at his side. Tomorrow night, she'd be in her own bed, receive him there, and he would return to his bed and sleep alone.

She kissed his shoulder and murmured a soft goodnight before relaxing completely, her sweet body molding against his.

Late in the night, he awoke to find her gone from his bed. Momentary panic eased when he spied her next to the window. He got out of bed and prowled toward her, naked. "Are you all right, Jane?"

"I'm quite all right, but I fear Grendel may be in for a shock."

He peered out into the night, but could see nothing. "I don't follow. What do you mean?"

"Listen carefully." She pushed open the sash and he heard a steady pounding, accompanied by sharp whinnies. "I believe she's gone into season and Pendragon is knocking at the edge of her stall."

Michael listened carefully and frowned. "I believe you're right." Where was the blasted stable master? Any of the grooms? He turned and went for his breeches. "I'll go and see what I can do, but if he's got to her, it's too late. He'll bite or kick anyone who comes near."

"I hope he hasn't injured himself."

He slid into his shirt and reached for his boots. "How old is Grendel?"

"Four years."

"Old enough, I suppose." He rose from the edge of the bed and went to the fire, tossing in a spade of coal and poking it about until it caught fire. There was a chill in the air, and she was barely covered by her gown. "If it's too late, I'll have to set them out to pasture and let it run its course for however many days she stays in season. I've other mounts in the stable, so we won't miss our ride in the morning." He moved next to her again. "I'm sorry, Jane. I'd not want my horse to harm yours."

"I doubt he will do so, Blixford. If anything, she's liable to kick Pendragon. She can be difficult. And she's not fond of him, you know."

He reached out and stroked her soft hair. "No, but then horses don't require affection to mate." Dropping his hand, he turned and left the room.

Outside, it was very close to cold, and he regretted not donning his coat, but the sound of the stallion's hooves beating against the wall drove him onward, despite the temperature. Good Lord, he was determined, wasn't he?

He found the stable master and the grooms standing at the far end of the block, wide eyed and frightened. Two of the suspended lanterns were lit, one halfway down and the other at the far end, where the men were congregated. "Hiyo, Benjamin, what goes on here?" he called, moving closer to Pendragon's stall.

"Your Grace, it be your stallion, busting the boards to get to Her Grace's mare. I tried to intervene, but he's in a devil of a rage and like as not to kill any one of us if we go near. I thought to move Grendel, hoping 'at would calm him a bit if she were not so close, but she'd have none o' that. Fair took a chunk out'n my arm, she did." He held it up and pointed to his torn sleeve. "All she got was my shirt, but I've a mind not to try again, lest she not miss next time."

Michael stopped and looked into the stall, impressed by the stallion's efforts. He'd repeatedly kicked so hard, he'd actually broken some of the boards. Moving on, he looked into Grendel's stall. She fretfully turned in circles, whinnying occasionally, as if egging him on. Every so often, she stopped, spread her legs and urinated, sending Pendragon into fits, his hooves pummeling the boards in a frenzy.

He was bound to hurt himself if he kept it up much longer. Michael waved the men back. "Close all the gates but the one into the paddock, then go inside the tack room and wait until I've let them out."

"Should ye do that, Your Grace? She's a might young 'un, she is. Reckon she may not be ready for breeding."

"She's four years." He gave the older man a wry smile. "Besides, what choice do we have, both of them unapproachable as they are? We could isolate them, perhaps, but we've only the one paddock."

Benjamin nodded. "Righto, then. Boys, get out of the way." They backed up and disappeared while Benjamin went to close the gates. When he was done, he followed the grooms.

Michael opened Grendel's stall door and she bolted out, hurried to the arched entry, then stopped, raised her head and whinnied.

Pendragon redoubled his efforts, unable to see her now, but still awash in her scent. Powerful indeed, Michael thought. He felt sorry for the beast, so determined to get to her, so frustrated. "There's a good man," he murmured. "Your wait is over."

Reaching for the latch, he stood to the side away from where the stallion was most likely to run, slammed it loose and allowed the stall door to swing back on its hinges. Pendragon was out like a shot, rushing toward Grendel, who urinated once more, then kicked out at the stallion when he moved close to catch her scent.

He watched them move outside, into the paddock behind the stable, clearly visible by the light of the full moon. Pendragon began to court her, raising his head, curling his lips, attempting to rub his nose along her flanks. Grendel wouldn't go easy, however. Unimpressed, she continued to elude him, kicking when he got too close to her rump.

Benjamin and the grooms came to see, and the old stable master clucked his tongue. "Ain't it jus' like a woman? Get all gussied up, get ye with a hankerin', then shut ye down, right fast-like. Poor Pendragon. He's a long road ahead of him tonight."

As one, they all nodded, male hearts sympathetic to the stallion's plight.

"Reckon he'll coax her along soon enough," one of the grooms said. "For all he's determined, he's a gentle soul, ain't that right, Your Grace?"

"Yes, he is. I expect Grendel could do a lot worse."

That appeared to be funny to them. They all laughed. Michael turned to face the first of the grooms. "What's your name?"

The lad tugged his forelock and said, "Wyler, Your Grace. Tom Wyler."

He looked to the next in line, a tall, lanky boy with hair the color of straw. He bobbed his head and smiled. "Faskin, Your Grace. Bob Faskin."

The third boy was stocky and not so tall, with freckles across his nose and a head of bright red hair. "I'd be Thomson, Your Grace. Harry Thomson."

"Well, then, lads, I trust you will keep an eye on the horses as things progress?"

They heartily agreed, all at once, and Michael nodded his approval before he looked to Benjamin. "In future, if circumstances are alarming, you are to alert me, regardless of the time of day or night."

"That I will, Yer Grace, that I will. You don't worry none about the horses, nor the busted stall. We'll watch 'em close, and first light, we'll send 'em out to the north pasture. Harry's good with carpentry and he'll work on gettin' them boards replaced."

He clasped the older man's shoulder by way of thanks. "Good night, then." Turning, he walked back to the other end of the stable block and made his way outside. He struck out for the house, but paused as he took a turn through the garden and glanced up toward their bedchamber window. Jane waved and smiled and had no idea she was backlit by the fire, revealing her shapely curves beneath the thin silk of her gown. He stood and stared for some time, until she opened the sash again and called down, "Blixford, you must come inside before you catch your death of cold."

He moved away then and into the house. Back upstairs, he told her how it was and she nodded, accepting. "Thank you for looking after things. I vow I'm not certain which of them I pity more, Grendel, who is a novice, or Pendragon, who must insist, even if she dislikes him. She will not be docile." She moved toward him. "You must be chilled, going about in only your shirtsleeves."

Michael was about to assure her he was not that cold, but she appeared intent upon getting his clothes off to warm him, and so he said nothing.

Within minutes, he was, indeed, very warm and cozy, Jane nestled next to him in the bed with her arm curled about his middle and her head tucked into his neck. He watched shadows dance across the ceiling, cast by the flickering light of the fire.

After a time, she whispered sleepily, "Good night, Michael."

"Good night, Jane." He held her more tightly, closed his eyes and decided he liked the sound of his name on her lips, in her low, sultry voice.

He was almost asleep when she murmured, "Thank you for marrying me. You really are a most remarkable man."

He didn't think he was remarkable, but then, much like her mare, she could have done a lot worse. He'd look after her, all the days of her life, and pray God she would weather childbirth without undue incident.

Sighing heavily, he tried to blank his mind and return to sleep, but his memories continued flashing mental pictures. There she was, stepping close to him while Miriam clung to his neck, sobbing about her child, and his 'cruel' marriage to another. No doubt most women would swoon in horror, or vent rage at his head. Not Jane. She calmly took Miriam in hand and solved the dilemma without theatrics of any kind, even going so far as to express sympathy for her husband's previous mistress.

He recalled her halting, sad tale of her abuse at the hands of her cousin. It had pained her greatly to tell him, but she had, and later, she opened herself up to him with complete trust that he wouldn't hurt her.

Perhaps most unsettling was her revelation at the

window after he inquired the reason for her grin and deep blush. Never in his life would he expect a woman to say such a thing. In his experience, women considered the aftermath of lovemaking distasteful, always hurrying to clean away his seed, as if it were dirty. Not Jane. She told him she found it *tantalizing*.

In the dim light of the banked fire, he smiled while he listened to her deep, even breaths. What a curious woman he'd taken to wife. He'd not had such an enjoyable day as this one in years. Perhaps never. He found himself anticipating the next day, wondering what further surprises she might have in store for him.

Genuinely lovely surprises.

Until she had an opportunity to make calls and let it be known she was in town and staying at Blixford's Cavendish Square house, Lucy was alone for the evening, with naught to occupy her. She'd sat with William during his supper, then read a bit to him before tucking him into bed. He liked the house, and the nursery, but he was understandably excited and a bit on edge, thanks to the different surroundings. He wanted to continue whittling a stick with his new pocketknife, as Sherbourne had demonstrated for him, but she told him there'd be time enough for that tomorrow. Just as Sherbourne had predicted, William cut his hand within minutes of receiving the knife. He's tried not to cry and failed, and she bandaged it, kissed it, then scolded him, and he subsequently handled the instrument with newfound care and respect.

It appeared to bother him that Blix was not in residence. When Lucy told him his uncle had married and gone to Beckinsale House for a wedding trip, he'd asked if they could go as well. He remembered Blix taking him out in a boat, rowing him across the lake, and he thought it would be a capital notion to visit and go about in the boat again. When she told him they couldn't, he wanted to know why. She finally said newly married people didn't know one another very well, and their wedding trip was a chance to become friends, which was accomplished much better without the intrusion of others. Then she talked about all that they would do while in London and he promptly forgot about Beckinsale House and Blix's jolly boat, eventually settling down to sleep.

Downstairs, she piddled about in the library a bit, until Peatrie announced dinner was served. At home, she typically took all of her meals in the morning room, and allowed William to breakfast with her, that she could teach him table manners. She hated eating by herself in the dining room, because it seemed to shout a reminder that she was very alone.

She wasn't comfortable requesting dinner anywhere but the dining room at Blix's house, so she went in and took a seat at the head of the long table. She almost forgot herself and asked after Peatrie's wife, until she remembered herself and remained silent. One didn't speak to servants while at table. Seemed utterly ridiculous, but there it was. She'd undoubtedly upset Peatrie if she broke stricture anyway, so it was just as well.

Eventually, she was done, and rose to retire to the drawing room for tea and a book she'd selected to peruse until she could retire for the evening. Peatrie had only just left after presenting the tea cart before he returned to the doorway and said stiffly, "A Mrs. Sherry here to call on you, Lady Bonderant. Shall I tell her you're out?"

Lucy didn't know a Mrs. Sherry, or, at least, she didn't think so. Perhaps she had met her previously and forgotten? She was terribly bad about that, wasn't she? Her mind was sometimes not on the matter at hand, especially when meeting new people. In any case, she had to wonder how the woman would know she was here. She peered at the butler, trying to discern his manner. He appeared to be cautious, but not offended. Mrs. Sherry must be only a small amount questionable. Ah, well, it wasn't as though she had anything else to do. Who knew when Sherbourne would arrive? If, indeed, he would at all. "Yes, Peatrie, do ask her to join me."

Moments later, Peatrie opened the door again and said formally, "Mrs. Sherry, my lady."

"Yes, of course. Thank you, Peatrie." Lucy stood and almost bit her tongue right off to keep from howling with laughter. Sherbourne walked in, his step mincing, his large body elegantly gowned in the first stare of matronly fashion, all purple satin and vanity flounces, his upper arms covered by elbow length sleeves and his lower arms encased in pearl-buttoned gloves, effectively hiding his muscled, hairy arms. His bosom was impressive, though modestly covered by the neckline of the gown, disallowing a peek at his cotton cleavage, or his hairy chest. A purple turban with matching, waving ostrich feathers covered his head, hiding his hair. An enormous amethyst brooch winked from the folds. He'd rouged his cheeks and painted his lips into a bow. In one hand, he clutched a lorgnette, which he held to his eyes as he looked toward her. Clever man, for it was enough of a distraction, one failed to notice his face was not particularly feminine. Actually, not in the least feminine. But he was a distractingly handsome man, and made a handsome woman. Even with the turban.

The best was yet to come. He would know, of course, that Peatrie wouldn't leave right away, but see that her guest was seated first, in the event anything was needed. Sherbourne minced toward her, padded hips swaying a tad too much, and swept into a deep curtsy. The distinct sound of creaking bones reverberated through the drawing room and Lucy noted Peatrie's widened eyes, no doubt worried he'd be called upon to haul the large lady from the floor if her decrepit knees gave out on her. Luckily for Peatrie, Mrs. Sherry returned to her full height, her very impressive height, without undue mishap.

"Lady Bonderant, you simply *must* forgive my impertinence to call upon you without prior notice, but I saw you in the park this afternoon and, as I told dear Mr. Sherry, there is Lady Bonderant and her sweet son, and he, of course, said, why yes, m'dear, so it is, and I said, well, I shall have to call on her as *soon* as possible and welcome her to town. Mr. Sherry said it was a splendid idea, but reminded me we are to leave in the morn for Northumberland, to visit his dying granny, poor dear, hasn't been well in an age, and I wonder if she's actually close to death, or merely anxious for a visit, but it's not for me to question, as it is, after all, Mr. Sherry's own, dear granny, but as you see, it will be *impossible* to call on you on the morrow as I'll be gone from town, so I am come tonight, instead, for I simply *could not* leave without saying hallo!"

Lucy blinked. If she didn't know better, she wouldn't believe this was Sherbourne, he of such strong, bold masculinity. His voice was pitch perfect, his manner of speaking spot on for a kowtowing matron. She avoided looking at his eyes, for she would surely break down and die laughing. Instead, she focused on the amethyst. It had to be paste, as it was so large as to be vulgar. "I'm honored, Mrs. Sherry. How lovely of you to call. Please, won't you sit down and enjoy a bit of tea?"

"Delighted!" He sailed toward the sofa and lowered himself in another fit of creaks and groans.

Lucy perched on the chair opposite and nodded at Peatrie. "That will be all, I believe. I'll ring if we require more tea."

"Yes, my lady." He bowed himself out and they were alone.

Lucy covered her mouth and let herself laugh until tears popped into her eyes. "Sherbourne," she whispered, "you are . . . " She couldn't speak, she was laughing too hard. "That turban! And my God, your bosom . . . it's . . . it's *huge*."

His blue eyes twinkled merrily. "Now, now, Lady Bonderant, shield your claws. I understand yours is quite impressive, but mine is colossal, which would, of course, send you into fits of envy." He drew an arm beneath his bosom and pushed it up a notch. "I daresay my stays are inadequate, however. Gravity, you know, is the very devil on a woman's bosom." His gaze moved to her bosom. "How do you manage to keep yours so uplifted and perky? I vow, I imagine your nipples must be positioned perfectly, for I can see their outline, and oh, my, you're a lucky, lucky woman, aren't you?"

She moved to the sofa and sat beside him. "Peatrie isn't one to eavesdrop, but if he were, he would doubtless find your observations unusual."

"Perhaps not. Connie had several Mrs. Sherrys who dropped by to kiss her feet, who complimented her on everything from her hair, to the way she held her teacup, to her fine figure, despite so many babies. I recall one woman actually told her she had a lovely, fine bosom, and asked her secret to keeping them perky." His gaze moved to hers, once again. "Hmm, it would appear I've a taste for perky breasts, would it not?" He reached up and removed one feather from his turban, then set about tickling her décolletage with it. "Let us hope Peatrie isn't peeking through the keyhole."

Lucy giggled and leaned back against the cushions, slapping at the feather. "Sherbourne, you are truly wonderful. I've not laughed so hard . . . ever, I believe." Her eyes widened. "But how shall we get to my bedchamber without detection?"

"We will be detected, but we won't care. In a little

while, you'll exclaim you've a new gown and hat, as well as some dress patterns my daughter would like, and we'll move to your bedchamber for a nice, womanly coze." His deep blue eyes looked into hers, still twinkling. How *did* he do that? "Then I'll take off your dress to see for myself how perky your beautiful breasts truly are, then take you to bed and make love to you until you scream and I have to cover your mouth, for surely we couldn't explain away your passionate, orgasmic cries when looking at dress patterns, now could we?"

Lucy stared.

"I vow, Lady Bonderant, you appear flabbergasted."

"It seems extremely odd to become aroused by a matronly woman in purple satin, but *I vow*, I cannot wait to take off *your* dress."

He pursed his painted bow lips and kissed the air. "Will you steal my rouge?"

Staring at his mouth, she was not laughing any longer. "I'll lick it off very slowly."

He wasn't laughing either. "You've no idea how long the day became after I brought you and William home. I've got you in my blood, Lucy."

She was gravitating toward him ever so slowly, until she caught herself and murmured, *"Now*, Sherbourne. I can't playact another moment. We will go and see my new bonnet and have our coze *now*." A movement caught her eye and she jerked her gaze to his lap, followed quickly by her hand. He was hot and hard beneath the satin and it was all she could do not to jerk his skirts up and straddle him. "Oh, God, I want this inside of me, so much." She sprang from the sofa and said in a loud voice, "Mrs. Sherry, you must come and see my new walking gown and bonnet! I've also a box of dress patterns for you daughter . . . Imogene. Shall we adjourn to my bedchamber for a nice coze?"

He stood quickly, belying the sound of creaking

knees.

She looked toward his skirts with a question in her eyes.

"Whalebone," he whispered, then said loudly as he followed her to the door, "What a lovely idea, Lady Bonderant, and how kind you are to take me to your bosom as though we are old friends, too long parted. But we are old friends, in a manner of speaking, are we not? Of course we are! As I said to dear Mr. Sherry, it was a happy day, indeed, when I met you at Twykham's summer solstice garden party, what has it been, now? Two years past? Such a dear thing you were, in your great hat and pretty summer gown. I vow, I envy your girlish figger, for I'm a veritable giant of a woman, although, of course, Mr. Sherry doesn't mind, even if he's scarcely to my shoulder, poor dear, and frequently accuses me of sitting upon him, which is most unfortunate and not at all the thing, but he seems to hide on occasion, and suddenly, there he is! Just where I sit. I say, His Grace, your brother, has done a lovely redecorate in this house, has he not? I don't recall this wallpaper. Is it Chinese? Beautiful! By the by, I heard Blixford married this morning, which, of course explains why you are in town, but do tell, is he really married to Lady Jane Lennox? You must give me details, my dear! Ah, here we are, in your chamber. I vow, those portieres are stunning. I must discover Blixford's decorator, because my house has become terribly dated, what with . . ." She closed the door and he stopped talking. He removed the turban and tossed it aside, along with his reticule and lorgnette, then reached out his arms, palms up, silently asking her to remove his gloves.

Lucy stepped close and bent her head to the task, fumbling in her haste. "Good heavens, Sherbourne, why ever did you purchase these gloves with all these infernal buttons?"

"So that you would stand very close to undo them

and I could look down your dress."

She jerked her gaze to his and saw that he was indeed, focused on her cleavage. "I like a man with a plan." She went back to work and eventually, she had his gloves off. He turned his back to her and she concentrated on the buttons of the gown. When it fell away, she saw that the false bosom was actually sewn into the bodice, as were the padded hips. "How much did you have to pay a modiste for her silence?"

He stepped out of the dress and turned to face her, devoid of stays or chemise, just him in all his muscled, hairy, stiff-cocked glory. And stockings lined in whalebone, held up by garters above his knees. She bent to remove them, keenly aware of his very erect shaft just next to her hair.

"An astonishing lot, but I've had the costume almost a year. I had it made for a practical joke I played upon Wrotham, last Season. He's a stick, you know, and because he can't allow himself to enter into sexual congress with a lady, he became quite desperate and decided to frequent a brothel. He made careful enquiries as to which might be most discreet, where he might go for an evening's entertainment and not be seen by anyone. Sticks can be like that, very hypocritical. Anyway, I, Mrs. Sherry, an avenging angel of morality and prudence, chose just that night, and just that brothel to crusade for the souls of the damned in the depraved fleshpots of London. Naturally, I happened to open the door of Wrotham's lady's chamber first and expressed my dismay at who was within, an earl, for heaven's sake, a pillar of London, surely, who had fallen so low, and how shameful it was."

He had her laughing again. "Did Wrotham faint?"

"On the contrary. He cast aside his woman and suggested he and I remove to an empty chamber, where we might discuss the matter in a more intimate fashion."

She stood and stared at him, slack-jawed, then at last said, "He propositioned you? An avenging angel?"

"It was the bosom, I'm certain. Some men would simply have to see the bosom without cover, for it is spectacular."

"But you're a matron!"

"True, but breasts are breasts, and very enormous ones are irresistible to some men. Wrotham was disappointed when I declined, and he didn't speak to me for a solid month after I removed the turban and revealed my identity. He eventually came round and forgave me and saw the humor, but I've watched my back ever after, waiting for payback. He will attack when I least expect it."

He was not fifty, but fifteen, surely. His love of practical jokes was legendary, and she could now see the intricate thought he put into them. She eyed him cautiously. "I've a grand sense of humor, Sherbourne, but please, don't play a practical joke upon me."

"Of course I wouldn't, Lucy. I doubt most people see the finer points of my pranks, that they're designed to gently, kindly, humorously point out some flaw in a person's character. Sometimes it works, sometimes not. Wrotham did leave off some of his stick tendencies after that, and took a proper mistress, as all gentlemen should do when they are not married."

"Some have mistresses even after they are married."

"Ah, but they are married to icebergs." He snatched her close and bent his head to hers. "You, my love, are anything but an iceberg. Whomever you marry will never, ever, in a thousand years, take a mistress, for you will keep him sated and replete and absolutely bound to your every breath."

"Suppose I marry you?"

"Then I shall have to search for an elixir that will allow me to keep up with you. I'm fifty, Lucy, and not able to make love to a woman multiple times in an evening."

"Just once, then?"He looked thoughtful. "Twice is possible, but three times is right out. Truthfully, once a man passes thirty, he loses the steam for three times, so I'm not far behind, am I?"

His doubt was endearing. "Sherbourne, you foolish man, I don't care how many times other men can work up the steam. I only want you, and if once is all I get, I'm content. If I get it twice, well, it's a fortunate day."

"You understand the multiple rule only applies to an evening? Over the course of a day, all bets are off."

"So you could make love to me of a morning, and in the afternoon, and again at night. Sounds divine, so what's the problem?"

"I suppose I'm beginning to be monotonous. Shall I stop reminding you of my age and limitations?"

"Not on my account, because I don't really pay attention. But perhaps you're too hard on yourself. I suggest you relax and enjoy our time together and keep it firmly fixed in your mind that I desire you an enormous lot, and cannot, have not, and most likely will not, find the slightest interest in another." Her hand closed around him and she sucked in a breath. "Ah, Mrs. Sherry, you are magnificent. Funny, warm, wonderful, kind, and absolutely a beautiful man. Given half a chance, I will fall wildly in love and make a cake of myself over you."

His arms tightened around her and he held her head to his shoulder. "I won't allow it, Lucy. We're going to find you a suitable husband, a man who can keep up, who will love you and give you more children, and who will live a very long time."

"Is this your way of saying you would never love me, or marry me?"

"It's my way of saying I want you to be happy, because I care for you, and am concerned for your future. It's far too soon to talk of love and marriage, anyway. We agreed to have our two weeks and reevaluate then, did we not?"

Her hand tightened around his cock. "So we did. Very well, I'll not mention it again, if you'll not mention your age again."

"It seems a fair bargain." His hands slid into her hair, knocking some of the pins loose. He brought his face close to hers and whispered, "You will lick it off, is that what you said?"

She was wet and hot and oh, so ready. "Slowly. I said I will lick it off . . . slowly." Releasing her hold on his cock, she reached up and cradled his face between her palms to keep him steady while she moved her tongue across his lips, first this way, then that. After a time, he groaned and opened his mouth to suck her tongue within. They kissed an eternity, and she knew, without a doubt, she'd never been kissed as Sherbourne kissed her. His entire body seemed to kiss her, his thighs spread to encompass hers, his heavy, muscular arms surrounding her, his body curled around hers, and his mouth solely focused upon hers. He made love to her mouth, sucking and licking and slowly, deliberately, languidly bringing her arousal to a fever pitch.

When she didn't think she could wait another moment to feel him inside of her, he lifted his head and whispered, "How shall I please you tonight, Lucy? Have you something in mind?"

Meeting his gaze, she smiled softly. "The chair, just over there." She nodded toward the fireplace, to the wingback she'd had removed from Blixford's room and delivered to hers, explaining to Peatrie that she frequently suffered insomnia and liked to read late in the night.

"Ah, it's a temptation you can't resist, and I know why." He spun her about and began undoing her buttons. "Shocking, Lucy, but you've no chemise, and no stays. Whatever were you thinking when you dressed for dinner?"

"Possibly the same thing you thought when you

failed to don drawers beneath your satin gown. Scandalous, naughty Mrs. Sherry."

"I admit to rather enjoying the sensation of satin against my nakedness. Hedonistic, I suppose." When her gown dropped to her waist, his hands captured her breasts and he stood just behind her, looking over her shoulder, watching his long fingers caress and massage until her dark nipples were hard and pointed. "Lovely Lucy, I've never been quite so intrigued with a woman's breasts. Yours are extraordinary. Exotic." He nibbled her ear, licked her lobe, sending shivers along her back, all the while continuing his particular attention to her bosom. "Did you know," he whispered in a low, husky voice, "a man can make love to a woman's breasts?"

Her entire pelvis exploded with desire so strong, she knew it would take but one touch to reach climax. She closed her eyes. It was too much, the gentle but firm pressure of his hands, his words, the sight of his strong fingers upon her. She couldn't watch another moment without going off. "I . . . suspected."

"Did you, Lucy? In your lonely bed, did you caress these perfect breasts and imagine the length of a man, nestled within your cleavage?"

"Will you be shocked if I admit I did?"

He chuckled low in his throat. "Nothing of you could shock me. I know who you are, understand the delightfully erotic thoughts that bump about in your beautiful head. I'm enchanted and fascinated with you." He turned her a bit, until she faced the fire —and the chair. "I've a fair idea of how you imagine it will be, but enlighten me anyway, in case I've got it wrong."

"You will sit, and I will be in your lap."

"Will you face me, or the fire?"

"I'd like to try both ways."

He made a sound that was close to a growl as he shoved her dress down until it pooled around her feet.

"Then you shall, but I suggest you face the fire to begin."

"Oh?" she asked as he bent to remove her slippers and garters. "Is there a reason?"

With his warm fingers against her legs, he replied, "Facing me, I'll be compelled to kiss you, and kiss your breasts, and you'll be compelled to look between us, where we are joined, and you'll climax long before you have the chance to turn round the other way." He stood and led her to the chair, where he sat and grinned up at her. "I've this lovely, open, needful lap, my lady. Won't you have a seat?"

Turning her back to him, she moved between his thighs and slowly sat upon him, savoring the feel of him as he slid inside. His long fingers grasped her about the waist and steadied her, held some of her weight, making it easier to move upon him, up and down. But she quickly tired of it, because she couldn't see him, couldn't touch him as she wanted to. Abruptly, she pulled away and stood.

"Was it something I said?" He was twinkling at her again, obviously funning her. He'd not said a word. Amazing. The man was simply amazing.

"I can't see your face that way, and it occurs to me that watching your face is terribly important." She bent one knee to the chair, then the other, straddling him, moving forward until she was there, just above him.

As she began to crouch lower, he met her gaze. "You wish to look, I know, so do so. Look now, my love. That's it, bow your head and watch."

Oh, but it was astonishing, erotic, arousing, incredible. He was so very large, and hard and hot and *hers*. She heard the sound of her body accepting his, felt every bit of him as she slowly slid down, saw him disappear into her curls. Jerking her head up, she moved closer and kissed him, hard, desperately, rocking her hips, thrusting her pelvis so that he moved in and out of her without any effort on his part. As she'd suspected, the position of him sitting and her in his lap brought his cock into perfectly aligned contact with her most sensitive spot, and her rocking hips built her desire hotter and higher.

Sherbourne watched her, his lids heavy, his eyes blazing with lust, one hand at her waist and the other fondling her breasts, which moved in tandem with her gyrating hips. "You've simply no idea how lovely you are, Lucy. The very earth."

She was beginning to gasp, knew she was close, wanted to slow down, to wait, to prolong their time together, and perhaps she might have, but Sherbourne deliberately sent her off.

He looked.

And spoke to her not as a gentleman, but as a man –a lusty, aroused man. It had always been a particularly favorite fantasy, that a lover would become so caught up, he would forget himself as a gentleman and she as a lady and speak as a man to a woman.

His gaze was upon hers, until it worked its way down, to her breasts, to her belly, and finally to where they were joined, to where she covered the essence of him, drawing away, pushing back, again and again and again. He murmured, "Come for me now, Luce. Let me see you take me in, all of me, down to my bollocks." His eyes didn't move from where they coupled. "Your cunny is so slick, hot, tight and beautiful, sliding along my cock, and it's all you can do to hold back. Don't wait any longer. Do it now, love, come for me and let me see."

His language, his eyes, his gruff voice, his focus on what they did, all served to send her off, and she was powerless to stop herself. With a suddenness that took her breath, her body was awash in wave after wave of heat and pleasure. Her back bowed inward, thrusting her breasts forward. His lips closed around one nipple and she did cry out, her climax prolonged, extended, exhausting.

She was still shaking, still coming, when he whispered, "Put your arms round my neck."

She complied and squeaked in surprise when he began to rise from the chair.

"Slide your legs about my hips."

He was still inside of her, still incomplete, still tremendously erect. "Where are we going?"

His grin was wolfish, she'd swear. "My turn, Lucy." He moved toward the bed, still a part of her, effortlessly carrying her while she clung to him like a burr. He laid her down, with her bottom almost off the edge of the mattress, and straightened, forcing her arms to let go of his neck. She started to move her legs, but he whispered, "No," and she kept them wrapped about his hips. He stood there, just stood there, for the longest while, his hands kneading her breasts, massaging firm circles, then softly rubbing her nipples before rolling their peaks between his fingers. And all the time, he was still within her body, unmoving, yet pulsing with the flow of his blood, thick and heated. "So beautiful, so sensual . . . needful. So . . . *mine.*"

He pulled back, then thrust so hard, she moved up on the bed. He did it again. And again. And all the while, his hands were on her breasts, his gaze upon his hands. He began to speak in a low, rough voice. "There are but two things a man cannot live without. The first is faith. Faith in his God, faith in himself, faith in love. Do you know what the second is, Lucy?"

Mutely, she shook her head, uncertain where he was going with this, but absolutely positive she was about to climax, yet again. Impossible! But there it was. His attention to her breasts, his violent thrusts, the look in his eyes, the sound of his voice, throbbing with need and passion, all contributed to the incredible exhilaration of climbing to a second orgasm.

He didn't increase the rhythm, didn't alter his

thrusts in any way, but continued to pound into her, hard and steady, until she was moved very far up on the bed. He grasped her waist and pulled her back, then hauled her up, almost to a sit, and held her there, his gaze intent upon hers while he worked magic within her body. "The other is this, in all its forms, and no man alive, young or old, can live long without it." A fine sheen of perspiration covered his face, his chest, his arms. "I'm waiting for you, Lucy, to have what I need, what I crave. Give over now and come for me again."

Staring into the blue of his eyes, those amazing eyes that could twinkle and laugh, or blaze with scorching lust, she wetted her lips and whispered, "Make me."

Something flared in his eyes that might have frightened her if it hadn't excited her so much. His hands tightened about her waist and she was in the air, snatched against his hard body. Instinctively, her arms went round his neck and her legs tightened about him. His hands moved to her hips and took control, alternately pushing and pulling her against him, then holding her steady while he thrust into her. He groaned, then growled, then kissed her deeply.

She ran her tongue across his lips before she moved her mouth to his jaw, to his throat. Her teeth nipped at his skin, slick and hot above his pulse. She opened her mouth and tasted him, licked him, her breath moving hot upon his flesh while his cock pumped faster, harder, pounding against her womb as he grew longer, his body tensed and poised for release.

"Now, Lucy. Come for me . . . *now!*"

She might have cried out, but she'd never know, because he captured her mouth with his at the same time his big body stiffened, every muscle tightening, and she felt him jerk and twitch deep inside, the contractions of her body greedily absorbing his essence.

Just after dawn, Jane met Benjamin, the stable master, and each of the grooms. She asked a few questions to ascertain their knowledge of horses and was well satisfied with each of the friendly, hardy lads. She was shocked at the damage Pendragon had done to the stall, expressing her dismay by exclaiming, "Blixford, I believe your stallion is half mad."

The grooms chuckled and moved away to begin their morning tasks.

Blixford tapped one shining black boot with the head of his crop and said evenly, "He's descended from Arabian stock, Jane."

Eyeing the splintered boards, she was in awe. "Are Arabians half mad?"

"Doubtful, but perhaps the line retains something of their wild nature." He waved toward the other stalls. "If you'll choose another mount, we may take our ride. There are only five available, being that Beckinsale House is the smallest of my estates. I never have visitors here, so the livestock are exercised by Benjamin and the grooms. The others here are the coach horses."

She went along the block and peered into each stall, settling on a brown bay gelding at the far end. A neatly painted wooden plaque upon the stall door told her his name was Morpheous. The horse didn't appear to live up to his name. Far from sleepy, he was feisty and full of spirit, poking his nose toward her and sniffing before he backed up and tossed his head.

He was saddled without delay, and before long, she was clattering out of the stable yard with Blixford at her side, himself seated on a roan mare.

They rode north, through a wooded area that eventually opened to a large pasture. "Did you spend your previous honeymoons at Beckinsale House?"

"No," he said simply and conclusively, his tone

clearly indicating he didn't like the question.

She couldn't help her curiosity, however, so she asked the next logical question. "If not here, then where?"

"All three of my previous brides were immediately settled into Eastchase Hall." His sigh spoke volumes, as though he knew she would continue to question him, regardless of his dislike of the subject. "I brought you here because I suspected you would like it, and I suppose in some respects I'm a superstitious sort. I thought to change the course in hopes the outcome would be different." He lifted his thumb and indicated the south, behind them. "This is also where I house my crossbreeding program. I believe you'll enjoy meeting Crofton, who oversees. He has a fascination with the possibilities presented by crossbreeding sheep that is equal to yours."

"Blixford, how marvelous! Thank you!"

He cast a look her way. "You are enjoying yourself?"

"Very much so." She looked ahead, toward the pasture. "Is this where Benjamin moved Grendel and Pendragon?"

"It is. Do you suppose they'll dislike our interruption?"

Jane laughed. "Doubtful. Unlike humans, horses don't mind an audience."

"I assume you'd have cause to know this?"

She jerked a startled look toward him. "Sherbourne has long maintained a breeding stable at Hornsby Grange. Surely you're aware? One of his won at Ascot only two years ago."

"Yes, I'm aware, but I'm surprised your father would allow you anywhere near the process of breeding horses. It's not typically an endeavor for unmarried young ladies."

She gave it some thought before she nodded. "I suppose not. My father is somewhat unorthodox, isn't he? He laments he didn't remarry after my mother's death, that my rearing in a houseful of males must surely have been to my detriment. Perhaps he's correct, but what's the point revisiting history? He didn't remarry and I grew up within a crowd of boisterous, decidedly masculine males, most of whom frequently forgot I was female. I daresay it wasn't until I matured into a feminine form and Sherbourne insisted I don a dress that they realized I was not, in fact, a boy."

"Do you mean to say you dressed in breeches as a child?"

"Will you be shocked if I confess that I did?"

"And rode astride, I'd warrant." He sighed at her nod. "I find myself less inclined to be shocked at anything you do, Jane." Suddenly, he widened his eyes and asked, "Is that how you traveled to Scotland without incident? Did you dress as a man?"

Laughing at the idea, she shook her head. "Heavens, no." Pointing at her full breasts, she stated the obvious. "No amount of men's clothing can hide my bosom, and I would not be so foolish to try."

"How then did you travel all that way without being accosted, as surely any lady traveling alone would be?"

"Are you certain you wish to know?"

"I will expire of curiosity if you don't tell me." They reached a gate and he opened it from horseback, held it so she could pass through, then closed it and resumed his position by her side.

She looked ahead, spying Grendel and Pendragon in the far reaches of the pasture. They were grazing together beneath a soaring oak. Evidently, the deed had been done, at least once, and they enjoyed a respite before he covered her again. She was glad and relieved to see Grendel appeared quite content. "It would perhaps be of benefit if I could demonstrate, but I left my costume in a trunk at Sherbourne's townhouse." Turning her head, she met his gaze. "With the assistance of my maid, I fashioned a false belly. I took three of her gowns and let them out in order to accommodate the false belly. When I stopped to rest each night, I quietly explained to the innkeeper that I was but a poor Scottish widow, en route to my home in the highlands to be delivered of my child in the bosom of my family. I explained the horse as a gift, given to my dead husband for his sterling service in the army."

Blixford was clearly fascinated. "Did you assume an accent?"

"Oh, but of course." She demonstrated and was pleased when he smiled. "It wasn't difficult and anyone who might have considered accosting me was surely put off by my pregnant state. I stopped at the border and waited for one of my brothers to catch up to me, as I knew they surely would. Once Julian arrived, I returned to being Lady Jane Lennox and he accompanied me to Castle MacDougal. I didn't dispose of my costume, however, and found cause to employ it again upon my return to London. It's how I was able to follow you for two days without discovery."

"Impossible. I'd have seen your face and recognized you."

"You don't look at servants, Blixford, unless, of course, they're your own. As a servant with child, walking along the street, I was invisible to you."

He was quiet for a while before he said, "Deuced clever of you, Jane."

"Thank you." She nodded toward the horses. "It would appear they've achieved a measure of harmony."

His gaze remained on her when he replied, "It would appear so because, I daresay, they have."

A bit flustered by his obvious double entendre, she cleared her throat and inhaled the fresh morning air. "I find myself anxious to run, Blixford."

"I'd ask that you wait until we reach the lane. This pasture is filled with rabbit holes and stones. It's never been cultivated."

"Very well."

They rode on in an awkward silence until they were halfway across. It was then that Pendragon resumed his amorous intentions and began circling Grendel. He lifted his head and curled his lips, as all stallions do when in the act of courtship. Jane always found it funny, and wondered if a mare was actually impressed, or if she found it funny as well.

Grendel, evidently, did not find him funny, but annoying, kicking out at him when he circled her rump. She snapped at his withers as he passed and he skittered away before he curled his lips again. She raised her tail as if in welcome, but moved away from him. Pendragon followed and she allowed him to catch her scent and rub his neck across her back before she slowed to a stop and spread her hind legs, bracing herself for his tremendous weight.

Jane knew she should look away, that watching them in Blixford's company would surely be terribly embarrassing, but she absolutely could not. She was indeed a naughty woman, but his stallion covering her mare took on erotic overtones that had nothing to do with the perfectly natural fundamentals of horse breeding. She had only to recall the night before, of Blixford mounting her from behind, and her center heated with strong desire. They were human, but still animals, with all the same instincts of Pendragon and his mare. It appealed to her elemental nature, and set her feminine soul to yearning.

Without conscious thought, they slowed their mounts to a stop, each of them staring across the pasture with rapt attention. At some point, Blixford murmured, "Really not the thing to watch, is it?"

"No."

"Why is it, then, that I'm unable to stop?"

"I've no idea, but it's quite impossible."

At last, Pendragon dropped to all fours and the excess of his seed spilled from the mare. He lifted his head and whinnied his triumph before he moved to her side. She turned to look and their noses met, ears flicking, coats twitching.

Blixford moved his mount closer to hers, his eyes intensely dark, smoldering even. "I'm one step away from abandoning ducal propriety and tossing my duchess in a pasture. Are you shocked?"

"No doubt I should be, but I'd be lying were I to say I was." Her gaze lingered at his lips. "Would you kiss me, husband?"

She'd barely spoken the words before she was hauled from her mount and seated before him, enveloped within his arms, her mouth assaulted by his. For a man of strict decorum, her duke was insanely passionate. His hands fell to her waist and he lifted her easily, commanding her to swing her leg over. She did so, and was straddled there, backward, her legs over his and her entire torso pressed against his as he kissed her again, their tongues twisted together, his prominent nose firmly against her cheek. He dropped one arm and it didn't become evident that he'd unfastened his breeches and shoved her skirts further up until she felt him there, close to her center. "Blix, how can we manage? We're atop a horse."

He kept his gaze upon hers while his hands lifted her once again and settled her down upon him, impaling her with his long, hard length. "Place your boots on top of mine," he whispered, his voice raw. "It will give you leverage. It appears you'll be required to do most of the work. I hope you don't mind?"

"Hard work . . . is its own reward." She followed his instruction, intrigued by the headiness of their distance from the ground, with the movement of the mare beneath them as she grazed, unconcerned by what took place upon her back. He kept his hands about her waist as she began to move, pushing up, then relaxing back onto him. Their positions lent a delicious feel to their joining, his solid, hot shaft sliding against her most exquisitely sensitive spot with every move of her body.

He kissed her again and she slowed a bit, drinking him in, enticed by the look in his eyes. She couldn't be certain, but she thought he was somehow different, less lighthearted than he'd been yesterday, much more intensely determined to take her. As if he were driven to it. Perhaps he was. She couldn't deny an answering need, as if everything depended on their coupling, immediately.

One of the horses whinnied and she glanced aside.

Pendragon was covering Grendel, yet again, this time turned in such a way to afford a clear view of his mighty, stiffened penis as he stroked the mare and sought release of his seed.

Jane refocused on Blixford, noting he had not looked again, but was watching her from beneath lids heavy with deliberate desire.

"You're increasingly very tight round me, Jane. I fear your voyeuristic arousal may be my undoing. Please . . . don't delay."

"Do you mean to say—"

"Jane, *please.*"

She rocked her body, moving her hips rhythmically, never taking her gaze from his. Slowly, surely, she built her desire until she exploded with deep pleasure, her head falling back and a sharp cry bursting from her throat. While her body reverberated with the after-effects of her release, she returned her gaze to his and was astonished by his expression. He looked at her as though he thought her simply wonderful. Suddenly, his shaft jumped within her, crowding her womb, and she immediately felt the warmth of him, saw his eyes close before he slumped forward to rest his chin upon her shoulder. "Good God, Jane, you must think me mad to take you atop a horse in an open pasture." He paused. "Only think of the danger if this mare bolted. Perhaps I am mad."

"Nonsense, Blixford. We are merely responding to

nature. It's your nature to pursue me, and it's my nature to find the sight of horses coupling somewhat exciting, although I have to confess I never thought so before today. You may have ruined me to breeding horses, because it will surely be disruptive and inconvenient if I become aroused every time I see a stallion cover a mare. I hope I don't respond in this way with sheep. Doubtful, I'd think, because really, sheep are less than elegant creatures. Horses, on the other hand, are truly lovely and graceful."

He raised up and slid his arms about her, holding her close to his breast. "Ah, Jane, ever sensible. I've not shocked you then?"

"Not at all, for surely you comprehend I enjoyed it as much as you?"

"I gathered that, yes." He sat up and nudged the mare close to the gelding before he lifted Jane and replaced her in the saddle. While she gathered the reins and adjusted her skirts, he fastened his breeches. "I'm starving. We'll have our run and return to the house for breakfast. Afterward, we'll visit Crofton and he'll give us an update on his progress."

She trotted along beside him to the farthest north end of the pasture where they passed through another gate and out onto a narrow lane. He pointed to the east. "That way lies the road to the village. Perhaps one day this week we'll go there for luncheon and visit some of the shops."

"I'd like that."

He pointed to the west. "This direction leads to the lane we traveled yesterday. It's a nice distance for a run, I believe." He glanced at her. "I'd prefer to forego a race this time, and merely enjoy a run, if that's acceptable to you."

She grinned at him and allowed the gelding to prance a bit. "Admit it, Blix, you're determined to remain the victor as long as possible."

His superior look and raised brow were all the

answer she needed.

"Very well, we'll wait for Grendel and Pendragon to end their courtship and come back to us before we race again."

"Have you considered she might not be so anxious to beat him next time out?"

"On the contrary, after he's bested her in yon pasture numerous times, I imagine she'll be ready to trounce him soundly."

Blixford moved closer. "Is this how you see it, Jane? Are we males merely besting females when we convince them to lay with us?"

"What a novel thought. It bears considering. Generally, females are not forthcoming of their own volition, but insist they be wooed. It's his instinct to impregnate her, and her instinct to seek superior seed, which would belong to the male best able to win her, whether through fighting other males, sheer persistence, or in the case of humans, the man she most admires. Once won, she then expects to be coaxed and wooed into submission. Because he is driven to it, he does whatever is necessary to have her. What do you think?"

His brows raised slightly. "I think I never before realized how much I hold in common with a horse." His eyes traveled the length of her before returning to her face. "'Tis true, it would seem, that I'm driven to have you, Jane. It's not my nature to be this amorous, but I find myself wanting you constantly."

"Whatever do you mean, it's not your nature? You've been misled, sir, for at your core you are a deeply sensual and passionate man. One need only watch you eat to ascertain the truth to it."

"I beg your pardon? How have we gone from sexual instincts to dining?"

"You carefully avoid certain foods, I suspect because the texture is not pleasing to your tongue. I noticed you bypassed Cook's yams and focused upon the steak and trifle. Every bite you take is enjoyed and relished, much as every sip of wine is fully appreciated." She settled the gelding and came up beside him. "While I lay between sleep and awake, I'm aware of you there, stroking my skin, unconsciously, because you enjoy the feel of it against the tips of your fingers. As to carnal instinct, perhaps you've never encountered your equal and this is why you assume yourself only prone to amorous urges when climbing into bed with a willing female. I am not merely willing, but enthusiastic. As I said, I find you fascinating."

"Am I not required to woo and coax you then?"

She laughed. "Of course you are, and do so, quite well, obviously. Only consider my anxiety, less than four and twenty hours ago, and now I have just made love to you atop a horse." She eyed him appreciatively. He really was quite handsome, Roman nose and all. "You are remarkable, Blixford, though you seem unaware."

His smile was wry. "I suspect you've a skewed opinion of me, Jane. For whatever reason, you see only my finer qualities, while blind to my lesser ones."

"Oh, pish! What lesser qualities? Granted, you're judgmental, crotchety at times, haughty, arrogant, and determined to keep others at a distance, but so what? Who among us isn't attached to less than sterling characteristics? To my mind, it's the man whose excellent qualities far outweigh the others that is worthy of my admiration. You are patient, kind hearted, exceedingly handsome, masculine and fearless, and tremendously loyal. You're also very adept at kissing."

"Crotchety? Am I?"

"Definitely. Although to be fair, I believe it's a condition pervasive amongst males. When they are tired or hungry, they become crotchety. Feed them, give them a rest, and they're back to their jolly selves again."

That earned a laugh. "I begin to see the benefits of marrying a woman with six brothers. You're astute in the ways of males."

"Very much so." She pointed toward the lane. "Shall we proceed, Blixford? I'm fair starving as well, and before long, I may be the one who becomes crotchety."

"Lead on, Duchess. Evidently, I'm compelled to follow, much like poor, besotted Pendragon. Male power is all an illusion, for it must surely be females who hold the trump card."

"Do you see? This is what I adore about you, Blixford. You realize your weaknesses and play them to your favor. What an intelligent man you are!" With that, she urged the gelding into a canter, and after a short while, nudged him into a run.

CHAPTER 11

She adored him.

Well.

That was intriguing, was it not? Unlikely and unexpected, but intriguing all the same.

Oh, he was not prone to humility, and was, undoubtedly, grievously arrogant. He was a duke, lower in rank only to a royal, the last of an ancient line of illustrious ancestral dukes. He was well read, well educated, and capable of reviving a bankrupt, failing ducal title into four thriving estates and a London townhouse equipped with all modern conveniences. His manners and tastes were impeccable, he was well respected in the political arena, and he was an excellent horseman and hunter.

Nevertheless, he was well aware of his shortcomings, some of them insurmountable and wholly unpleasant. Unlovable. He couldn't forget his first three wives. They didn't adore him. They feared him in the beginning, were intimidated by him in the end. Even Annabel, whom he'd held in great regard and mild affection, had never looked at him in even the smallest manner of adoration. She came to respect him and they enjoyed a friendly marriage, but she'd no doubt thought him cold, arrogant, and tiresomely proper.

Sometimes he really was a stick.

Except when in a pasture with his last duchess,

observing the mating rituals of horses. Great God, he'd dragged her off her mount to make love to her right there in his saddle. Any number of men might have happened by, but he'd not thought of anything but her, of her soft, hot center, convinced he'd lose his mind if he didn't take her, right then. Immediately.

Any of his first three brides would have expired in a faint. Upon revival, they'd have called him a horrid animal. A beast of no fine sensibilities. They'd be correct.

Jane thought he was remarkable. Fascinating. Deeply passionate and sensual.

Michael admitted his response to her was much like a trained hound who responds to pocket treats and his master's praise. He'd never been lauded and hailed remarkable by anyone, least of all a woman. The cynic in him wanted to pass it off as her attempt to smooth the way for a trouble-free marriage, to stroke and pet him until he became malleable to whatever she wanted.

He couldn't believe that. If Jane wanted something, she would never resort to manipulation to get it. She would stand up, demand it, and if given no adequate reason why she might not have it, she would go and get it anyway. Whether it was refusal to marry an arrogant, cruel duke, or provide for a cast off mistress and her bastard child, Jane would have her way.

Possibly her best characteristic was her blunt, unapologetic honesty. In one moment, she might rip him up for implying she would bear him children because of duty, and extol his intelligence the next, but she was never anything but sincere. He rather thought he'd know instantly if she lied, or attempted to bamboozle him. Her gaze would not be so direct and bold.

He enjoyed their run, as he enjoyed breakfast and her ability to eat heartily without false feminine apology, but what truly made the morning excellent was her response to his crossbreds. She and Crofton hit it off immediately, falling into an easy conversation about the ins and outs of sheep breeding that would fly over most heads. He himself occasionally had a difficult time following them. Jane waved her hands about, scowled severely at times, appeared deep in concentration at others. Overriding everything, however, was her sheer delight in his program. She would glance at Michael every so often and grin cheekily, conveying her happiness. At one point, she said enthusiastically, "Isn't this amazing? You are sure to be famous, Blixford, along with Mr. Crofton. Not to mention, rich beyond all imagination. When you finally take the crossbreds to market, oh, my, they will fetch a fortune. You'll be the envy of every sheep farmer in England and Scotland. In all the world."

He eventually dragged her away, enabling Crofton to get back to his work, promising she could return in the morning. He took her back to the house, then left to visit his tenants, but he'd gone only half the distance to the first of them when he turned about and went back, remembering he'd promised to show her the fields.

She was working up an inventory of the household with Hester, but seemed happy to accompany him. In fact, she thanked him a number of times, and exclaimed over the excellent state of the farms, of his obvious talent for management, and made comment of the tenants' open admiration of him. She noticed every detail, from the state of the tenants' cottages, all repaired, clean and sturdy, to the neat and orderly implement barn. He was astonished at her knowledge and answered her questions much as he would had they been asked by the steward, Mr. Pottinger. He had to remind himself she was his wife, that it was odd in the extreme, her interest and comprehension. She even made a few suggestions he found helpful.

At the end of rounds, which didn't take more than

the remainder of the morning because Beckinsale House was a very small estate, they took a picnic into the wilderness and walked almost an hour before he led her to the place he liked to imagine no one else knew of. It was not a stretch to believe, particularly because getting there required winding through a narrow, scarcely visible trail, cut between the encroaching vegetation. Eventually, they reached a tiny clearing, no larger than their bedchamber, enclosed completely by towering trees and thick undergrowth, its singular feature a huge boulder, hollowed out along one side, providing the illusion of a cave.

As he'd expected, Jane was enchanted. She spread their blanket beneath the boulder's overhang and they ate their lunch with great relish, the long walk having built strong appetites. Afterward, he removed her clothing, released her hair from its long braid, and made slow, deliberate love to her with an audience of chirping birds. They slept a bit, then packed up the picnic and made their way to the lake. She was, of course, an apt pupil at rowing, laughing at her first, awkward attempts, then fiercely concentrating until she realized it was unnecessary to move half the lake with each stroke of her oars. Eventually, she gave over and declared her arms quite tired. He had removed his hat, coat and shirt, and she stared at him as he rowed, declaring him positively beautiful, there in the spring sunshine, his muscled arms shown to tremendous advantage. He set the oars, hauled her close and kissed her madly. They drifted for a while, until the sun was low in the west.

He docked the boat and they slowly made their way home.

They declined to dress for dinner and dined at one end of the table, well aware Clive was shocked, despite his jovial manner.

Bathing was equally as enjoyable as it had been the

day before, as was bedtime. He moved down her body and took her with his mouth, almost laughing when she exclaimed, "You wicked man!" and then, "Don't stop!"

It was not until they were wrapped up together and drifting off to sleep that he remembered his plan to have her removed to another bedroom. But he was tired after an energetic day and resolved to do so on the morrow. He kissed her forehead and went to sleep.

The following days fell into a similar pattern, a comfortable routine of early morning runs, estate business after breakfast, long walks and leisurely boating in the afternoons, and in between, at random moments, they made love to each other. It was always the same, yet always different. Sometimes they went at it very slowly, drawing their lovemaking out into a long, languorous, immensely gratifying experience. Other times, it didn't seem they could come together quickly enough, occasionally tearing garments in their haste to couple. Every night, after they turned in, he introduced her to something different and she slowly became attuned to him, as he was to her. He couldn't shock her, it seemed. Jane was like a child in some ways, always game for a new experience and additional knowledge of an activity she enjoyed. And there was no doubt Jane enjoyed lovemaking a great deal. One thing remained constant, and that was their mutual satisfaction. She never failed to respond, never came away dissatisfied and unfulfilled. As for himself, he couldn't appease his need for her, his mind constantly entertaining possibilities, his imagination filled with her.

Every night, with her in his bed, their arms and legs tangled together as they fell asleep, he remembered he'd intended to have her removed from his room. And every night, he was too tired to worry about it.

On Friday, he took her into the village and they lunched at the Honking Goose, after which they stopped in some of the shops and she purchased a few baubles, along with gifts for her father and brothers. She purchased an embroidered handkerchief for Lucy and a set of knitted baby boots for Miriam. He suspected her purchases were more in the vein of supporting the local villagers than any true interest in shopping. Everything was done in a bit of a rush, her impatience evident to him by the tapping of her boot, although she was warm and courteous to everyone. She held herself as a duchess ought, with just the right combination of kindness and aristocratic demeanor. He remembered worrying she would embarrass him and was ashamed to have thought it. Jane was magnificent.

On Sunday, they attended services because she insisted. "I will not rot in Hell, and neither will you." She greeted the vicar afterward and invited him and his wife and daughter to tea in the afternoon.

When afternoon arrived, she appeared in the parlor dressed in a lovely, demure gown of rose muslin, her hair dressed perfectly, her demeanor gracious and welcoming when the vicar arrived with his lady and daughter, who vaguely reminded him of Bella, the vicar's daughter at Eastchase. He wondered if all vicars daughters tended to be plain and mousy. As soon as they'd left, Jane declared the man a dead bore, but a man of God, so very worthy, surely.

He laughed far too loudly and she told him to shush, that God would hear and doom him to Hell.

It quickly became evident to him that Jane had a healthy fear of Hell. He asked why and she explained, "When I was a little girl, my nurse said I was the devil's spawn, that I would die and he would take me back to live with him in Hell. She also said I was the cause of my mother's death, that the good woman could not live with the knowledge she'd borne a child of Satan."

Michael was horrified.

He assured her they would always attend services, to ensure she didn't go to Hell. Then he prayed fervently that she would not entertain the possibility of Heaven or Hell until she was one hundred years old and he'd been gone twenty, at least.

Slowly, he began to fret. He wondered if she was with child, and couldn't believe it when he hoped she was not. He would lose his mind, surely, worried she wouldn't make it through childbirth. There was also his promise to himself that he would take her to Eastchase Hall and leave her there until the last month of her confinement. He was nowhere near ready to leave her. He'd become quite attached to her, would miss her dreadfully when she was not at his side. How had he slept almost thirty years without her in his bed? He finally admitted to himself that he could not, would not, remove her to another room.

He considered their daily, multiple, sometimes desperate couplings and couldn't imagine she wasn't with child. They'd been after one another enough to put even the most prolific of rabbits to shame.

During the second week of their stay, six days before they were to return to London, he awoke before her, made his way to the dressing room and the screened commode, then returned to the bed to awaken her with a kiss. He mostly decided upon it to aggravate her, because she didn't like morning kisses until after she'd rinsed her mouth, exclaiming they both had horrible breath and it was not in the least romantic.

He reached for the sheet and tossed it back, thinking to shock her awake, but it was he who had the shock.

There was blood everywhere.

Bright and red, screaming of pain and death.

His mind exploded with memories of Grace's slender body, writhing in agony, her legs and the bed covered in blood.

A terrible howling keened through his soul. "*Jane!* Oh, dear God, *Jane!*" He scooped her up and cradled her against him, rocking her to and fro, close to hysteria. "Jane, love, please, *please*, wake up! Do not be dead. I won't allow it, do you hear? *Jane!*"

"Michael, be calm. I am not dead, you see." Her arms circled his neck and she nuzzled into his throat. "Have you no knowledge of a woman's monthly courses? It would appear I'm not with child, despite our earnest attempts."

He held her and stared at the sheets, completely floored. "How can you bleed so and not die? Great God, it's inhuman. What pain you must feel."

"Am I to assume you have no experience in these matters?"

"None at all. I was always told when it wasn't convenient. Until you, I've not slept all the night through with any woman." He couldn't stop staring at the sheets. "It's so much, I can't believe you aren't faint and ill."

"Nonsense. It's not so much as it appears. I'm terribly sorry you've had such a shock, and it bothers me that you're so distressed, but assuredly, it is neither painful, nor life threatening. I've been doing this for years upon years, and expect I will do so for any number more." She lifted her head and looked into his eyes. "Are you upset I'm not with child?"

Crushing her to him, his voice shook. "No, Jane, not at all. It will happen in God's own time, and truthfully, I will sorely miss making love to you once you do become pregnant."

"Why will you miss it? Do you intend not to make love to me after I conceive?"

"Of course I will not. It will harm the babe."

"Ah, Blix, you are clearly undereducated when it comes to women. I shall have to redirect your thinking, I see. In the meantime, I believe you should set me down, as I'm undoubtedly making a mess of you, go and get dressed and leave me to my privacy. I'll not subject you to further knowledge of all this."

He did set her down, on the edge of the bed, but his curiosity was high. "How do you go about, Jane? I'd not realized there was such a large amount of blood with a woman's courses."

She sighed and looked up at him. "I have cloths just for this purpose. They are folded and pinned inside a set of drawers I wear during my time. I change the cloths several times during the day, and wash them out to be used again, later during my time, or the following month."

"What a great bother it must be."

"Indeed. But it's necessary, is it not? Otherwise, we wouldn't have children."

"I feel rather . . . incompetent."

"Because there's really nothing you can do to relieve me of this? Even dukes must bow to nature, you know."

"Do you mean to say, you don't mind?"

"Not so much. One grows accustomed to it, truthfully. Now do go away, Blixford. I find myself somewhat at odds about all this."

"Why?"

She glanced over her shoulder at the sheets and murmured, "If you must know, this is something I've always dealt with on my own. It's intensely private."

"Understandable, but answer me one question before I go."

"Very well." Her face was still averted.

He was thinking about her upbringing in a houseful of males, with no mother to direct her in the ways of women. "How did you begin? How did you know how to go on?"

She didn't answer for some time. He was about to say she didn't have to, that he was sorry for prying, when she spoke very softly. "I was twelve years old and had not the slightest idea why I would be bleeding, except I was surely dying. I dressed and went to say goodbye to my family. When they realized I thought I would die, they were naturally confused and asked why, was I ill? It was horrible, truly, because of where I bled. I ran off and stayed in the woodsman's hut that night and all of the next day, until Old Maudie came and found me there. She was said to be fey, and made her living by telling people their fortunes whilst she smoked a long pipe. She said she kenned I was in trouble and sought me out, then took me home with her and showed me what I was to do, and explained why I bled. I vowed I would never marry, never have children, because it was simply too ghastly to contemplate. Old Maudie said I was wrong, that I would marry and have seven children, as my mother had. I thought she said it only to make me feel better. When I went home, Sherbourne and my brothers never mentioned the incident again, or asked where I'd been. But I later found out through the housekeeper that they'd taken turns watching the hut. I suspect they knew, and Papa probably sent Old Maudie to see me, because I liked and trusted her."

Michael decided to find Old Maudie, if she was still living, and press a great deal of money upon her. Perhaps he'd have her tell him his fortune while he was at it. Stepping close to his duchess, he petted her hair before bending to kiss the top of her head. "What a lonely little girl you were, in spite of all your brothers. You had no female friend to confide in."

"I had Annabel. But she was always so proper, and not one with whom I could discuss anything so personal. She was forever determined to make me into a girl, and I didn't want it. My brothers would never have allowed me to join them if I was a girl in a dress."

"Was it so important to join them?"

At last she looked at him. "It meant everything, Blix. I adored them, all of them. They were fun and jolly and able to do most anything, it seemed. Have you not figured out this is why I'm so mad about you? I'm always attracted to and inspired by those with tremendous ability and strength of character. For all that my brothers can be insensitive clods, occasionally very badly behaved, they're each of them amazing men. Just like you."

He blinked several times and rested his hands upon her head, stroking downward, tangling his fingers in her hair.

"If you say I'm too kind, or I'm blind, or some other such rubbish, I'll plant you a facer. Women can be tetchy during their courses."

Laughter bubbled up in his throat, though he was certain it was a knee-jerk reaction to counteract and bypass the lump that had formed there. "Very well, I won't speak rubbish. I've no doubt you could indeed plant me a facer of significant wallop."

"Oh, Blixford," she said around a sob, "I'm so sorry!"

What was this? He drew her to her feet and wrapped his arms around her. "What are you sorry for?"

She mumbled into his shoulder, "I don't mean to be mannish, truly I don't, but it just pops out there, and I know how much you dislike it. I'm so sorry I've made a mess of things, and you will not want me, ever again, because now this is in your mind and you won't be able to forget it, and oh! I'm not with child, which I know must disappoint you, no matter what you say. It is, after all, the only reason you married me, and I've failed you. Now you'll leave me alone at Eastchase and I'll die of missing you. Please don't do that. I'll try again, truly I will, and surely I'll be successful this time, and we'll never think of the sheets again. Tell me you won't. Say you will still want me."

He was hard pressed not to laugh, which was terribly unkind, he knew, but she was babbling as she cried, clearly overset in the extreme. He decided it was a product of her courses, surely. It was unlike his Jane to carry on like this. He held her and petted her hair and assured her he would want her until he was old and gray and unable to service her any longer. "And you are not mannish. You must forget I ever said that, promise me you will. As for your mess, would you think me base, crude and common if I told you I find it rather endearing? It's who you are, the soul of your femininity. There's a good girl, stop crying now and know that I won't leave you at Eastchase, for I would not be able to sleep without you."

She hugged him with great gusto, pressing the breath out of him. "Oh, God, I don't deserve you, I do not."

"Now you *are* speaking rubbish."

"Are you going to plant me a facer, Blixford?"

"I'd not hurt a hair on your head, Jane." He stood there and kept her close to him for a very long while, until she pulled away and reached for the corner of the sheet, which she used to dry her tears. "Oh dear, this is certainly an unusual turn of events."

"How so? It happens every month."

She blinked at him. "We're still in our honeymoon, and this will put a great damper on things."

"Only because we can't make love to each other?"

"Of course. It is what people do on honeymoons."

"Doubtful many do it so much as we have," he said dryly. "It's of no consequence to me. You'll stop your courses in a few days, and we'll go on until then just as we have, with one exception." He turned and headed for their dressing room. "I'll have to resist taking you whenever the mood strikes, but I'll work hard not to mind."

"As you know, hard work—"

"Is its own reward," he finished for her. "Today may be a bit different, however. I've got some business in Dover, so I thought perhaps we'd go there together and have a late luncheon."

"Really?"

She sounded like a little girl, anticipating a grand treat. He turned and grinned at her. "Yes, really. You may not feel up to riding, in which case we can take the carriage. Now, I'm going to throw on some clothes, go for a ride, and return to shave and dress properly before we have breakfast. Shall I send your maid up?"

She cast a look toward the sheets. "Not just yet. I'll have to clean up first, then I'll ring for her and request a bath."

"Is it not the duty of a maid to clean up messes made by a duchess?"

Her eyes were wide when she looked at him. "I can't allow it, Blix. I'd surely faint of shame and embarrassment."

What an unusual woman he had married. "Will you launder the sheets yourself?"

"I'll take them to the wash house and rinse them out before I give them over to be properly laundered. I daresay the topmost feather mattress is ruined. Deuced shame to waste, but I truly didn't anticipate this. I thought surely I must have conceived. We've certainly tried hard enough, have we not?"

Something in that didn't sit well with him. "Is conception all we've been about?"

"Well, I'd be lying if I said it was my only objective. In truth, it has been tucked away in the back of my mind as a lovely possible outcome, but I confess not my main concern, as it is yours." Her expression became defensive. "However, I don't think I can apologize, because I'm not sorry. You knew I was a hoyden when you married me." The expression instantly changed to anxiety. "You *do* understand that I *want* to conceive?" Now she looked very perplexed. "Perhaps it's because I've not thought about it with enough concentration. Mayhap I should go forward with conception uppermost in my mind. Do you suppose one's thoughts can make a difference?"

Fascinating. His wife was absolutely captivating.

"First of all, I should also confess that conception has not been much on my mind, but rather, like you, somewhere in hiding, though definitely there. As to you being a hoyden, I don't believe that would explain your enjoyment of conjugal relations. I certainly understand that you do, indeed, wish to conceive, but I don't think focusing on it will make the slightest difference. Only think of all the children born on the wrong side of the blanket. They were undoubtedly not thought of with great intensity before conceived. I believe we should carry on as we have, and let nature take its course. If you're meant to conceive, you will. If not, my line will die and my ancestors will have to forgive me. It can't be said I've not attempted to do my duty."

"Very sensible, Blixford. I agree, and will apprise you the moment my courses are done so that we may resume our efforts."

He turned for the dressing room, was almost through the doorway when he heard her voice, low and soft.

"It pleases me much to discover that making love to me is not all about your heir."

He looked over his shoulder at her, standing there beside the bed, her fine, lawn night rail splotched with blood, her long, dark hair mussed, a faint red line across her cheek, from where she'd slept upon a wrinkle in her pillow. Her lovely blue eyes were filled with an emotion he didn't dare name.

He formed a number of reasonable responses, but spoke none of them. Instead, he impulsively said, "Hell and damn, Jane, I'm not only a blasted duke! I'm a human being, a man, a living soul who craves intimacy and acceptance as much as the rest of poor, pathetic humanity. Is it such a stretch to imagine I make love to you three, sometimes four times a day because I *want* you, at times because I *need* you? Do you think I took you about with me every day, everywhere, merely on the off chance I would find an opportunity to toss your skirts up and get a babe on you? Did it never occur to you that making love to my wife anywhere outside this room is not something I'd ever rationally contemplate? I did it because *I could not help myself.*"

His voice became louder, her eyes became wider, but he seemed unable to stop. He turned away from the dressing room to face her and shouted, "For God's sake, if my only motivation was conception, would I take you *atop a horse?*"

"I don't understand your anger. I merely thought to express my appreciation."

"Well, stop it. I don't make love to you out of duty, or because I expect you to appreciate it, or for any other reason than because I cannot keep my hands off of you."

"And this makes you angry?"

"Yes!" He sucked in a deep breath. *"No!"* The howling in his head resumed and he clenched his hands into fists of frustration. He stared at her and decided he was well on his way to losing his mind. He was doomed. Just like his poor, mad papa. "I'm at a loss why a man like me would risk everything for a woman like you. I do not lose control, *ever.* It's a sign of weakness and I *hate* it. Around you, however, it's as though my mind is not my own, that I *will* have you, *must* have you, and my will be damned."

"I've unintentionally wounded you, for which I'm deeply sorry. I hold you in high regard and great affection, and God help me, I am as impetuous as you are. We have the great fortune of being married to one we find attractive and irresistible. That we come together in unconventional ways and places surely can't be wrong, or ill-advised, can it?"

"That is not the issue, and well you know it. Have you become a coward, Jane? Will you sidestep my meaning and hide behind a deliberate misconception?"

She paced to the end of the bed, then halted quickly

and grasped the fabric of her gown, bunching it into a ball within her hands, as if she'd only just remembered the blood. Her eyes were flashing.

He let out a heavy breath. She was angry, thank God. He could deal with her anger, even her rage. He couldn't deal with that other look.

"You hate losing control, and I'm evidently the cause of this perceived weakness, so am I to surmise that you hate *me*? Shall I dress in sackcloth and crop my hair like a boy, perhaps have a tooth pulled, or eat enough to grow fat? Maybe I should turn myself into a shrew?" With the gown still balled into her hands, she moved toward him. "Would it make you *feel* better if I *never* said yes, if I lay upon the bed like a board and cried?" She dropped the gown and poked a finger into his chest. "*You* are the coward. You're so afraid you might actually grow to like the part of me that grows above my neck, you've resorted to claiming to hate the part of me that extends below my neck."

He stared down at her, knew she was dead on the money, but he would poke out his eye before he'd admit it. "Did you just call me a coward, ma'am?"

"I believe I did."

"If you were a man, I'd call you out."

Her eyes fairly glittered. She was incredibly beautiful. Her bosom moved enticingly with her increased breathing, a direct result of her anger. "If you did, you'd be grievously injured. I'm a crack shot. My mannish tendencies, you know."

"Dammit, Jane! I told you to forget I said that. You don't fight fair."

She stepped closer still and glared up at him. "I don't forget wounds which caused me great pain, and I assure you, I won't forget this morning. You've as much as said you hate me." Her eyes welled with furious tears. "Unlike you, I'm unable even to think of something to say that might hurt you, and if I did, I could not, *would* not say it. I beg you to call me out.

Give me an excuse to shoot you, for physical pain appears to be all that I'm able to inflict."

His peripheral vision caught the sight of the blood on her gown –*her* blood. Only minutes ago, he'd thought she might be dead, and he'd wanted to die too. Why, and how, could he be cruel to her? Now she was crying, wounded and asking for some way to defend herself. He was truly a despicable man.

What he did next took every ounce of courage he had, but he knew if he didn't, they would be set upon a road that afforded no return.

He snatched her to him and nearly smothered her in his embrace. "I don't hate you at all, Jane, and you're correct, as usual. I admire and desire you. I enjoy your company, your body, your intelligence. I hold you in great affection, surely you know this." He stroked her hair with one hand and clasped her close with the other. "I told you once, I don't want to tender any affection for my wife. I thought you'd gone from me only a while ago and I went a little mad. It's what I fear above all things, and it's best you understand it."

He felt her arms as they went round him and he sighed. She would forgive him, thank God. "After my mother's death in childbed, my father did go mad. He imagined she was still there, would sit at table and speak to her, pause on the stairs and crook his arm, as though she placed her hand there. He even imagined the babe was alive and well, would go into the nursery and rock an empty cradle. Sometimes he was lucid, and knew he was gone quite mad. It was during one of those times that he realized he might pose a danger to me and Lucy, and he summarily packed us off to live with his sister. I never saw him again. He died alone some ten years later, while I was at Cambridge. They told me his hair was down to his hips, his fingernails were grotesquely long, and he wandered the halls of Eastchase in his nightshirt, talking to his duchess."

She didn't speak, but rubbed her nose against his

throat and made a soft sound of pain, as if what he said was terribly hurtful. He had no choice but to continue.

"He'd allowed the estates to fall into disrepair and was perilously close to completely destitute. I inherited a pile in Devonshire, another in Yorkshire, one in Cornwall, and Beckinsale House. He'd long since sold the London townhouse and gave the money to a man who came to the kitchen door at Eastchase, offering to repair Cook's pots. He sold everything that wasn't entailed, including all of the family jewelry, some pieces hundreds of years old, and gave that money away as well. I had Lucy to think of, and my first order of business was to get her away from our aunt as quickly as possible. She's four years my junior, was only fourteen at the time, but already worn down by the hateful, cold woman it pains me to call kin. We moved back to Eastchase Hall and were close to penniless when I began to rebuild what my father had lost, amongst the evidence of his madness. He'd broken all the mirrors in the house and destroyed the ancestral portraits. He removed the carved balustrade from the grand staircase and burned it, piece by piece. He died when he tripped on the stairs and tumbled from the edge to the hall below."

Her voice was a whisper against his neck. "Why did someone not take him to an asylum, where he could be watched and unable to harm himself?"

"His sister was the only one who could do it, his only relative of age, and she never acknowledged his madness, wouldn't see it because she did not wish to. Even after his death, while I worked to rebuild all he'd lost, she insisted my father merely had a run of bad luck. She demanded to have a hand in my business and it was difficult to dissuade her. She insisted upon sponsoring Lucy when she came out, but I wouldn't allow it. I asked Twykham's previous wife, and she was kind enough to lend her assistance. Once Lucy married Bonderant, I felt a great weight lifted, except that I still had the duty of providing an heir to the title and holdings. I felt I owed it to my ancestors to retain all of it, especially the title, as some measure of recompense for the tarnish it was given by my father."

His arms tightened round her and he sighed into her hair. "There are times I wonder if I'm cursed, Jane. I'm responsible for the deaths of three women, all of them very young, completely innocent. I purposefully didn't marry for love, or even affection, though I did grow to be fond of Annabel. Surely you can understand why I'll never be able to truly love you as you deserve? I like you, want to be with you, desire you, but to love you, knowing the risk of losing you, I cannot do. I can't go mad, Jane. Too many depend upon me, and I'll not abandon them as my father did."

"I don't ask for or expect you to love me, Michael. I only ask for your respect, and that you not lash out and be cruel when you perceive I'm too close."

"You have my respect and I'll do my best not to be cruel, even unintentionally." Looking over the top of her head, with her soft, lovely body melded against his own, he spied the bloody sheets, remembered the horror of thinking she was dying, and felt a pain in his chest. He was, indeed, doomed. "As for you being too close, I believe it's far too late for me to keep you at arm's length. I've grown quite attached to you, and even if you do conceive, I daresay my intention to leave you alone, to avoid you, is completely ludicrous. Near, or far, you'll always be in my thoughts, and I'd worry more about you at a distance. There's also the issue of sleeping. I've not slept so well my entire life as I do with you beside me. I won't give that up."

She was quiet a moment, then asked, "If your goal has been to keep me at arm's length, if you wanted not to be attached, why, then, did you arrange for us to share this chamber? Why have you taken me about the estate, even when you did not have to, and I did not expect it? Today, you will take me with you to Dover, on a matter of business, even though I wouldn't consider it odd to be left behind. We've been together, in every possible way, awake and asleep, since we arrived at Beckinsale House."

He tangled his fingers in her hair and inhaled the faint scent of lemons while he considered her question, and his answer. "Will you think me ridiculous if I say I haven't any idea? I sent instructions to Hester and I thought I told her to place you in a different chamber, but perhaps I did not. Once we arrived, I thought to have you moved, but every day, I forgot, and after a while, I abandoned the notion. There are no connecting rooms in this house, so maybe I unconsciously didn't like the idea of traipsing down the hall each night in my dressing robe." He smiled, in spite of the seriousness of her question. "I won't be coy and say I didn't intend to make love to you and enjoy it thoroughly, so perhaps I was being hopeful we would not be limited to once of an evening. I don't know about you, but I think some of our very best times have been just at dawn, with the birds chirping and the sun peeking over the horizon and you with your sleepy eyes."

Her arms tightened about him. "It is wonderful to wake up to you, Michael. You are somehow . . . different in the mornings."

His smile faded. "I've liked you from the start, Jane, and knew this would not be anything like my previous marriages, that we would be friends, as well as lovers. I suppose most would say I am a lonely person, usually going about life in a solitary fashion. That you're familiar with the workings of an estate, that I can speak with you about these things and you understand completely, even take an avid interest, is really kind of marvelous. But again, there was no forethought to any of it. I asked you to accompany me, you did, we enjoyed it, and beyond that, I don't suppose I thought about it."

He leaned back a bit to look into her face. "It would appear I've been at cross purposes to my intent of keeping a distance."

Her blue-eyed gaze was filled with that look she had, as though he were the only man in the world. "I'm glad, Blix, and love, or no love, it's been a glorious honeymoon. I'd not change a thing."

"I feel the same, even if I fear I've become too attached." He thought of their return to London, and eventually, Eastchase Hall. He pictured the large suite of rooms they would occupy in each house, one chamber and dressing room for him, another of like size for her. The rooms were connected, but he would still detest it. "When we go to London, and later to Eastchase, will you stay with me, Jane? Would you grievously mind sharing my bed, not having your own bedchamber?"

"No, Blix, I wouldn't mind at all. On the contrary, in my own bed, I believe I'd miss you awfully. As we go forward, we'll be friends and lovers, and hold one another in affection, because we do all of these things already. I'm content to go on as we are, and if I conceive and die, you'll bury me and keep living and remember me fondly. You won't go mad, I assure you."

"How can you be so certain?"

She was solemn in her gaze. "You're not only your father's child. You're also your mother's, as Lucy is. I happen to know she loved her husband much, and when he died, she didn't go mad. She seems relatively happy and content. I'm also unaware of any history of madness in your family, so I don't believe it's hereditary." She cupped his cheek within her palm. "You have to allow me to love you, if it comes to that. Promise me that much, at least. I believe I'm halfway there already. You are such a re—"

"—markable man," he finished for her, crushing her to him, yet again. "Ah, Jane, what a devil of a time I have given you, and you so deserving of a whole, capable husband who would love you without hesitation. You'll forgive me this morning's cruelty, surely, because I can't bear the thought of hurting you."

"Yes, I forgive you, and I'll never again mention that you called me mannish." She paused. "To be fair, there is a little truth to it, which is undoubtedly the only reason it was so dreadful of you to say it. I even sound like a man at times. I despise it, but one must deal with what one is given."

He kissed her then, and murmured against her lips, "I love your voice, Jane. On several occasions, you've said something without intention of sounding seductive and I have grown hard, simply because your voice is so appealing."

"Truly?"

"Yes, truly." He kissed her again and willed his cock to not respond, but of course, as always with Jane in his arms, with the scent of lemons in his nose, his body was powerless to resist. "Ignore it," he whispered. "I wish to kiss you, and it's an unfortunate result I can't control."

"I've yet to rinse my mouth."

"I've yet to care." He covered her mouth with his, plunged deep within and kissed her with great passion and tenderness and the closest he would ever come to love.

CHAPTER 12

The rest of the day and all of the following passed much as the previous days, with one notable exception. Although he kissed her often, frequently embraced her, seemed always to have a hand upon her in some fashion, whether holding hers, or riding his large palm against the curve of her spine, or gently stroking her hair, they didn't couple. His nearness, despite knowing he couldn't take her, was terribly endearing, and his sad, horrible tale of his father's madness had catapulted her the final distance. Jane was deeply in love with her husband.

She chose not to say so, certain he would feel bad for his inability to return her love. Instead, she was content to know he held her in his affections. Most of her anxiety fell away and she became ever more comfortable with him. She noted he laughed more, that he hid a wicked sense of humor, and at his core, he was truly a gentle, kind soul. He took great pains to mask it, to present a hard, cold, aristocratic face to the world, but she wasn't fooled one iota.

Remembering Julian's tale of the suspicion that swirled around Blixford's mother's death, and that of the neighbor, the old Viscount Radcliffe, she wondered how it fit with what Blixford told her. Were the rumors only cruel lies, or was there some element of truth to them? If the old duke killed his wife because he believed she betrayed him, and yet he loved her, would his crime not drive him mad? It certainly seemed so, but Jane couldn't believe it. The duchess had been friendly with Radcliffe, who was shot by a highwayman just after she died in childbed. It was a tragic coincidence, surely.

Two days after she'd begun her courses and they'd had their heart to heart, they were having breakfast when Clive brought a silver salver into the dining room and presented it to her. "You've a letter from town, Your Grace. Appears to be from your father. I hope he's well."

"Yes, thank you, Clive," she murmured, stifling a grin. He and Hester were very dear, not like servants at all, always conspiring to provide opportunities for romantic interludes for her and Blix. They evidently found their marriage enormously entertaining, frequently making comments that were not too forward to be impertinent, but not exactly respectful either. They'd been at Beckinsale House since they were very young, had in fact married while in the old duke's employ, and clearly considered themselves something beyond mere servants.

Jane agreed, and found it charming in her husband that he held them in high regard. She'd noticed he was especially kind and thoughtful to all the servants, had taken an interest in young Harry's ability at carpentry and suggested he would support his tutelage in the craft, if he had a mind to pursue it. Harry was still mulling over the prospect, and obviously had a good amount of hero worship for Blixford. They all did, in truth. He couldn't retain his aristocratic hauteur, no matter how hard he tried.

She broke the letter's seal and began to read, becoming a bit breathless as she did so. "Blix, are you aware that Lucy remained in London after we left?"

He was concentrating on slathering his toast with marmalade. "Yes, she mentioned it in her letter of a few days ago. Did I not tell you?"

"If you did, I don't recall. Sherbourne says he's squiring her about, determined to find her a suitable match, and wonders if I think Blaisdale too dull, or March too wild, or Dowling too self-important. Good heavens, Blix. My father, a matchmaker? This is absurd!"

Shocking her completely, Blix shrugged and continued munching his toast, a drop of marmalade clinging to his lips. "I daresay your papa knows what's what and who's who and can see the make of a man with far greater ability than most. It would please me much to see Lucy wed again, and if she's willing to allow your father to find a suitable husband, I say he's a good man and a brave soul, and where's the harm?"

Jane read the letter again, intuition allowing her to read between the lines. Her papa was not, in fact, looking for a husband for Lucy. He might say he was, give all appearances of doing so, but he was not. He spoke of her fine character, her excellent qualities, her devotion to her child, her rather unexpected sense of humor. He mentioned that he was having the devil of a time finding a man worthy of her, that he'd not realized until now how very slim the choices of decent men in polite society, that they were all a rather depraved lot, and he was becoming disgusted. Lady Bonderant deserved and needed a man of high character and strong affections, one who would hold her in great regard and honor her as the high born, lovely lady she was.

Jane sipped her coffee and wondered what Blix would say if he realized her father, the Earl of Sherbourne, was deeply in love with his sister? Would he be so understanding?

She didn't think so. Blix was terribly protective of Lucy, and he would surely not look favorably upon her marriage to a man of fifty.

Leaning back in her chair, she watched him eat his eggs and pondered her own feelings on the subject. On the one hand, it would please her very much if her father was happy, and she did like Lucy, would wish for her happiness as well. But the notion of the two of them, together . . . it was a trifle uncomfortable to consider. She had only to think of what transpired between herself and Blixford, and imagine the same between her father and Lucy, and it gave her a queasy feeling in the pit of her stomach.

It appeared she was again mannish in her demeanor. Hadn't he said men shy away from thoughts of their female relatives in a man's passionate embrace? She could no more think of her father in that way than she might sprout wings and fly about the dining room.

Of course, if she were fair, she had to see that he was a man before he was her father. With seven children and a few bastards to his credit, he was clearly very much a man, with all the incumbent characteristics of such.

But, Lucy? She pictured her quiet, dignified beauty, then considered her father's hearty laugh, his love of the outdoors, his enjoyment of ribald jokes and elaborate pranks, and it didn't add up.

She read the letter a third time, and concluded she was correct. Her papa was head over heels in love with a woman half his age, his own daughter's sister-in-law.

Blixford would not like it, she was certain.

Oh, dear. Returning to London was going to be even more trying than she'd imagined.

All the more reason to enjoy the last three days of their peaceful interlude in Kent.

He was ridiculous. He was besotted. He was falling deeply in love with Lady Lucy Bonderant. Sherbourne spent most days telling himself all the reasons why he couldn't have her, why she needed a young man, why it was wrong, in myriad ways, for him to attend to her needful appetites with complete abandon. Despite his stern lectures to himself, every night found him in her bedchamber, doing just that. She was truly insatiable, and he'd found a hidden well of strength and stamina that allowed him to keep up. But it was an illusion, surely, bound to wane soon, and she'd be disappointed.

He waltzed her across the Morrison ballroom just after midnight on Friday and debated his plan for the evening. Over the past week and a half, he'd concocted a number of inspired ideas for ways in which he could gain access to her bed without anyone the wiser — particularly Blixford's servants –for all servants, even the most trusted and regarded, had a tendency to gossip. He would not subject Lucy to gossip.

But he was all out of ideas tonight, and almost of a mind to simply take her home, follow her up to her chamber, close the door and stay until morning. He would love sleeping with her, nestling her sweet body close to his as they slumbered. He would love to see her of a morn, her hair mussed, her eyes sleepy, her body pink and warmed by his. He would love her all the days of his life, and attend to her with care and consideration.

If he were not fifty years old, and she but four and twenty.

In some ways, he regretted his impetuous decision to take her the day of Jane's wedding. Had he but followed his head, he'd have gently discouraged her, sent her home, and that would have been an end to it.

But he didn't. Instead, he plunged himself into her soft heat, and subsequently, into her life. They had become fast friends, sharing a hundred and one confidences, allowing private, intimate views into the darkest recesses of their minds and souls. He'd discovered a great deal about her during their sojourns in and about London each day, William usually in tow. In the night, when they were complete and sated, lying in each other's arms, he learned of the cloistered life she'd led in the days, weeks and years since Bonderant's death, of her unfulfilled needs, and the fantasies and imaginings she'd concocted to pass the lonely nights. She confessed she didn't buy her erotic books, but wrote them herself. He was astonished, intrigued, and exacted a promise from her that she would allow him to read one of her books.

All in all, she'd had something of a sad and forlorn life. He admired her good nature and sense of humor, cultivated in spite of her somewhat gloomy circumstances. He loved to make her laugh, was captivated by her smile, her enjoyment of him. He was hopelessly in love. He wanted to pet her and spoil her and shower her with all the affection that had been missing from most of her life. He was pleased to know Blixford was, at least privately, an extraordinarily warm, kind man, who clearly loved her much.

But he was only her brother, and it was very clear, Lucy needed a husband. A lover. A champion. A father for her son.

His growing affection for William almost caused him pain, for he knew when it was over between him and the boy's mother, he wouldn't see the child again. He was a bundle of energy, a sponge who soaked up all that Sherbourne taught. He was mad about archery, and loved to go to the park each afternoon and practice with his wee bow, becoming better with every session. Sherbourne always promised an ice if he applied himself diligently, but he was certain no bribe was required. It made him feel good to see the boy exert his masculinity, then point out to his mama what an excellent archer he was becoming, or gift her with yet another sharp stick, whittled carefully and lovingly by his small hands.

He also rather liked the way Lucy looked at him in those moments, as if he'd handed her a tremendous gift. She told him she could well understand how he'd ended up with such an accomplished, honorable brood, for he was surely the very best of fathers.

It had taken every ounce of his self-discipline not to ask for her hand, right then, and promise to give her many more children, with whom he would be an equally attentive father.

He had not. He was fifty, no doubt bound for the cold ground in twenty years or so. She wouldn't recover from losing another husband, and he couldn't put her through it. He wouldn't. He had too much regard for her. Too much love.

"Sherbourne, you're not yourself," she murmured, looking up into his eyes. "You're almost brooding. Has something upset you?"

Shaking off his mood, he smiled down at her. "No, my love, I'm only pondering how I shall come to you tonight."

Her expression was inscrutable when she said airily, "As much as I've delighted and progressed in my education, for which I'm most thankful to you, I don't believe I'm ready to introduce a third party into my bed. Frankly, it isn't something I find at all interesting. Perhaps I'm less adventuresome than I thought."

Confused, he swept her across the floor in a series of turns before he asked for clarification. "Did I suggest a third party?"

Her gaze was fixed upon his shoulder. "In truth, you would be the third party, and a bit of an intrusion, as I've agreed to an assignation with one of your prospects. I'd thought him disinterested, but it turns out, he's simply mad about me. Naturally, I can't contemplate marriage unless I am certain he's . . . up to the task, shall we say? I suggested we get to know one another in a more intimate fashion and he was decidedly amenable to the idea."

Without thinking, he waltzed her straight out the open doors and onto the terrace, to the far end, in the shadows. He brought them to a standstill, dropped his arms and faced her, determined not to throw his head back and shout, to scream or howl and vent the blood-boiling rage sweeping through him. "No doubt he's amenable." The sodding, bloody bastard! "Who's the lucky fellow?" Amazing how calm he sounded.

"I'd rather not say until I'm certain I wish to marry him." She spun about and stared out at the gardens, lit by paper lanterns in the trees. "It's clear you're merely biding your time until the end of the fortnight, and that you're frustrated by the lack of a suitable gentleman to take me to wife. I realize you thought the task would be fairly simple and quick, and didn't foresee a protracted process, so I'm releasing you from your promise three days early, and taking the matter of finding a husband into my own hands. I daresay it's better this way, Sherbourne. To continue as we have, knowing we will part, that our friendship will end –for surely, sir, I cannot be your friend after all we have shared –is self-inflicted cruelty. I will, of course, miss you terribly, but I really feel I must move on. I can't go back to my lonely existence at Margrave Park, and I can't have you, so I will instead marry a man who satisfies me, who can be an adequate masculine influence for William. The gentleman I speak of will do nicely, if he proves tolerable in bed."

Good Lord, he actually felt tears prick the corners of his eyes. "I see." But he didn't see, didn't want to see. That another man would know her as he had known her would surely kill him. Ah, God, he couldn't bear it. "I feel it's my duty to Blixford to look after you in his absence, Lucy, so I would know with whom you've made an assignation."

"I'm not your responsibility, Sherbourne, now, or ever. It doesn't concern you."

"Oh, but it does. Suppose you've conceived? If you lay with another, there will be a question of paternity. I assure you, if I have got a child on you, it will be raised by me, and no other. Have you learned nothing of me? Do you not see I place my family above all else, that any child of mine, and especially were he to be a child of yours, would bring me the greatest joy, and you couldn't run from me, couldn't find completion in another man's arms without ensuring his immediate death?" He couldn't help himself from grasping her slender shoulders and moving just behind her, pressing his belly against her back. "Lucy," he whispered, his voice cracking, "please, God, don't do this." Sweet Christ, he was going to cry. He'd not done so since he buried dear Connie. "I shall die, truly."

"Oh? Why is that, Sherbourne? Is the thought of me finding pleasure with another man's cock inside of me bothersome to you?"

His hands squeezed her shoulders and he couldn't stop his eyes watering. "Bothersome is far too small a word to express the depth of my anguish." He would kill him. Whoever this man was, he would have to kill him.

"You fail to see the problem, my lord. You deny me yourself, but you would deny me all others, as well. We've now considered every unmarried man in London, and even some beyond, in absentia, and none have lived up to your exacting specifications. Indeed, it would appear you've discarded any possible match for me, and in the end, there is only you. Yet, you will not have me."

So focused on his Lucy, her petite, feminine form, her lovely scent, her warmth beneath his hands, he forgot the humiliation of weeping and allowed a tear to roll down his cheek, unchecked. "You deserve so much more than me. I love you, Lucy, truly I do, and it's because I love you that I won't see you widowed again. You deserve a young man who will stay and grow old with you."

"I deserve to be happy, and I won't be happy without you, but I may, at least, find some outlet for my carnality in another man, and I've decided to begin tonight."

He couldn't speak. Instead, he could only force an odd sound from his constricted throat, one of pain so great, he was dizzy with it. He'd felt thus only once before in his life, and that was the day Constance died.

Her shoulders relaxed a bit and she sighed. "Ah, Sherbourne, you are a foolish man. You won't believe that it doesn't matter to me if I have you by my side for thirty years, or only thirty days. You won't see what even a blind man could see, that the erotic side to our friendship is but a part of the bigger picture. You won't trust me enough to know my own heart and mind." At last, she turned, and slid her arms about his middle. "Does it not occur to you that I am wildly, insanely, completely, helplessly, hopelessly in love with you? That even the mere thought of another's hands upon me is out of the question? Do you really believe I'd invite another into my bed?"

He blinked in confusion before the reality of what she'd just done smacked him in the face with the force of a slap. "Well, you are scrupulously honest. What choice do I have but to believe you?" He gathered her close, bent his head and kissed her deeply, uncaring who saw, what they thought, whether it was right, or wrong. When at last he raised his lips from hers, he mumbled, "It was the very devil of a practical joke, Luce. I may never recover. I began to cry, for God's sake. I believe my bollocks have shriveled to prunes."

"It occurs to me that a practical joke can sometimes be the best method of pointing out another's decidedly ridiculous, wrong-headed notions. I'm sorry it wasn't humorous, but I'm a novice, and didn't know any way to go about it that would be funny. I felt I had to force the issue because I'm so impatient to begin a life with you that doesn't require you dressing up as a matron, or attending to my pretend illness as a humpbacked, bespectacled physician. You'll soon have to resort to climbing the ivy, or sliding down the chimney. I want you in my bed without risk to your life, Sherbourne. I want you there all the night through. I'm bereft after you leave me, and don't wish to be without you, ever again. Besides, I wish to see if your boast of making love to me morning, noon and night is true." She gazed up at him, expectantly. "Well?"

His arms tightened convulsively, and he clasped her to him, the thought of losing her bringing yet another prick of tears to his eyes. "Marry me, Lucy," he murmured, heart pounding, "and I'll try not to leave you too soon, will be a good father to William, will give you more babies and live to raise them, and love you deeply, madly, until there's no breath left in my body." He kissed her again, uncaring of the audience they'd gained at the other end of the terrace. Looking down into her beautiful eyes, he solemnly said, "Please, marry me. I do love you so."

Someone in their audience called, "Oh, do marry him, Lady Bonderant! He's a wonderfully marvelous man!"

"Deuced havey-cavey, Sherbourne, casting about to catch one for the lady when it was you on the line all along."

"Lord have mercy, whatever will Blixford say?"

"Won't like it by half. He's a stick, you know."

"I say, Sherbourne, congratulations!"

He finally looked toward them, his face split with a grin. "She's yet to say yes."

They broke out, all of them, into urgent directives. "Lady Bonderant, 'tis a father the young viscount needs."

"Dashed fine father, Sherbourne is. You could do a lot worse."

"He loves you madly. Of course you must marry him!"

"Isn't this lovely? So romantic! Oh, do say yes, Lady Bonderant!"

He looked into her sweet face and they both began

to laugh. She boldly planted a kiss on his lips before she said, still laughing, "Yes! Oh, yes, of course I will marry you!"

The impromptu audience applauded, rushed forward and surrounded them, gently directing them back into the ballroom. Before Sherbourne could protest, Morrison had been pressed into making an announcement.

Within the space of half an hour, he'd gone from the depths of despair and a bleak future without her, to the pinnacle of happiness and a future certain to hold many lovely surprises, Lucy at the center of it all.

Jane didn't get her three days, thanks to her father. The day after she received his letter, the man himself arrived. It was late in the afternoon and she and Blix had only just returned from a lengthy sojourn at the lake. The weather was especially warm and they had bathed and made love on the grassy bank, especially amorous as this was the first opportunity they'd had since she'd done with her courses. Later, they'd wandered through the wilderness, searching for a gigantic, bright, yellow butterfly she claimed to have seen and he would not believe. They eventually gave up when they found themselves in the small clearing with the boulder and their interest turned from butterflies and focused on each other.

She'd not braided her hair, but left it loose to dry. She carried her damp chemise in one hand and held her husband's hand in the other. He was in his shirtsleeves, his coat and waistcoat slung across one shoulder. Anyone happening along who caught sight of them would have no doubt how they'd spent their afternoon. But Beckinsale House was well off in a world of its own, offering privacy and seclusion, so they had tended to relax further as time passed.

How could they have known Sherbourne would

arrive without notice, or that Hester would situate him in the parlor, and after he tired of waiting, he'd take a stroll in the garden? They could not know, of course, and thus it was that as they tripped up the garden path, grinning at one another and exchanging suggestive remarks, headed for the garden door and ultimately their bedchamber, where they had plans for the remainder of the day until dinner, they instead ran into Sherbourne.

Her face flaming, she curtsied and greeted him. "Papa, how nice to see you. Isn't this a lovely surprise." She suspected she knew the nature of his visit and her stomach instantly tied itself into knots. Blixford was certain to go off, very soon.

Sherbourne shook Blixford's hand before he swept her into his arms and embraced her tightly. "I've a guess that you've been swimming, daughter." He set her back and smiled down at her. "How is your backstroke these days?"

It had always been what gave her the most trouble, and had taken years to perfect. Beaming with pride, she announced she'd gone halfway across the lake on only her backstroke. "I aimed for a target and swam directly to it, instead of going about in circles. You may ask Blix if you don't believe me."

He petted her hair and nodded approval. "Took to the water like a fish, almost from the time you could walk." He smiled and nodded toward Blix. "Not that I don't trust your husband, but he'd naturally sing your praises, whether you swam competently, or sank like a stone, eh, Blixford?"

Appearing to relax a bit from his initial stiff, obviously horrified stance, Blix gave a short nod and waved toward the house. "Won't you come inside, Sherbourne, and have a refreshment?"

"Yes, of course. Thank you."

Looping her arm through his, she walked with her father as they followed Blix to the door. "Will you stay for dinner and spend the night as our guest, Papa?"

"I hate to intrude, I do, but yes, Jane, I believe I will. Something has come up and I felt it best to come and discuss it with Blixford immediately."

They stepped inside, into the central hallway that led to the front hall and the stairs. "Does this have something to do with my sister, and your recent attempt to find a suitable husband for her?"

Sherbourne nodded solemnly. "It does, indeed."

"Have you met with any success?"

"As a matter of fact, I have. She received an offer, only last night. I felt it incumbent upon me to come and discuss it with you, posthaste."

"I appreciate it. If you'll excuse us, we'll just go and freshen up, and meet you in the parlor directly."

"Of course, please, take your time. I apologize for arriving unannounced."

"Do not concern yourself," Blix said, heading for the stairs without waiting for Jane.

When he was out of earshot, she whispered to her papa, "Did *you* propose to Lucy?"

He was clearly shocked. "Why do you ask?"

"I read between the lines. So, did you? And did she accept? Oh, Papa, he isn't going to like it. He's so very protective of her."

He looked decidedly uncomfortable. "It's neither here nor there, Jane, and I won't discuss this with you until I've spoken to Blixford. In fact, perhaps you might send him down and remain above stairs an extra while. I'd like to get this done and over so that I may enjoy our visit." He smiled then. "You look very happy and content, child. I'm so glad."

"Thank you, sir, yes, I'm happy. He's a complicated man, but I believe we suit quite well, and time can only bring a better understanding between us." She turned toward the stairs, but stopped and looked back over her shoulder. "I wish you well, Papa. Do try and not lose your temper."

"Yes, Jane, I will try."

"Now," Michael said as he leaned back upon a chair in the parlor, a cup and saucer cradled in his hand, "tell me who's proposed to Lucy. I'm assuming you don't approve, or there wouldn't be this apparent immediacy to tell me."

His father-in-law appeared relaxed, his fingers idly twirling his quizzing glass, an affectation Sherbourne never employed, other than to toy with it. He looked directly at Michael and said, "I approve, most definitely, but I suspect you may not, at least initially."

"What of Lucy? She is, of course, my only concern. Does she appear satisfied with this prospect?"

"Rather a lot, actually. She tells me she's in love, that she can't imagine marrying another, that he'll be an excellent father to young William. In short, Blixford, the prospect is myself. I beg your forbearance before you pass judgment, and listen to what has transpired since you left London."

He was speechless with shock. Sherbourne? Lucy had fallen in love with *Sherbourne?* He was twice her age. He remained composed and didn't allow any expression to cross his face as Jane's father told him of how they initially struck it well, of the days that followed, the time they had spent together, the search for a suitable husband, her disappointment, and Sherbourne's dissatisfaction with each and every prospect. They had become friends, he became attached to William, they realized they held each other in great affection. She indicated she wouldn't be happy with anyone but him, and he proposed. He wasn't passionate in his speech, but Michael could see the sparkle in his eyes, could hear the inflection in his voice. The man was completely gone for Lucy. He didn't doubt they'd been intimate. His mind turned that over once, twice, then firmly shoved it aside. It was bad enough, imagining his baby sister, but with *Sherbourne?* Good God! It was . . . disturbing.

If it were not his sister, he would find it equally funny and rather romantic. Here was a man widowed some twenty-two years ago, one who loved his first wife so much he'd never taken another, but instead, raised seven children, alone. Now, he was besotted with a woman half his age. Michael could see why the age difference was of no concern to either of them. Sherbourne was young for his age, and Lucy had always been mature far beyond her years.

In point of fact, despite Lucy's eventual heartbreak, for she was bound to outlive him by many years, he could see that the match made perfect sense, would probably be enormously successful.

But for one thing. He cleared his throat at last and began, "Sherbourne, it can't happen. I'm sorry, but you simply cannot marry my sister."

"Why not?"

"Frankly, because of what happened to Jane in Scotland."

His father-in-law frowned. "I fail to see the correlation, Blixford. Perhaps you'll enlighten me?"

"I don't intend to slight your skills as a parent, nor do I disparage or call into question your affection for your children, but your lack of oversight concerning Jane's welfare is beyond the pale, unacceptable, and not something I can forgive, or forget. She was misused terribly, and I place the blame squarely upon your shoulders. How can I entrust my sister and nephew's welfare to you, a man who allowed his only daughter to rusticate in the far reaches of Scotland for four long years, and never once visited? I can't allow it, Sherbourne. You believe you have her best interests at heart, and I don't doubt that, but you show a lack of wisdom and diligence that may put Lucy and William in a bad spot. Perhaps even in danger."

"Well." Sherbourne was obviously set back on his

heels. He'd undoubtedly expected Michael to disapprove of the match because of their age difference, not because of his failure as a parent. "She can marry me without your approval, of course, but she won't, and I wouldn't want her to. I'm a bit taken aback, Blixford. I'd ask you to give this serious thought before you give your final answer."

"It's unnecessary, Sherbourne. I won't change my mind."

Suddenly, the door burst open and his wife rushed into the room, eyes flashing, bosom heaving, arms waving. She was in termagant mode, fully in a rage. Unfortunately, her rage was directed at him. He suspected his wife had fallen to the rather low endeavor of eavesdropping. She confirmed his suspicion when she stopped close to his chair and glared at him, her hands balled into fists at her side. "How dare you! I told you something in deepest confidence, something which brings me tremendous shame and humiliation, and you *told my father?* Michael, how *could you?*"

"Jane, I didn't tell him."

"You just said I was misused terribly. What else could he think? And it's clear he already knew, so you must have told him the day we married. All this time, I was so glad to know my father would never learn of his daughter's shame, and you had already told him. You are a cad! By all that's holy, I've married a *cad.* And by God, it's grossly unfair to accuse him of negligence. He didn't come to visit because I *would not allow it.* I didn't want to see him, nor any of my brothers. If you had a farthing of sense, you'd understand why. I was ruined! As much as my running away humiliated you, how do you think it was for them? I couldn't bear to see them, knowing I'd brought such shame upon my family. I said if any of them came to see me, I wouldn't be there. I'd go away until they left. He wrote to me every single week, for four years! He sent money and gifts and begged me to return home. He sent a distant cousin to act as companion and chaperone and I sent her back. I won't stand by and allow you to ruin his and Lucy's chance at happiness because you're a bloody *stick*."

She turned to leave and marched for the door. "I won't be able to get past this betrayal, Blixford. You will return to London to your duties in Parliament and I will retire to Eastchase Hall and settle into the duchess's chambers that I may take up my duties as mistress of the house."

Had she tossed a barrel of iced water upon him, he couldn't have been as stunned and shaken. She wouldn't stay with him in his bed. She would become as his first three duchesses, available only at night, in her chamber.

"Jane," Sherbourne called, rising from his seat, "he didn't tell me. He said he thought it odd you hadn't taken a husband while in Scotland, then told me you requested he meet you in the park, early that morning, that you could tell him something of significance that transpired in Scotland. I surmised his meaning. He said only that much so that I would realize your motivation for marrying him, that to dissect him was really rather pointless, when you had such a great weight upon your heart. He did it out of concern for you, so that your obtuse father would accept your choice of husband and stop inadvertently heaping additional guilt upon your head."

He strode toward her and turned her round to embrace her. "I am nevertheless at fault, no matter that you insisted I not come to Scotland. I should not have allowed you to run, and should never have allowed you to stay. Your husband is right, and I will ever feel I failed as a parent, but you should know I love you most dearly, treasure you as my only daughter. I'd sooner cut off my arm than any harm come to you."

She did not cry. She did not relax her posture. She did not say a word.

Michael knew her well enough by now to know, she was too angry to hear what her father said, too filled with rage to listen to reason. Eventually, Sherbourne released her and she turned and walked out, closing the door quietly behind her.

His father-in-law gave him a pained, questioning look.

"Do sit down, and permit me to offer you a brandy."

He got up to pour each of them a hefty portion, delivered Sherbourne's and resumed his seat. "It appears our honeymoon is over, and as my business here at Beckinsale House is concluded, we'll return to London tomorrow. I'll speak to Lucy and make a decision then." He took a deep drink of brandy and stared down at the pattern in the parlor rug, admitting to himself he was a dismal failure at marital harmony. He had only to think of how it had been, how very much he had enjoyed, reveled even, in the past days, of their understanding of one another, and the swift loss of everything made him want to hit something. To cast his brandy across the room. To shout and howl and stomp upstairs and demand she recognize he did *not* betray her, wouldn't contemplate such a thing, and he ever had her best interests and happiness at heart.

"She's been in love with you from the start, of course. Never stopped, despite her running off and insisting she'd never see you again. In every letter, she asked after you, wondered if you'd yet got your heir, if I had seen you, if you seemed happy. She fretted endlessly about jilting you, afraid it would serve a permanent scar upon your reputation. I dutifully reported your comings and goings, your acquisition of a new bride, her sad and untimely demise, and later, the third bride, and her death. She wrote and expressed her sorrow and concern, and there was a good amount of splotched ink in those letters. Jane was never one to cry, but you have the singular distinction of one with the ability to bring her emotions to the fore. I daresay because she loves you."

Michael remembered she'd said she had wept over a letter from home. He had taken a third wife, and the news made her cry. The truth of it hit Michael and he felt a bit short of breath. She hadn't come back to marry him because he was the only way she could reinstate her respectability. She had come back to marry him because she loved him. How could he be so blind? Her words of only a few mornings ago came back to him. *You have to allow me to love you, if it comes to that. Promise me that much, at least. I believe I'm halfway there already.*

What must she have thought when he told her he would never love her, that he couldn't allow it, couldn't risk madness if he were to lose her? She'd said it didn't matter, that she was content merely to be in his affections. Now, she perceived that he'd betrayed her, and she must surely be grieving, upstairs in their bedchamber. He had unintentionally hurt her, yet again, and he didn't know if she would be able to forgive him this time.

The thought was so depressing, he slumped in his chair and wondered how a methodical, rational, reasonable man could make such a mess of things.

Sherbourne took a drink of his brandy and gave him a long, silent look before he said softly, "It won't be easy to convince her your betrayal was slight, and meant only for her benefit, but I suspect you're up to it. The love of a woman is always worth whatever price must be paid."

Michael eyed his father-in-law curiously. He began to understand how Lucy might have fallen in love with him. "Sherbourne, you astonish me. Am I forgiven, then, for ravishing her, for maligning her afterward, for angering her to such an extent, she took off for

Scotland, rather than marry me?"

He appeared to give it some thought, rather than rushing to reassure him. Michael's respect for the man inched further upward.

At last, he said, "Perhaps when you have a daughter of your own, you'll better understand my feelings. I admit I'm in no way objective when it comes to Jane. To me, she is simply wonderful, can do no wrong. If I'm forced to see any shortcoming, it angers me, not at her, but at the one forcing me to look. I'm not sure if this makes any sense at all, but I knew, that morning, you were not entirely the villain. She was in love with you, was quite obvious in her attentions. I should have told her to contain herself, but I didn't, because I spoiled her and let her have her way all of her life. I imagine what you said to her was in way of admonishment for traipsing about the house half dressed, in the middle of the night. I'd also assume you were less than impressed with her choices of masculine pastimes. I'd been called to task for this on a number of occasions by my brother's widow, but I didn't listen. I insisted Jane was not one for feminine pursuits, but in truth, it was selfishness on my part, because I wasn't interested, and had no patience for such things."

He drank more of his brandy and smiled, albeit a bit sadly. "I truly enjoy children, and loved every moment of raising mine. Jane was my last, and so like her mother. I wanted her with me, as much as possible, and as I wasn't going to begin stitching, or watercolors, or any proper missish activities in order to spend time with her, I took her about with me to the sheep farms, to see the crops, and visit tenants. I taught her to shoot, and ride, showed her the fundamentals of horse breeding. It was selfish on my part, and I regret she's not accomplished in ladylike pursuits, but as I said, I can see no fault in my child. To me, she is perfection, a loving, compassionate, capable woman. I see that to one who is not her doting papa, she may be lacking.

Your obvious distaste for her pursuits, despite your attraction to her as a female, rather painfully pointed this out to me that morning, and I wanted to kill you for it."

"Perhaps I should thank you for your forbearance?"

He lifted a brow. "I most likely would have killed you, except that I knew Jane loved you, I suspected you had some feelings for her, as you would not have taken liberties if you did not, and I believed insisting she marry you was possibly the best of outcomes. I figured, over time, the two of you would work out your differences and be sublimely happy. I didn't foresee that she would run, and once she did, I couldn't force her to come back and see it through." He sighed. "Would that I had."

After a pause, he sat up a bit straighter and met Michael's gaze directly. "After your third duchess passed, I wrote to Jane and suggested she come home, at last, and see you, to apologize in person and put the past behind her, so she could move on and perhaps find some peace and contentment. I mentioned that you would undoubtedly have some difficulty finding a fourth bride, owing to your misfortunes with the first three, then casually suggested she might still marry, despite her ruination, that there were a number of gentlemen of reduced circumstances who'd be willing to look past all that and love her for her fortune."

Michael was shocked. Truly astounded. "Surely you didn't say such a thing to her!"

"Oh, but I did. I knew it would get her back up, but I also knew it would set her to thinking, to wondering, now that you were free again, if perhaps she might marry you, after all. I was convinced, from four years of letters asking after you, that she was still in love with you. Within a month of my letter, she wrote to say she would come home, at last, and asked my assistance to see you again, that she could apologize." He glanced around the parlor. "And here we are, not quite three weeks since your meeting at the Manderly ball. I do hope you'll give this your best effort, Blixford. I have come to see you in a far different light, and am convinced, despite my earlier anger with you and disappointment over the entire situation, that you and Jane are extremely well suited, and have the prospect of a very happy union. Unfortunately, I believe you'll have to be the impetus to make this happen." He sighed deeply. "It will require a fair amount of hard work."

"I've heard it said that hard work is its own reward." Despite the pall cast upon him, Michael smiled. "She's certainly an unusual woman, and I'm constantly surprised by her. In truth, I wouldn't have her any other way. She's devoted to you and her brothers, and I'm well able to see why she would be so upset that you know anything of what happened to her. She sees it as her fault, her shame, and won't allow that she was duped and misused by a blackguard of no honor. I'm planning his comeuppance, by the bye."

Sherbourne's eyes glittered with relish. "You will, of course, allow me to assist you, if at all possible?"

"I'll be only too happy to do so. After today, I'll be even more committed to the task, for it appears that, even now, he's interfering in my wife's happiness."

"Poor Jane, my heart breaks for her. I wish she'd see that this doesn't lower my estimation of her, but she will believe it until I prove otherwise. It will be difficult, but I'll succeed."

"You must have some intrinsic understanding of women, because she respects and loves you so much. You also apparently had a harmonious and happy marriage. I wonder how you went about it? What is the secret to providing a wife with happiness?"

"It's not so very difficult." His father-in-law relaxed in his chair and smiled at him. "Within reason, when possible, admit you are wrong, even when you're convinced you're right. You should say you're sorry, even when you cannot fathom how you have erred, or why she's so angry with you. It's also wise to bestow gifts, not necessarily of value, but thoughtful tokens. Just last week, I gave your sister a set of pencils and a package of drawing paper, because she hadn't brought any from home, not planning to stay longer than one night. You'd have thought I handed her the crown jewels."

He took another drink and stared intently at the portrait of Mrs. Hopping that hung above the mantel. "Never criticize her family. No matter how much she may criticize them, never vocally agree with her, even if you do. If she asks if she appears to have put on weight, deny it, even if she's grown heavy with child and fair waddles. These things should all be applied in double doses when she's in her courses. They're downright mean at times, and you're powerless in the face of it, trust me. No amount of reason will work. Just get down and grovel and be done with it."

"Wise words, but sometimes difficult to put into action."

"True, but it does become worth it, you know. Women don't expect so much, in truth. They need to know they are cared for, that they are loved, respected and appreciated, and they require a certain amount of affection. They're also deuced sensitive about the offspring, so have a care before you criticize her mothering skills. I've come to believe they view it much as we would react were another man to call us dishonorable. It is the greatest insult. Truth be told, they generally know, much better than we do, the physical needs of a child."

Michael drained his brandy and went for more. "You'll forgive me for speaking plainly, as this does concern your daughter, but I'd say after today, it may be many, many years before we have any offspring." He looked toward the door. Would she let him in her bed at all? "I suspect I'll be sleeping down the hall tonight." He looked at Sherbourne and a bit of his helplessness must have shown.

He stood and came for another round, then paced to the fireplace and looked up at Mrs. Hopping. "Relative?"

"No. The original owner's wife."

"I thought it was a smudge, but I see it is not. Damned if she don't have a moustache." He turned and rested a boot against the fire screen, leaning an elbow on the mantel. "There's a fine art to groveling, Blix. Get it wrong and you'll not be down the hall, but outside with the hounds." He nursed his brandy, appearing to be lost in thought. "I'll tell you a story to demonstrate. When I'd been married less than a year, with Connie only just delivered of our first child, I made the grievous error of siding with my mother when she insisted Constance employ a wet nurse. My mother thought it common and low for a lady to nurse a child. Before it was said and done, Connie was cast as an ignorant Scottish peasant, less than common, even. I found it rather endearing that she wished to nurse our son, but I didn't say so. I allowed my mother to interfere, and suddenly, somehow, it all got away from me, all because I didn't stand up for Connie and tell my mother to mind her own business."

Michael retook his seat and listened, wondering where this was going.

"She packed up and left me. Took the babe and went all the way to Scotland, she did, to her own mama. I was young and proud and stupid and determined she would be brought to heel, so I wrote and told her she should hie herself back home, or suffer the consequences."

"What were the consequences?"

Sherbourne barked a laugh. "Hell if I had any idea. I thought certainly she'd shake in her boots and rush back to me. Instead, she sent me her wedding ring and told me to pawn it for coin and buy myself a brain."

Michael couldn't help a chuckle. "Did you go after her then?"

"Oh, no, I was righteous at that point, furious, of course, and determined to wait her out." He swirled the brandy in his snifter. "I waited another six months in a cold bed, until I thought I'd expire of loneliness and missing her. I wrote every week and she sent the letters back, every blasted one. I had a son and I was missing everything, wouldn't see him grow up. Then I ran into someone who'd done some business with her father and found out, through him, a relative stranger, that Constance was with child again. I'd had enough. I went to Scotland, well prepared to grovel. Or so I thought. I brought her an expensive gift of jewelry, said I was sorry, that I would never go against her in future, and surely now she would come home? She wouldn't allow me to stay, made me go into the village, where there was no inn, and I lived two weeks with an old harridan of a woman and slept in her hayloft."

By now, Michael was laughing right out. "A hayloft? You're funning me!"

"No, no, I don't exaggerate. She had a foul tempered goat whose head butts I tried and failed to dodge every night on my way to the loft ladder. He was quick and wily and I could scarcely sit for the bruises on my bum. Time passed and I went to see Constance every day, bearing gifts, begging her to return home with me. The gifts were not accepted and the answer was always no. I was exhausted, depressed and wondering how everything had become so dismal. She loved me, I knew she did, but she wouldn't relent. Oddly enough, it was that nasty old woman who made me see the light. She wanted me out of her hayloft, in spite of the coin I gave her, and she told me one morn, if I'd just be sincere, and tell Constance how I felt, how I really, truly felt, she would forgive me. The old woman said too much unhappiness comes from pride, that it's the downfall of every man, and the one who is able to swallow it turns out to be the one who always wins, who has most to be proud of. I went back to Connie's father's house, but this time without a gift, with nothing but humility. She was there, I recall, in the nursery, nursing James in a rocking chair, her belly round with my child, and I thought I'd fair die of loving her. I went down on my knees and told her so, swore she was my life, my heart."

"And she forgave you?"

Sherbourne swallowed the last of his brandy. "She told me I was ruining a perfectly good pair of breeches. Always wasteful, she said to me. If I wasn't careful, I'd go through all of our money and we'd be destitute and have to live in a cold garret, and she'd have to take in laundry. I stayed on my knees and said I would do half the laundry, if it came to that, but I wasn't getting up until she forgave me."

Michael thought it was perhaps the best story he'd ever heard. Maybe because it was true. Perhaps because it was a bit of Jane's history. Or maybe because it was so very different from his own parents' marriage. "Did you take her home then?"

"Couldn't. She was too far along. We stayed until after Jack was born, and returned to Hornsby Grange when he was six months old." He lifted a brow suggestively. "Our twins, Henry and Julian, were conceived on the return trip. Lot to be said for groveling, Blix, but as I said, there's an art to it." He nodded toward the door Jane had recently exited. "I suggest you get to it. Don't allow her to go to Eastchase Hall, or you'll be spending the next few months in a cold bed and wind up doing what you can do right now."

"How will you occupy yourself? This may take a while."

"If you don't mind, perhaps I'll go and take a look at your crossbreds."

Michael stood and set aside his empty glass. "Be my guest. Crofton is no doubt still at the cottage we're using for the office. Go south of the house and pick up the lane to the west. There's a small barn you can see from the lane, and the cottage is just there, along with the pens. Help yourself to a mount, but you should avoid Grendel." He moved toward the door. "She may be breeding. Went into season last week and before I could isolate her, Pendragon got to her." His mind flashed a picture of Jane, watching, then kissing him atop his mount, moving her body on his.

"You don't say. Now *that* will be an interesting foal, will it not?"

"Indeed. Jane and I have decided to hope she is pregnant. Until we know, Jane's not been riding her. If you like, take Pendragon. He's rather chipper of late."

Sherbourne laughed. "No doubt. Well, then, Blix, I have to say, I appreciate your brandy, your hospitality, and your friendship, and I hope, most sincerely, you'll see your way clear to allow me to marry Lucy."

With his hand on the doorknob, Michael turned and met his gaze. Sherbourne's eyes twinkled. How *did* he do that? "Will you fair die of loving her?"

He expected him to laugh. Instead, the man shocked him completely when he said soberly, "She is my heart and my life, and you must believe I will never, so long as I am breathing, allow any harm to come to her, or William, nor any children we may have between us. I won't pretend this isn't most humbling for me, and I certainly feel ridiculous, being fifty years old and wanting to marry a woman half my age, but that is the way of it." He paused. "The answer is yes, Blixford, I may fair die of loving her."

CHAPTER 13

He expected to find a blaze of fury and a flurry of packing activity when he opened his chamber door. Instead, all was quiet within. He was about to turn to leave and go in search of her when he spotted the top of her dark head, peeking above the back of a chair before the fireplace. He glanced toward the dressing table. Her things were still there, resting next to his.

Reassured, he walked into the room, closed the door and went to sit on the chair to the other side of the grate. She met his gaze directly. "Is your conversation with my father done?"

"Yes, Jane."

"Will you allow him to marry Lady Bonderant?"

"If she confirms it's what she wants, yes."

"That's good. They will be very happy, and it pleases me for lovely people to have their happiness."

Silence followed and they gazed at one another for what seemed an eternity. He formed a thousand sentences in his head and didn't speak even one. He knew, instinctively, he couldn't make it right to her, couldn't explain enough for her to understand his motivation.

He couldn't tell her he loved her, that she was his life, his heart. She couldn't be, and she would know he lied, would despise him further than she did already. Sherbourne's tale to demonstrate the power of groveling had been marvelous, but nothing of it applied to Michael. He was sincere in his insistence that he didn't betray her, but she wouldn't respond to that, regardless of how sincere.

The situation was hopeless.

Her words confirmed it.

"I'm not angry," she said at last. "I'm not upset, nor sad, nor hurt. More than anything, I'm astonished that a man of your sensibilities could so monumentally miss the significance of what you've done. You've destroyed any chance we had for happiness and harmony, Blix. We might have lived together for years upon years, raised a large brood and found pleasure in one another's company. We might have shared our lives. We would have been friends and lovers, as we agreed. But it's impossible without trust, and I can never again trust you."

"Your father believes you love me."

"He is, as usual, correct, but love without trust means nothing. I can never tell you anything, share any part of myself, of who I am. Sharing one's soul is something of a cornerstone to a close marriage, I believe. As it stands now, I would be hard pressed to confide in you my favorite flavor of ice at Gunther's. I don't expect you to understand, but try and imagine if I betrayed your confidence. I had never heard that your father was mad, and I suspect your aunt managed to hide it, to keep his condition from the outside world. Suppose I told someone whom you hold in high regard of your father's madness, and your deep fear of becoming like him? I believe you would be stunned that I could do such a thing."

"It is not the same thing. He's your father. He needed to know something happened to you, needs to reassure you that the blame for it is his, not yours."

"How can he be to blame when it was I who allowed it to happen to me?"

"If he or one of your brothers had been a presence there, do you believe MacDougal would have lied to gain your acquiescence for liberties, subsequently assaulted you, even when you said no, then insulted you grievously? No, Jane, he would not. You were essentially alone there, without protection from a blackguard of no honor. That he's your kin only makes it worse. You said he backed off after a time, but renewed his insistence after he discovered your ruination. He saw it that you were already fallen, that you were his to take. Because no one of your family was there, he assumed they had cast you aside, banished you, that they wouldn't care what happened to you."

He rose and went to the window, staring out at the gardens and the wilderness beyond. "Sherbourne doesn't in any way see this as your shame. You have to believe that, if you don't believe anything else I say. He loves you very much."

"You really don't understand at all, do you? I don't fret that he'll think less of me because MacDougal assaulted me, or even because I allowed myself to be duped so completely. I'm his daughter, someone he cherishes and loves and considers very dear. From now on, he'll think of MacDougal when he looks at me. He'll feel guilty about it, and treat me differently than he did before. He'll think me wounded, and won't be as open with me. It will alter our relationship permanently and I don't know how I'll bear it."

It was not something he'd considered. She was undoubtedly correct in her thinking, but he still believed Sherbourne needed to know, had a right to know. He was quiet for a time, giving significant thought to her words as he looked out the window.

From the corner of his eye, he caught a movement along the edge of the house, close to the garden. Turning his head, he saw Lucy and William walk into view. She must have only just arrived, undoubtedly anxious to convince him to allow her marriage to Jane's father. Why had Hester not shown her into the parlor? Then he saw Sherbourne striding toward her from the direction of the stables. He must have seen her drive up, and returned his mount in order to greet her.

He knew he shouldn't look, but he was compelled. Grinning happily, Sherbourne swept her up into his arms, lifted her feet from the ground and twirled her about. Lucy laughed, and her face, he could see even from this distance, was lit with joy. When Sherbourne set her down, he kissed her, then stepped away to reach for William. He ruffled his hair and greeted him before lifting him up to his shoulders. William looked very happy, his ordinarily serious face split with a wide grin. With an arm about Lucy's shoulders, her arm about his middle, and William riding upon his shoulders, Sherbourne walked away, toward the wilderness.

Michael suspected he told Lucy they should spend some time away from the house.

His father-in-law was an eternal optimist, no doubt believing all would be well upon their return.

When they were out of sight, he turned to look at his wife.

She had folded her hands in her lap and her head was down, as if she stared at them. Her voice, when she spoke, was soft and quiet. "We are married and I've agreed to bear you an heir. I will do so. After I'm delivered of a son, my promise will be fulfilled. I will raise him at Eastchase Hall and ensure he receives an upbringing and education befitting the heir of a duke." She looked up and met his gaze. "I'll be your duchess and mistress of your homes. I'll entertain and present a respectable face to the world. I'll never embarrass you. However, I will not go beyond my obligations as your wife and your duchess. We won't be friends. We won't be lovers. We'll couple as needed that I may conceive, but I expect you to perform the duty with all due haste as I cannot bear the idea of intimacy with you after today."

Every word was like another slamming door. He must have flinched, because she sounded haughtily disgusted.

"You should be happy, I'd think, because there will be no likelihood of forming any feeling for me at all. Over time, whatever affection you now have will dissipate as though it never was, and the possibility of following in your father's footsteps will become ever more remote. I won't be emotionally accessible in any way. I won't trust you at all. I had but one secret to share, and you promptly told the only person I would hate to know it above anyone else. You may fool yourself that you did it for my benefit, but in truth, it was to protect yourself from his censure, to smooth your way, to shift his anger toward another. How could he remain upset with you over the arrival of your mistress on his doorstep, when another man was a far worse villain? He fell right in, didn't he? As soon as he learned what happened to me, that you nobly married me in spite of it, he saw you in a much more favorable light, which was as you intended, whether you did it with conscious thought, or not. You damaged the bond between my father and me for the sake of your own comfort and pride."

Her gaze dropped to her hands again. "It would appear the marriage I ran away from is the marriage I came back to. That it is now I who dislikes you would be hysterically ironic if it weren't such a travesty. This is all I never wanted." She sighed. "I expect you'll want to take a mistress. I don't care. I ask only that you be discreet and that I never know of her existence, nor of any children she may bear you."

She stood. "I'm going to ring for Rose that she can assist me in packing for my departure tomorrow. I'll travel with my father."

"What of Grendel?"

An expression of pain crossed her features. "I'd

prefer she remain here until Benjamin determines if she's breeding. If not, I will have her taken to the block and sold. She deserves a mistress who will ride her, and I don't wish even to see her."

He moved toward her but stopped when she turned her back to him. "Jane, I've barely spoken, not had the opportunity to tell you any of my thoughts."

"Why waste time and breath? It won't matter what you say, or how convincing you may be. I've made my plan, and as it follows yours exactly, you can hardly complain."

Had he sounded so cold, so distant, so unfeeling? He suspected that he had. She had loved him and married him in spite of his autocratic cold scheme, insisting only that he dismiss Miriam, determined he stay only in her bed, no doubt because sex was the most she could hope for in the way of affection from him.

She moved toward the dressing room. "I'll await you in London, at the house in Cavendish Square."

"You've abandoned the notion of going directly to Eastchase?"

"On further reflection, yes. I cannot become pregnant without you, so I will remain in London until I'm breeding. The instant I become aware of conception, I'll retire to the country and await the child's birth. If the child is female, we will try again." She stopped at the doorway to the dressing room and looked at him over her shoulder. "Unless I die in childbed. In that event, my obligation to you will be at an end, along with this farce of a marriage."

Their eyes met and held for several long moments. Michael was certain he could say something, do something that would melt the ice in her gaze, but he had no idea what it might be. He was an intelligent man, capable and courageous, but faced with making things right with Jane, he didn't know how to go on. "You said you love me. Is all this your way of expressing it?"

"Yes, it is. If I didn't love you, I would leave you. Because I love you, I will stay and bear you a son so that you may have peace of mind."

"You love me, yet you dislike me?"

"I cannot stop loving you. It has become a habit, a part of me. But I'm unable to like one I distrust." Her expression softened, infinitesimally. "Poor Michael, you've lost something you never knew you wanted, haven't you? An adoring wife who found as much pleasure in you as you for her, an amiable, intelligent companion, a helpmate, a friend." She shrugged. "Ah, well, you're back to where you started, as when you first married Annabel. You can take comfort in knowing your best laid plans will come to fruition, at last. You'll have a stranger for a wife, and you'll have your heir. You'll do your duty, no matter the cost." She turned away. "I'm going to pack. We are done." Stepping into the dressing room, she closed the door.

Lucy's joy over Blix's unexpected acquiescence to her marriage to Sherbourne was significantly dampened when she learned of what transpired. Sherbourne wouldn't say what transgression her brother had committed, but told her Jane was terribly upset with him, that she intended to go to Eastchase Hall on the morrow, rather than return to London with her husband.

"It's a damn shame," he said to her as they returned to the house after a lengthy travail across the lake in one of the old boats. William dashed ahead of them on the path through the wilderness, searching for grasshoppers. "When I arrived, unexpected, of course, they were out and I spent my time awaiting their return by taking a stroll in the garden. When they appeared on the garden path that leads from the lake, not knowing I was there, he was half dressed, her hair was down and I've not seen two people more in love."

He smiled down at her. "I daresay because I'm unable to observe the two of us."

Lucy squeezed his hand and returned his smile. "Oh, Sherbourne, I'm so glad Blix wasn't a mule about us marrying. It appears I made the trip for no reason." She glanced at William. "Though I can't be sorry. He loves it here." She looked up at him again. "And I began to miss you after an hour of your leaving."

"It took an hour? I'm crushed." He stopped and drew her close to kiss her. "I'm glad you came, Lucy. We'll discuss the arrangements this evening and hopefully, by this time two days hence, we'll be married."

William ran up to them and tugged her dress and Sherbourne's coat. "Mama, sir, I have found the very largest grasshopper in all the world. Stop kissing and come and see!"

Chuckling, Sherbourne dropped his arms and stepped back to look at William. "The very largest? You don't say! Well, lead on, my man." He winked at Lucy before following William into the brush. There was a narrow trail cut into the undergrowth that eventually led to a small clearing, dominated by a gigantic boulder. "I didn't know this was here."

Sherbourne moved away, expressing hearty interest in William's bug. They both forgot about her as they extolled the gargantuan size, the handsome legs, the intriguing shape of its head.

Lucy walked toward the boulder, spying a bit of fabric tucked into a pocket in the stone. She reached for it and realized it was a stocking. Glancing down at the grass beneath her feet, she could see it was pressed close to the ground. Good heavens, her brother, ever proper, had made love to Jane outdoors, not so very long ago, it would seem. How very interesting.

Eventually, the grasshopper became weary of his admirers and hopped away, and they returned to the main path. As they neared the garden, Sherbourne said, "I'm hopeful they've worked things out and are back to a happy state, but if not, perhaps you might speak to him, see if you can help. I suspect you're the only person he'll listen to."

"I'll do my best, but it would be helpful to know what caused the disagreement."

He slowed and looked conflicted. "It would be a breach of confidence to tell you particulars, but I believe I can at least say Blixford alluded to a secret of Jane's, something she wanted to keep from me. She fell to the temptation of eavesdropping upon our conversation, and the subject came up. She burst into the room, righteously furious, and called him a cad."

"Oh, my. Why would Blix do such a thing? How could he betray her like that?"

"He did so out of concern for her, but Jane won't see it that way. As much as I want to believe Blix can make it up to her and she'll forgive him, I know my daughter, and once she's taken a wound to heart, it's the very devil to find her good graces. Poor Blix may be sleeping in the stable tonight."

Their approach had been observed, it seemed, and as they came into the garden and up the path toward the house, Blix was there to greet them. She noticed Jane was not with him. It appeared they had not worked things out. Her brother embraced her and shook William's hand before turning to lead them into the house. Sherbourne expressed an interest in the nursery and suggested he and William climb to the second floor to investigate what toys might have been left behind by the last boy who lived there.

When they were gone, Blix escorted her back outside, into the garden. They strolled to the arbor and she sat upon a bench while he leaned against the arch. "I confess I was quite shocked when Sherbourne said the prospect he'd found was himself. Are you certain this is what you want, Lucy?"

"I've never been more certain of anything. We will

suit very well."

"Do you hold him in affection?"

She beamed up at him. "I love him madly. I suppose it seems odd, because of our age difference, but truthfully, I don't think of it at all when we're together. He's far from what I'd consider old. And he's truly marvelous with William. Oh, Blix, I'd never thought to feel like this again. I must thank you for your approval, for I might surely have died had you not approved."

His dark gaze was intent upon hers. "You want it this much, then?"

"Oh, yes. He's an amazing man, funny and warm and wise, and tremendously affectionate. It's difficult to express in words how right this feels, and how ecstatically happy I am."

A fleeting expression of pain crossed his features before he quickly assumed his usual somewhat inscrutable regard. "Then I'm happy for you, Luce. Sherbourne does seem to exemplify the best of fathering skills, so William will no doubt benefit greatly from his influence. I wonder, what will you do about Margrave Park? I assume you'll live at Hornsby Grange."

"I suggested closing up the house and perhaps hiring an assistant for Mr. Timms to help oversee the tenants, but Sherbourne won't hear of it. He says William must stay connected to the house, and the land, and we'll spend a month, at least, of every year there. He indicates he'll visit with you about administration, to see if perhaps you'd like to share the responsibility. I assumed he would take it over, but he believes your involvement with the estate will help retain your relationship with William, that as he grows, he may need some guidance." She lost a bit of her smile. "I'm certain he worries he'll become senile, or die, and he wants you to remain an important part of William's life as he grows into his own responsibilities."

"Well." He turned away and looked beyond the bramble roses, toward the stables. "There is a depth to the man one wouldn't expect to find, considering his love of a grand joke."

Remembering Sherbourne's tale of the jest he pulled on Wrotham, Lucy said, "His jokes are not meant to be only funny. I believe he plots and plans them because it's his way of gently pointing out another's flaw, something which keeps them from realizing their happiness. He doesn't do it merely to provoke a laugh."

He was quiet for a long while, until at last he said, "In many ways, you've had a dreary life, and nothing will make me happier than to see you settled and content. I regret that the man you've fallen for is so much older, simply because it must necessarily bring you unhappiness at some point in the future, but you've always had an amazing ability to recover, to be optimistic."

"It's only that I refuse to anticipate unhappiness, Blix. If I'm happy now, today, that's all that really matters. For all we know, I may die first, and he will be the one to mourn. The future is God's to know, not ours. The best we can do is make the most of today. I'm ever grateful to have found him, and will express my thanks by being happy now, and for as long as he is with me."

Turning toward her, he moved close and reached out his hands. She grasped them and they looked at one another for a long moment. "I do love you so, Blix, and it wounds me that you appear unhappy. I'd thought marriage to Jane would be the answer, but perhaps I was wrong."

He squeezed her hands before letting go, then offered his arm. "Walk with me, sister."

She stood and did so, hoping he would reveal something of what occurred.

Instead, he asked a question. "Do you suppose if our

mother hadn't died, our father might still have gone mad?"

It was unexpected and she had to concentrate to shift her mind in another direction. In all their years together, they'd never openly spoken of their father's insanity, of how he lived the last ten years of his life, or how he died. They referred to him on occasion, but they never actually discussed it. That Blix wanted to do so now seemed somehow significant. She remembered various things she's heard over the years, and in particular, a conversation she'd overheard between the housekeeper and the butler at Eastchase, just after she returned to live there. She'd never told Blix. The subject of their father always upset him, it seemed. "I believe he suffered a head injury not long after I was born, when you were but four years old, and he never fully recovered. It didn't impair him physically, but he was not the same afterward. He became irrational and ill tempered, and was convinced that our mother was involved with the old Viscount Radcliffe."

Blix was quiet, then said, almost in a whisper, "A head injury. I didn't know. How did you?"

"I shamelessly eavesdropped on the servants after I returned to Eastchase Hall. I was terribly curious to understand why I'd been forced to live with horrid Aunt Reid, instead of at home, with my father. She always said he was busy, that he didn't have time for children, and until he took another wife, she would be responsible for our upbringing. I was never so glad in my life than when you came down from Cambridge and took me away."

"Poor Lucy, you did have the worst of it. I was gone off to Eton within a year of moving to her house, and was only there for short periods afterward. I hate that you had to endure her cruelty. At the same time, I've always admired that you hold no lasting scars, that you bear no grudge. I suppose it's your nature to forgive, isn't it?"

She smiled at that. "Don't make me into a saint, Blix. It's too droll of you, really. I don't hold a grudge because it will do nothing to her, and everything bad to me. I choose to forget her and move on. She may rot in her miserable, pathetic life, and I care not a whit what she does, or how she goes on. Hardly saintly."

"I suppose not," he agreed. "A true saint would attempt to make her into something different, to see the error of her ways." He patted her hand upon his arm. "All the same, I admire your ability to put her out of your mind." They walked along a bit further before he said, "It's ironic and a bit humbling to admit, but I've long worried I'd follow our father into madness, and a great many of my decisions have been made with that fear in mind. It could almost be funny, if it weren't so wrong. All these years, I was convinced it was her death that brought on his insanity. Now, to know it was most likely the result of a severe blow to the head . . . well, it's a surprise."

Lucy's heart flipped over and tears welled in her eyes. "Oh, Blix, I didn't know, had no idea. All this time!" No wonder he'd insisted upon marrying women he couldn't love, who would never love him, could never understand his complicated nature. She understood, at last, why he'd resisted marriage to Jane. He knew he wouldn't be able to keep his distance, that he would grow to love her, worried she would die, and he would go mad. Her tears spilled over and rolled down her cheeks. "If only I'd seen this, I might have told you the truth of it and you wouldn't have suffered such a misconception. But we've never discussed it, have we? It's as though we believed not talking about it would make it less real, less painful."

He took a deep breath and let it out slowly. "Do you think she was involved with Radcliffe?"

"No. In my days of eavesdropping, I came to understand she was well thought of, respected by the servants and all who knew her. It appears her life became very difficult after our father was injured and began to doubt her, but she remained faithful." The sun was setting, but she was loathe to return to the house just yet. Blix needed to know all of it, and this was the time to tell him. "The servants speculated that her death was not entirely due to complications in childbirth, that she'd been dosed with something to bring on labor and cause excessive bleeding. They also believed the old viscount was not shot by a highwayman, but by our father, disguised as one."

"I can't believe it. Can you?"

"I'd rather not believe it, Blix, but he was truly mad, I think, even before she died. Who can say? What can it matter now? I'd ask you to not dwell upon the past, to look ahead and live life on your own terms, in a way that will bring you peace and joy."

He came to a halt and stared across the garden toward the sun at the horizon. "You've always had a wisdom that belies your age and experience. I do love you very much, you know."

Her tears began anew. He had never said so. Oh, she knew it, of course, but hearing him say it aloud made her weep. She stepped close and embraced him. "Yes, I know. Have always known. You've been my champion, all of my life, Michael, and I love you. I wish for you to find happiness, to lay aside this restlessness that has dogged you so long."

Returning her embrace, he said against her hair, "I believe I will. I've only to convince my wife I'm not a cad, and all will be well."

"Do you want to talk about it?"

He let her go and turned toward the house, offering his arm again. "No, I think it best to follow my own instincts. You mustn't fret, Luce, or allow anything you may observe between Jane and myself to dampen your spirits. We'll plan your wedding, and enjoy a nice visit, and tomorrow, we'll all return to London where

I'll begin to search for all this happiness you're so mad about."

"Sherbourne indicated Jane would go directly to Eastchase Hall."

"Lucky for me, she's changed her mind." His dark gaze glittered. "I believe I'm rather looking forward to finishing out the Season this year."

Lucy grinned up at him. "Oh, Blix, how lovely! You're going to win her heart, aren't you?"

"I'm going to try, Lucy, but it won't be easy. It seems I've married a termagant with a head fashioned of granite."

They were almost to the door when she said softly, "You know, a good beginning would be an apology for whatever wrong you've committed."

"But I'm not wrong."

"Perhaps, but she *thinks* you're wrong, and that makes all the difference. Trying to convince her you're in the right will only make her more determined to believe you're not. Mayhap you should suggest she is right, after all, and say you're sorry." He was reaching for the door when she asked, "Do you love her, Blix?"

He paused. "I've only recently realized I may fair die of it, Luce."

"Well then, all will be well. You'll figure out a way to win her, I'm certain, and I'll enjoy watching you go about it." He opened the door into the hallway and as they stepped inside, there was Jane, coming toward her, a wide smile upon her beautiful face.

"Lucy, what a lovely surprise. How good of you to come and see us, and how pleased I am to know you will marry my father." Her blue eyes twinkled, much like Sherbourne's. "I daresay I won't call you mama, however, because it would be only too strange, would it not?" She laughed and moved close, looping her arm with Lucy's, urging her toward the front of the house and to the stairs. "Come along and I'll show you to your bedchamber. Is this not a lovely house? I told Blix

I wouldn't mind staying here on a regular schedule, for it is so warm and inviting and cozy. You must be tired from your journey. I'll send Polly up with hot water, and you must rest a while before dinner, which will be steak and kidney pie. It's Blix's favorite and I asked Cook to prepare it, especially for him. Oh, I am so glad you've come!" She kissed her cheek as they reached the landing, the scent of lemons drifting around her. "You're so very lovely and kind, it's no wonder Papa is mad about you. I've always admired your quiet, dignified beauty."

Lucy returned her smile, even while Sherbourne's gruff, aroused voice echoed in her head. *The very earth.* "Thank you, Jane, and I do apologize for intruding upon your honeymoon. Things got away from us last night at the Morrison's ball and before we knew it, an announcement had been made. Sherbourne thought it best he come to Kent, straightaway, before Blix heard it from someone else."

"Wise decision," she said conspiratorially as they made their way down the hallway. "Blix is so protective of you, and had he heard it from anyone other than Papa, I don't doubt we would not be anticipating your wedding right now." She stopped at a door and pushed it open, then followed her into the room. "You've only to ring, of course, if you require anything. Don't worry about William. I've just left him and Sherbourne in the nursery, playing a rousing game of miniature ninepins." She continued to smile, and Lucy noticed when it became less forced. "He's a beautiful, sweet child, and Papa is clearly crazy for him. He's always loved children, and I'd call William lucky indeed to acquire such a father as Sherbourne."

"Yes, I've thought much the same." She watched Jane go to the door. "Thank you for your kindness and hospitality, despite our dropping in without announcement, or invitation."

"Nonsense! You're welcome in our home whenever

you like, and surely no announcement is necessary among family." She moved into the hall, and pulled the door closed behind her.

Lucy stared after her for some time before her lips curved into a wide grin. Oh, yes, it was going to be great fun to watch Blix find his happiness. Jane hadn't a prayer of resisting.

"Thank you for dinner. I believe that was the very tastiest steak and kidney pie I ever did eat. Lucy appears ecstatically happy, and I'd say your father is in as fine of spirits as I've ever seen him."

Jane didn't reply, but lay in his bed, stiff as a board, waiting for him to take her so she could go down the hall to another bedroom.

He appeared to be not ready, and in no hurry, continuing to speak as though nothing was wrong, as though he hadn't betrayed her in the worst possible way, as though he could simply ignore this terrible travesty and it would somehow magically disappear.

She sighed into the dim bedchamber, staring up at the flickering shadows against the ceiling. Why would he not get on with it? She was so tired, after swimming, and then all the high drama and emotion of the remaining afternoon, then sitting through dinner, acting as though everything was well, that she was a blushing, happy bride.

It had been torture. She'd even resented him his favorite meal, and crossly wished she'd had Cook serve up a hefty portion of smoked trout. She'd not have cared. She wasn't able to do more than pick at her food anyway.

He continued talking, his long, warm, hairy leg nestled intimately next to hers, his arms folded behind his head. "I've decided we should not begin slowly, Jane."

Alarmed, she stiffened further. "Begin? Begin

what?"

"Your reintroduction into society. A soiree or musicale is too tame by half. Let's begin with a grand ball, and invite absolutely everyone, even wicked Aunt Reid. We'll have it to honor Lucy and Sherbourne's marriage."

"As you wish, Your Grace." Thank God. He'd only been speaking of a party. She could handle that with one hand tied behind her back.

The other . . . Well, he was kidding himself if he thought she'd melt into a puddle when he reached for her. Fast, slow, or anywhere in between, she would hate it. She hated that she had to submit to him in any way at all. How long would it take to conceive?

"I remember a ball from many years ago that had a nautical theme. I believe it would be intriguing to do something similar." He went off about the idea, talking and talking about what manner of decoration they might employ, what they might serve, how they might dress to reflect the theme of water and sailing.

After a time, he moved on to William, and what a lovely lad he was, and how proud Bonderant would be of him.

Eventually, he worked his way into a discourse on Crofton's crossbreds and the auction coming up in June, and how they would go to Newmarket together, make a trip of it and perhaps buy some cattle for the property in Cornwall, for the population was scarce, and they would go down and visit at summer's end, and bathe in the sea, for she had never been, and she would like it, and on he went.

Her eyes drifted closed without her realization and when they opened, it was just dawn, she was wrapped up in him and he was pressing soft, feathery kisses to her forehead. He was warm and solid and delicious. She forgot her usual insistence of rinsing her mouth and returned his kiss with tremendous passion. He was on top of her, sliding into her with a slow, insistent push before she came fully awake and remembered that she disliked him.

"You promised," he whispered when she stiffened beneath him. "You may dislike me in a little while, love, but for now, please do not."

She closed her eyes and said angrily, "Hurry up, then."

He didn't hurry up. He made love to her body, to her lips, to her face, moving over her with tenderness and gentle but firm hands.

She would have to literally be made of stone not to respond.

Her climax only served to make her more angry. As soon as he was spent, she scrambled out from under him and leapt from the bed to rush for the dressing room.

He followed, but didn't say anything as rang for his valet. Instead, he smiled at her. Why did he have to be so handsome? Why did a smile change his face to make it even more handsome? Why did even his eyes have to smile at her, look at her as though she was simply wonderful?

Within an hour, she was dressed and Rose had gone down to ask Clive to call for the carriage. She followed shortly and went into the dining room for coffee and a piece of toast. She'd only just buttered the crusty, warm bread when Blixford strolled in, smiling as he fixed his plate at the side board. She noted he was in dress clothes, not riding breeches, and she was alarmed. Did he intend to attend services with her? How could she tell him he was unwelcome? It was church, and surely no one, even a wife who disliked him, had the right to refuse him worship. She would instantly be sent to Hell, she was certain.

When she was done with her toast, she rose from the table and walked out of the dining room, despite the fact he was in the midst of a small speech about the remainder of the day, that they should stop at the

Red Lion Inn to say hallo to Mr. and Mrs. Osgood, and Lucy and Sherbourne were sure to enjoy that good lady's victuals.

She was just stepping into the carriage when he came out of the house and bounded up beside her, smiling still, as though the world pleased him enormously. "We're in for another lovely day, it appears. It will make for good traveling, will it not?"

She stared out the window and didn't reply. What the devil was he about? Did he think he could wile his way back into her good graces, merely by being cheerful? If so, he had another think coming.

He sang loudly during services and she was astonished. He'd not sung at all when they attended previously, but now, he sang as though he thought to call Abraham down from Heaven. That his rich baritone was truly lovely only served to increase her anger. She didn't want to admire anything about him. He was a cad, a bounder, a terrible betrayer. A selfish autocrat.

As the day progressed and they traveled back to London, he didn't change his demeanor. She and Lucy rode in Lucy's traveling coach while Blix and Sherbourne rode alongside, her husband astride Pendragon and her father riding the brown bay gelding, Morpheous, with William perched just in front of him. His own and Blixford's traveling coaches came behind, carrying her and Lucy's maids, Blix and Sherbourne's valets, and William's nurse, along with their trunks and bags. And young Harry, who'd decided to go up to London and begin his instruction in carpentry, under the tutelage of one of the best known cabinetmakers in all England. Blixford was to pay his way.

How could he be so kind and generous, so warm and wonderful, yet be a bounder? It was grossly unfair, that's what it was.

The Osgoods remembered them well, and hovered

about them as they dined right in front, in the public room because Blixford insisted it was such a lovely place, and he liked rubbing shoulders with the common man. Sure enough, he struck up a sheep conversation with a man seated at their long table, and before long, at least six men had gravitated into the lively discussion. Sherbourne was in the thick of it, as well, and by the time they were done with luncheon, he'd exacted a promise from one of the men to travel to Hornsby Grange and demonstrate his sheep shear invention. Blixford insisted he be allowed to observe and said he'd back the man if his claims proved true. Sherbourne declared they would be partners. Then Blix did something most unusual. He turned and indicated her, his wife. "You'd best be diligent in your demonstration, sir, for the duchess is difficult to impress. Quite the expert when it comes to sheep."

The man grinned at her and bobbed his head. "Reckon you'll be impressed enough, Yer Grace. Ain't nobody wot can shear 'em sheep quick as ol' Bob, and that's a fact."

He was clearly very proud. She smiled and said easily, "I'll look forward to it, sir. Your invention sounds most intriguing."

He beamed his pleasure and she'd swear he blushed.

Then they were on their way again. While William napped in the seat opposite them, she and Lucy discussed the wedding, although it was to be a very small affair, as hers had been. They gossiped a bit and Jane caught up on the comings and goings of old friends in London for the Season. She asked about Lucy and Sherbourne's wedding trip and was not terribly surprised when Lucy said they would wait until summer to take one. She didn't want to leave William just yet, not until he was more comfortable in his new surroundings.

They talked of many things, but they didn't talk

about Blixford, or the disaster that was their marriage. Jane thought Lucy wanted to talk about it, but wouldn't be so rude to inquire. She waited for a cue, which Jane was careful not to give. What was done was done, and continuing to talk of it or wish it were different was pointless. Besides, why depress the dear woman on the eve of her own wedding?

They arrived in London late in the afternoon and Sherbourne went off immediately to obtain a special license before it was too late in the day. Lucy declared herself exhausted and cried off of dinner, asking if they'd mind terribly if she dined in her room and made an early night of it?

Of course they did not, and within minutes of arriving at the house in Cavendish Square, she and Blixford were alone.

He was still smiling. He had done so all day. She had the low desire to slap him and demand he stop being so bloody cheerful. Their marriage, for all intents and purposes, was over. How dare he go about smiling as though all was right with his world?

She was introduced to the household staff, a veritable army, all under the direction of a very proper butler called Peatrie. Finally, she was able to go to her bedchamber and freshen up, wash her face, answer nature's call, and change into a clean gown. Afterward, she met with the housekeeper, Mrs. Humphries, and discussed what they would serve for Lucy's wedding breakfast. She asked that smoked trout be the highlighted offering.

Dinner was long and boring, with her at one end of the table and Blixford at the other, a mile away, it seemed. All the better, she thought. She'd scarcely risen and left him to his port before he was in the drawing room with her, cozying up beside her upon the sofa to read a sheaf of papers he said was a manuscript Mr. Pipkin wanted him to peruse. She attempted to read an already published book, but he constantly interrupted, laughing and reading passages from the manuscript. She finally gave up on her own story and set it aside to listen as he continued to read aloud.

Peatrie eventually brought the tea cart and she poured while Blix read. She absolutely couldn't help smiling at some of the passages. It appeared Mr. Pipkin had indeed found a new prodigy authoress. She was a young lady from Yorkshire whose story was an honest, slightly painful look at the sometimes ridiculous strictures of the *ton*, of the elaborate rituals of the upper crust of English society.

She dropped her spoon and when she bent to retrieve it, spied something purple beneath the sofa. Reaching for it, she withdrew a long ostrich plume, dyed a most awful shade of purple. Her memory flashed a story Robert had relayed to her in a letter, of one of Sherbourne's practical jokes that had to do with Wrotham being a stick and Sherbourne dressing as a matron in full purple regalia. He gave no details, so she suspected it had to do with lightskirts, probably that Wrotham was involved with one, or some such. She'd wished she had seen Sherbourne, and had laughed merely at the thought of him dressed as a matron.

"What have you got there?" her husband asked curiously.

She waved it about. "I believe this belongs to Mrs. Sherry's turban." Briefly, she told him the story, then watched as realization dawned on his face. He quickly resumed reading, but when Peatrie returned to inquire if they needed anything, he asked, "Did Mrs. Sherry pay a visit to my sister while I was gone?"

"Yes, Your Grace, she did." His brows lifted slightly. "She's quite a large lady, with bad knees. I believe Lady Bonderant was happy to receive her, however, and they spent a good amount of time in her bedchamber, having a nice coze. Mrs. Sherry was delighted to take home some dress patterns for her daughter, Imogene."

Blix shot her a glance before nodding thoughtfully toward the butler. "Very good, Peatrie. Thank you. We've discovered a part of Mrs. Sherry's headpiece here beneath the sofa. I wonder if you'd be so good as to have it delivered to her, with my compliments for attending my sister in my absence? I believe she's staying in Grosvenor Square with the Earl of Sherbourne."

"I'll do so immediately, Your Grace." Peatrie made his way toward Jane and took the plume before bowing himself out.

When the drawing room door closed, Jane blinked at her husband. "I'd not have thought it of you, Blixford. A practical joke?"

He shrugged as he looked back to the manuscript, but not before she caught the distinct twinkle of devilment in his eyes. "Shall I continue?"

"I suppose," she said, trying not to sound too interested, even though she was dying to know how Miss Engstrom would manage to get Mr. Donovan to come up to scratch, or how her sister, Lucinda, would fare during her first country dance, or, in fact, how Mr. Tenwhistle might manage to convince his uncle, the marquess, to fund his exploratory trip to the continent of Africa.

The hour grew late by the time he was finished. He looked up and asked, "What say you? Shall we publish Miss G.'s manuscript?"

"Of course. It's delightful." She rose from the sofa and almost, *almost* thanked him for reading it to her.

But she did not.

She went upstairs and made ready for bed, then climbed in and awaited him. He wasn't long opening the door from her dressing room, which connected to his, and his bedchamber beyond. He strode in, completely naked, his shaft already partially erect.

Good. He would do the deed and be gone quickly.

He was *still* smiling. Surely his face would crack if he kept it up much longer.

Moving next to the bed, he hauled her to a sit and quickly discarded her night rail, despite her protests. "I want you naked," he said simply as he slid in beside her and drew her near to hold her close and kiss her, apparently unconcerned with her total lack of response and the absence of any limberness in her body. She was as a plank of wood. It took a great amount of concentration to remain so. He was determined not to be fair at all, not to honor her request that he be done with his conjugal duties as swiftly as possible.

No, instead he moved his mouth across her skin, very slowly, lingering at her breasts before he moved on to the apex of her thighs. He spread them apart and kissed her there, before he opened his mouth and licked her. She closed her eyes and thought about sheep. She thought of the book she'd been reading.

He began to suck her essence, the sounds he made reverberating about the room, making her even more aware of what he was doing. She almost moaned when he slid a finger inside of her. She bit her lip and concentrated on moving her thoughts far away. Tomorrow, she would go over the household with Mrs. Humphries, make a list of linens and dishes and . . . oh, dear God, now he was loving her with his tongue, mimicking his finger, which had reemployed itself by rubbing firm circles around her nipple, coaxing it into a hard peak.

"Do get on with it, Your Grace." She'd intended to sound cold and imperious. Instead, she sounded deliriously breathless and needy. She may as well have said, *Please, for the love of God, come into me, right this instant, because I can't wait another moment!* He might be a cad, but he was very smart, for he wisely made no comment as he moved back up her body. He paid particular attention to her breasts, making her shiver, before he crouched above her and slowly, deliberately pushed inside of her.

She waited for him to move.

He did not.

She waited a while longer.

He remained still, poised above her, resting most of the weight of his upper body along his forearms, his belly against hers, his thighs against the mattress, nestled within hers. He stared down at her, mere inches between their faces. Then she felt it. He jumped within her. He did it again. It was intensely erotic, both of them so still, it was impossible not to focus on where they were joined, at the length and heat of him buried within her body, jumping. How did he do that? Why did she enjoy it so much? *Bloody hell.*

At long last, he began to move, slowly at first, increasing his rhythm as he went along, then suddenly, with no warning at all, he withdrew and moved to the bed beside her, turned her to face away from him and slid up into her from behind, spooning her body against his, one arm around her, his hand massaging her breasts, the other hand holding her leg up that he could have access to her center as he pounded into her.

Against her will, she climaxed. It was like a slap to her pride that she didn't simply reach orgasm —she fairly came off the bed, and let out a short, tight scream of surprise and euphoric pleasure.

Again, he didn't say a word, but kept her there, next to him, while he stroked again and again, until at last, he completed with a deep, happy groan.

She immediately tried to move away from him, but his arm was a vice lock about her, holding her still. "Stay, Jane, just a while, just until I am not hard any longer."

Relaxing against him, his shaft still buried in her body, she waited and waited, and didn't realize when her eyes drifted shut.

When they opened, it was dawn, she was wrapped up in his arms, their legs tangled together, and he was there, as he'd been the previous morning, pressing soft kisses to her forehead. Unlike before, she was aware of the circumstances, remembered that she disliked him. But she was also aware he wouldn't let her get up until he'd had his way, until he'd found an ease for the throbbing erection she felt against her belly. He wouldn't allow her to lie still and stiff and unresponsive, and she hated that she had not enough discipline to resist him. Once again, he moved over her and brought her to climax, and afterward, instead of scurrying from the bed, she rolled away, dejected that this was not going as she'd planned, not at all, and promptly went back to sleep.

Incredibly, when she awoke, he was there, yet again, his groin against her bottom, his cock slipping between her thighs, still slick with his seed from before. He knew she was awake, and his lips moved close to her ear to whisper, "There is nothing in all the world so beautiful as you when you come for me, Jane." He moved against her, his member there, between her legs, sliding back and forth along the slickness he'd left behind an hour ago. "I'm all over you, as you're all over me, and just the scent of us, together, is enough to make me want you again." He moved away and rolled her over, to her back, then stacked all of the bed pillows beneath her head and shoulders. Rising to his knees, he moved between her legs and sat on his heels before reaching for her feet and placing them flat upon the mattress, just next to his thickly muscled thighs. He lifted her hips and moved beneath her, positioned himself, watched her face as he filled her. She was not sitting up, but the pillows had raised her enough that she could see them, could watch what he did to her.

She shouldn't look. It was too erotic, too stimulating. Forcing herself to meet his gaze, to not look again, she managed to whisper, "I dislike you more and more." To her dismay, it came out as though she said, *I'm mad about you, deeply in love with you, can never live without you.*

Evidently unconcerned that she disliked him more and more, he smiled slowly and continued to stroke her, his gaze moving between them, along with his warm fingers, drawing her eyes to follow. This time, she couldn't look away, was mesmerized and fascinated enough to temporarily forget that she disliked him, that she was furious with him, that she didn't want to speak to him.

"Ah, love, I've come to know your body, to know when you are close . . . so close. This is a gift you give me, each and every time. I'm in awe, truly."

"If I could stop . . . I would." She was panting, trying hard to hold back, to not give in, to not give him *anything*, most especially a gift.

His smile never faltered, and neither did his body, or his fingers. "But you can't stop, can you, love? You were born with a passionate, hungry soul, and starving it would be cruel. Surely you wouldn't deny your very soul?"

It didn't make sense on any rational, logical level that the sight of his thick, hard cock sliding into her curls could be this intensely exciting, but it was. Amazingly so. He was beautiful, from the top of his silky, dark haired head, to his handsome, strong face, to his broad, masculine chest, to his flat belly, to the long length of his member, which could bring her such tremendous gratification. It was unfair. She could so much more easily despise him if he were stooped, corpulent, and ugly, with a wart upon his nose and a failing penis, unable to rise to the occasion. Instead, he was masculine beauty and raw power and smoldering sexuality, irresistible to her.

He was also dead on the money about her. Despite her pathetic attempt to hold out, to get up from the bed without giving him what he wanted, she stepped close to the edge of reason and leapt, her body soaring with undeniable, indescribable bliss.

His expression became almost fierce as his smile suddenly and swiftly disappeared. He rose to his knees, lifted her legs to rest against his shoulders, and his slow, languid strokes became hard, violent thrusts. She was falling from her peak, gasping for breath as though she'd run a great distance, but the look on his face, possessive and concentrated with desire, coupled with the movement of his body in hers and the sound of their skin coming together, again and again and again, brought her back to the edge. She knew, with but a bit of strong stimulation, she would go off again, and she wanted to, oh how she wanted to. A second time, just after the first, would be incredible, wouldn't it? She had to know, demanded he give it to her.

Without consciously thinking about it, she began to urge him on, to beg, to plead, to insist. "Please, Michael, don't slow down! I want . . . faster! Yes, hard like that! Harder!" Her body writhed upon the sheets, desperate for release again, out of her control, far away from her will, which she'd left behind many moments ago. She met his eyes and could see he was close. If he went before she did, this would be lost, and she would die of need, surely she would. "No, not yet! Please, *please* wait for me! Oh, God, make me come . . . now . . . *do it now!*"

His fingers curled around her ankles and pushed until her legs bent at the knees. He pressed them against her breasts, until she was curled in upon herself, leaving her bottom and her core completely open and vulnerable. He moved closer, his thighs surrounding her. His thrusts slowed, but she could feel each one that much more intensely, moaned when he touched her womb, he was so very long, stretched and ready. "Now, Jane, it's almost time, you're almost there, and I'm waiting. I'm patient and would wait forever, but don't make me. Come for me, love, gift me again, quickly, for I'm out of my mind with wanting you."

She reached for his hands, clutching her ankles, and held tight as every drop of blood within her body caught fire and screamed through her, until she was sweating and shaking uncontrollably. Her head went back, digging into the pillows, her throat stretched taut, making her voice sound foreign and strange to her ears when she shouted in mad, delirious glee. It was glorious. It was like the first, but a thousand times more intense. Exhausting. Incredible.

Perhaps it was so marvelous because he met her at the top, and for the first time since they married, he expressed a loud cry, almost a shout. His big body went rigid and she felt him, deep inside, pulsing and plentiful.

When it was over —and it seemed to take a very long time for it to be over, each of them panting and perspiring and staring at the other with looks that didn't speak of a ruined marriage —and as they drifted back to earth, he said in a raw, shaking voice, "You're mine, Jane, will always be mine, and no force of your will, or your anger, or your dislike of me will keep me away from you. I'd not cause you distress within yourself, always fighting to resist this, so I'm telling you, straight out, you can give up and feel safe in the knowledge that it is I who makes you succumb, not a weak will. To speak plainly, you have no choice. I'll not love a board, and will always do whatever I must to coax your desire from where you would hide it."

She wetted her lips, as they were incredibly dry. "Why?"

He stayed there, on his knees, still inside of her, still partially hard, and said roughly, "Because I want you. I need you. I desire you and no other. I will not take a mistress, will not lay with another woman. Even if you become pregnant, Jane, I will ask this of you —nay demand it. Even if you give me ten sons, and feel your duty has been done, I will not be able to leave you alone. Ever."

Staring up at him, she could think of no argument, no way to persuade him. It appeared she would not have a loving husband, but she would have a lusty one.

For the first time since she'd overheard his words to her father and realized how horribly he'd betrayed her, she wished he would apologize. She'd not thought it would do any good, but of a sudden, she wanted him to say he was sorry, to admit he was wrong, to ask forgiveness. She looked up at his determined expression and sighed, knowing he never would. He was too caught up in his own pride, his need to be right. A true aristocratic autocrat. He would never be sorry because he could never allow himself to be wrong.

CHAPTER 14

Several hours later, Michael stood with Jane on the front steps of the London house and waved goodbye to Lucy and Sherbourne and young William as their carriage drove away, headed for Sherbourne's house in Grosvenor Square. Jane's brothers had recently taken their leave as well. Michael had not asked the newlyweds' plans for the day, but William volunteered that they were to go to the park, where he would practice his archery, and afterward, they would go for an ice at Gunther's. Michael thought it sounded grand, and decided he and Jane would take their son to the park to practice archery, and take him for an ice at Gunther's afterward.

Just as soon as they had a son.

His father-in-law had pressed a note into his hand as he left and Michael glanced down at it, curious. Turning back to the house, he stepped inside and as Peatrie closed the door, he broke the seal and read Sherbourne's strong, elegant script. The note indicated poor Mrs. Sherry had expired the moment she heard he was to marry Lucy, that the dear lady felt her existence was no longer required. He would not mourn, he said, because he wasn't overly fond of her, but sweet Lucy had taken quite a liking to her, said she would always remember their lovely coze. He went on to suggest that Michael take a cue from dear Mrs. Sherry, for she well knew, surprise and spontaneous delights were easily accomplished, and irresistible to women. The ending of the note was of a serious nature. He expressed gratitude for his blessing of Lucy's marriage, his friendship, and his patience with Jane. Then he reminded him of haylofts and harridans and nasty, mean goats, and urged him to be sincere, that the taste of a wife's love and esteem was far more pleasing than a dish of pride. He'd given it up years ago, and didn't miss it in the least.

He tucked the note into his coat pocket and went in search of his wife, who'd taken off to parts unknown as soon as they came back inside. He found her in the kitchen, conferring with Cook about dinner. He excused her, drew her aside and said in a low voice, "I've an errand to run, but will be back for luncheon. Afterward, I believe we should make our calls, don't you?"

"Yes, Your Grace."

He sucked in a deep breath and let it out slowly. Calmly. "If you continue to address me in that manner, I'll insist you practice at the pianoforte two hours, each day."

"Yes, Your . . . Blixford."

Turning to leave, he spied the leftover smoked trout and turned back around. "By the by, the cat was most pleased with your selections for the wedding breakfast. Regrettably, we will soon be overrun with rodents, as he is now too fat and lazy to catch them. Might I suggest we not serve smoked trout again anytime soon?"

He swore her eyes were laughing, but her voice was sober when she repeated, "Yes, Your . . . Blixford."

He left then and went about his errand as quickly as possible, but it took much more time than he anticipated, and by the time he returned home, she'd already had lunch and was cooling her heels in the drawing room, pacing about, clearly anxious and nervous about the calls. He realized she was afraid of her reception, that perhaps people wouldn't receive her, despite her marriage to him. Deciding not to reassure her, because it would necessarily point out that he was aware of her anxiety and she would hate that, he instead asked if she would ring for tea, and have some mince pie brought up along with it. He was very hungry, having not eaten much breakfast, and missing luncheon. He was feeling a bit out of sorts, but after a cup of tea and the pie, he was in a better frame of mind, ready to go out.

She looked very fetching in a walking gown the color of peaches, with long sleeves and a trim of dark orange about the waist. Her bonnet was simple, but elegant, and she carried a matching reticule, into which she placed the cards he'd ordered for her before they left London. He'd had an odd, very sentimental moment when he went round to the print shop to collect the cards. Seeing her name there, coupled with his, made it all seem much more permanent, and it pleased him.

As they left the house in the curricle, he considered his course of action and toyed with a number of ideas, but he couldn't determine which would ensure the desired result.

He'd thought of Sherbourne and Lucy's advice, many times, for lengthy periods, but it didn't fit, wouldn't work. His and Jane's marriage wasn't ordinary, and to bow at her feet, admit he was wrong, humbly apologize, and declare undying love for her, no matter how sincere he might be, would not make the lasting impression he needed. Within a month, some other dilemma was bound to crawl from the wainscot, and they would be at loggerheads, yet again. He was tired of drama, of worry and anxiety and unhappiness. He was not intended to be gloomy, surely. There was a time when he rather looked forward to things, anticipated the day when he rose of a morning.

Not until Jane came to live with him did he remember those days, and long for them. Perhaps because waking up beside her filled him with hope and eager anticipation of what the day might bring. Even now, with her wishing him to the devil, he loved reaching for her warm, soft body in the chill of early dawn, dozing with her wrapped around him, slowly waking with quiet desire.

Soon, very soon, she wouldn't wish him to the devil. She would look at him as she did before, as though she expected the sun to rise and set in him. He'd become accustomed to it in a very short time, and now that it was gone, he missed it dreadfully. That he loved her had not been such a startling revelation, but the realization that he could, that he might want to die if he lost her, but would not go mad after all, was certainly amazing.

It changed everything. He was simply unsure how to go about telling her, how to set things back to rights. He continued to think about it, confident he would come up with something.

They decided to call on the Marchioness of Bloomsbury first. As she was undoubtedly the staunchest, most persnickety of all society matrons, a stalwart guard of the respectability of the *ton*, passing muster with the old battle-axe would be a clear indication of their reception in other homes.

Jane was brave and held herself as a duchess, the slight tremor of her hand upon his arm as they climbed the steps of the Bloomsbury house the only indication of her anxiety. He patted her hand and smiled down at her before he lifted the knocker. "You are very beautiful. Is this a new gown?"

"Actually, no, it's from several years ago."

"We will go to the modiste and order some new frocks if you like." For the moment, while she was afraid and nervous, she forgot to dislike him. Her smile was tremulous, her blue eyes wide, her fingers tightening against his arm. "Yes, Blix, that would be lovely, thank you. I really should update, I suppose, especially if we are to attend any social engagements. Oh! Here is the butler . . . oh, my." She grew an inch, straightening her back as they were waved into the front hall.

He presented his card and said in his best aristocratic, imperious tone, "The Duke and Duchess of Blixford, to call upon Lady Bloomsbury."

They were shown into a small parlor to the east side of the hall, and asked to wait while the butler went to see if the marchioness was in.

Jane remained on his arm while he glanced at his watch. Even if they were received, it might be accounted for as a mere courtesy to him. The true test was a matter of time. The longer they were made to wait before being escorted to the drawing room, the less they were deemed acceptable.

Minutes crawled by and with every one, his wife's eyes widened a bit further.

After ten minutes, she was pale and shaky. "Please," she whispered, "can we go?"

"Not until we've been told she's not in." She was mortified. He was livid with rage. What went on here? He'd not actually expected to receive a cut of any kind. She was a duchess. The daughter of an earl. Her past indiscretion of jilting the man who ruined her was not beyond the pale, was completely reconciled by their marriage. Something was very wrong. They stood in the center of the parlor and waited another ten minutes before the butler returned and asked them to accompany him up the stairs.

They were announced in the drawing room and all within immediately became silent.

As they crossed the room toward the marchioness, who rose from her seat and watched their progress, he noted friends and acquaintances seated about the room, none of them looking in his and Jane's direction. It was a cut from all sides. It was a disaster.

Jane apparently held a well of hidden courage and

he admired her tremendously when she swept into a beautiful curtsy and smiled perfectly —not too friendly, not too coldly —at the marchioness. The older woman didn't return the smile, and didn't greet her. She didn't, in fact, look at Jane at all, but rather focused on him. "Good afternoon, Duke."

He sketched a bow that was close to an insult, it was so slight. He was hard pressed not to strangle the old biddy and demand to know by what right she would give Jane the cut direct. "Good afternoon, Lady Bloomsbury." He stepped back, offered his arm to Jane, they turned and left.

Back on the sidewalk, he handed her up into the curricle, tossed a coin to the groom and they were off. She didn't speak. She didn't cry. She was a statue.

He took her home and pressed a kiss to her palm before watching her ascend the stairs. Somehow, he'd known not to say anything, or try to reassure her. Truthfully, he had no reassurances. It was clear her marriage to him had changed nothing. She was still a pariah, shunned by society.

It made no sense, and he was determined to discover what went on. He left again and went to his club, acting as though all was well as he took a brandy and walked about, greeting friends, smiling affably. He was offered congratulations upon Lucy's marriage to Sherbourne, but no one mentioned his marriage to Jane.

At last, he decided to step outside propriety in order to discover what the devil was going on. He cornered Wrotham and after a few polite congenials, said smoothly, "The duchess and I paid a call to Lady Bloomsbury this afternoon."

Wrotham, his shirt points so tall and stiff it was surely difficult to turn his head, sniffed meaningfully. "How did you find that lady?"

"I reckon cozying up to an iceberg would provide more warmth. After waiting twenty minutes to be shown into the drawing room, Jane was handed the cut direct and we were not invited to sit." He lowered his voice. "It would be most helpful if you might shed some light on this matter, Wrotham. I'd certainly thought marriage to me would bring Jane back into the fold."

The man was clearly very uncomfortable, his face flaming with color as he drained his glass and waved to the steward for another. When at last he met Michael's gaze, he sighed as if in defeat. "I'd ask you not kill the messenger, Blixford."

"On the contrary, I'd be humbly grateful for information from the messenger and not in the least inclined to inflict harm upon him."

"You may change your mind." He handed his empty to the steward and accepted another brandy before he said, almost in a whisper, "Just after your marriage, after you'd gone from London, a rumor began to circulate, and as with all rumors, it caught like wildfire. Seems a gentleman returned from business in Edinburgh, a transaction involving some crossbreds offered by a Brian MacDougal, recently become the Earl of Haversham, after his father's death. Haversham indicated to this gentleman that he'd heard Lady Jane was returned to England then jested about her attempt to regain her respectability. He insinuated he had been . . ." he paused and swallowed a large gulp of brandy before he finished, "intimate with her, that she was in fact his mistress, all the years she was in Scotland. He hoped the gentleman would convey to London society the nature of her pilgrimage to Scotland, that an unwary suitor might avoid being caught in marriage with a . . ." he took another great gulp, "harlot."

Somehow, he wasn't surprised. He'd wondered if the man might exact his revenge on Jane for shooting him in his bollocks, and here it was. He was amazed how calm he was. It was simple, really. He would kill

MacDougal. He would stretch things out and ensure it was painful and horrible, that the man would beg for death to relieve him of his misery. "Wrotham, you're a good chap, and I've no doubt I'll have the honor of returning this favor in future."

He looked nonplussed. "How can you take this so easily, Blix? Good God, man, it is the worst thing. The very worst! It's untrue, of course, as I well know. Why, I've known Lady Jane since she was in the schoolroom, can call Sherbourne one of my closest friends. But there are those who don't know her true, sweet nature, who only see her pistols and hard riding and talk of farming. Her very unconventional behavior only lends credibility to a rumor such as this." He drained the brandy and his shoulders slumped. "This will kill Sherbourne, surely. I believe the only reason he's not aware of it is because of his friendship with Lady Bonderant. They spent a great deal of time together these past weeks, and I daresay he was not attuned to much else, or he'd have heard . . . something. I'd pray God he never hear of it, but that's not possible. Just as you have surmised there is a problem, so will he. Were I not an abject coward, I would go and tell him myself, that he would be forewarned."

"Do you suppose her brothers are aware?"

Wrotham shook his head, but only just barely. Those shirt points bordered on ridiculous. "They're all known for their over-the-top protective stance toward Jane. I've no doubt not a soul in London would have the nerve to even whisper about Jane when any of them are present. That person might wind up feeding the fishes in the Thames." His look was sympathetic. "I'm terribly sorry you've had to find out this way, Blix, and it wounds me for Lady Jane to be hurt so."

He grasped Wrotham's shoulder. "If I were to ask your assistance, would you be willing?"

His eyes widened. "Blix, will you call him out? Do you ask me to act as second?"

"Nothing of the kind. Calling a gentleman out suggests he deserves the honor of a request for satisfaction."

Wrotham's eyes widened further. "Revenge, then?"

"It's said revenge is a dish best served cold, but in this situation, I believe straight from the oven is what's called for. May I count on you?"

"It would be my pleasure and honor." He stood straight once more. "What do you plan?"

"Please, let us have a seat and I'll tell you."

Half an hour later, he thanked Wrotham and took his leave, then headed for Sherbourne's townhouse. He wouldn't ask his assistance, but he believed her father deserved to hear the blasted rumor from his son-in-law, instead of via sly innuendos in a social setting.

Sherbourne was out, having taken Lucy and William to the park. Michael returned to his curricle and went there directly, driving through, searching. When he located them, he noted William was very adept with his small bow and short arrows. He noted Lucy was beaming proudly, and Sherbourne was staring at her as though he expected her to disappear. If he were not in a cold rage, he'd be warmed and fairly amused by Sherbourne's obvious besotted state.

His father-in-law, now also brother-in-law —and wasn't that odd? —turned as he drove up, his expression changing from rapt admiration to concern in a blink. "Blix, what's this?"

"Will you come up with me for a turn about the park?" He nodded at Lucy. "I've need to borrow your husband for a moment, sister. I pray you won't mind?"

"Of course not. Is everything all right, Blix? Is Jane well?"

"Yes, she's fine." Actually, she wasn't fine at all, but he didn't wish to say so to Lucy. "I'd ask your forbearance, Luce, and allow me to speak to Sherbourne at once."

He climbed into the curricle and Michael took off.

He didn't wait, didn't mince words. Straight out, he told Sherbourne what had happened and what he'd learned.

Her father was quiet as they drove along, then said, "If you don't kill him, surely you know I will."

"I admit, that was my first resolution, but I don't believe it's for the best. For one thing, if the man's dead, he can't refute what he's said. For another, it will be murder, no two ways about it, regardless of justification, and Jane would never get past it. She hates the man, of course, but she doesn't hate me, and she'll be convinced I'm doomed to Hell were I to commit murder. Jane worries much about Hell."

"You don't say. I don't suppose I knew."

He told him about her nurse.

"Never did like that woman. She was there only a short while before I dismissed her, but it appears she was with Jane long enough to inflict her demented cruelty upon her." He paused, then asked, "If you won't kill him, what do you plan?"

"While I was away, I had my solicitor make some enquiries and he tells me MacDougal is likewise invested in a crossbreeding program. I was pondering how I might use this information to gain satisfaction for his ill treatment of Jane, but my plans didn't involve anything of a public nature, for obvious reasons." He leveled a look at his father-in-law. "Now it appears his comeuppance must be made very public."

Sherbourne was a quick study. "You'll draw him to London."

"Wrotham has agreed to assist. He'll write to MacDougal and express interest in his crossbreds, making mention of several other gentlemen who are likewise interested. My solicitor tells me MacDougal is in financial straits since the death of his father and the discovery of some significant debt. The woman he was to marry cried off and he must now find a wealthy bride to save him from debtors' prison. Wrotham will suggest he come for a visit, to discuss the possibility of him investing in MacDougal's program, and to enjoy the remainder of the Season."

"He'll be unable to resist temptation, with an eye toward Wrotham's money, and the possibility of securing an heiress."

"That's my hope. To ensure he has no worry of meeting Jane or myself, she and I will retire to Eastchase Hall until he arrives in London, when we will return, but not openly. With your permission, we'll stay with you until it's done, that no one knows we're in town. With Wrotham to assist, we'll determine which engagement might draw the largest crowd, and when things are in full swing, Jane and I will arrive. It will, I am certain, bring the matter to a head, and the truth will out."

Sherbourne turned to look at him. "Blixford, I'm astonished."

He listened for a disapproving note to accompany his words, but heard none. In fact, he appeared to be astonished in a rather good way. "Why is that?"

"I've long understood your desire to live reclusively and your determination to retain your privacy, and have an even finer understanding after learning more details of your past from Lucy. That you would do something like this, in essence air dirty laundry before all of society, knowing it could well backfire and exacerbate the situation, which will make you as much a pariah as Jane, is, simply, astonishing. I find myself quite proud of you, if you don't mind me saying so."

Focused on the drive, Michael smiled, despite the depressing situation. "I don't mind, Sherbourne. Thank you. As to becoming a pariah with Jane, I'd far rather join her than leave her alone in her shunned state. But I suspect this will work, that Jane will be as competent at supervising the washing of our metaphorical laundry as she is with the real thing."

They went along in silence for a while before Michael said quietly, "It remains to be seen, however, if I'll be able to keep myself from killing him, risk of Hell be damned." He would never, so long as he lived, forget the look in Jane's lovely eyes when Lady Bloomsbury gave her the cut. He couldn't blame the marchioness, as much as he'd like to do so. MacDougal was considered a gentleman, his word above reproach. No one thought to question him, and if he claimed she had been his mistress, it must surely be true. Her elevation to duchess couldn't absolve her of anything so low and common as becoming a man's mistress. Until MacDougal publicly recanted, Jane would never be accepted.

As sure as he was that his plan would work, he decided upon an additional course of action, just in case. He would acquire an ace in his pocket that MacDougal wouldn't expect.

"I'm sorry to ruin your wedding day, but I wouldn't want you to learn of this from out of nowhere, from someone not your family."

"Of course, and I appreciate it, Blix. As to my wedding day being ruined, never think it. As soon as you set me down, I know you will take care of things, that you'll see to Jane's comfort and safety, and all will be well. Oh, I'll worry about her, of course, and be saddened for her hurt, but I assure you, my day isn't ruined. I'm married now to a woman I hold in high regard, her son is a delight, the sun is shining, my son-in-law is clever enough to plot my daughter's revenge, and in an hour or so, I will be enjoying an ice at Gunther's. Not ruined at all, Blix. Do call on me when you learn anything else, and keep me apprised of your progress, won't you?"

He nodded as he drew the horses to a standstill. "I'll write from Eastchase. I expect we'll leave tomorrow morning."

"Safe travels, son, and do give a kiss to Jane from

her papa and remind her how much I love her." He bounded down from the curricle and they all waved goodbye as Michael drove away.

He was out of the park gates and halfway home when he realized Sherbourne had called him son.

As soon as she arrived home, Jane had undressed and crawled into bed, uncharacteristically weepy and feeling cold and horrid. When Blixford returned, he didn't knock, but came right in and sat upon the bed and massaged her shoulders until she was relaxed and sleepy. She drifted off, and when she awoke, he was still there, but in his dressing robe. The sun had set, though dusk still lit the room. "I've asked dinner to be served here, Jane, so we may speak in privacy and you can continue to rest."

Listless and depressed, she only nodded. What did it matter?

He drew the portieres and lit the fire, along with the candles. A short while later, dinner was delivered and laid out upon a small table from the drawing room, brought up by a footman and placed before the fire. As they ate, Blixford told her of his activities during the remainder of the afternoon, of what he'd learned from Wrotham. Jane was stunned.

Then he told her of his plan and she was impressed at his cleverness.

Staring at her plate, at her mostly uneaten food, she said quietly, "I'm so very sorry. I've brought shame upon you and I'm most humbly apologetic."

"You've nothing to apologize for, so I cannot accept."

She didn't argue, but drank more of her wine, then got up and crawled back into her bed. "If it's acceptable to you, I believe I'll wait until morning to call Rose to come and help me pack. I've not the energy to do so just now."

He got into bed with her and gathered her in his

arms. "All will be well, Jane, wait and see. We'll deal with the blackguard and he'll never hurt you again."

"I wish now I had killed him when I had the chance. I believe it might be worth going to Hell, just for the satisfaction." Her tears returned. "I don't understand, Michael, truly I don't. How can anyone be so cruel and horrible, so lacking in honor? I feel . . . this is just how I felt when . . . after he . . ." She clung to him and cried until she was hiccupping.

He never let her go, but somehow produced a handkerchief. He dried her tears and she blew her nose, then settled down in his arms, the storm past. "Thank you."

"You're welcome."

"I love you, Michael," she said, just before she hiccupped, "but I'm afraid I still dislike you."

"It's quite all right, love. I'm working on that problem, as well."

"You are?"

"Hmm. You'll see. Just relax now and go to sleep, and when you wake up, you'll feel much better, I promise."

"Will not." She hiccupped again. "You're going to make love to me and I'll dislike you more and more."

"Will it be how you disliked me this morning?"

"I hope so," she said, her eyes drifting closed.

She slept hard, dreamless and unmoving, then came awake of a sudden, instinctively reaching for him. The bed was empty. She sat up and saw him in the chair next to the fire, a brandy snifter in one long fingered hand. "Blix," she called out sleepily, "what are you doing?"

"Watching you sleep."

"Well do stop and come to bed. I'm cold."

His smile was interesting. "In a while, love."

Lying down, she burrowed into the covers and dropped back to sleep. Later, she knew not how much later, she woke again and reached for an empty space.

She sat up. He stood at the window, the portiere's open, moonlight streaming in. "Michael, what are you doing?"

"Watching you sleep."

"Looks to me like you're watching the moon."

He turned and he was magnificent in moonlight. He was naked. In spite of herself, she heated with desire. "Aren't you chilled?"

"On the contrary," he replied, "I'm quite warm."

She noticed then, he was fully erect. "Did I mention that I'm cold? Won't you please come to bed?"

He did, and it didn't take long for her to be quite warm as well. Afterward, she went to sleep in his arms and didn't wake again until the sun was up, having spent the remainder of the night spooned into his warm, solid form.

Eastchase Hall was just as she remembered, a pleasing blend of old and new architecture. The stone walls of the central, cavernous hall, built over three centuries earlier, were hung with standards, each bearing the Blixford coat of arms and varying symbols and colors of characteristics considered necessary to the ducal title: courage, faith, honor, loyalty to the crown, and stewardship. A fireplace twice as tall as herself and doubled in width was set into the wall opposite the massive, oak doors, flanked on one side by a curving staircase and on the other by an old fashioned minstrel gallery, its screen an elaborately carved section of juniper. An enormous, intricate iron chandelier, maneuverable by heavy chain and pulleys, hung above all, fashioned to hold two hundred candles. The central building included the hall, the kitchens, a morning room, a dining room, an extensive library, a study, and a drawing room surely large enough to host a small ball. An actual ballroom had been added above stairs, directly above the hall, adjacent to a long portrait gallery, which was notable for its absence of portraits. Three separate wings went off from the central hall section of the house, one occupied entirely by the army of servants employed by the estate, another reserved for guests, and the third housing the ducal family apartments.

Jane remembered worrying she would get lost, the house was so enormous, but Annabel had drawn it out for her, and once she had a clear idea of the layout, she found it easy to navigate. Everything was oversized, from the doors, to the rooms, even the furniture. The bed in her chamber was of ordinary size, but the bed in Blixford's chamber was huge, long and wide. He said she would sleep with him, and he wouldn't allow her to hide in the massive thing, no matter how far he had to come after her. She argued that she desired her own chamber, and he relented to her own dressing room, but drew a hard line at her own chamber. What was the point? he asked. If she would sleep in her own bed, he would be there anyway, so why not make use of his enormous, extremely soft one?

Their journey had taken all afternoon and the better part of the following day. They stopped at an inn to spend the night and left mid-morning, Blixford saying they were in no hurry, so may as well go along at a leisurely pace.

Once they arrived at Eastchase Hall, she was introduced to the upper servants; the housekeeper, Mrs. Daniels, a dour-faced woman with small eyes, the butler, Bagwell, a starchy man of indeterminate years, the majordomo, Hopkins, who appeared to be into the wine a bit too much, his breath scented and his cheeks red, and the head gardener, Moseby, whose hands were entirely too clean for a man in his position. Cook was the sole servant who appeared the least bit friendly and helpful. As much as anything, Jane resented the obvious attitude of the others, as if they clearly didn't need to pay her much attention. She was the duchess, and mistress of Eastchase Hall, but she was most likely doomed to die within a year, so why bother paying her any mind? Or respect?

Jane had been in residence exactly two days when she caught Mrs. Daniels pilfering the wax candles, no doubt intending to sell them and pocket the money. Wax candles were very dear and Jane was beyond incensed. She dismissed the woman on the spot, but Mrs. Daniels refused to leave, saying the duke hired her, and if he wanted her gone, he would say so. Within ten minutes, he did just that, and informed the remainder of the servants that Jane was the mistress of his home, and her word was as his. Nevertheless, Bagwell was openly surly and after he failed to answer her ring from the drawing room the following afternoon, he too was sent packing. When a clearly inebriated Hopkins stumbled and landed in her lap as he attempted to deliver a letter, he was dismissed. That left Moseby, who apparently saw his future a bit more clearly, and of a sudden, he had dirty hands.

She spent the following week interviewing prospective replacements and was pleased with her choices. Blixford noted Mr. and Mrs. Dashing, a lively, portly couple recently out of work due to the death of their longtime employer, were very similar to Hester and Clive at Beckinsale House. She hadn't noticed, but his observation was spot on, and she wrote to Hester of the new additions to the staff at Eastchase, and that they were missed, evidently even more than Jane realized. She and Mrs. Dashing, with the able assistance of Mr. Dashing, spent a great deal of time preparing an inventory of the house, making a list of items needed for purchase, or repair. She left it to Mr. Dashing to find a replacement majordomo, and within a few days, Geoffrey had joined the ranks. He quickly and adequately rallied the footmen into shape, seeing that their livery was cleaned and repaired, instructing them in proper footman form.

The second week of her stay at Eastchase, she received a letter from Miriam, indicating her direction, a lovely, cozy manor house near to Twykham, in Shropshire. Blixford said he'd purchased the home from Lord Twykham, along with several surrounding acres. Jane was pleased and wrote to Miriam, sending along the wee baby boots she'd purchased in Kent, and expressing her good will and hopes for the safe progress of her pregnancy, reminding her to advise Jane if she required anything at all.

They settled into a routine, as they had at Beckinsale House. They rose early and rode, returned for breakfast, then went about estate business, Jane going along at Blixford's insistence. She was amazed and impressed at the vastness of Eastchase, and couldn't help but admire her husband's evident talent for managing it. The tenants' respect for him was clear, and the two stewards he employed, Mr. O'Brien and his assistant, Mr. Perkins, were able and competent and obviously thought much of Blixford. He made a point of telling each of them, if he was ever absent and they needed any sort of direction, they were to come to her, for she was knowledgeable and capable. Despite her enduring dislike of him, she was warmed by his praise and confidence.

In the afternoons, she worked about the house with the Dashings while Blixford closeted himself in his study to work on his investments and to read his sheep literature, published monthly by a fellow farmer in Yorkshire. They took dinner early and after a relaxing sojourn in the drawing room, where they read to one another, or played cards, or discussed estate matters, they retired usually by ten o'clock. Sometimes he made love to her, sometimes he simply gathered her close and they drifted off to sleep. He never failed, however, to wake her of a morn with a strong erection and passionate kisses.

It seemed they were biding their time, waiting for

word from Wrotham that they could move on to the next part of Blixford's plan.

She was surprised one night when, as they went off to sleep, he mumbled against her hair, "I love you, Jane. Pleasant dreams." She did indeed have pleasant dreams, and wondered if he was aware he'd spoken aloud to her. He didn't repeat it, so she thought perhaps not. He continued to call her *love*, however — had done so since that horrible day she learned of his betrayal. In fact, his whole manner seemed different, as though he did, most truly, love her. But he never said so.

She was content, despite an underlying sorrow that her husband would not make his betrayal right, that he wouldn't budge from his certainty that he'd done nothing for which to apologize.

Not that she asked. She avoided the subject and retained a cool demeanor toward him. He appeared not to notice, maintaining his cheerful disposition, acting as though nothing was wrong. At least he was kind enough not to point out how very much she did not dislike him in bed. She was ashamed enough of her lack of self-control and discipline. It would pain her to be audibly reminded of it by him.

Every Sunday they went to services in the nearby village of Blixford and the third Sunday, Jane invited the vicar, Mr. Pool, and his daughter, Miss Bella, to tea. Mr. Pool was a pious man, given to sermonizing even when not in the pulpit, and it was a dreary, long afternoon before he and his painfully shy daughter finally took their leave. Jane remembered Miss Bella from her stay at Eastchase Hall during Annabel's confinement, but it had been a long time ago and she'd tried to put it out of her mind, for it was painful and sad to remember. Mostly what she recalled of Miss Bella was how she read scripture all that long day when Annabel was laboring, and in so much pain. Something about the girl had set her teeth on edge, though she could never quite discover why. She gained no additional insight during tea, simply because Miss Bella scarcely spoke, keeping her eyes downcast almost the entire time.

The Sundays following, she didn't extend another invitation, although Miss Bella always made a point to seek them out before they left the church, clearly angling for an invitation. Jane felt guilty, for surely the poor girl had little enough of a social life. Her father was overprotective of her and wouldn't allow her much freedom to leave the vicarage, unless he accompanied her. At four and twenty, Miss Bella was on the shelf, and her prospects dismal. Blixford was a wee village, and her father appeared to have a stranglehold on her movements, disallowing her to venture out. Otherwise, she might have struck up a friendship with Mr. O'Brien, or Mr. Perkins, the stewards at Eastchase, or perhaps Mr. Ball, the steward at the ever absent Viscount Radcliffe's neighboring estate. Jane thought Miss Bella would benefit from clothing not so drab and brown, perhaps a new hairstyle, and a smile upon her face. She was such a dour woman.

Six weeks into their sojourn in Devon, Miss Bella pulled her aside before services, when Blixford was engaged in conversation with the vicar, and asked, quite bluntly, "Your Grace, are you with child?"

So startled by the young woman's rude question, Jane was too sunned to speak.

"I only ask because you've that look about you. The other duchesses looked just like this, and so I wondered." She didn't smile. "If so, if you are to bear the duke's child, I will pray for you."

What a strange one she was. Unsure how to respond, Jane finally said simply, "Thank you, Miss Bella." She cast a sidelong glance at Blixford. "If you'll excuse me, I believe we should take our seats now." Discomfiture overrode guilt and she didn't invite

Reverend Pool and Miss Bella to tea that afternoon, as she'd planned.

She didn't mention the incident to Blixford, primarily because she didn't want to get his hopes up, if indeed she wasn't pregnant. She was late, but she wanted to be certain, so she said nothing.

Later that week, on Wednesday, he seemed even more cheerful than usual at luncheon, and as soon as she'd rested her knife and fork, he came round the table and produced a wooden box from behind his back. "I've your wedding gift here, Jane." He set it upon the table, just next to her plate. "Open it."

A gift? She suspected jewels, but the case was rather large for jewels. She lifted the gold latch and opened the hinged top, gasping in surprise. Inside, nestled in a bed of soft linen, was a small pistol. The stock was inlaid with mother of pearl, and the barrel engraved in an intricate design. Jerking her gaze to his, she didn't attempt to hide her shock. "Blixford, this is most unexpected."

He grinned as he nodded toward the box. "I had it made especially for you, Jane, to fit your smaller hand. It was delivered just this morning. Do you like it?"

"Of course." She was stunned. "It's lovely, and such a thoughtful gift. Thank you."

"Come along and we'll try it out, shall we?" He reached inside the box for the pistol and handed it to her, his teeth white in his tanned face as he beamed at her.

She accepted it, then went to retrieve her apron, to protect her clothing from any loose gunpowder. Following him outside, they passed through the extensive, formal gardens until they reached the rolling expanse of lawn south of the house. A target had been erected some distance away. "I've long heard of your prowess, but have never seen it for myself. Will you demonstrate, Jane?"

With calm hands, she loaded the weapon with a

bullet he produced from his pocket then eyed the target, remembering her father's many lessons. *Be the missile, travel along as the missile and find your target. Aim is everything. Make your hand, your eye, the missile and the target as one, in harmony.*

She fired and a hole appeared in the target, just left of center. She reloaded again and that bullet hit close to the same spot. "It fires a bit left." She corrected her aim by moving to the right ever so slightly, and hit the target dead center. "Now you try."

He did, but his shots were several inches to the left of center. "It has less of a kick than I'm accustomed to. Quite nice, don't you think?"

"Extremely nice, Blix. It isn't so heavy as my father's pistols."

He reloaded and handed it to her, expecting her to take another shot, his smile slight, his look a bit anxious. "Do you really like it, Jane, or are you only being kind?"

It was impossible to remain cool toward him in that moment, he was so very anxious to please her. How could she not express her gratitude? She took the pistol and smiled her pleasure. "It is, without a doubt, the very best, most wonderful gift I've ever received. Yes, it is a very fine piece and I shall be proud to own it. I'm astounded you would give it to me, as I thought you disliked my enjoyment of pistols."

He became very sober and looked away, toward the target. "I wish for you to be happy, Jane. Anything that gives you pleasure is a good thing, to my mind. Sherbourne shed some light on the reasons behind your unusual interests, that he wanted you with him, instead of learning to stitch, or play the pianoforte. How ignoble it would be of me to dislike anything you learned to enjoy under those circumstances. He's terribly proud of you and loves you very much. I've come to respect him a great deal, for many reasons, but perhaps most of all because he raised you." His dark gaze turned to hers. "As we go on, I only become more fascinated with you, for you've so many lovely surprises. I see now that you are, indeed, a crack shot. How many men can claim anything so marvelous as to be married to one such as you? I foresee myself the envy of every male of my acquaintance and suspect it will become all the rage for wives to take up pistols."

It was a ludicrous notion, but she understood his point. Far from disliking her ability at pistols, he was proud. "Thank you, Michael."

They stared at each other for several long moments and she had the feeling he was about to say something terribly important, but the moment passed and he looked away. Clearing his throat, he turned toward the stables and strode off, leaving her alone with the pistol, the target, and the sudden realization, he was waiting for *her* to speak. In his way, he had apologized, and she had missed it, hadn't forgiven him.

Men were, indeed, very strange, driven, it seemed, by pride. He wouldn't say it aloud, but he was sorry, she was certain. She was also very sure he loved her. Why, then, would he not speak it? Did he fear she would reject him, that she wouldn't return his feelings? Good Lord, what a complicated man she'd married. Tonight, she decided, they would talk. She would begin and see where it led, if perhaps they could put the past away and start afresh. She was weary of the fight, yet unable to move forward until he acknowledged the wrong he'd committed by betraying her confidence.

With a deep sigh, she tucked the pistol into the pocket of her apron and wandered back to the house, lost in thought.

As she reached the back terrace and climbed the steps to the door, Mr. Dashing came out and greeted her. "Your Grace, you've a caller. The vicar's daughter, Miss Bella Pool. I've put her in the drawing room while I came to see if you are in."

Remembering the woman's strange demeanor of Sunday, Jane almost said no, she was not in. But Miss Bella had most likely walked all the way from the village, and she didn't have the heart to turn her away.

"No, Dashing, it's quite all right. I'll go and receive her."

Inside, she made her way to the drawing room, but didn't remove her apron. She and Mrs. Dashing planned to reorganize the vegetable cellar that afternoon, and the sooner she said goodbye to Miss Bella, the better. Her apron would send a message that she was busy, so perhaps the woman would take her leave that much quicker.

"Good afternoon, Miss Bella," she said as she came into the drawing room.

"Good afternoon, Your Grace." She didn't apologize for her unannounced arrival, nor did she explain the reason for her visit.

Fearing it was to be a long hour ahead, Jane invited her to sit, then rang for tea. Within minutes, she knew exactly why Miss Bella had set her teeth on edge, all those years ago. Perhaps age and experience had lent her further intuition, or perhaps Miss Bella's character was more pronounced. She was a different person by herself, without her stern, starchy father's presence. No longer a girl, of course, two years older than Jane, six years of maturity had unfortunately not made Miss Bella more attractive, for she was decidedly plain, with a strong overbite and a weak chin, underscored by a thick neck and body. As the minutes ticked past, whatever sympathy Jane had felt toward Miss Bella vanished. Her haughty, brusque, and decidedly antagonistic manner didn't lend itself to sympathy.

They exchanged stilted pleasantries and Miss Bella interjected a few hidden barbs until the tea cart arrived. Then she leapt from her chair and insisted Jane allow her to pour, that she would be most honored. It was an unusual request, but the woman appeared enamored of the idea, and pleaded in a far kinder tone than she'd previously expressed, "It's so rare I'm able to perform the service. My father doesn't allow me to entertain at the vicarage. I'd consider it a great favor, Your Grace, if you'll permit me to serve you."

She acquiesced, all the while thinking Miss Bella was a strange sort. She was, quite simply, unlikable.

Almost as soon as she'd handed Jane her cup and seated herself on the chair opposite, she asked after Mrs. Daniels. "She and I were particular friends," she said with a sniff after Jane informed her the housekeeper had been replaced, "and as our village is so very far removed from other villages, it's not a simple endeavor to acquire friends. My father is very particular about who I associate with, and Mrs. Daniels was one I could visit without his knowledge, when he goes on his Wednesday visits to the orphanage. I do wonder how I shall go on without her companionship?"

Jane might have said then that Miss Bella could count on her friendship, but she did not, for it was untrue. She disliked the woman, could feel a strong sense of hostility emanating from her, and wished she would make her visit short. She was also possessed of a great need to answer nature's call, as she'd been very frequently of late. She set aside her tea after only a few sips, thinking it best not to encourage her need of the privy. "I hope you'll convey to your father how very much his grace and I enjoyed his sermon, Sunday last. It's regrettable we've not had the opportunity to invite him to call again, but we've been rather inundated with getting the household in order. As you know, hard work is its own reward, but it appears there's been a lack of any sort of work here at Eastchase, hard or otherwise. Much remains to be done." In only a few statements, she gave Miss Bella a setdown for her temerity in calling without invitation and aired her low opinion of Mrs. Daniels' competency.

Miss Bella's back went up and her gloved hand obviously tightened about her teacup. "Perhaps Your Grace's standards are higher than most. I believe the previous duchesses were pleased with Mrs. Daniels' abilities."

"It's of no consequence, Miss Bella, as those dear ladies have all departed from here and ascended to God, have they not?"

"One would hope so, but who can say? It's said in the Bible, we must not judge, lest we be judged, and whether for good, or bad, I believe this holds true, don't you?"

"I daresay one's hope of a departed soul's ascension to Heaven cannot be considered passing judgment, but we're all entitled to our own interpretation of God's word."

Miss Bella looked quite superior in that moment, as though she were the duchess and Jane a mere underling. It was bizarre in the extreme. "I'd not expect a woman of your reputation to be learned of the Good Book, nor to comprehend its significance to the souls of good, decent, Christian folk." Her brown eyes were cold and hard. "Blixford is a small village, but not completely shut off from the world. I have heard of your ruination, of the sin in which you lived while in Scotland."

Jane was astounded by her bold, rude insult. She was about to remind Miss Bella of her place, and ask that she leave, immediately, but before she could say a word, Blixford strolled into the drawing room. Dressed in his riding breeches and a coat of blue superfine, he looked handsome and fresh, his cheeks and nose pinked by the sun, his dark hair overly long at the moment and tousled by the breeze. "I understand Miss Bella has come to call," he announced as he came in, heading directly toward the vicar's daughter, a wide smile upon his lips. "How good of you to come, Miss Bella. How are you?" He bowed to her curtsy and grasped her extended hand most courteously before releasing it to step back and beam down at her.

Astonished, Jane watched the change in Miss Bella's demeanor. She retook her seat, blushed, and batted her lashes at Blixford as she said very prettily, "Simply marvelous, Your Grace, and oh, so much better now that I have seen you. It appears you are in the very best of health, for which I am glad."

"You're also looking fit, Miss Bella. How go things at the vicarage?"

While Jane watched in complete fascination, Miss Bella expounded on the good works of her father, the progress of the village school, and plans being made for a spring fete, to be held for the benefit of the orphans. "I do hope you'll extend your help, Your Grace. We require the support of our benefactor to make it a success."

"Of course!" He looked toward Jane. "You'll lend your aid, certainly, won't you?"

She could hardly refuse, and she nodded her head. He looked a bit confused at her lack of enthusiasm, but turned back to Miss Bella and said, "The duchess is quite accomplished at organization, having grown up in a houseful of many brothers. With her assistance, I'm certain you'll do quite well." He smiled again. "I say, it is good to see you, Miss Bella. I must leave you now, though it pains me to depart good company, but I've promised to attend Mr. O'Brien on an estate matter. Do give my best to your father, won't you, and tell him how very much the duchess and I enjoyed his sermon, Sunday last."

"Oh, yes, of course I will," she said, a bit breathlessly. "You are too kind, Your Grace."

Good heavens, she was in love with him! No wonder she was so hostile toward Jane. A part of her wanted to be sympathetic. Surely unrequited love was a stone about one's neck, but the greater part of her couldn't be sympathetic. Those with two faces had always bothered her. MacDougal was such a person, extending a jolly good nature to the world, while harboring a nasty side he kept hidden. Miss Bella was her enemy, she was certain, and her clear hostility toward Jane was alarming.

As she watched her interact with Blixford, a thought took hold, but she dismissed it. No, it couldn't be. Surely not.

Then he left and Miss Bella returned to her sour expression and blatant dislike of Jane. "When I heard of your marriage, I was beyond shocked. In truth, I couldn't imagine his grace sullying the ducal position by taking to wife a woman such as yourself. I didn't wish to pay this call, but I felt it my duty, as a woman of God, to come and attempt to lead you from sin, that upon your death, you're not doomed to hellfire. Would you pray with me, Jane?"

Upon her death. The thought returned and wouldn't let go. The look in Miss Bella's eyes was not one of a rational person. She looked to be a bit mad.

Jane's memory raced back in time, to the day Annabel died. Miss Bella was there, in the chamber where Annabel labored, praying, reading scripture, sometimes so loudly, the midwife had to shush her. Jane had been overset, of course, Annabel in so much agony, writhing upon the bed. The midwife had commented, several times, that her labor seemed strange, too strong, too painful. Annabel screamed and screamed, and began to bleed. Copious amounts of blood. The midwife was alarmed and said the womb must have ruptured, that Annabel was in grave danger, and if she survived, she would never have another child.

All the while, Miss Bella prayed and read scripture. She didn't approach the bed, didn't offer words of comfort. Jane was so young then, with no knowledge of such matters, and extremely hysterical over her friend's imminent death. In the midst of Annabel's horrible, agonizing pain, she didn't find it odd that Miss Bella, who claimed also to be Annabel's friend, didn't offer comfort, but instead stood back and read aloud a somber, depressing Psalm. Looking back upon it, she realized it was very strange, that Miss Bella's demeanor had been cold and uncaring, as though her only duty was to read the Bible and intone long prayers asking God not to save Annabel's life, but rather to save her soul from the devil.

She looked at Miss Bella, at her expression of hatred, and instinct told her she was correct. The vicar's daughter must surely have given something to Annabel, and most likely Blixford's next two brides, to bring on labor, and cause hemorrhaging. Fear crept down her neck and settled in her spine. Remembering Miss Bella's rude question as to whether she was with child, and her insistence just now upon pouring tea, she glanced at her teacup and praised God she'd only barely sipped it, then said to Miss Bella, "I'd ask that you return to your home and there you may pray all you like." Rising, she gave the woman a hard look. "You'll forgive me if I don't express appreciation for your call, or welcome your return to Eastchase Hall in future."

"I do not call on you, but upon the duke. He would be dejected and sad if I didn't come and see him. He has long loved me."

She was, truly, mad as a hatter. Jane felt nauseous. "I'm sure he does, Miss Bella. This is why he's taken four wives and none of them you."

"Oh," she said with a wave of her hand, "he'll marry me, eventually. It's only that he feels he must marry a lady of consequence, and I'm merely the daughter of a vicar. He'll come round, however, and realize our love cannot be denied, that consequence matters naught when God has fated two to be together."

"I see." She did indeed. "Does his current state of marriage not deter your thinking?"

"Of course not. I foresee you'll have similar problems with breeding as the previous duchesses, and after you're gone, his grace will finally see the truth to things, that he cannot deny our love, our divine fate." She assumed a pitying look. "I'm sorry you'll have to die, but it's God's will. I know this because my mother told me, long ago, I was to be the duchess, that she had been fated to marry the old duke, but he succumbed to the sins of the flesh and was led astray by his harlot wife, so it will be I who fulfills our family's destiny to marry into this, the most ancient of ducal titles. His grace is a fine, Christian soul, and not prone to sins of the flesh. He will come round, most assuredly."

Jane walked to the door, now overcome with nausea, no doubt the result of fear, but denied herself the urge to run. Miss Bella was frightening in her insanity and Jane was so ill at ease, she truly felt sick. "Please take your leave, Miss Bella, and do not return."

The woman swept forward and as she passed, she gave Jane a sly look. "I ken that I'm correct and you are breeding, even as we speak. What a pity you won't live to see your child, and he'll die along with you." Then she was gone.

Jane leaned against the door, feeling decidedly dizzy. Of a sudden, she knew she would be sick and ran into the great hall, but quickly determined she wouldn't make it to the privy. Spying the flower filled urn resting upon the long table that ran down the middle of the hall, she ran to it, tossed aside the flowers and was violently sick.

Mr. Dashing hurried to her and placed his hands upon her back. "Your Grace, what's this? You are ill!"

In between her retches into the mouth of the urn, she managed to choke out, "Michael! Please go and . . . *Michael.*"

The butler forgot himself enough to shout, "I say, Mathilda! Come at once! Her Grace is ill!" He patted her comfortingly. "There, there, fear not. I'll go for your husband. Ah, here's Mrs. Dashing." His hands went away, replaced by his wife's.

"Poor angel! We must get you upstairs. Oh dear, this is distressing, Your Grace. Can you stand?"

Jane thought her belly might well explode, she was in such pain. "I believe I've been poisoned," she said as she stood erect, then immediately doubled over in pain. She felt a rush of liquid between her legs. Great God, had she wet herself? Could this be more frightening, or humiliating?

"Poisoned? Oh, surely not, Your Grace!"

"Miss Bella . . . crazy as . . . Oh! God, this is horrible!"

"Come along and I'll get you to your bed." With Mrs. Dashing's assistance, she made it up the stairs and into the bedchamber connecting to the one she shared with Blix. When she was laid out, she reached for her skirts and pulled them up.

Mrs. Dashing's eyes widened. "Oh, Your Grace, you're bleeding!"

Ah, so she had not wet herself. The rush she'd felt was blood. Jane gasped for breath around the severe cramps in her abdomen. "Send for the physician, and find out if there's an herbalist in the village. Bring them here, as quickly as possible. Send Rose to look after me. Go, now!"

Mrs. Dashing hurried away and Jane lay still, her knees drawn up, praying fervently that God wouldn't let her die. She knew the truth of it, that she was pregnant.

Now, it appeared she was losing the babe, even before his father knew of his existence.

She didn't weep, the pain keeping grief at bay. She thought to sit up, to remove her apron and dress, but the attempt sent jabs of pain through her abdomen and she fell back to the bed.

Out of nowhere it seemed, Miss Bella appeared, an open Bible in her thick hands. She moved close and intoned a solemn prayer that Jane would be saved from the evil clutches of Satan.

"Go . . . *away*." She couldn't bear it.

Miss Bella began to read a Psalm in a loud voice and Jane kicked out at her. "Leave! Now! Horrible murderer! You've killed my baby, *may you rot in Hell*."

The vicar's daughter merely moved back a pace and continued as though Jane wasn't screaming at her.

That's when Blixford ran into the chamber, eyes wide, face pale. "Jane, what goes on? Dashing says you are . . . oh, dear God!" He came to the bed and saw the blood. "Is it your courses?"

Grimacing when another wave of nausea struck, she managed to roll over and retch from the side of the bed. "Poison . . . Miss Bella in love . . . with you. Mad . . . completely mad." She retched again. "A babe, Michael. We were to have a . . ." She didn't finish because she lost consciousness.

CHAPTER 15

It was his worst nightmare. He bent a knee to the bed, reached for Jane and turned her over, his eyes welling with tears, his heart pounding so hard, he was dizzy. "Jane, love, do not die. Please, Jane —*wake up*." She was so pale and one glance told him she was bleeding heavily, her very life flowing from her before his eyes. He couldn't bear it. Petting her hair, he begged her to live, prayed to God to save her. "The doctor is coming, love." How long would it take?

He noticed Miss Bella then, standing beside the bed, holding a Bible, reading in a loud monotone. "What have you done to Jane?" She didn't look at him, but continued to read. Leaping from the bed, he grabbed the Bible, closed it with a snap and dropped it to the floor before grasping her shoulders and shaking her. "*What have you done to Jane?*"

She drew herself up and said importantly, "It is the will of God, and I am his handmaiden. *She* is evil, a wanton harlot unworthy of the ducal title, unfit to be your duchess. You must face your responsibilities now, Your Grace. We must marry and *I* will give birth to the next Duke of Blixford. I will raise him up to be a holy, shining example to all England of the nobility of this ancient peerage. The shame brought upon it by your mad father and his whore of a wife must be undone. She had to die, to ensure the sin of her loins, begat in her wicked unfaithfulness, was never allowed to be born."

"How? *How did my mother die?*"

Her wild eyes turned toward Jane. "With a babe in her belly, put there by the seed of a man not her husband, by the horrible devil in his breeches." She looked up at him and smiled the smile of one completely off balance. "My own mother was to be the duchess, but your father was tricked into marrying a whore of no honor, who lay with the devil and would bear his bastard to further degrade the ducal title. To save her soul, to save the title from blemish, it was my mother's duty to kill the child, his harlot mother, and the devil who betrayed the duke."

Could it be that the vicar's wife had killed his mother and the old Viscount Radcliffe? It was so outlandish, he couldn't believe it. Miss Bella was insane, making her own reality. His hands were still against her shoulders and he squeezed hard, his fingers digging into her thick flesh. "How could you know this? You were but a child."

"All of my life, until her death, my mother told me it was my duty to succeed where she had failed, that I would become the duchess, and renew the honor and dignity of the title."

Honor and dignity through the murder of innocents and the babes they carried. Michael was breathless with the realization, cold with deadly fury and heart stopping fear. Jane was so still, the blood was so much. How could she survive? He fought himself to keep from strangling the life from Bella Pool.

"Say you will marry me, that you'll respect the title and bring honor upon it by taking to wife one who is pure, who knows the face of God, hears his divine voice in the dark of night when my father pierces me with his holiness. It is I, Bella, who understands the purity of God's plan for a man and a woman." She shot a disgusted look at Jane. "She understands only carnal knowledge and cannot fathom what it is to find God within her body."

Michael felt ill, even while he was consumed with rage. Bella's words could mean only one thing —she had been molested by her father, the pious vicar. In another time, another place, he'd have felt sorry for her plight. But his Jane was dying by this woman's hand, and he couldn't find sympathy anywhere in his soul for her.

"You will leave now, so that I may take care of my wife."

"No! She must die. She *will* die. You will marry *me!*"

He modulated his voice, hoping his even tone would calm her. "I don't wish for my duchess to die. I love her very much and it will cause me great pain and sorrow if she's gone from me."

Jerking away from his hands, she withdrew a small knife from her reticule and held it up for him to see. "You cannot save her. She must die so that we may be married and become as one, as it says in the Bible, as I am with my father. I must bear your child, the next duke."

He saw her intent even before she lunged toward Jane, and caught her, but she was possessed of unnatural strength and he struggled to wrest the knife from her.

"I see now that you are no better than your father, tempted by the sins of the flesh, by a harlot's body, *blind to her evil.* If you'll not seek God's truth with me, *you shall go to the devil and live there in Hell.*"

He was startled when he felt the blade slice through his coat sleeve, into his arm, and loosened his hold upon her just long enough for her to twist about and raise the knife, ready to plunge it into his heart.

Michael tried to move away, to dodge the stab, but he saw he would not be fast enough and only was able to turn enough to keep the blade from his heart. Instead, she buried it into his shoulder. She drew back, intent upon trying again, her breathing labored, eyes wild, hair coming loose from its pins. Her arm was raised, the bloody knife clutched within her fingers, when the room exploded with noise and smoke. Miss Bella's eyes widened in shock before she crumpled to the floor at his feet.

He looked toward the bed just as Jane fell back, the smoking pistol in her hand.

In the hours that followed, he died a thousand deaths. Each time she awakened he was reborn, over and over, hope that she would survive burgeoning in his chest. Then she would cry out in pain and eventually lose consciousness again and he would be dashed to bits, his soul howling with despair.

He wouldn't allow her maid to attend to her, but instead instructed her to bring clean bedding, a stack of towels, and fresh, warm water. He didn't like to move Jane. She moaned when he tried, so he asked for a pair of scissors and cut her garments away. He washed her gently, then carefully cradled her in his arms while Rose quickly removed the bedding, discarded the soiled topmost feather mattress, and spread out clean sheets. She placed the towels just so and he bent to lay Jane upon them.

Within moments, the towels were soiled, and it became clear to him they fought a losing battle.

The physician arrived and said there was little he could do, that the best thing was to give it time and keep a close watch on Jane. Two footmen had removed Bella from the room and the physician declared what he already knew, that she was dead, Jane's bullet having pierced her heart. Michael instructed Dashing to send for the constable and the vicar, and have them wait in the library until he could attend them. He allowed the physician to bind the wounds on his arm and shoulder before he put on a clean shirt and resumed his vigil at Jane's bedside.

The herbalist, an old woman named Dora, arrived soon after. After inspecting Jane's teacup, saved and not rinsed due to Mrs. Dashing's quick thinking, Dora declared it was rife with a powder long used by prostitutes to rid themselves of unwanted pregnancies. Under his watchful eye, she dosed Jane with a concoction she said would thicken her blood, and perhaps lessen the flow. She said Jane was, indeed, pregnant, but when it was done, she wouldn't be any longer. Her prognosis was good, however, because she'd not ingested very much of the tea.

He set aside his grief over the news that she'd lost the babe and prayed constantly that God would allow her to live, that he didn't care if they ever had a child, but he couldn't survive without Jane.

When pressed to reveal how Miss Bella came into possession of such a powder, Dora confessed to Michael that she'd been giving it to her for years upon years, due to her repeated pregnancies, which were the result of her father's molestation. In a small dose, it would start the process of miscarriage or labor, depending upon how far along the mother was, but if the dose was too great, it would cause severe bleeding, even hemorrhaging, and ultimately, death.

He faced the cold truth that his first three wives had not died of complications in childbirth as all had believed, but were, in fact, murdered by the vicar's daughter, who thought herself ordained by God to become his duchess. Perhaps due to the horror of her life at the vicarage, the sequestered existence demanded by her rapist father, Miss Bella had formed her own reality, wherein he would rescue her and she would be exalted and hailed as good and worthy. Considering how her life was lived behind closed doors, was it any wonder the woman was mad?

Dora also revealed she had given the same powder to Bella's mother. She'd married the vicar at a very young age, just fifteen, and as she matured, and after she gave birth to Bella, he evidently lost interest in her. "Mrs. Pool was a pretty woman, but prone to spinning tales. When she came to me and said she was with the child of the old Viscount Radcliffe, I didn't believe her. She became hysterical, and said her husband would kill her if he knew she was with child, that it could not be his and he would know it. I relented and gave her the powder. She came back to me a year later, pregnant again and very angry, certain the duchess, your mother, was also expecting the viscount's child. Mrs. Pool claimed she had once been betrothed to your father, but he cast her aside for the duchess, and now she was taking away the viscount as well. I told her she was wrong, that the duchess was a good woman, but she was convinced." Dora shook her head, her wrinkled face filled with regret. "Would that I had not given her the powder. I've only just realized she most likely was not increasing, but lied to get the powder, and gave it to the duchess."

Michael thought of his poor, mad papa, wandering the halls at Eastchase, imagining his wife was still with him. "Do you think Mrs. Pool also killed Radcliffe?"

The old woman shook her head. "I believe the vicar discovered his wife's betrayal and he killed him. Of course I had no way to prove it, and who would believe me? He's so pious and none suspect his evil heart. When Miss Bella first came to me, I thought to tell you of what went on, even considered alerting the constable, but she begged me not to, insisted her father would kill her. Her mother took her own life, but I wondered if she had discovered what her husband was doing to Bella, threatened to expose his perfidy, and he killed her to keep his secret."

Had she not tried to kill Jane, were she not responsible for the deaths of three innocent women and the babes they carried, he would have felt a great deal of sympathy for Miss Bella. As it was, while he hated what her life had been, he harbored great rage toward her.

He held a far greater rage toward her father, however, and as soon as he and the constable arrived, he went down to the library to meet with them, leaving Rose and Mrs. Dashing to keep watch over Jane. He asked Dora to accompany him, to bear witness to what she knew, and she agreed, saying, "Too long has he been allowed to terrorize his family, and I pray he'll pay for his wrongs."

Michael intended to do much more than pray. He was brief and succinct when he spoke to the constable, then turned to the vicar. "I can't fathom what goes through a mind like yours, and thank God I cannot, for surely you are eaten alive by the worms of depravity and evil. I will see you hang, Mr. Pool."

Incredibly, the man looked insulted. "I've done nothing wrong, nothing to be ashamed of. Bella was a homely, plain girl who could never attract a husband. I merely stepped in to comfort her in her loneliness, as any good father should do."

Michael narrowed his eyes in disgust. "You're a disgrace to fathers everywhere and a blight on humanity." Turning, he left the constable to arrest Mr. Pool and strode to the stairs, climbing them two at a time.

Jane drifted in and out of consciousness all the rest of the day and late into the night. He wouldn't leave her side. Sometime after midnight, she roused up and appeared coherent, her face wan, her hand shaking as she reached for his. "I've not died," she whispered. "I was certain I would, and it made me so angry."

He rose from his chair, bent to the bed and slid his arms about her to hold her gently. "I have prayed much, and promised many things to God. I shall have to leave you and become a monk and bring peace to the world in order to fulfill all of my promises."

She began to cry, softly, brokenly. "I thought I had conceived, but wanted to be sure before I told you, and now . . ." She clutched him tightly. "As sorrowful as I am at the loss, I have to thank God I'm alive to try again. Oh, Blix, poor Annabel. I've dreamed of her, over and over, in this very bed, crying and . . . and screaming, in so much pain, and all because of a madwoman. I was there, in the drawing room, when we had tea, when Annabel drank it, not knowing it would kill her. If only I'd seen what Miss Bella was about, if only . . . my heart is broken, truly, at the senselessness of it all."

He debated telling her what he'd learned, and decided it should wait. "Hush, love, you couldn't have known, couldn't have prevented it. Annabel is with God now, and she knows, she understands."

That appeared to soothe her and her desperate grasp about his neck eased. "Miss Bella, is she—"

"Yes, love, she's gone. You saved my life."

Her arms tightened about him again and she whispered, "God forgive me, but I can't be sorry she's dead. I have only to remember her wild eyes, that knife in her hand, and you, so close . . ." She began to cry again.

"It's over now, Jane, and all will be well. Rest and regain your strength. We'll talk later, when you're better."

"Yes, Michael. I wonder . . . might I rinse my mouth? The taste is truly horrid."

He set about bringing her the rinse, and the washbowl from her dressing room. When she was done he removed it and sat again on the chair at her bedside, to watch her sleep. She was more restful, her body relaxed and still, instead of tense and fretful, as she'd been since the afternoon. She was safe, she would live, and someday, with an excellent chance of surviving the experience, she would bring a child into the world. The realization brought tears of gratitude to his eyes. There, in the quiet of the chamber, with only the soft sound of her even breaths breaking the stillness, he allowed himself to cry, and sent silent prayers of thanksgiving to God for bringing Jane into his life. He allowed himself to cry for the lost lives of three innocent souls and the babes gone with them. And perhaps some of his tears were for his mother and his mad papa.

After a time, he bent forward and rested his upper body upon the bed, holding her small hand within his as he faded to sleep.

When he awoke, her fingers were in his hair, petting him softly. He raised his head and blinked at her. There was some color in her cheeks. "How do you feel?"

She stared at him, her blue eyes filled with emotion. "I love you madly, you know. Always have, even when I ran away. I came home to marry you because I couldn't bear to see you marry another. Not again. I wanted you for myself."

"Yes. I know. Your father had the right of it when he told me he suspected as much."

He drew in a breath, deciding now was the time, but before he could speak another word, she whispered, "It all seems so small now, Michael, so ridiculous in the face of death and the end of it all. I realize you don't feel the need for forgiveness, but I feel the need to give it, and there, you have it. I don't dislike you at all, no matter that you're an autocrat. It appears you'll ever do wrongheaded things with the very best intentions, and I'd be an ungrateful wretch to hold it against you." She smiled weakly. "It also occurs to me, you never had a father, not really, and perhaps what you did was an unconscious attempt to establish a kinship with Sherbourne. You clearly think much of him, and why not? He's a marvelous man, a tremendous father. How selfish I would be not to share."

Great God, his eyes filled with tears again. He

dropped his head back to the bed and did not speak for a very long while. When finally he had his emotions under control, he looked at her, lying there, pale and wan, smiling at him with her heart in her gaze. "Ah, Jane," he managed to say, though his voice sounded rough and raw to his ears, "it's so like you to steal my thunder. Have you any notion how long I've plotted and planned the best way to tell you how very sorry I am for hurting you, and how deeply I love you? Now, here you are just from death's door, forgiving me before I've asked, offering a gift of such magnitude, nothing I can offer could compare. You're a termagant, a hoyden, and simply wonderful. I love you so, you've no idea."

Her fingers were still in his hair. "I've some idea, but perhaps, if you work very hard, you can convince me just how much."

He moved up to stretch out upon the bed and gather her close, holding her carefully, gently to his breast. "I will, Jane. After all, hard work—"

"—is its own reward," she finished for him. After a while, she said, "In retrospect, that's a singularly ridiculous statement. One doesn't work hard but for a certain outcome to the work. Why ever would anyone work hard, simply to work, with no end of toil, no result for the effort? If I didn't anticipate the fruits of labor, I would become like the lazy cat, fed too much smoked trout for its own good, and lie about doing nothing all day and all night."

"Nothing, Jane?"

"Well," she said after a moment, "I suppose I'd do *something*, but that can hardly be called work." She paused. "Although in some respects, it is work to you, is it not? You've got the short end of it, now I think on it. Why, you're made to be most athletic in the endeavor, while I'm merely required to enjoy myself. Hmm, I believe in future, I may need to exert myself a bit more, and take some of the strain off of you. It seems only fair and—"

"Oh, no, Jane. You may shoot your pistols and ride neck-or-nothing and extol the wonders of crossbreeding sheep, but a man has to draw the line somewhere, and this is mine. You must allow me my masculine pride."

"Do you mean to say you don't mind having to exert most of the effort?"

He held her a bit tighter and smiled with such happiness, with such love for her, he thought he'd fair die of it. "It's part and parcel of what gives me such pleasure with you. Your satisfaction, and those delightful cries you make, are the fruits of my labor, and it is sweet fruit, indeed." He stroked her lovely dark hair and sighed. "I'll ring for breakfast now, and insist you eat every bite, that you'll be back in good health as soon as possible."

"So you can get back to work?"

"Hmm. That too, but I was speaking of returning to London. Yesterday, I received a letter from Wrotham. MacDougal has accepted his invitation and is expected to arrive a week from tomorrow."

Sherbourne was late to bed, remaining in the library with Wrotham several hours after Miss North and her parents departed and Lucy had retired. It had been a while since he'd had a long conversation with Wrotham, and he felt he owed it to his old friend. Thus far, Wrotham had declined invitations to dinner, undoubtedly avoiding him because of his discomfiture over the scandal surrounding Jane, but perhaps also because he wished to escape Lucy's matchmaking. She'd declared him in need of a wife and appointed herself the task of finding him one, posthaste. Wrotham was alarmed, but Sherbourne told him he may as well play along. His wife would have her way, hell or high water.

To be fair to Lucy's ability of choosing wisely, he thought Wrotham was taken with Miss North, herself something of a female version of a stick. A very large-breasted stick, but a stick, nonetheless. He suspected she would bend quite nicely, given the opportunity, and he rather enjoyed the notion of Wrotham applying the pressure. Besides, wasn't it said one could start a fire by rubbing two sticks together?

After several brandies and a deep philosophical discussion of the merits of matrimony, Wrotham declared himself ready for his bed. As he took his leave, he said, "I hope I'm up to Blixford's task and can pretend a friendship with that rotter, MacDougal. He's to arrive at my home on the morrow." His shirt points had wilted during the evening and he was almost animated in his determination to call the blackguard to heel. "I have only to think of dear Jane, and my hope that she and Blixford may take their rightful places in the world, and I most certainly can do whatever is needed."

Feeling grateful for his friendship, Sherbourne wished him good night and made his way upstairs to his chamber, shared now with Lucy. He dismissed his valet as soon as he had removed his coat and boots, anxious to be alone with his thoughts. And his sleeping wife.

In his shirtsleeves and stockings, he poured himself another brandy and went to the fire, thinking to sit and watch her sleep for a while. Instead, he found a slender book upon the chair. Bound with red ribbons looped through holes cut into the thick paper cover, a fine, elegant script penned across the front read simply, *Volume Seven*.

He opened the book, began to read, and within moments, he was forced to stop and adjust himself because he grew hard within his tight-fitting breeches. He read on, and looked at her drawings, and could only wonder at her imagination. By the time he reached the end of the story —and it was, truly, a love story —he was so aroused, he couldn't let it be, yet didn't wish to simply take himself in hand and be done with it. He wanted Lucy beneath him.

He woke her up and took her within the minute, her half asleep and he absolutely, incredibly explosive with need. That she climaxed was a miracle, for he'd given her almost no time.

In the aftermath, he whispered in the dim glow of the room, lit only by the dying fire, "I'm in awe, my love. I had no notion you have such an artistic talent, and your ability to pen a lovely story is tremendous, but truly, what bowls me over is your imagination. If I didn't know better, I'd think that book was written and drawn by a courtesan, with years upon years of experience. What a strange little thing you are, and what an amazing mind."

"You liked it, then?"

"Lucy, I've just assaulted you in your sleep, I became so aroused. I much more than liked it —I loved it. Will you allow me to read the first six volumes?"

"Do you really wish to, or are you only being kind?"

"I really wish to."

"Very well. Suppose you read one, each night, rather than all at once? I find after a time, one becomes a bit numb and the story loses its power."

"I will read them as you give them to me, and be delighted."

They settled into the bed and began to drift into slumber, until he asked, in the darkness, "When did you write *Volume Seven?*"

"Three years ago. Why?"

He grinned and pulled her closer. "I noted the count's face bears a remarkable resemblance to someone I see in the glass every morning. I wonder why?"

She didn't answer for a while. He thought perhaps she'd fallen asleep, but suddenly, she said, "I wanted perfection. The count was invented for my enjoyment, and I had the ability to make him any way I chose. I'd guess your face was fixed firmly in my mind as one of perfection, and so it wound up belonging to the count as well. Does this bother you, Sherbourne?"

He chuckled. "Not in the least. I'm not too old to respond to flattery, and really, Lucy, that's about as good as it gets. I do have to wonder, however, where you ever saw a cock that large? Surely Bonderant was not so well endowed?"

"No, he was not. I've never seen any other than his and yours, so the answer, of course, is nowhere have I seen such. I made it up. As I said, the count was my idea of perfection, though it took me a very long time to get his legs right. They were always out of proportion."

"I don't wonder. To support such masculinity, a man would need legs of iron." He considered his next question and despised himself for asking, but was compelled. "Lucy, is it ever a disappointment to you that—"

"Oh, good heavens, Sherbourne! I knew I shouldn't let you read my books, because this was sure to be a problem." She pushed him to his back and moved to lie on top of him, her toes tickling his shins. "I know there is no man of that size, just as I know it's impossible for two human beings, regardless of how fit, or carnal, to engage in that much lovemaking, or employ such novel approaches and positions. It's a fantasy, husband, and you'll admit, your own fantasies bear little resemblance to reality. Were you to draw yours out, I'd guess your countess would have breasts so large, they'd smother her lover, and if you were truly honest, the count's cock would be as big as my count's, perhaps bigger."

"Hmm, yes, I begin to see your point. You know, it's interesting your female protagonist is a countess, and here you are, also a countess." His hands ran along her back and ended at her sweet bottom, cupping a cheek within each hand. He began to stir again. "All this talk of sex and cocks and breasts and your very luscious body rubbing against mine is keeping me awake. Whatever shall I do about it, Countess?"

Lowering her voice to a small soft whisper, she told him rather graphically what he should do, and that was all it took for him to rise to the request.

Half an hour later, they were back to falling asleep when she murmured against his chest, "Sherbourne, I'm late."

He nearly squeezed her to death, he was so elated. "Have I told you how very much I love you?"

"Not nearly enough." She sighed contentedly. "You are happy, then?"

"Ecstatic. Ah, Lucy, you're beautiful and splendid. I do love you so."

"And I love you. Goodnight, Sherbourne."

"You really must begin calling me by my Christian name."

"It's difficult, being as you have the same name as my son."

"I understand. Perhaps, then you can call me Sherry, when we are alone."

She laughed. "Capital notion! Yes, I like that . . . Sherry. It will keep a favorite memory alive, as well. Goodnight then, Sherry. I love you."

He fell into slumber at last, sated, happy and content. Wonder of wonders, he was to be a father again. Life was so very good, was it not?

Early summer had arrived, Parliament was in its last sessions, and the Season was coming to an end. The rounds of parties were beginning to thin, with some people already gone from town, but the majority remained. No one wished to miss the Bloomsbury ball. It was rumored that Brian MacDougal, sixth Earl of

Haversham and Wrotham's houseguest the past week, would be in attendance. He'd been spotted at a few occasions, and proved to be an amiable chap. There were some matchmaking mamas, those whose daughters had tried and failed to secure an offer during the Season, who eyed him with interest. It was difficult to determine anything of his fortune, but there were those who didn't consider it important, who wished to see their daughter become a countess, even if it meant a move to the wilds of Scotland.

But of course his being a jolly chap and a possible match for the remaining unmarried misses on the marriage mart wasn't the reason so many were anxious to attend the Bloomsbury ball and make his acquaintance. The Earl of Haversham was at the heart of the year's juiciest scandal, an exclamation point at the end of a seemingly endless list of scandals, all surrounding Lady Jane Lennox, now the Duchess of Blixford.

The night of the ball, Jane was oddly calm. When Michael commented upon it, she said simply, "Either the truth will out, or it will not. Whatever comes, I'm ready to face. I've knocked on death's door, along with my husband, and nothing after that seems so terribly important. Truthfully, I'm more hopeful we're successful for your sake than for mine. I could be happy with only you and our family and our servants for company until I am very old."

"Strangely, I feel much the same." He shook his head. "It always seemed so critical to keep the title sterling and pristine, and I find now that how others see it is irrelevant. How you and I live as the Duke and Duchess of Blixford is all that matters, and I believe we honor the position."

He looked delicious in his formal attire and she wondered at how much she loved him. "Yes, I believe we do. If we didn't have the future of our children to consider, I might suggest we stay in tonight and leave

MacDougal to God. But we can't bring children into the world beneath a cloud of scandal, so I suppose we must go through with this."

Offering his arm as they reached the top of the stairs in her father's house, he smiled down at her. "You grow more lovely every day, Jane. It's good to see the bloom back in your cheeks. If you grow overly tired, you'll let me know at once?"

"Yes, I will, but I'm feeling quite well and foresee we'll enjoy a waltz or two."

"Perhaps this time we'll have company on the dance floor."

Papa and Lucy were there in the hall, waiting for them, and they all went out to the Sherbourne coach to ride the short distance to Lady Bloomsbury's house. It was near midnight, and most everyone who planned to attend the ball would be there by now.

Indeed, they were. Lady Bloomsbury may have waited until late in the Season to host a grand ball, but it was a smashing success, a veritable crush.

When they arrived and were announced, she came toward their group and greeted Blixford first, Sherbourne second, Lucy third, and Jane not at all. It was as though she were invisible.

Remembering her hurt from the last time she entered the hallowed halls of the Bloomsbury home, Jane could almost laugh. How long ago it seemed, and how unimportant.

The announcement of their names had most everyone within the ballroom straining to look their way, openly staring as they made their way around the periphery, Blix leading them toward a less populated section of the wall.

Jane stood next to her husband, shoulders back, head held high, meeting the gazes of those she would call friend, but for a viscous lie. They returned her gaze, unsmiling, unwelcoming, but in some, she detected perhaps a trace of admiration. That she would attend the ball was courageous, they thought. How could they know that any fear she harbored was not due to being shunned and ignored, but because she was to face MacDougal for the first time since the night she leveled her pistol and shot him in the bollocks?

Determined not to show the slightest crack in her demeanor, she remained by her husband and gained strength from the support of his warm, muscled arm beneath her gloved hand.

Within five minutes, she spotted MacDougal across the room, conversing with Wrotham and Miss North, along with a handful of other young unmarried misses. She stared. Blixford stared. Sherbourne and Lucy stared. Eventually, half the ballroom stared.

At precisely the moment MacDougal realized he was being studied much like a bug in a jar, the Bloomsbury butler announced in an excessively loud voice, "James Lennox, Viscount Hildebrand. Lady Northern. Mr. John Lennox. Mr. Henry Lennox. Mr. Julian Lennox. Mr. Bramwell Lennox. Mr. Robert Lennox. Recently of Scotland, Miss Mary Anna MacGruder." The last he practically shouted, and a hush fell over the ballroom.

Stunned, Jane didn't move her gaze from MacDougal, but whispered beneath her breath, "What a remarkable man you are."

"I can't take all the credit," Blix replied softly. "She replied to my letter immediately and enthusiastically vowed her assistance. Seems she also determined the make of the man, luckily before she married him. Your Aunt Northern was gracious and welcomed her as her houseguest. As to your brothers appearing en masse, I believe you've your father to thank for that. He sent notes around this afternoon, mentioning you would be in attendance tonight."

Her eyes devoured them. How she had missed them while she lived in Scotland, and barely back in England, she'd married and had gone from them again. She vowed to ask them to Eastchase Hall in summer. They would catch up at last.

Miss MacGruder was a lovely woman, fair and blond, with incongruously dark eyes. Her petite form in the midst of Jane's brothers made quite an impression. Those who were not already staring stopped what they were doing and joined the others.

While they stared, Miss Mary Anna MacGruder of Scotland, on the arm of Mr. Henry Lennox, walked straight up to the earl of Haversham and said in a loud, but cultured voice, lightly accented by a soft burr, "By all the saints, my lord, this is a surprise! You've grown courage, it seems." Her gaze darted toward Jane before returning to MacDougal. "Are you not afeared your cousin might again produce a pistol and shoot to unman you? She's as great a reason to try now as she had last time, does she not? She suffered from your lies, and now suffers again." She looked to Jane. "Ma'am, you have my sympathy for the stone about your neck that is your cousin. I've the great fortune of not being related to him, and praise God I cried off of marrying the louse when I realized his true character. If I could shoot half as well as you, I believe I'd finish what you attempted."

Jane realized it was her cue. Reaching into Blixford's pocket, her hand closed around the small pistol he had given her, the beautiful wee thing with a pearl handle and engraved barrel. Lifting it free, she pointed it toward MacDougal. A collective gasp resounded through the ballroom and the distance between she and MacDougal hastily cleared of people, all of them moving back out of her line of fire. "It occurs to me, Miss MacGruder, that you're correct. I'm shunned, so what have I to lose by shooting him? I will, at least, gain satisfaction for myself, my husband and my family. Blixford would have called you out, MacDougal, but it would imply you deserve the honor of a level field. Instead, you'll be shot by a woman and thus unmanned in more ways than one." She lowered the barrel and pointed the pistol directly at his crotch, her hand amazingly steady.

His eyes widened with fear. "Jane, you would not!" He looked about at the shocked faces of Lady Bloomsbury's guests before refocusing on her –and her pistol. "Tell them the truth, Jane. Despite being ruined to any gentleman, you pursued me endlessly, determined I would marry you, instead of merely keeping you as my mistress. When my betrothal to Anna was announced, you went into a fury and shot me."

The tide turned, he sounded so certain, his tone and demeanor lending an air of reality to his words. It was remembered then that she'd been ruined when she arrived in Scotland. More credence to his claim was given.

Jane ignored the accusing faces of the guests and her world narrowed. There was only him and her, the pistol and the lie. "I'm married now to the man I fell in love with when I was but sixteen. Circumstances kept us from our happiness and I fled to Scotland, to the bosom of my mother's family, where I thought I could safely nurse my grief. Instead I spent much of my time deflecting your advances. When Blixford didn't come after me, as I wished him to, and instead took a third bride, my sorrow led me to finally accept your proposal, to allow liberties afforded a fiancé, only to hear your father's announcement of your betrothal to Miss MacGruder, *that very night.*"

The tide turned again as another collective gasp went up round the room.

"That is why I shot you. Now, you again misuse me by your lies, and I'm compelled to respond." Closing her right eye, she aimed carefully. *Be the missile. Eye, hand, missile and target in harmony –all are one.*

He didn't believe she'd do it. He didn't move.

She fired, someone screamed, and when the smoke

cleared enough to see across the room, she saw that MacDougal sat upon the floor, clutching his thigh. "Hell and damn," she said to her husband, "I forgot it kicks a bit to the left."

"Hmm, yes, so it does. I should have reminded you."

"I say, daughter, excellent shot! But you may have missed your mark slightly."

In truth, she had aimed exactly right, hitting him with but a graze across the fleshy part of his thigh, just enough of a wound to bleed impressively. The ball would be found somewhere behind him. She held the pistol before her and looked quizzical. "Shall I try again?"

MacDougal shouted, "No! Mother of God! I cannot believe you shot me!" He paused. "*Again!*"

She walked with Blixford across the dance floor and they stared down at MacDougal, at the bloom of blood spreading from his leg.

Blixford raised his quizzing glass and observed in a detached manner before he frowned his displeasure. "You must get up at once. You are bleeding all over Lady Bloomsbury's floor."

Her cousin clearly remembered it was what he had said to her, after taking her virginity, that she should get up immediately as she was bleeding on his mama's divan. He had the good grace to look ashamed. And the good sense to look worried.

"Lady Bloomsbury," Jane called, "I believe a set of footmen might be useful." She looked at the blood. "I daresay a parlor maid is also in order." The marchioness moved toward them. It was the moment of reckoning. If she ignored Jane, their little stage play had not worked and she and Blixford would be shunned forever. As she drew close, Jane said in her very best duchess voice, "My heartfelt and sincere apologies, ma'am. It appears I've disrupted your lovely ball, and injured this man such that he is making rather a mess upon your floor. I hope and pray you can forgive me."

The older woman tapped her fan against her multitude of chins as she looked at Jane, then down to MacDougal, then to Anna. She looked at Blixford, at Sherbourne, Lucy, and all of her brothers, who'd moved close, and finally, she looked around at the faces of her guests.

"For God's sake, woman, have you no mercy? I'm in danger of bleeding to death while you decide whether to forgive my cousin for *shooting me!*"

The marchioness's expression didn't change at all. She remained inscrutable as she looked down at MacDougal. "It's unfortunate that you're bleeding to death, but I cannot find it within me to call for assistance until I know the truth."

"I've told you the truth. She was my mistress. That she coerced marriage to a duke would be laughable, if it were not so pathetic."

"Deuced rude to call you pathetic, Blix," Wrotham said. "And I believe he called Lady Bloomsbury 'woman'. Such disrespect should surely not go unpunished."

"I agree. Jane, love, would you be so good?" He handed her a bullet from his pocket.

"Delighted, husband." She loaded the pistol and pointed it at MacDougal's crotch.

Incredibly, the marchioness said, rather loudly, "You're a tremendously good shot, Duchess, and I believe I may just take up pistols as well. I believe I might be up to the challenge, but it's really not very sporting to shoot him at this close range." She waved her arms, shooing the guests back. "Do step away and give the man a chance to save his manhood."

For the barest moment, she met the older lady's eyes and saw admiration and acceptance reflected there. She and Blixford stepped back and she aimed once again.

MacDougal cried out and cowered into a ball of fear.

"Do not do it, Jane! I beg of you!"

"I will pull the trigger if you don't tell the truth."

This time, he believed her, which was rather ignorant on his part because she wouldn't shoot him again. He might die if she did, and she wouldn't kill him, no matter the provocation.

"All right! It's untrue that you were my mistress." He glared at her with bitter resentment. "But it's not a lie that I bedded you! That you allowed it!"

The third gasp of the evening rose to the very high ceiling of the ballroom.

Blixford moved forward then, reached down, grasped his collar and hauled him to his feet. "She didn't allow it," he said in a low, even voice. "She said *no*." He drew back his arm and planted MacDougal a facer, sending him flying backward. Blixford followed and bent to repeat the process, but MacDougal was unconscious. Raising up, he turned to face Jane. "I'm sorry, love, but he's ruined his comeuppance by fainting." He moved close and crooked his arm. "Perhaps you'll waltz with me while I wait for him to wake up."

She looked to Lady Bloomsbury. "With your permission, ma'am?"

Their hostess nodded. And smiled. "By all means." She waved at the orchestra leader. "A waltz, my good man!"

Two hours later, after dancing with Miss MacGruder, Lucy, Aunt Northern, and the Marchioness of Bloomsbury, then going down to supper and feeding bits of smoked trout to the marchioness's mouser, Michael waltzed again with Jane. The floor was crowded and he thought he'd never been smiled upon quite so much. "Perhaps we should create another scandal, only so we might have the dance floor to ourselves."

"The idea has merit, but let's wait a while."

Spying the open doors to the garden terrace, he waltzed her in that direction until they were outside.

"Blix, what's this? I thought you wanted to waltz."

He led her down the steps. "We have done so. Now I'd like to stroll through the garden with you. Ah, what lovely paper lanterns the marchioness displays in her trees. Hmm, but what's this? They appear only to illuminate the front half of the garden, and back here, it's quite dark, but for the moonlight through the leaves. Quite romantic, you'd have to agree. Now, if only the opportunity would present itself to engage in sexual congress with my wife. I say, will you look at that, Jane? A lovely bower we might duck into. Can you see me? No? Ah, well, no matter. I've no doubt you can work my fastenings with your eyes closed, and as for your gown, well it's quite easy to lift, as you see . . . well, I suppose you can't see, but you get the idea. Where the devil are your lips? I've found your eye it appears, and your eyes are lovely, but not what I had in mind at the moment."

He dove into a kiss, sucking her bottom lip between his teeth, kissing her as no gentleman ever kisses a lady.

After a time, when he was so hard he was afraid he'd climax before he'd yet touched her, he continued, "I've missed taking you in unusual places, had a dream, in fact, just the other night, and I made love to you atop a horse. Yes, love, there is a bench, I'm certain. Place your hands there, and I will be just here, behind . . . forgive me for blathering, but anyone who ventures near will hear the sound of a voice and go away, though I am speaking quietly so hopefully they couldn't know what we're about. As I was saying, I suggest we try it again, as soon as we return to Eastchase, though not on Grendel, since she's breeding and possibly more tetchy than usual . . . ah, love, yes, this is marvelous. You are marvelous and I love you so,

I may fair die of it . . . if this doesn't kill me first. Amazing how we fit together, is it not? I have missed this, more than you know, and I'm probably a brute not to ask first. Jane, I'm not hurting you? I'd rather die . . . ah, good, you are fine . . . what's that? Better than fine? Yes, I begin to comprehend, for I can feel . . . great God, Jane, you are already . . . ? I'm sorry to half smother you, but we can't have you crying out and announcing our activity. I was only joking about creating another scandal. Ah, love, you've no idea what you do to me, so tight, so beautiful, so. . ." Curled around her, covering her, feeling the weight of her breasts in his palms, he exploded within her softness and couldn't speak any longer.

Breathing so hard, she was panting, Jane turned to throw her arms around him, the hem of her gown returning to her ankles. "Will you take me home now, Michael?"

His embrace was fierce and tight.

Home.

It had the loveliest sound to it.

"Yes, Duchess, let's go home."

ABOUT THE AUTHOR

Author of the RITA winning Pink Files series, Stephanie Feagan has had a love affair with romance novels since she was eleven and discovered there are kissing scenes in Victoria Holt books. Stephanie also writes Young Adult and New Adult paranormal romance as Trinity Faegen. A practicing CPA who loves travel, books, new pencils, old keys, and smart guys, she lives in the oilfields of west Texas with her engineer husband and a mean cat. She'd love to hear from you.

She answers to Stephanie, Trinity, Hey Lady, and Mom, and can be reached at Stephanie@StephanieFeagan.com or Trinity@TrinityFaegen.com.

For information about upcoming releases, please visit www.stephaniefeagan.com.

COMING SOON!

The next sexy book in the Lennox Series, *The Iron Duchess*.

He wanted easy. Instead, he got Helen.

After walking away from a love affair gone horribly wrong, Henry Lennox is all about easy. He wants a wife who is pleasant, affectionate, and passably pretty, but despite an abundance of potential brides, he can't muster the enthusiasm to woo any of them. Instead, he's constantly, irresistibly drawn into a battle of wills with the Duchess of Hartsborough, a striking widow who taunts him from behind an impenetrable wall of iron. He really can't abide the woman, yet he can't stop thinking about her, can't resist sparring with her, can't control imagining her in his bed. And he's certain she's hiding something troubling, that she's in peril. As much as he wants to walk away, he can't. Not this time.

After her husband and his brother died in an accident five years ago, Helen discovered the Hartsborough dukedom was bankrupt. For her sister-in-law, Lara, and her infant nephew, now the Duke of Hartsborough, Helen works tirelessly with the family solicitor to regain what her weak husband and his wastrel brother lost, all while maintaining a façade of wealth and idle privilege. Focused on her goal, she has neither interest in nor time for men, but when Henry Lennox keeps turning up like a bad dream, she finds it harder and harder to ignore him. The handsome devil is infuriating, rudely inquisitive, and far too observant.

Then Lara falls for a fortune-hunter, and unless Helen can convince her he's a bounder, everything she has worked for will be lost. Even worse, her beloved, gentle sister-in-law will be ill-used and hurt. As disaster looms, Helen is determined to beat the cad at his own game, but when outfoxing the fox becomes dangerous and she fears all is lost, she needs an ally. Who better than Henry Lennox and his knowing blue eyes? All she has to do is ask his help, get rid of the threat, and save the dukedom. Then she can walk away from Henry Lennox. Easy.

Visit www.stephaniefeagan.com for more information about upcoming releases.

www.ingramcontent.com/pod-product-compliance
Lightning Source LLC
Chambersburg PA
CBHW030549180626
46816CB00005B/1469